...ook Buyers' Best
...ed and was a finalist in the National Readers' Choice awards. She is married and has three children. One of eleven siblings, she loves to write about the complexity of families and totally believes in the power of love.

An ex au-pair, bookseller, marketing manager and sea-front trader, **Jessica Gilmore** now works for an environmental charity in York. Married with one daughter, one fluffy dog and two dog-loathing cats, she spends her time avoiding house-work and can usually be found with her nose in a book. Jessica writes emotional romance with a hint of humour, a splash of sunshine and a great deal of delicious food—and equally delicious heroes.

Caroline Anderson describes herself: 'Mother, writer, arm-chair gardener, unofficial tearoom researcher and eater of lovely cakes. Not necessarily in that order. I love my family, my friends, reading, writing contemporary love stories, hearing from readers, walks by the sea with coffee/ice-cream/cake thrown in, torrential rain, sunshine in spring/autumn. What I hate: revising manuscripts, losing my pets, fighting with my family, cold weather, hot weather, computers, clothes-shopping. My plans? To keep smiling and writing!'

Susan Meier is the author of over fifty books for Mills & Boon. *The Tycoon's Secret Daughter* was a RITA finalist and *Nanny for the Millionaire's Twins* won the Book Buyer's Best award and was a finalist in the National Readers' Choice Awards and the Book of the Year Award for Romance Writers of America. She is married and has three children. One of eleven children herself, she loves to write about the complexities of family.

One Passionate Night

SUSAN MEIER
JESSICA GILMORE
CAROLINE ANDERSON

MILLS & BOON

First Published in Great Britain 2018
by Mills & Boon, an imprint of HarperCollins*Publishers*
1 London Bridge Street, London, SE1 9GF

ONE PASSIONATE NIGHT © 2018 Harlequin Books S. A.

Her Brooding Italian Boss © Linda Susan Meier 2015
The Heiress's Secret Baby © Jessica Gilmore 2015
Best Friend To Wife And Mother? © Caroline Anderson 2015

ISBN: 978-0-263-26618-4

05-0218

MIX
Paper from
responsible sources
FSC™ C007454

Printed and bound in Spain
by CPI, Barcelona

HER BROODING
ITALIAN BOSS

SUSAN MEIER

CHAPTER ONE

LAURA BETH MATTHEWS sat on the rim of the old porcelain tub in the New York City apartment she had to vacate by the next morning. Her long brown hair had been swirled into a sophisticated French twist. Her lilac organza bridesmaid gown was an original Eloise Vaughn design. A pregnancy test shook in her right hand.

Tears pooled in her eyes. There was no question now. She was going to have a baby.

"Laura Beth! Come on!" Eloise called from the hall as she knocked on the bathroom door. "I'm the bride! I should at least get ten minutes in the bathroom to check my makeup."

"Sorry!" She swiped at her tears and quickly examined her face in the medicine cabinet mirror. No real mascara smudges yet, but the day was young.

For the first time since she, Eloise and their third original roommate, Olivia Prentiss Engle, had decided to spend the night before Eloise's wedding together and dress together, Laura Beth regretted it. She was pregnant. The father of her child, one of Olivia's husband's vice presidents, had called her a slut when she'd told him she was late and they might be parents. And now she didn't just have to smile her way through a wedding; she had to hide a pregnancy test in a tiny bathroom.

She glanced around. "I'll be two more seconds." Out of time, she wrapped the stick in toilet paper and tossed it in the little wastebasket. Satisfied neither Olivia nor Eloise would rummage through the trash, she sucked in a breath, pasted on a happy smile and opened the door.

Eloise stood before her, glowing, a vision in her original Artie Best gown, designed specifically by her boss, the one and only Artie Best. Smooth silk rode Eloise's feminine curves. Rhinestones sparkled across the sweetheart neckline. And real diamonds—enough to support the population of a third-world country for a decade—glittered at her throat.

Tears pooled in Laura Beth's eyes again, but this time they were tears of joy for her friend. Eloise, Olivia and Laura Beth had moved to New York City with stars in their eyes. Now Olivia was a married mom. Eloise would be married in a few hours. And Laura Beth was pregnant, with a deadbeat for her child's father and twenty-four hours to vacate her apartment.

She was in deep trouble.

Antonio Bartulocci studied his shoulder-length curly black hair in the mirror. He'd gotten it cut for Ricky and Eloise's wedding, but he still debated tying it back, out of the way. He looked to the left, then the right, and decided he was worrying over nothing. Eloise and Ricky were his friends because they liked him just as he was. They didn't care that he was a tad bohemian. Most artists were.

He straightened his silver tie one last time before he walked out of the bedroom of his suite in his father's Park Avenue penthouse and headed for the main room.

Comfortable aqua sofas faced each other atop a pale gray area rug, flanked by white Queen Anne chairs. A gray stone fireplace took up the back wall, and a dark walnut wet bar sat in the corner. The view of the New York City skyline from the wall of windows in the back had taken Antonio's breath away when he first saw it. Since his wife's death, it barely registered.

"Hurry up, Antonio," his father called from the bar as he poured bourbon into a crystal glass. He wore a simple black suit, a white shirt and yellow striped tie that would be replaced by a tuxedo for the reception later that night. Though he was well into his seventies and a few pounds overweight, Italian billionaire Constanzo Bartulocci was a dashing man. A man whose looks spoke of money and power, who lived not in an ordinary world, but in one he could control. Unlike Antonio's world, where passion, inspiration and luck ruled.

"I'm right behind you."

Constanzo jumped and faced his son, his right hand over his heart. "You scare me."

Antonio laughed. "I'll bet I do."

After downing his drink in one long swallow, Constanzo pointed at the door. "Let's get going. I don't want to end up in a crush of reporters like we did the last time we went somewhere."

Antonio straightened his tie one more time. "Hey, you made me the paparazzi monster I am today."

"You are not a monster." The lilt of an Italian accent warmed his father's voice. "You could be one of the most important painters of the twenty-first century. You are a talent."

He knew that, of course. But having talent wasn't what most people imagined. He didn't put his gift away in a shiny box and take it out when he needed it. Talent, the need to paint, the breathtaking yearning to explore life on a canvas, were what drove him. But for the past two years he hadn't even been able to pick up a brush. Forget about painting, accepting commissions, having a purpose in life. Now, he ate, drank, slept—but didn't really live. Because he'd made millions on his art in the past few years, and, with his savvy businessman father's help, he'd parlayed those millions into hundreds of millions through investments, money wasn't an issue. He had the freedom and the resources to ignore his calling.

The private elevator door silently opened. Antonio and his father stepped inside. Constanzo sighed. "If you had a personal assistant, this wouldn't have happened."

Antonio worked to hide a wince. He didn't have to ask what his father meant. He knew. "I'm sorry."

"I wanted you to be the artist who did the murals for Tucker's new building. Those works would have been seen by thousands of people. Ordinary people. You would have brought art to the masses in a concrete way. But you missed the deadline."

"I don't have a brain for remembering dates."

"Which is exactly why you need a personal assistant."

Antonio fought the urge to squeeze his eyes shut. What he needed was to be left alone. Or maybe to roll back the clock so far that he hadn't married the woman who'd betrayed him. But that wasn't going to happen. He was stuck in a combination of grief and guilt that paralyzed him.

Constanzo's limousine awaited them on the street. They walked under the building portico without speaking. Antonio motioned for his father to enter first.

When he slid in behind him, soft white leather greeted him. A discreet minibar sat near the media controls. His father hit a few buttons and classical music quietly entered the space.

The driver closed the door and in less than a minute the limo pulled onto the street.

"A PA could also handle some of the Gisella problems that remain."

Antonio's jaw twitched.

Constanzo sighed. "Well, you don't seem to want to handle them." He sighed again, more deeply this time. "Antonio, it's been two years. You cannot grieve forever."

Antonio glanced at his father. He let his lips lift into a small smile. Pretending he was grieving had been the only way he'd survived the years since his wife's death. Beautiful Gisella had burst into his life like a whirlwind. Twenty-four hours after they'd met they'd been in bed. Twenty-four weeks after that they were married. He'd been so smitten, so hopelessly in love, that days, weeks, months hadn't mattered. But looking back, he recognized the signs he should have seen. Her modeling career hadn't tanked, but it had been teetering, and marriage to the newly famous Italian painter had put her in the limelight again. Her sudden interest in international causes hadn't cropped up until she found a way to use them to keep herself, her name, in the papers and on everybody's lips. She'd even spoken at the UN. He'd been so proud…so stupid.

"My son, I know adult children don't like nagging, meddling parents, but this time I am correct. You must move on."

Without replying, he looked out the window at the hustle and bustle of New York City in the spring. Bumper-to-bumper traffic, most of it taxicabs. Optimistic residents walking up and down the sidewalk in lightweight coats. The sun glittering off the glass of towering buildings. At one time he'd loved this city more than he'd loved the

Italian countryside that was his home. But she'd even ruined that for him.

"Please do not spoil Ricky and Eloise's day with your sadness."

"I'm not sad, Dad. I'm fine."

The limo stopped. They exited and headed into the enormous gray stone cathedral.

The ceremony was long and Antonio's mind wandered to his own wedding, in this same church, to a woman who hadn't really loved him.

No, he wasn't sad. He was angry, so furious some days his heart beat slow and heavy with it. But he couldn't ruin the reputation of a woman who'd used him to become a cultural icon any more than he could pretend she'd been the perfect wife she'd portrayed.

Which meant he couldn't have a PA digging through papers in his office or documents on his computer.

The ceremony ended. The priest said, "I now introduce Mr. and Mrs. Richard Langley."

His best friend, Ricky, and his beautiful new wife, Eloise, turned and faced the crowd of friends and relatives sitting in the pews. A round of applause burst through the church and Ricky and Eloise headed down the aisle. Matron of honor Olivia Engle and best man Tucker Engle, also husband and wife, followed them out of the church. Antonio walked to the center aisle to meet his partner, Laura Beth Matthews.

Laura Beth was a sweet young woman he'd met and had gotten to know fairly well over the years when she'd visited Olivia and Tucker at their Italian villa, and every time there was a baptism, birthday or holiday party at the Engle penthouse on Park Avenue. Unfortunately, she had usually been with an annoying boyfriend, someone who didn't fit into Tucker Engle's world or Ricky Langley's, but who desperately tried to.

Laura Beth slid her hand to Antonio's elbow and he smiled at her before they walked down the aisle and out of the church.

As Ricky and Eloise greeted the long line of guests filing through the vestibule, Antonio turned to Laura Beth. "You look lovely."

She glanced down at the pale purple dress. "Eloise designs the most beautiful gowns."

"Ah, so she did this herself."

Laura Beth nodded. When she brought her gaze back to his, though, her green eyes were dull. Not sad for the change in her life that the marriage of her last room-mate would bring, but lifeless.

He caught her forearm to bring her attention to him. "Are you okay?"

She suddenly brightened. "Sure. Yes. I'm fine. Wonderful. It was just a stressful morning."

"Tell me about it. Have you ever tried traveling with a billionaire who expects everybody and everything to be at his fingertips?"

Laura Beth laughed. "Oh, come on. I love your father! He's not a prima donna."

"You've only dealt with him when you were on vacation or at a party for one of Tucker and Olivia's kids. Just try flying across the Atlantic with him."

She laughed again and something lightened in Antonio's chest. With her dark brown hair and bright green eyes, Laura Beth was much too pretty to be so—

He paused, not able to put a label on her mood. Nervous didn't quite hit the mark. Unhappy wasn't it either. She seemed more like distant. As if she were preoccupied.

Seeing Ricky and Eloise still had a line of guests filing out of the church, he said, "So what's up?"

Her head snapped in his direction. "Up?"

"You're here one minute, but your mind is gone the next. You're obviously mulling something over. Or trying to figure something out."

"I…um…well, I have to be out of my apartment tomorrow before noon."

His eyebrows rose. "And you're not packed?"

"No, I'm packed. I just don't have anywhere to go."

"You could stay at Constanzo's penthouse. We leave tomorrow morning."

She blushed. "Yeah, I could stay at Tucker and Olivia's, too." The red of her face deepened. "I'm always taking advantage of other people's goodwill."

The greeting line for wedding guests suddenly ended. Ricky and Eloise headed outside. Antonio caught Laura Beth's hand and led her to the side door. "Let's go. We want to be outside to toss confetti when they come out."

When Antonio took her hand and guided her out into the warm spring day, Laura Beth's heart tugged. With his shoulder-length curly black hair and penetrating dark eyes, he was the epitome of the sexy artist. But that wasn't why her heart skipped a beat. His very casual way of making her feel a part of things, when her brain kept dragging her away, lifted her spirits. He was a good man, with a big heart and so much talent she almost couldn't fathom it.

She'd had a crush on him from the day she'd met him. But she'd been dating Bruce. Then Antonio had gotten married, and two short years after that he was mourning the loss of his beautiful, equally talented, dedicated wife. So though she'd crushed on him, she'd never even let the thought of flirting with him fully form. And now, pregnant, she only let the thought flit through her brain. She absolutely wouldn't act on it.

She should just get off her self-pity train and help Antonio enjoy the wedding, not expect him to help her.

So she made light, happy conversation while they posed for pictures as members of the wedding party, and hours later in the ballroom of the Waldorf, while they ate dinner. Antonio laughed in all the right places, but Laura Beth could see the glimmer of sadness in his eyes. As much as she wanted to be able to entertain him, she was failing. Her own troubles weighed her down, just as his dampened his mood. They'd both run out of jokes and neutral topics and even fun-filled facts. Worse, every time he turned his dark, brooding eyes on her, she wanted to flirt. Flirt! He had troubles. She had troubles. And she wanted to flirt? Ridiculous. So after the wedding party dance, she shuffled off to the ladies' room.

She sat on the cushioned sofa along the back wall and took several deep breaths. She might be able to hide out in her apartment one more night, but then she seriously had to decide where she'd sleep tomorrow. In Tucker and Olivia's penthouse? Or Constanzo Bartulocci's? Once again accepting charity.

How long could she live like this? She did not have a home. She did not have a full-time job. She was *pregnant* by a man who thought her a slut. She was a failure.

Tears filled her eyes.

Oh, great. Now she'd upset herself.

She sucked in a breath, brushed away her tears and rose from the comfortable sofa. She might not be able to pretend she wasn't in financial trouble, but for the next few hours she still had to feign happiness and fulfill her bridesmaid responsibilities.

In the plush hall outside the ladies' room, she straightened her shoulders and drank in another fortifying breath. She could do this.

The first person she saw as she entered the ballroom was Antonio, so she walked in the other direction. The pull of her attraction to him was so strong today she could have melted in his arms when they danced, and that was just wrong. He was grieving a wonderful woman whom he'd adored. And Laura Beth herself had problems to solve before she could even consider flirting with someone, let alone melting into his arms.

Walking past laughing entrepreneurs, happy socialites and waiters serving champagne, she had a strange epiphany, or maybe a rush of reality. She was only here because of her roommates. In the four years since she'd been invited into this rarified world by Olivia and Eloise, they had not only found their true callings, but they had fallen for the loves of their lives—while she hadn't found squat. Rubbing elbows with executives, she hadn't been able to prove herself enough to anyone to get a full-time job. And despite being in front of all these gorgeous eligible bachelors, she hadn't yet found a man who wanted her.

Maybe her problem wasn't that there was something wrong with her. Maybe she was in the wrong class of people. After all, she'd grown up blue-collar. Why did she believe that just because her friends fit into the glitzy, glamorous world of billionaires, she should fit in, too?

Maybe this whole mess—her inability to get a full-time job, her inability to keep her apartment and her pregnancy—was a wake-up call from the universe. *Hey,*

Laura Beth, you're in the wrong crowd. That's why you're failing!

It made so much sense that she stopped short, not quite at the open bar.

The answer was so obvious it stunned her. Though she would always be friends with Olivia and Eloise, she didn't belong in this part of their world. She was common. Normal. Not that there was anything wrong with that. It was more that a common person, someone who didn't fit in this world, would always come up short. But if she were to jump off her high horse and get a normal job, she would probably be very happy right now.

If only because she would get to be herself.

Antonio almost groaned when his dad sidled up to him at the bar. "So have you given any thought to my suggestion about a personal assistant?"

As much as Antonio loved his dad, he did have moments when he wished the old billionaire would just get lost.

"Dad, how about letting this go?"

"I think it's the answer to your problems."

Out of the corner of his eye, he saw his partner for the wedding, Laura Beth, walk up beside him and order a ginger ale from the bartender. He would only have to tap her arm and snag her attention to get himself out of this conversation. But how fair was that? Not only did he need to put his foot down with his dad, but Laura Beth obviously wanted to be left alone. It wouldn't be right to drag her into his drama.

He sucked in a breath and smiled at his dad. There was only one way to stop Constanzo—pretend to agree. Albeit temporarily. "You know what? I will think about the PA." It really wasn't a lie. He would *think* about hiring a PA, but that was as far as it would go. There was no way he wanted a stranger in his house. No way he wanted someone going through his things. No way he wanted a stranger to accidentally stumble upon any of his wife's deceit when rummaging through papers or files or phone records while trying to organize him.

Constanzo's face lit. "You will?"

"Sure."

"And maybe start painting again?"

He stole a glance at Laura Beth, suddenly wishing he could capture that faraway look in her eyes, the expression that was half-wistful, half-sad. She was so naturally beautiful. High cheekbones gave her face a sculpted look that would serve her well as she aged. And her bounty of hair? He could see himself undoing that fancy hairdo and fanning his fingers through the silken strands to loosen it, right before he kissed her.

What? Where had that come from?

He shook his head to clear it, deciding it was time to get away from his dad before he had any more crazy thoughts.

He faced Constanzo. "I'll paint when I paint. Now, I need to get mingling again."

As he walked away from the bar, he noticed his dad bridging the gap between himself and Laura Beth and sighed with relief. This meant his dad wouldn't follow him. Besides which, it would help Laura Beth get her mind off her troubles. When he wasn't hounding Antonio about something or another in his life, Constanzo Bartulocci could be a very funny guy.

Laura Beth glanced at Constanzo and pasted a smile on her face. Now that she recognized she didn't belong in this crowd, that she was pretending to be someone she wasn't, she knew exactly what to do: enjoy the rest of the wedding, then get busy finding a normal job and some new roommates. Whoever she chose couldn't ever replace Olivia and Eloise—no one would ever replace her two best friends—but she'd make it work.

"You seem sad tonight."

Laura Beth nodded and smiled at Constanzo. He was like everybody's rich uncle. But he didn't flaunt his money. He made people laugh. He'd made *her* laugh at more than one of Olivia and Tucker's family events. It wasn't unusual or out of line for her to confide. She simply wouldn't tell him everything.

"My second roommate got married today," she said, taking advantage of the obvious. "I'm not exactly an old maid, but I'm on the road."

Constanzo laughed. "You Americans. What is this old maid thing? Can't a woman mature and enjoy life without being married?"

She laughed lightly. That was exactly the attitude she needed to cultivate. "Actually, yes, she can."

"Good. A woman doesn't need a man. She should *want* a man in her life. But he should complement her, not define her."

She toasted him with her glass of ginger ale. "Wise words."

"So, now that we've settled the old maid issue, what else has made you sad?"

"I'm fine."

He studied her face, then shook his head. "I don't think so."

"Jeez. You're as perceptive as Antonio."

"Where do you think he gets it?"

"I thought it was the artist in him."

Constanzo shook his head sadly. "Unfortunately,

since his wife's death, I think the artist in my son is withering and dying."

His gaze drifted to Antonio, and Laura Beth followed his line of sight. Antonio was stunning in his tuxedo, with his hair a little wild. Every woman he passed eyed him with interest. The spark of her crush lit again, the desire to walk over and suggest another dance rising up in her. But that was wrong. Not only did she have troubles she had to solve before she got involved with another man, but as every woman around him drooled, Antonio didn't seem to see anybody.

"The death of a spouse is difficult."

Constanzo accepted that with a slight nod of his head. "I don't want him to lose his entire life over this."

"He'll come around."

"He needs a nudge."

Laura Beth laughed. "A nudge?"

Constanzo sucked in a breath. "Yes, he needs to hire help. An assistant. Somebody who can live with him and get him on track."

"Sounds like a tall order."

"I don't think so. We've been talking about him hiring a personal assistant, and he's finally agreeable, which means he's finally ready to heal and get back into life. I think once an assistant gets rid of the two years of junk he's let accumulate in his office, Antonio will be able to see his future—not his past."

Laura Beth mulled that over for a second. "Oddly, Constanzo, that actually makes sense."

Constanzo laughed. "I like that you understand us. It's part of why I find you to chat to at parties."

She smiled. "There's not much to understand. You're a dad who loves his son. He's a son who appreciates having a dad. All the rest is just stuff."

He laughed again. "I wish I could hire you to be his PA."

Laura Beth paused her ginger ale halfway to her lips.

"But I'm sure you wouldn't want to live in Italy. And then there's matter of the job itself. I'm sure you're accustomed to much loftier employment."

She sniffed a laugh. "My degree has gotten me nothing but temp jobs."

His eyebrows rose. "So you're interested?"

She thought that through. A real full-time job, that came with room and board? In a country away from her family and friends, so she could think through what to do about her pregnancy before she announced it?

"Yes. I'm interested."

CHAPTER TWO

THE NEXT MORNING, as instructed by Constanzo, Laura Beth took a taxi to Tucker Engle's private airstrip. She pulled her measly suitcase out of the backseat and paid the driver one-fifth of the money she had, leaving her a mere pittance. If this job didn't pan out, she'd be penniless. But since she was already in trouble, and knew Antonio and Constanzo well, taking work as Antonio's personal assistant wasn't much of a risk.

A swirl of April air kicked up dust on the tarmac as she walked to the plane. Two pilots stood beside the lowered stairway, comparing information in logbooks. As she approached, one of the men saw her and smiled. He said something in Italian and she winced.

"Sorry. I don't speak Italian."

The pilot laughed. "I speak English. What can we do for you?"

"I'm Laura Beth Matthews. Constanzo told me he would call you to add my name to your passenger list."

The pilot looked down, then back up again. But the second pilot pointed at the list.

"Ah, *sì*. Here you are." He reached for her pathetic suitcase. "I will take care of this."

Fear ruffled through her as a man she didn't know

took the entirety of her possessions out of her hand and walked away. But the second pilot pointed up the steps.

She sucked in a breath. She needed to get away. She needed time to think. She needed a job. She climbed the stairs.

At the doorway she stopped and gasped. The main area looked more like a living room than a plane. Rows of seats had been replaced by long, comfortable-looking sofas. Tables beside the sofas provided places for books, drinks or food. A desk and wet bar in the back filled the remaining space.

She eased toward the sofas, wondering where the heck Constanzo and Antonio were. Sitting on the soft leather, she leaned back, enjoying the feel of it against her nape. She'd been so nervous the night before she hadn't slept, and part of her just wanted to nod off. Before she got too comfortable, though, a commotion sounded outside. She jumped up and looked out the window.

A big white limo had pulled up. Antonio got out and held the door for his dad. She tilted her head, watching them.

Dressed in jeans and an open dress shirt over a white T-shirt, Antonio looked totally different. She usually saw him in tuxedos at gallery openings or formal events, or trousers and white shirts at parties for Olivia and Tucker's kids. Seeing him so casual sent a jolt of attraction through her. Especially with the way the breeze blew through his long curly hair, making her wonder if it was as soft as it looked.

She shook her head at her stupidity and raced back to her seat. She'd just gotten settled when Constanzo boarded the plane.

"*Carissima.* You made it."

She rose, just in case she was sitting in the wrong place. "I did."

Antonio entered behind his dad. He stopped when he saw her, his brow wrinkling. "Laura Beth?"

Though Antonio had been raised in the United States, he'd spent the past five years in Italy. Speaking Italian had changed the timbre of his voice. Her name rolled off his tongue sensually. A shiver breezed along her skin. And another thought suddenly hit her—this man was now her boss. She wouldn't just be working to organize him. They'd be living together.

Oh, wow. No wonder her thoughts ran amok. *She was going to be living with the guy she'd had a crush on for five years.*

Right. Plain Jane Laura Beth would be living with a famous artist, who still grieved his equally gorgeous, equally wonderful wife. Common sense plucked away her fear. She had nothing to worry about.

She smiled and said, "Hello."

Constanzo ambled to the back of the plane. "Can I get you a drink?"

She turned to watch Constanzo as he approached the bar. "No. Thanks."

Antonio stopped in front of her. With his windblown hair and sun-kissed skin, he looked so good, so sexy, that her mouth watered. Especially when his dark eyes met hers.

"What are you doing here?"

Reminding herself Antonio wouldn't ever be attracted to her and she had to get rid of this crush, she peeked back at Constanzo again.

He batted a hand. "I hired her. She's out of her apartment and had no permanent job. It was perfect timing."

Antonio's lips lifted into a smile that would have

stopped her heart if she hadn't known he was off-limits. "Oh. That's great."

The pilot announced they'd been cleared for takeoff. Antonio pointed at the leather sofa, indicating Laura Beth should sit, then he sat beside her. Close enough to touch. Close enough that if they hit turbulence, they'd tumble together.

She squeezed her eyes shut. *Stop!*

She had to get ahold of these wayward thoughts or she'd drive herself crazy living with him! She was not in this guy's league. She'd figured all this out yesterday. She was common, pregnant and needed a job more than a crush.

They both buckled in. The little jet taxied to the runway of the small airstrip and took off smoothly. It climbed for a few minutes and leveled off before the fasten-seat-belts light blinked off and the pilot announced they anticipated an uneventful flight, so they could move about the cabin.

To settle her nerves and maybe waylay the attraction that zapped her every time she looked down and saw Antonio's thigh mere inches away from hers, Laura Beth pulled a book from her purse.

"Ah. I loved that novel."

She glanced at the book, then at Antonio. "I never took you for a science fiction fan."

"Are you kidding? Some of the best art is in science fiction. The imaginations and imagery required are magnificent."

Laura Beth smiled, glad they had something normal to talk about, but her stomach picked that exact second to growl. Her face flushed.

Antonio laughed. "You skipped breakfast."

She hadn't been able eat breakfast. It seemed that

now that she knew she was pregnant, morning sickness had kicked in.

"Um, I wasn't hungry when I got up this morning."

Antonio unbuckled his seat belt. He reached for her hand. "Come with me."

She undid her seat belt and took the hand he'd offered. Her fingers tingled when his warm hand wrapped around them. As he pulled her up to stand, she reminded herself to stop noticing these things and followed him to the back of the plane.

The area she'd believed was a wet bar was actually a small kitchenette. She gaped at it. "You have to be kidding me."

Antonio nudged his head in the direction of his dad, who had fallen asleep on the sofa across from the one where Antonio and Laura Beth had been sitting.

"Anything my dad could possibly want is always stocked on the plane. When we arrive at our destination, any food not eaten will be donated to a charity." He laughed and opened the small fridge. "How about eggs and toast?"

Her stomach didn't lurch at the thought, so she nodded.

Antonio studied her. "Hmm. Not very enthusiastic. So let's try French toast."

"I love French toast." And she hadn't had it in forever.

He motioned for her to sit at one of the bar stools, obviously needing her out of the way in the tiny space. He hit a button and what looked to be a grill appeared.

"This is so cool."

"This is the life of a billionaire."

She glanced around. Remembering her thoughts from the night before, she didn't look at the plane as somebody who someday wanted to own one. She counted her blessings that she was here and had a job and a place to stay.

"It's kind of fun getting to see things that I wouldn't normally see."

He frowned. "I don't understand."

"Well, I'm never going to be a billionaire. So I'm never going to own a plane like this."

"Ah." He broke two eggs in a bowl, added milk, vanilla and a dash of what appeared to be cinnamon, beat the mixture, then rummaged for bread. When he found it, he dipped two slices into the egg mixture and put them on the small griddle. They sizzled.

She sniffed the vanilla. "Yum."

"You really must be hungry."

"I am."

He turned to flip the two pieces of French toast. She tilted her head, taking in the details that made him who he was. Sexy dark hair. Wide shoulders. Trim hips. But his face was the showstopper. Dark, dark eyes in olive skin. A square jaw. High cheekbones.

Something soft and warm floated through her. She was just about to curse herself for looking at him again when she realized she'd never felt like this with Bruce. She'd liked Bruce—actually, she'd believed she'd loved him. But she'd never felt this odd combination of attraction and curiosity that mixed and mingled with the warmth of their friendship and turned her feelings into something more…something special.

She cleared her throat. What was she doing? Fantasizing again? This guy was her boss! Not only that, but he was a widower. Someone who'd lost his wife and still grieved her so much he no longer painted. What would he want with her? Plain, simple Laura Beth Matthews, who—oh, by the way—was also pregnant with another man's child. Her job was to organize him back to the land of the living, not drool over him.

He made eight pieces of French toast, divided them onto two plates and handed one to her.

Her stomach rumbled again. "Thanks."

He passed the syrup across the bar. She slathered it on her French toast, but waited for him to pick up his fork before she picked up hers. If there was one thing she'd learned from her years of attending Olivia and Tucker's baby events and Ricky and Eloise's elaborate parties, it was to follow the lead of the host and hostess.

He took a bite of his French toast, then smiled at her. "So getting a job where you get to live in was a pretty nifty way to handle the apartment problem."

She reddened to the roots of her hair. "Does it seem sleazy?"

"No. It's smart. After I rotated out of the foster-care system, I'd have killed for a job that got me off the streets."

"Yeah, but then you wouldn't have scrounged your way to Italy, where your dad found you."

"Scrounged." He grinned. "I love American words."

"Hey, you're half-American!"

"Yes, I am. And proud of it. I use both worlds." He frowned. "Or did." Then he brightened. "Never mind. How's the toast?"

"I love it." She pushed her plate away having eaten only two slices. "But I'm full."

Antonio took her plate and his and set them in a metal drawer, which he closed. "Staff will get this when we land."

She laughed. "Wow."

"Hey, you better get used to living like this."

Though she didn't think Antonio was as persnickety or as pampered as his dad, she decided not to argue the point. Especially since she'd had a sleepless night, agonizing over her problems. With her tummy full and the lull of the plane, she just wanted to curl up on one of the sofas.

She wandered back to her seat, buckled herself in—in case they hit turbulence—and almost immediately fell asleep.

She awoke to the feeling of someone shaking her. "Laura Beth...we're here."

She snuggled into the blanket someone had thrown over her. "We're where?"

"In Italy."

Her eyes popped open. When she found herself staring into the gorgeous face of Antonio Bartulocci, it all tumbled back. They were on a plane to Italy. His dad had hired her. She didn't have an apartment. She was pregnant.

Her stomach dropped.

She was pregnant. In a foreign country. Starting a new job. Working for Antonio, who needed her. But she was attracted to him. She thought he was the sexiest, most gorgeous man alive and she would be living with him. But he didn't feel the same way about her.

That relaxed her. It could be a good thing if he only saw her as a friend. As long as she hid her crush, there'd be no problem. Plus, being on call twenty-four-seven to help him get his life back would keep her from dwelling on her problems.

That was the real silver lining. Not just the money. Not just a place to live. But someone to take care of, so she could forget about herself.

She pushed aside the soft cover. Her days of daydreaming she belonged in this world as anything other than an employee were over. She could take this job and run with it, create a halfway decent life for herself and her baby. Everything would be fine.

"Thanks for the blanket."

Antonio smiled. "My pleasure."

She found her purse and tucked her science fiction novel inside. Two gentlemen, Antonio and Constanzo waited for her to exit first.

Constanzo paused to say something to the pilots, but quickly joined them on the tarmac below the steps.

She glanced around. The sky was blue, as perfect as any she'd seen in Kentucky. Tall green grass in the fields surrounding the airstrip swayed in a subtle breeze that cut through the heat. "Another private airstrip?"

"You don't think my dad's going to have a plane and suffer the torment of going to a real airport and waiting to take off and land, do you?"

Pushing a strand of her hair off her face, she laughed. "Right. Spoiled."

"Incredibly spoiled. You're going to need to remember that."

She frowned. It was the second time he'd said something odd about her getting accustomed to his dad. Still, he was her boss now. They might have been able to relate like friends on the plane, but here on Italian soil, his home turf, her role kicked in. She was his assistant. Basically, a secretary. But this was better than anything she'd even come close to finding in New York.

This was her life now.

Constanzo walked over. "Bags are on their way to the limo."

Laura Beth said, "Wow. Fast."

Antonio laughed. "So much for you to get used to

about my dad." He nudged his father's shoulder. "Exactly how do you intend to explain to Bernice that you hired someone to help her?"

Laura Beth's brow wrinkled.

Constanzo's face reddened.

Laura Beth gasped as she faced Antonio. "You think Constanzo hired me to work for *him*?"

This time Antonio's brow wrinkled. "You're not working for my dad?"

Constanzo's face reddened even more as both Laura Beth and Antonio turned to him.

"I did not hire her to help my PA. I hired her to be yours."

Antonio's mouth fell open at his father's audacity. Anger whispered across his skin, causing his temper to bubble. He took a minute to pull in a breath and remind himself that his father hiring a PA was nothing compared to his deceased wife's handiwork.

Still, when he spoke, his voice was harsh, angry. "Why are you meddling in my life?"

Constanzo headed for the limo again. "I'm not meddling." He strolled across the quiet tarmac. "You said last night that you were thinking about this. When Laura Beth and I struck up a conversation and I realized she'd be perfect for the job, I did what I do best... I anticipated."

He almost cursed. "You meddled!"

Laura Beth touched his arm to get his attention. Her fingertips warmed his skin, caused his breathing to stutter.

"I didn't realize he didn't have your permission."

Constanzo bristled. "I did not need my son's permission. He said last night he was agreeable. I *anticipated*."

Antonio stayed outside the limo, unable to get himself to move into the car with his dad and Laura Beth, who had hesitantly climbed inside. Confusion and resentment clamored inside him. He wasn't just angry about his dad hiring someone for him; his reactions to Laura Beth were wrong.

He'd always liked her. And, yes, he supposed there was a bit of an attraction there. But suddenly, today, maybe because they'd had such an intimate chat on the plane, he was feeling things he shouldn't feel. Good God, she was a sweet girl trying to find her way in life. And he was an angry widower. He did not want to be attracted to her, and if she were smart she wouldn't want to be attracted to him. Worse, they should not be living together.

He had to fire her.

No...*Constanzo* had to fire her.

Behind him, the chauffeur wheeled their luggage to the rear of the limo. One scruffy brown bag stood out.

It had to be Laura Beth's.

Just one bag. And it was worn. So worn he would consider it unusable. But that was her best.

He scrubbed his hand across his mouth as a picture formed in his brain. Her two roommates hadn't just found the loves of their lives, they'd made careers for themselves and she was still working temp jobs.

Damn it.

He couldn't embarrass her by refusing to let her work for him. But he didn't want to be living with an attractive woman—the first woman to stir something inside him since Gisella. Worse, he didn't want someone rifling through his things.

He'd give Laura Beth a few days to rest in his country house, then gently explain that he didn't want a PA.

Since he was essentially firing her, he'd send her back to the US with a good-sized severance check and the codes for his dad's penthouse so she'd be okay until she found a new job.

But today, once he had her settled, he intended to have this out with his dad.

CHAPTER THREE

LAURA BETH WATCHED Antonio climb into the limo. He didn't say a word the entire drive to his father's house.

Nerves skittered along her skin. He didn't want her. It seemed he didn't want a PA at all...*Constanzo* did. And the second he got out of the car, Antonio would fire her.

They reached Constanzo's beautiful country home and he unceremoniously got out. Angry, too, he didn't say a word to his son. When the limo began moving again, she couldn't take the quiet.

"I'm so sorry."

Antonio stared out the window. "Not your fault. As I told you on the plane, my dad has the mistaken belief that everything he wants should be there when he wants it. Sometimes that translates into a belief that everyone in his life should do what he wants when he wants it done."

With that the car got quiet again. Any second now she expected him to apologize and fire her. But he didn't. The twenty-minute drive was extremely quiet, but with every mile that passed without him saying, "You're fired," her spirits lifted a bit. They drove up to his gorgeous country home and he got out as if nothing were amiss.

Exiting the limo, she glanced around. Antonio's

home was nestled in a silent stretch of Italian countryside. Hills and valleys layered in rich green grass with a spattering of wildflowers surrounded the new house. A smaller, much older house sat at the end of a stone path.

As if seeing the direction of her gaze, Antonio said, "That's my studio."

She tilted her head as she studied it. In some ways the old stone house was more beautiful than the big elaborate home that had obviously been built within the past few years—probably for his wife.

Her face heated as envy tightened her chest, so she quickly reprimanded herself. This man she thought so handsome had had a wife, someone he'd adored. She'd been hired to be a glorified secretary. She was pregnant with another man's child. *And* she'd also decided the night before that she was no longer going to try to fit herself into a world too grand for her. Being jealous of Antonio's dead wife, being attracted to a famous artist slated to inherit the estate of one of the world's wealthiest men…that was foolishness that she'd nip in the bud every time it popped into her head, until it left for good.

Antonio motioned to the door and she walked before him into the grand foyer of his home. A wide circular stairway and marble floors welcomed her. To the right, a painting of what looked to be the field outside his house brightened the huge foyer with its rich greens and striking blues of both the flowers and sky.

"I've seen this before."

He laughed. "In Tucker and Olivia's Montauk mansion."

She faced him. "That's right!"

"I bought it back from them."

"I can see why. It's beautiful."

"It was the first thing I painted when I rented the run-down shack I now use as a studio."

He walked up behind her. Little pinpricks of awareness danced up her spine. "The second I set foot on Italian soil, I knew this was my home, that the time I'd spent in foster care in America was an aberration. An accident." He pointed at the painting. "This picture captures all the happiness of that discovery."

"I see it."

He sniffed a laugh. "Tucker did too. Made me pay him a pretty penny to get it back." He motioned to the stairs. "Let me show you to your room."

Taken aback by the abrupt change of mood, she almost didn't follow him. Her skin was prickly and hot from his nearness, her breathing shallow. Still, she smiled and started up the steps, reminding herself that he was off-limits and she should be paying attention to the layout of the house rather than the nearness of her boss.

At the top of the staircase, Antonio directed her down a short hall. A glance to the left and right showed her the upstairs had been designed in such a way that private hallways led to individual rooms. And each wall had a painting. Some stark and stunning. Some warm and rich with color.

They finally stopped at a closed door. Antonio opened it and directed her inside. She gasped as she entered. Thick white carpets protected golden hardwood floors. A white headboard matched the white furniture, which was all brightened by an aqua comforter and bed skirt and sheer aqua curtains that billowed in the breeze of the open window.

"It's beautiful." She'd tried not to sound so pedestrian

and poor, but the simple color scheme in the huge room with such beautiful furniture took her breath away.

"Thank you. I did this room myself."

"You did?" She turned with a happy smile on her face, but her smile died when she saw him looking around oddly. "What?"

He shook his head. "It's nothing. Foolish."

"Come on." She used the cajoling voice she'd use with her older brother when he had a secret. If they were going to be working together—and she hoped his recent change in mood was an indicator that they were—she needed to get him to trust her. "We're friends. You can tell me."

He sucked in a breath, walked a bit farther into the room. "Most men let their wives decorate, but mine was away—" He caught her gaze. "Traveling. She also showed no interest in the samples the designer sent to her, and one day I just decided to look at the whole house as a canvas and—" he shrugged "—here we are."

"Well, if the rest of the rooms are as beautiful as this one, I can't wait to see everything."

He smiled slightly. "I'll give you a tour tonight."

She said, "Great," but her heart sank. Talking about his wife had made him sad. He might give her the tour, but it would be grudgingly. The disparity of their stations in life and the reality of her situation poured through her. She might be trying to get him to trust her, but if she were simply a new assistant not a friend of friends, he wouldn't give her the tour of his house. She might not even get such a grand bedroom. He probably wouldn't have told her the tidbit about decorating it himself. And he wouldn't be sad.

Maybe it was time to put herself in her place with him—*for* him.

"You don't have to." She laughed lightly, trying to sound like an employee, not a friend. "This is your home. There might be areas you wish to keep private."

He faced her, his expression filled with sadness. "People in the public eye quickly realize there is no such thing as privacy. If you sense hesitancy about my showing you the house, it's because the house reminds me of better times."

She struggled to hold back a wince at her stupidity. Of course, memories of his dead wife affected him more than the oddness of having a friend working for him. "I'm sorry."

"I'm sorry too." He glanced around at her room again. "I'd love to have my inspiration back. I'd love to paint again." He drew in a breath, as if erasing whatever memories had come to mind and faced her. "I need to go to my father's for an hour or so. But it's already late. Especially considering we're five hours ahead of New York here. You may just want to turn in for the night."

"Are you kidding? I had a seven-hour nap! Plus, I'm still on New York time."

"Maybe you'd like to read by the pool? Or make yourself something to eat. The staff doesn't return until tomorrow, but the kitchen is all yours."

He left her then and she fell to the bed, trepidation filling her. So much for thinking he'd changed his mind about keeping her. He was going to Constanzo's to confront him about hiring her. When he came back, he'd probably tell her that her services were no longer needed.

She wanted to stay. Not just because she needed a job, loved getting room and board and wanted some time away from everyone to figure out her life, but also because Antonio was so sad. Somebody needed to help him.

Empathy for Constanzo rippled through her, total understanding of why he desperately wanted to do something to lift his son out of his sadness. Antonio was a good man. Life had treated him abysmally by taking away his beloved wife. He deserved to have someone nudge him back into the real world. And having someone to help actually gave her a way to forget about her own troubles. It could be the perfect situation for both of them.

Except Antonio didn't want her.

Her stomach rumbled and she rose. Might as well find the kitchen and make herself something to eat. Because this time tomorrow she'd probably be on a plane back to New York.

A failure again.

But on her way to the kitchen, the beauty of the house superseded her need for food as it lured her from one room to the next. She hadn't expected a stuffy, formal house. Antonio was too creative for that. But she also hadn't expected to be so charmed by paintings and sculptures that added life and energy to brightly colored sofas, or the eclectic dining room that had a long wood table and sixteen different-styled chairs around it.

Eventually she found herself at the door of a room with a desk and a tall-backed chair, which fronted a huge office with an enormous window through which she could see the pool and the field of flowers behind it.

His office?

With an office in front? For an assistant?

Had he had an assistant before? Could Constanzo be right? Was he ready for someone again?

She entered hesitantly. Stacks of papers littered the first desk, the desk she believed would belong to an assistant. But his room was empty, his desk dusty though free of clutter.

She walked in slowly, ran her fingers through the dust on his desk, curious again. From the coating of dust alone, she'd swear he hadn't been in this room since his wife died.

At the wall of glass, she stopped. The window was actually a series of doors, which she slid aside. A warm breeze fluttered in, bringing the scent of the pool not more than twenty feet away. When forced to do paperwork, Antonio could be poolside.

Sheesh. The rich really knew how to live.

With a sigh, she closed the doors. But as she walked into the outer office, she saw all those papers piled high on the assistant's desk. A film of dust dulled the white of envelopes. Dust covered the arms of the desk chair. But that was nothing compared to the sheer volume of untouched paperwork, unopened mail.

Glancing around, she combed her fingers through her hair. It was no wonder Constanzo wanted his son to hire a PA. He clearly needed some assistance.

And, technically, helping him straighten this mess was her job—

If she kept it.

She walked to the desk, lifted a piece of paper and realized it was a thank-you from a fan. Reading it, she lowered herself to the chair. Obviously, Antonio didn't know the letter's author. So a simple note to express appreciation for his kindness in writing would suffice as a reply.

She leaned back. A box of fancy letterhead caught her eye. A beautiful script *A* on Antonio linked with the

B in Bartulocci. What fan wouldn't want to get a thank-you on the actual letterhead of the artist he admired?

The desire to turn on the computer and write a quick thank-you tempted her. She faced the monitor that sat on the side arm of the desk. She could press the button that would turn it on...

No. She couldn't. It wasn't right.

Still, somebody had to help him, and she needed a way to prove herself.

She lifted her hand to the start button again, but paused halfway and bit her lip. The computer software would probably be in Italian—

Though Antonio had been raised in the US—

She shook her head. It was one thing to look at a few pieces of mail, quite another to actually write letters for him without his permission.

But how else would she prove herself?

Antonio stopped his motorcycle at the front door of his father's country house. He didn't knock. He just entered the foyer and walked back to his father's game room. Sure enough, there he was, playing pool.

"I see the nap you had on the plane gave you energy too."

He set down his cue stick. "Antonio! Why aren't you home?"

"With the PA you hired for me?" He shook his head. "Because I don't want a PA and because your meddling in my life has to stop."

"I don't meddle. I anticipate."

Antonio groaned. "You meddle, Dad. And I can't have it anymore. Not just because it infuriates me, but because this time you're hurting an innocent woman. She's going to be devastated when I send her home."

"So if you're the one sending her home, how can you say that I'm the one hurting her?"

"Because you're the one who brought her here under false pretenses!"

"I did no such thing. You need her."

Antonio groaned again. "There's no reasoning with you. You always see what you want to see."

"True. But that's also why I win so much." He walked to the wall of pool sticks, chose one and offered it to Antonio. "Here is a place you sometimes beat me."

Antonio snatched the stick away from his dad. "If you win, I keep her. If I win, she goes home after a few weeks of rest. But you pay her severance and you let her stay in your penthouse in New York."

Constanzo grinned. "You're on."

They decided on best out of three. Constanzo played pool constantly in his spare time, and was very, very good. But Antonio needed to prove a point, to get it across to his dad that he couldn't take every matter into his own hands. He didn't just want to win. He had to win. In the end, he beat his dad by one shot.

Constanzo sighed. "This is a big mistake. You need her. And she needs a break."

Antonio headed for the door. "That's why I'm going to let her stay a few weeks. It'll give her time to relax enough that she can think through her problems." He turned and faced his dad. "And *you* pay her a big enough severance that she can get a decent apartment."

Constanzo sighed. "It is wrong to send her home. But I lost the bet and I agree. If she must go, I'm the one who owes her severance."

Antonio got back on his bike feeling only slightly better. He didn't want to hurt Laura Beth, and he didn't like the fact that he'd had to gamble to get his way in a situation that his father shouldn't have interfered with. But he'd won.

Revving the bike's engine, he shot along the hills, past the green fields to his house, the wind blowing his hair and teasing his face. By the time he got home, darkness had fully descended and he noticed a light coming from his office. Confused, he parked in the garage and entered through the series of doors that took him from the garage, through the butler's pantry and kitchen to the main living area.

Because there were no lights in the pool area, he thought Laura Beth must have been more tired than she'd thought and retired to her room. Glad he didn't have to face her until the next day, he headed back to the office to turn off the light.

But when he stepped inside, he stopped dead in his tracks. There, behind the stacks of unopened mail and the wide computer monitor, was Laura Beth.

He raced to the desk. "What are you doing?"

She looked up at him. "I've been sitting here fighting the temptation to read your mail." She pointed at one open fan letter. "I know you well enough that I could answer that for you. And any letter like it."

Fear collided with anger. But the stacks appeared to be untouched. The computer hadn't been turned on. She couldn't have seen anything.

His head began to pound anyway. Still, he calmed his voice before he said, "You went into my office without permission."

"I didn't touch anything but this one letter that was already open." She met his gaze. "Plus, it's my job to get you organized."

He sucked in a breath. Memories of finding his wife's itineraries and the matching itineraries of her lovers swam through him, making him shake with anger. Not at Laura Beth, but at his wife. At her shameless audacity. And his just plain stupidity. Add to that the abortion information. The appointment on the calendar. The payment in her check registry. The way she hadn't even tried to hide the fact that she'd taken his child from him.

How the hell could he face that? How could he face another person knowing that his wife hadn't even told him of the pregnancy?

It took great effort for him to soften his voice, but he did it. "I'm not ready for this."

She pointed at the stacks of papers again. "You don't have to be ready. If most of this is fan mail, I can answer it. I can create lists of requests for charitable events. I can coordinate your schedule with Olivia," she said, referring to her friend, who was also his manager. "And I think that's Constanzo's point. A smart PA could do a lot of this work for you."

"I don't want you in here! I don't want anybody in here!"

His shout echoed off the walls of the quiet office. Laura Beth shrank back, her big green eyes round and frightened.

He ran his hand along his nape. "I'm sorry. But this will not work for me." He motioned for her to rise. "Please come out from behind the desk."

She rose and stepped away from his desk.

"You are welcome to stay for the next two weeks. Rest in the sun. Be a tourist. Hell, I can take you around to see the sights. But I do not want a PA."

To his great dismay, her lower lip trembled.

"Seriously. When you return to New York, you can stay in Constanzo's penthouse. And Constanzo is writing a check for a huge severance."

The lower lip stopped trembling as fire came into her green eyes. "What?"

"This is Constanzo's mistake. He will pay for it."

"I don't want your severance! I want a job. I'm insulted by your charity when it's pretty clear I could earn my keep, and even more clear that you need me."

To his surprise, she propelled herself toward him and stood directly in front of him. The tinge of flush in her cheeks matched the glitter of anger in her green eyes. Heat poured from her, triggering his attraction. He'd always loved the way she could stand up for herself.

"I don't want to go home! I want this job. I need this job!"

She stepped closer. The raw power in her glittering eyes hit him like a punch in the gut. He hadn't seen this kind of passion in years. Hadn't felt it himself in forever. It was everything he could do not to pull her to him and kiss her senseless to capture it.

He stepped back. "You think you want this job. You think living in Italy will be a grand adventure. But trust me. You will miss your city and your family."

She eliminated the distance between them again. The fire in his belly spiked. He caught her gaze. Was she daring him to kiss her?

She didn't back down. She stood toe to toe with him. Fire matching fire. "And you can trust me when I tell you that I will not regret being thousands of miles away from my family. I need to be here. I want this job!"

He snorted in derision. He was feeling passion. She was talking about a job. He must really be tired to be so far off base, thinking a woman was daring him to kiss her when she was simply fighting to keep her job.

He turned away, started walking to the door.

Quiet, but close, as if she'd followed him, her voice

drifted to him. "Antonio, I need to be away from my family and friends. For a while. I have more than job troubles to figure out." She said nothing until he faced her again, then she caught his gaze. "I'm pregnant."

CHAPTER FOUR

"PREGNANT?"

Laura Beth watched Antonio, her heart chugging, her nerve endings glittering. Her announcement might have settled him down, but while they'd argued, she'd seen something in his eyes. She'd expected anger and had been prepared to deal with it, but the smoldering gazes? Sweet, considerate Antonio had been replaced by sexy Antonio, a man who looked as though he wanted to kiss her.

The only way she could think to deal with it was to tell him the truth, and now here they were, talking about something she wasn't even ready to announce.

She stepped back. "I'm only two months along, but pregnant all the same."

He rubbed his hands across his eyes, as if confused. Whatever had been happening with him in that argument had disappeared, and he was back to being sweet Antonio, her friend.

"I'm a man. Right now I have no idea if it's appropriate to say congratulations or offer sympathy. I mean, I know this is trouble for you, but babies are wonderful." He shook his head. "And my dad? He goes bananas over babies. Boy or girl. It doesn't matter. He's a cuddler."

A laugh bubbled up. Not just from relief. He'd made

her think about the baby as a baby. A little girl. Or a little boy. She wasn't just going to be a mother; she was getting a baby.

"Congratulations are what I want."

"So the father's on board?"

She swallowed hard, not sure what to say. But she'd be answering this question for the remaining seven months of her pregnancy, so she might as well get used to it.

"No." She cleared her throat. "Let's just say his response was less than enthusiastic."

"And there's no wedding in your future?"

"He doesn't want to see me again or see the baby at all."

Antonio pointed a finger at her. "With my dad's lawyers, we can force him to be part of the baby's life."

She shook her head. "I don't want him to. He said he would send child support, but only if no one knows it's coming from him."

"I think you just blew that by telling me."

She paced away. "If he doesn't want to be part of our baby's life, then I don't want him to be. I think an angry dad would do more harm than good. And I don't want his money."

Thankfully, Antonio refrained from pointing out the obvious: that she needed money too much to turn any down. Instead, he asked, "What do you want?"

She shrugged and spread her hands. "Time. I have to tell my conservative parents that their little girl is about to become a mom with no father for her child. Ultimately, I'll need a job that supports not just me, but me and a baby. So working for you kind of solved all my problems."

He winced. "You can stay."

Hope blossomed in her chest. Being here was the perfect opportunity for her. But she couldn't take charity. "And be your assistant?"

"You're my friend. You don't have to work for your keep."

She stormed over to him. "Yes! I do! I can't be a charity case. Don't you see?"

He sighed and shook his head. "All I see is a woman with a lot of pride."

"Oh, yeah?" She crossed her arms on her chest. "What I see is a man with a lot of pride. You're fighting with your dad about hiring one measly assistant—whom you need—and you won't budge an inch! Why won't you let me work for you?"

"We're friends. I should be able to let you stay in my home as a guest, not an employee."

"That's not why you're fighting Constanzo."

He gaped at her. "Now you're telling me how I feel?"

"Before you knew I was pregnant, you didn't want me working for you. You said you don't want a PA. But it's clear you need one. So obviously there's a reason you're fighting having someone work for you."

He sighed.

"Fine. Don't tell me. Because I don't care. What I do care about is earning my keep. And just from the glance I got at your mail, it was clear that I could at least answer your fan letters. I minored in accounting, so I could also keep track of your money. Anything else in your office, in your life, in your world, I wouldn't care about."

He sighed again. "You are a pregnant woman who needs a rest. Just take the time here with me to have some fun."

She raised her chin. "No. If you won't let me work,

I won't take your charity. Not even your offer of Constanzo's penthouse. I'm going home."

"You don't have a home to go back to."

"I'll think of something."

"If I tell Constanzo you're pregnant and refusing a few weeks of rest, he won't let you use his plane."

"Then I'll fly commercial."

He raised his hands in defeat and slapped them down again. "You can't afford that."

"I know. But I'll be fine."

"No. You won't!"

"Then let me stay here for two weeks as your assistant. If you don't like what I do or still feel you don't need someone at the end of two weeks, I'll take another two weeks to rest and then go home."

He stalled, as if unaccustomed to someone compromising. His brow furrowed. His expression and demeanor were so different than five minutes ago that confusion billowed through her. When they'd first begun arguing, before he'd known she was pregnant, his eyes had been sharp. Glowing. She could have sworn he wanted to kiss her.

Her eyes narrowed again. He might have been seductive Antonio, but he hadn't made a move to kiss her. It was as if he had been daring *her* to step closer—

Had he been daring her to step closer?

He might have been. But to what end? She'd been close enough to kiss, yet he hadn't kissed her.

She swallowed just as he said, "Really? If I let you work for me for two weeks then you'll spend another two weeks resting and not arguing about going home?"

"Yes, I'll get out of your hair if you let me work for two weeks and rest for two more. But that's if you still want me to go home." Her voice shook a bit as she considered that he might have actually been attracted to her. If she hadn't told him about being pregnant…he might have kissed her. Just the thought almost made her swoon.

Telling herself it was foolishness to deal in *what if*s, she said, "But who knows? You might—" she swallowed again "—like me."

Her heart thrummed as their gazes met. He didn't seem to get the double meaning.

He broke their connection and stepped back. "Constanzo can help you find a job in New York."

She smiled sadly. Before he'd discovered she was pregnant he might have found her attractive, but he didn't now. Though something in her heart pinched, it was okay. It had to be okay. She had bigger worries than disappointment over being wanted one minute and discarded the next. After all, why would a man who'd been married to a supermodel want a pregnant commoner?

She took a step back too. "I'd have to make a ton of money to be able to live in New York on my own, especially with the added expense of a baby. If I couldn't make it as a single woman, it's pretty far-fetched to think I could make it as a single mom. At the wedding, I thought about finding new roommates, but I now realize it might be impossible to find two women who want to share the small amount of space we could afford with an infant. I think, in the end, I'm going to have to go back to Kentucky. Live with my parents until the baby is born and then hope I can find a job."

The sadness in her voice sat on Antonio's shoulders like a cold, wet coat. Two minutes ago, she'd been so fiery he'd wanted to kiss her. But suddenly she'd become meek, docile.

Not that he wasn't glad. Now that he knew she was pregnant, everything inside him had frozen with a new kind of fear. The last thing he needed in his life was someone who would remind him of the child he had lost. He might be able to keep her in his home for the four weeks of rest she needed, four weeks before her pregnancy showed…but he couldn't handle watching another man's baby grow when he knew his own child had been cast aside.

She pointed behind her to the door. "If you don't mind, I'd like to go to the kitchen to make a sandwich."

"I'll show you—"

She waved a hand to stop him. "I'm fine. I really do need some time by myself."

She turned and walked out of the room, and he fell to the tall-backed chair behind the desk and rubbed his hands down his face. The man who loved peace and quiet now had a constantly hungry pregnant woman in his home. Pregnant. As in with child. Here was a single woman with no money who was willing to beg and sacrifice to figure out what to do with her life so she could keep her child—and his wealthy wife, who could have hired all the help in the world, had aborted his baby.

He squeezed his eyes shut. He had to get her out of his house before her pregnancy showed, before the constant reminder drove him insane with sadness and anger.

But he wouldn't do it at the expense of her feelings. She'd left his office believing she'd done something wrong, when she had done nothing wrong. His jumbled emotions had caused him to react poorly.

He should apologize tonight, before she went to bed,

so she didn't take the weight of this job loss on her shoulders like one more mistake.

He bounced out of his chair and headed for the kitchen, but when he got there it was empty. And clean. Not even a bread crumb on a countertop.

Regret tightened his stomach. He hoped to God he hadn't upset her so much she'd decided not to eat. Thinking that she might have gone outside for some fresh air before making her snack, he waited in the kitchen for twenty minutes. But she never came in.

Irritation with himself poured through him. Of course he'd upset her by telling her she couldn't stay. She was pregnant and sensitive. Right now she was probably taking responsibility for everything that happened to her.

Knowing he had to apologize and make her see it wasn't her fault that he couldn't keep her, he headed upstairs to her room. The strip of light below the white door to her bedroom indicated she was inside, and he knocked once.

"Laura Beth?"

There was no answer, but the light told him she was still awake, probably reading the science fiction novel she'd had on the plane.

He knocked again. "Laura Beth?"

This time when she didn't answer, he sighed heavily. She might want her privacy, but he didn't want a sleepless night, angry with himself for being the cause of her anxiety and going to bed hungry. And he didn't want her upset with herself.

He twisted the knob. "I'm coming in."

As soon as the door opened, he knew why she hadn't answered. Sprawled across the bed, wrapped in the bath towel she'd used after showering, lay his houseguest.

Her toes hung off the side. Her hair fell down her long, sleek back. The towel cruised across her round buttocks.

The fact that she was angry with him disappeared from his brain like a puff of smoke as interest and curiosity fluttered inside him. He told himself to get out of her room. She was sleeping. Obviously exhausted. And tiptoeing closer was not a very gentlemanly thing to do.

But right at that moment, he didn't feel like a gentleman. The artist in him awoke and cautiously eyed the smooth lines of her back, the long sweep that spoke of classic femininity, the perfect milk-white skin interrupted by dark locks of hair that shimmered when she sniffed and shifted in her sleep.

Longing to paint coiled through him. Swift and sharp, it stole his breath. His fingers twitched, yearning for the slim wooden handle of a paintbrush, and also pulling him out of his trance.

Oh, dear God.

He squeezed his eyes shut. *He'd wanted to paint her.* For real. At the wedding he'd wanted to capture the expression in her eyes, but that had been more like a wish.

What he'd just felt was a genuine yearning to see her form on a canvas, to bring her essence to life.

Excitement raced through him and he studied her back, her hair, her peaceful face against the soft white pillow. His unwanted attraction to her blossomed, but the desire to paint didn't return.

Anguish filled him, but he brushed it off. He couldn't explain the fleeting moment of wanting to paint her, but it was gone and that might be for the best. His decision to let her go was a good one. Even if his ability to paint returned, he could not paint her. It could take weeks to get the image of her he wanted and by that time she'd be showing and he'd experience all the sadness of the loss of his child a hundred times over.

He quietly tiptoed backward toward the door and left her as she lay.

The next morning, Laura Beth awakened to the bright Italian sun peeking in through the blinds behind the sheer aqua curtains. She stretched luxuriously on the smooth, cool sheets that felt like—terry cloth?

Her brow furrowed and she looked down with a gasp as the events of the night before tumbled back. She'd been too tired to make herself something to eat but had forced herself to shower, then she'd fallen asleep before she could even get into pajamas. Pregnancy was full of surprises.

But that was fine. Today was the second day of her life as a realist. No more dreaming or rhapsodizing for her. She had a child to consider. She might have told Antonio the night before that she envisioned herself going back to Kentucky, but that wasn't the optimal plan. Her parents would eventually come around and love the baby, no matter that it didn't have a participating father and that their daughter wasn't married. But there weren't a lot of jobs for IT—information technology—people in Starlight, Kentucky, the small town in which she'd grown up. If she was going to earn a decent living, it would be by getting a job where she could use her degree. And that was what she needed to consider while she had this one-month reprieve. She had to think about exactly what kind of job she could do and in what city she would find it.

She dressed in her best jeans—which were nonetheless worn—and a pink tank top, then ambled downstairs feeling a little better. Because she'd slept later than she normally did, her morning sickness was barely noticeable. Antonio might not be giving her a shot to prove that she could be a good assistant, but she needed time to really think through her options. And he was giving it to her. In beautiful Italy.

Technically, she was lucky.

Very lucky.

When she opened the door to the huge stainless-steel kitchen, the noise of shuffling pots and chatting servants greeted her. Antonio's staff hadn't been around the day before. He'd mentioned giving them time off while he was in New York for the two weeks for Eloise and Ricky's wedding. But today they were in the kitchen, going about what looked to be typical duties.

"Good morning!"

The three women froze. Dressed in yellow uniforms, with their hair tucked into neat buns at the backs of their heads, they could have been triplets, except the woman at the stove appeared to be in her seventies. The woman at the table was probably in her thirties. And the woman with the dust cloth looked to be in her early twenties.

The oldest woman said, "Good morning," but it sounded more like "*Goot* morning."

Laura Beth eased a little farther into the room. "I'm a friend of Antonio's. I'm staying here for a few weeks. Hopefully, I'm going to be helping him clean his outer office."

The youngest woman smiled. Her big brown eyes brightened. *"Sì."*

The oldest woman batted a hand. "Her English isn't good. God only knows what she thought you said." She walked from behind the huge center island that housed the six-burner chef's stove. "Would you like some coffee?"

"She can't drink coffee." Antonio's words were followed by the sound of the swinging door behind Laura Beth closing. "She's pregnant."

The eyes of all three women grew round, then bright with happiness.

Caught like a child with her hand in the cookie jar, Laura Beth spun around. Antonio's usually wild hair had been tied back, and the curve of a tattoo rose above the crew neck of his T-shirt, teasing her, tempting her to wonder what an artist would have chosen to have drawn on his shoulder. Rumor had it that he had a huge dragon tattooed from his neck to his lower back and that it was magnificent.

Interest turned to real curiosity, the kind that sent a tingle through her and made her long to ask him to take off his shirt.

Their gazes caught and her stomach cartwheeled. The attraction she felt for him rippled through her, reminding her of the look he'd given her the night before. She told herself she wasn't allowed to be attracted to her boss—even if he was gorgeous and sexy with his dark eyes that seemed to hold secrets, and the unruly hair that framed the strong face of an aristocrat. But after their encounter in the office the night before, everything about him seemed amplified.

He'd wanted to kiss her. She was just about positive of it. So why hadn't he?

Her curiosity spiked. Something soft and warm shivered in the pit of her stomach.

Oh…that had been a bad question to ask.

The oldest housekeeper's excited voice broke the trance. "We will have a baby here!"

"No." Antonio faced his staff and said, "We will have a pregnant woman here for about four weeks."

"Ah. *Sì*."

Antonio pointed at her. "This is Rosina. She supervises Carmella and Francesca."

Laura Beth stepped forward to shake their hands. "It's nice to meet you."

They giggled.

"They aren't accustomed to guests shaking their hands."

"But I'm an employee, just as they are." She turned to Antonio. Her gaze met his simmering brown eyes and her stomach fell. Good grief, he was hot.

She took a step back, but swayed. She hoped her morning sickness was back because she'd hate to think she'd actually faint over a good-looking guy.

He caught her elbows and kept her upright. "Let's get you to the dining room and get some food in that stomach."

As he led her into the ultramodern dining room, dominated by the large rectangular table with mismatched chairs, her skin prickled from the touch of his fingers on her arm.

She reminded herself that he was only a friend helping her because she'd swayed. And she was pregnant—with another man's child. She didn't know how Italian men were about these things, but lots of American men would think long and hard before they took on the responsibility for another man's child. And Antonio was half-American.

Damn it! Why was she even thinking about this?

He pulled out her chair and helped her sit, but immediately excused himself. "I'll need five minutes. By the time I get back, the staff will have breakfast ready."

She nodded and he left. Nervous, she shifted on her chair, until the pool beyond the wall of glass caught her eye. Past the shimmering water were lush gardens, and beyond that, the blue sky. She'd been to Italy before, but this place, the place Antonio had chosen, was so perfect it seemed to have been carved out of heaven. The peace and quiet of it settled over her.

The door swung open and Antonio returned to the table. "I'm sorry about that."

As he spoke, Rosina entered behind him, carrying two plates of eggs, bacon and toast. She served their breakfasts and exited. Antonio opened his napkin and picked up his fork.

"I trust eggs and bacon are good for you this morning."

She nodded eagerly, her stomach rumbling from the scent of warm bacon. "It's great. I'm starving."

His fork halfway to his plate, he paused. "You should be. You didn't eat last night. I went into the kitchen ten minutes after you said you'd be getting a snack, but you weren't there."

"Too tired. Honestly, Antonio, everybody talks about things like morning sickness, but nobody ever mentions the exhaustion."

He fussed with the silverware beside his plate. "When I told Rosina you had fallen asleep last night without even changing into pajamas, she said women are very tired for the first three months and fall asleep often."

She heard everything he said as a jumble of words. Her brain stalled then exploded after he said he knew she'd fallen asleep without changing. For him to know that, he had to have checked up on her. Which meant he'd seen her lying naked across her bed. Her face blossomed with heat.

"What?"

She sucked in a breath. "You came looking for me last night?"

"Yes."

She groaned.

He frowned. "What?"

"You saw me naked."

He busied himself with his silverware again. "No. I saw you lying on the bed with a towel wrapped around you. You weren't naked."

"Oh, way to split hairs."

"Americans are prudish."

She squeezed her eyes shut. Was she making too much of this? "You're half-American!"

He laughed. "What are you worried about? You have a beautiful, long, sleek back. I'd love to paint you, but I'd replace the towel with a swatch of silk—" He stopped. His brow furrowed.

This time she frowned. "What?"

He picked up his napkin. "It's my turn to say nothing."

"Really? Because I wouldn't mind sitting for a portrait."

He sniffed a laugh. "Then you'd be sitting for a long time. I haven't painted for two years."

Since his wife died. She knew that. And knowing he'd grieved for two long years, a smart person wouldn't push, wouldn't question any further. She reached for her toast.

Rosina walked into the dining room. "Excuse me, Mr. B. Your package has arrived. I sent it back to the office as you requested."

He rose. "Thank you, Rosina."

Laura Beth looked from Antonio to Rosina and back again. But the oldest maid smiled and walked away. Antonio set his napkin on his plate. "That would be your computer."

"My computer?"

"Yes. I ordered you a new one, since you insist on playing secretary for two weeks. Come back to the office whenever you're ready. I'll have it set up."

An odd feeling stole through Laura Beth as he walked out of the room. Why had he gotten her a new computer when there were two perfectly good computers in his office? She remembered the software might have commands in Italian and she didn't speak Italian, and went back to eating.

She finished her breakfast, wishing she could eat more. Not because she was hungry but because she simply wanted more food. But in the end, she knew if she didn't soon get ahold of her appetite, she'd be big as a house when this baby was born.

After washing her hands and brushing her teeth in her room, she made her way to the office.

As she entered, she gasped. "Wow. Look at this." Everything on the desk had been stacked in neat piles. The old computer had been removed and sat on the floor in a corner.

He pointed at his office behind her. "Everything in that room is to be left alone." He motioned to the piles on the smaller secretarial desk. "This fan mail you can answer."

"What about the other stacks?"

"Some are requests for portraits or for me to paint specific scenes or commissioned work for someone's home or office. Those we will answer together."

She nodded. Obviously considering the conversation over, he walked to the computer sitting in the corner, picked up the monitor and took it into his office. He returned and did the same with the computer tower and the keyboard. When he was done, he pulled the office door closed and locked it.

She tried to catch his gaze, but he avoided her by keeping his attention on the keys he shoved into his pocket.

"I have some errands in town. I'll be back at noon to read any letters you've drafted."

She nodded and said, "Yes," but before the word was fully out of her mouth he was gone.

She sat at her desk, glancing at the new computer, which he'd set up while she finished breakfast. When she saw that everything was in English, she reminded herself that was why he'd bought a new computer.

But that made her frown. If the computer had instructions and menus in a language she didn't speak, why would he feel the need to hide it behind closed doors?

Why hide it at all?

CHAPTER FIVE

ANTONIO RETURNED A little after three. Angry with himself for being so obvious about hiding the computer, he'd avoided his office. But he couldn't stay away any longer.

With a resigned sigh, he walked down the long quiet hall. About two feet before he reached the door, he heard the click, clack of the computer keys. He sucked in a breath and stepped inside. Laura Beth immediately looked up.

Her green eyes sparkled. Obviously, she loved to work, and he had to admit she looked right sitting behind the long, flat computer screen, her brown hair knotted away from her face and held together by two pencils.

"Love your hair."

She laughed and stretched her arms above her head, revealing her perfect bosom to him. Her pink tank top expanded to its limits. The long lines of her slender neck all but outlined themselves for him. The slope of her breasts above the pale pink material made his fingers twitch.

The desire to paint her tightened his chest and he had to fight to stop a groan. She was the last woman in the world he needed to have in his house right now. He didn't want to give their attraction the chance to grow when he knew there was no future for them. Not only did he not want to hurt her, but he also could not handle seeing her pregnancy.

But, oh, how he wanted to paint. How he longed for brushstrokes. For the joy of finding just the right light, just the right angle…and he could see all of it with her.

She pointed at her head. "I forgot that my hair gets in my way. So I had to improvise."

She lowered her arms and his vision of painting her crumbled like the walls of the Coliseum. One second the urge to paint was so strong he could see the brushstrokes in his mind's eye; the next minute it was gone and in its wake was a cold, hollow space.

He wanted to curse. He'd finally gotten adjusted to not painting. He'd lost the hunger. He didn't awaken every morning trembling with sorrow over losing himself, his identity, his passion.

And she'd brought it all back.

He fought the impulse to turn and walk out of the office, telling himself anything to do with painting wasn't Laura Beth's fault. These were his demons, left behind by the betrayal of a narcissistic wife and his own stupidity in tumbling into a disastrous marriage with her. He couldn't take any of this out on Laura Beth.

As casually as possible, he said, "Well, your hair is certainly interesting." He motioned to the stacks of letters. "I see you made headway."

"It's fun pretending to be you, thanking people for adoring my work."

He sniffed a laugh and leaned his hip against the corner of the desk. "Give me a pen and I'll sign them."

Like a good assistant, she rummaged for a pen. When she found one, she handed it to him along with the first stack of replies to fan letters. He looked down only long enough to find the place for his signature, then began writing.

He'd signed three letters before she grabbed the stack and pulled it away from him.

A look of sheer horror darkened her face. "You're not reading them!"

"I don't need to read them. I trust you."

"That's nice, but aren't you at least a little curious about what I'm telling people?"

"No. I assume you're saying thanks, and that you homed in on some detail of their letter to me, some comment, and you addressed that to make each letter sound personal."

She fell back to her chair. "Yes. But you should still want to read them."

He took the stack of letters from her again. "One would think you'd be happier that I trust you."

She crossed her arms on her chest. "One would, except I don't think you trust me as much as you're disinterested."

"I'm not sure I see the difference."

"I did a good job!"

"Oh, you want me to read them so I can praise you?"

She tossed her hands in the air. "You're impossible."

"Actually, I'm very simple to understand. None of this interests me because I was a painter. Now I'm not."

She frowned. "But you said this morning that you'd like to paint me."

He had wanted to paint her. Twice. But both times the feeling had come and gone. Now that he had a minute of distance from it, it was easy to see the urge was unreliable. Not something to take seriously. Certainly not something to change the stable course of his life. Given that he was attracted to her and she was pregnant—while he still wrestled with the loss of his own child—that was for the best.

"A momentary slip."

She frowned at him. "Really? Because it might actually be your desire to paint coming back, and like I told you, I wouldn't mind sitting for a portrait."

He chuckled at her innocence. "Trust me. You wouldn't want to sit for a portrait."

She rose and came around the desk to face him. Leaning on the corner, he didn't have to look down to catch her gaze. They were eye level.

"I have the chance to be painted by the most sought-after artist in the world. How could that not be fun?"

He licked his suddenly dry lips. She stood inches away. Close enough that he could touch her. His desire to paint her took second place his desire to kiss her. If wanting to paint a pregnant woman was a bad idea, being attracted to that woman was a hundred times worse. Spending the amount of time together that they'd need for a portrait would be asking for trouble.

"I didn't say it wouldn't be fun. But it wouldn't be what you think."

Her eyes lit. "That's what makes it great. I have no idea about so many things in life. I might have lived in one of the most wonderful cities in the world, but I was broke and couldn't experience any of it. Now, here I am in gorgeous Italy and I feel like the whole world is opened up to me." She stepped closer, put her hands on his shoulders. "Paint me, Antonio."

Her simple words sent a raging fire through him and the desire to paint reared up. Having to turn down the chance to get his life back hurt almost as much as the betrayal that had brought him here. But though his attraction to her was very real, there was no guarantee this yearning to paint was. He could take her to his studio, risk his sanity, feed his attraction to her, and then be unable to hold a brush.

"I told you. It wouldn't be what you think."

"Then tell me." Her eyelids blinked over her incredibly big, incredibly innocent green eyes. "Please."

Attraction stole through him, reminding him that his desire to paint her and his attraction to her were somehow knitted together, something he'd never felt before, adding to the untrustworthiness of his desire to paint. He refused to embarrass himself by taking her to his studio and freezing. And maybe it was time to be honest with her so she'd know the truth and they wouldn't have this discussion again.

"Last night, seeing your back, I might have wanted to paint you, but the feelings were different than any other I'd had when I saw something—*someone*—I wanted to paint."

Her head tilted. "How?"

He'd always known, even before he'd studied painting, that the eyes were the windows to the soul. With his gaze connected to Laura Beth's, he could see the naïveté, see that she really didn't understand a lot about life. How could he explain that the reasons he wanted to paint her were all wrapped up in an appreciation of her beauty that tipped into physical desire, when he wasn't 100 percent sure he understood it himself?

When he didn't answer, she stepped back. The innocent joy on her face disappeared. "It's okay. I get it."

"I don't think you do."

"Sure, I do. It's been two years since you've painted and suddenly you're feeling the urge again. It's not me. It's your talent waking up."

He should have agreed and let it go, but her eyes were just so sad. "It is you."

"Oh, come on, Antonio. Look at me. I'm a green-eyed brunette. A common combination. I've never stood out. Not anywhere. Not because of anything."

He stifled a laugh, then realized she was serious. "You don't think you're beautiful?"

She sniffed and turned away. "Right."

Pushing off the desk, he headed toward her. He pulled the pencils from her hair, tossed them beside the computer and watched as the smooth brown locks swayed gracefully to her shoulders. He turned her to face the mirror on the wall by the door. "Still don't think you're beautiful?"

Her mouth went dry. Her gaze latched onto his, and the heat she saw in his eyes made her knees wobble. "What are you doing?"

"I want you to see what I see when I look at you." He watched his finger as it traced along her jaw, down her neck to her collarbone. A thin line of fire sparked along her skin.

"You think you're common. I see classic beauty." His dark eyes heated even more. Anticipation trickled through her, tightening her chest, stealing her breath.

"A woman on the verge of life, about to become a mother. With everything in front of her. The painting wouldn't be simple. It would be as complex as the wonder I see in your eyes every time I look at you. And it would take time. Lots of time." His gaze met hers. "Still want me to paint you?"

Good God, yes.

The words didn't come out, but she knew they were in her eyes. She couldn't tell if he wanted to paint her because he saw something in her eyes, or if he saw something in her eyes because he wanted to paint her. But did it matter? Right at that second, with her attraction to him creating an ache in her chest...did it really freaking matter?

She waited. He waited. The electricity of longing passed between them. He longed to paint. She suddenly, fervently, wished he liked her.

Finally, her voice a mere whisper, she said, "You said this doesn't happen often?"

He shook his head. "It's never happened at all."

She swallowed. "Wow."

He spun around and stepped away. "Oh, Lord! Don't be so naive! I have no idea what this feeling is, but it's powerful." He met her gaze again. "And it could let me down. We could spend hours in my studio and I could freeze. Or your portrait could be the most exciting, most important of my life."

"Antonio, if you're trying to dissuade me, you're going at it all wrong. What woman in the world wouldn't want to hear that?"

"You shouldn't!" The words were hot, clipped. "This feeling could be nothing but my talent tormenting me." He picked up the stack of letters. "Go freshen up for dinner while I sign these."

She stayed where she stood, frozen, suddenly understanding. To him she wasn't an opportunity, but a torment.

"Now!"

She pivoted and raced from the room, but even before she reached the stairs she'd decided Antonio was wrong. He couldn't know that he would freeze unless he tried to paint her.

She might have lost tonight's fight, but the next time they had this discussion, she wouldn't lose.

They managed to get through dinner by skirting the elephant in the room. He feared picking up a brush and she longed for him to paint her. Or maybe she was just curious. After all, Bruce dumping her had made her feel worthless. She'd spent every moment of every date trying to get Bruce to say something special, something romantic, and she'd failed. But Antonio wanted to paint her. He thought she was classically beautiful. That her painting might become the most important of his life.

She knew he hadn't meant it as romantic, but she was so starved for affection that it felt romantic. And she was supposed to ignore it? Not want it? Not be curious?

But that night in her bed, she scolded herself for being such a schoolgirl. Yes, she'd never had a man think her beautiful enough to be a work of art. And, yes, she'd never been attracted to anyone the way she was to Antonio...but was that good? Or bad? She was a pregnant woman with responsibilities to think about. She shouldn't be daydreaming. Fantasizing.

She spent an almost sleepless night, and in the morning groaned when she knew she had to get up. The truth was Antonio would probably like it if she slept in and didn't do any work. They both knew the job was temporary. She was going home in a few weeks. He didn't want the feelings that he had around her, and her going home would settle all that for him.

But like it or not, Antonio needed a PA and she had a baby to support. She should have been able to prove herself and keep this job, but that crazy feeling or need he had to paint her had ruined everything.

She pulled a pair of old, worn jeans and a big gray

T-shirt from her closet. The staff might wear uniforms, but Antonio wore T-shirts—

An idea came and her eyes narrowed as she thought it through. She dug through her clothes until she found her three skirts, three pairs of dress trousers and a few tops that she typically wore for work. This might be Italy, and Antonio might dress like a beach bum, but she was supposed to be a PA. Maybe if she dressed like one, he'd stop wanting to paint her and see her as the worker she was supposed to be.

She slipped into a gray skirt and white blouse that looked like a man's shirt, pulled her hair back into a bun at her nape, sans pencils this time, and slid into gray flats. Instead of her contacts, she wore brown-framed glasses.

Antonio wasn't at breakfast that morning, so she ate quickly and headed for the office. He wasn't there either. But that was fine. She still had plenty of fan letters to answer. She ate lunch alone, fighting the urge to ask Rosina if she knew where Antonio was. She was a secretary, not his girlfriend. Or even his friend. If she wanted to keep her job, then she couldn't see herself as his friend anymore. She had to work the job correctly. Not insinuate herself into his life.

Not secretly long for a relationship with him.

But when he wasn't there at supper time or for breakfast the next morning, she got nervous, antsy. What if his plan was to avoid her for two weeks, tell her the PA thing hadn't worked out and give her another two weeks of alone time to rest? What if she was working to prove herself when there really was no possibility of her keeping this job?

In the office, she lifted the final three fan letters. In an hour, she'd have nothing to do. She answered the last pieces of fan mail and set the letters on top of the stack she'd generated the day before.

He hadn't even come in to sign the letters.

Where was he?

Was she going to let him avoid her so he could take the easy way out? Just send her off with a pat on her head?

She straightened her shoulders. She'd be damned if yet another man would send her off with a pat on her head. And if she had to drag him into this office by the scruff of the neck, he would see that one of two things was going to happen here. Either he would let her work for him—really work—or she was going home. She did not take charity.

Still, she needed the job more than her pride. She was not going to let him slide out of giving her a chance to prove herself by avoiding her. He was going to answer the requests for commissioned paintings with her. He was going to do his job, damn it!

All fired up, she marched out of the office and into the kitchen. "Rosina?"

The maid looked up. *"Si?"*

"Where is Mr. Bartulocci?"

She frowned. "He say not to tell you."

She shoved her shoulders back even farther. "Oh, really? Would you like me to tell his father that you stood in the way of him getting the help in his office that he needs?"

"No, ma'am."

"Then let me suggest you tell me where he is."

Rosina sighed. "Mr. Constanzo might be bossy, but Antonio is my boss."

She spun on her heel. "Fine. Then I'll simply find him myself."

"Okay. Just don't go into his studio."

Her hand on the swinging door, Laura Beth paused, turned and faced Rosina. "His studio?"

Rosina went back to kneading her bread. "I said nothing."

Laura Beth's lips rose slowly. "I wasn't even in the kitchen."

His strong reaction to painting her had led her to believe his studio would be the last place he'd want to be. So it confused her that he'd be in the old, crumbling house that reminded him he couldn't paint.

But whatever. The plan was to find him, no matter where he was, and force him to see she could be a good employee for him.

It took a few minutes to locate the door that led to the studio. The old stone path had been repaired, but appeared to be the original walkway. The house's door was so old the bottom looked to have been gnawed by wild animals. She tried the knob and it moved, granting her entrance.

The cluttered front room held everything *but* canvases and frames. Paint cans—not artist's paint, but house paint—sat on the floor. Strips of fabric lay haphazardly on metal shelves. She recognized one of the swatches as the fabric for one of the chairs in his dining room.

She glanced around. Most of this stuff corresponded to something in his house. He'd stored leftovers and castoffs here.

He'd said he hadn't painted since his wife's death. But if the items in this room were any indicator, it had been longer than that.

She stepped over a small stack of lumber and around some paint cans and walked through a door that took her into the huge back room, empty save for Antonio, who sat on a stool, staring at a blank canvas.

Light poured in from a bank of windows on the back wall and set the entire room aglow. She didn't know much about painting, but she imagined lots of light was essential.

"Think of the devil and look who appears."

She walked a little farther into the room. "Are you calling me Satan?"

"I'm telling you I was thinking about you."

In a room with a blank canvas.

Because he wanted to paint her.

Because he thought she was classically beautiful.

Tingles pirouetted along her skin. She told herself to ignore them. He didn't want what he felt for her and she did want this job. Acting like a PA had jarred her out of her feelings, so maybe forcing him to see her as a PA would jar him out of his.

She cleared her throat. "I have nothing to do."

He sucked in a long breath and said, "Fine," as he turned on the stool. But when he saw her, he burst out laughing. "Trying to tune in to my librarian fantasy?"

She pushed her glasses up her nose. "I'm trying to look like a PA so I get a fair shot at working for you."

He rose from the stool and walked toward her, stopping mere inches in front of her. "You still want to work for me?"

Her heart jumped. The pirouetting tingles became little brush fires. A smart girl might take Constanzo's severance and run. But though Laura Beth prided herself on being smart, she was also a woman who didn't take charity and who liked a long-term plan. This one, working for Antonio, living in Italy, was a good one.

She couldn't afford New York. She didn't want to burden her parents. Keeping this job was the right move.

Instead of stepping back, she stepped forward, into his personal space, showing him he couldn't intimidate her. "Yes. I still want to work for you."

"You're a crazy woman."

"I'm a desperate woman. Your confusion about painting me isn't going to scare me."

He out and out laughed at that. "Fine."

She motioned to the door. "So let's get back to the office and tackle those letters requesting commissions."

He almost followed her to the door, but hesitated. He'd been thinking about painting her. Imagining it. Mentally feeling the sway of his brush along the canvas. The ease of movement of his arm and hand as they applied color and life to a blank space.

But his hand had shaken when he'd reached for a brush. His heart had pounded. His fingers refused to wrap around the thin handle.

"Come on, mister. I don't have all day."

He laughed. Dear God, how he wished he could get *that* on a canvas. Sensuality, sass and sense of humor. A few years ago, capturing that wouldn't even have been a challenge. It would have been a joy. Today, he couldn't pick up a brush.

He ran his shaky hand along his forehead as sadness poured through him. This place of being trapped between desire to paint and the reality that he couldn't even pick up a brush was as hot and barren as hell.

And maybe she *was* Satan.

He glanced at her simple skirt, the shirt made for a man, the too-big glasses. Or maybe she was right. Maybe she was just a single woman looking to make a life for herself, and *he* was Satan—depriving her because he worried that he couldn't endure seeing her pregnancy, watching another man's child get the chance for life his child hadn't. Watching her joy over becoming a mom.

"I'm not ready to answer the letters about commissions yet." He wasn't sure why he'd said that, except that turning everything down really was like telling the world his career was over. "But maybe it's time I looked at some of the invitations."

"Invitations?"

"To parties and galas and gallery openings." He caught her gaze. "Maybe it's time for me to get out into the world again."

Who would have thought it would be running from a pretty girl that would force him back into the world he didn't want to face? If it weren't for his fears around her, he'd be staying right where he was—hiding.

Instead, he was about to face his greatest fear—getting back into the public eye.

CHAPTER SIX

ANTONIO MANAGED TO find a gallery opening for that weekend. He called Olivia, his manager, putting his phone on speaker, and Laura Beth heard the astonishment in her friend's voice when Antonio told her he would be leaving for Barcelona that evening and would be at the event on Saturday night.

"I hadn't planned on going myself," Olivia said, her voice the kind of astonished happy that made Laura Beth stifle a laugh, since Olivia didn't know Laura Beth was in the room, or even that she was in Italy, working for Antonio. "But I can be on Tucker's plane tomorrow morning. In fact, my parents can stay with the kids and Tucker and I will both come. We'll make a romantic weekend of it."

Laura Beth glanced at Antonio, who quickly looked away. "You know I'd love to see you, but I'll be okay on my own."

"Oh, no, you won't!" Olivia immediately corrected. "You'll probably start telling people you never want to paint again, and all those great commission offers will be off the table. I'm going."

He laughed and Laura Beth watched him, a mixture of curiosity and admiration tumbling around inside her like black and white towels in a dryer. *She* saw a dark, unhappy side of Antonio when he talked about painting. But with Olivia he could joke about it. So who was he showing the real Antonio? Her or Olivia?

He disconnected the call and rose from his desk. "I will be gone for the next few days. You have two choices. Enjoy the pool or sightsee."

Watching him walk to the door, she swallowed. Had he just used work to get out of work? Maybe to show her she wasn't needed?

When she didn't answer him, Antonio motioned toward the door. "Come on, missy. I don't have all day."

Knowing she had no right to question him, she rose from her chair. "No fair using my own lines against me."

He followed her out the door. "All's fair."

In love and war.

She knew the quote. She just didn't know if he thought wanting to paint her was love or war.

Sitting alone in the huge, echoing dining room two nights later, Laura Beth felt like an idiot. She gathered her dish and silver and carried them into the kitchen.

Rosina about had a heart attack. "You are done? You barely ate two bites!"

"I'm lonely. I thought I'd come in here for company."

"Francesca and Carmella are gone."

She walked to the table and set down her plate. "But you're still here."

Rosina winced. *"Sì."*

"Then I'll talk to you."

"You are a guest! You shouldn't be in here and we're not supposed to talk to you."

"Did Antonio tell you that?"

"No. It's good manners."

"I'm not a guest. I'm an employee, like you. I should be eating in here. I *would* be eating in here with you if it weren't for my friend Olivia, who is Antonio's manager."

Rosina eased to the table, slowly took a seat. "*Sì*, Miss Olivia."

"I'm actually an IT person." At Rosina's frown, she clarified. "Information technology." She took a bite of ravioli and groaned. "This is great."

"You should eat lots of it."

Laura Beth laughed. "And get big as a house?"

"You're pregnant. You don't need to worry about gaining a little weight."

"Thanks."

"You're welcome."

They chatted a bit about Rosina's grandchildren. But the whole time they talked, Rosina looked over her shoulder, as if she was worried Antonio would arrive and scold her for fraternizing with his guests.

Respecting Rosina's fear, Laura Beth ate breakfast by herself Friday morning, but by lunch she couldn't stand being alone another second. She wandered into the kitchen long before noon and actually made her own sandwich, which seemed to scandalize Carmella.

She tried to eat alone at dinnertime, but the quiet closed in on her, and she took her plate and silver into the kitchen again.

Rosina sighed but joined her at the table.

"I'm sorry. I just hate being alone."

Rosina shook her head. "This isn't the way it works in a house with staff."

"I know. I know. But I still say we're both employees and we should be allowed to talk."

The sound of the doorbell echoed in the huge kitchen.

Rosina's face glowed with relief as she bounced off her chair. It almost seemed as if she'd been expecting the interruption. Maybe even waiting for it.

"I will get it."

As Rosina raced away, Laura Beth frowned, unable to figure out who'd be at the door. It was a little late for a delivery, though what did she know? She was in Italy, not the US. The country might be beautiful, but it was unfamiliar. Antonio had run from her. Rosina was afraid to talk to her.

This wasn't working out any better than New York would be. Though Italy offered her a way to raise her child in the sunny countryside, rather than being stifled in the kind of run-down New York City apartment she could afford, what good would it do to be raised in a home where people ignored him or her?

The kitchen door swung open. *"Cara!"* Constanzo boomed. Dressed in a lightweight suit, he strode over to her. "What are you doing here when your boss is in Spain?"

She shrugged. "He never asked me to go with him."

"You are his assistant. He needs you." He tapped her chair twice. "Go pack."

She gaped at him. "Go pack? No way! Antonio will be really mad at me if I just pop up in Barcelona!"

"Then you will go as my guest. You can't sit around here moping for days."

She'd actually thought something similar sitting by the pool that afternoon.

"And since you're in Europe, why not enjoy the sights? If you don't want to find your boss, we'll make a weekend of it. I will show you Barcelona, then take you to the gallery opening myself."

Her heart thrummed with interest. She'd never seen

Spain. Still, she was in Italy to work, not race around Europe with her boss's dad. "I can't. I'm supposed to be working."

"And did my son leave you anything to do?"

She winced.

"I didn't think so."

The pragmatist in her just wouldn't give up. "It really sounds like fun, and part of me would love to go, but I didn't pack for vacation. I packed to work. I shipped most of my fun clothes home to my parents. I don't think I have anything to wear."

"You have…what you call it…a sundress? Something light and airy? Something pretty?"

"Won't women be wearing gowns at the gallery opening?" She frowned. "Or at least cocktail dresses?"

Constanzo waved his hands. "Who cares? You will be with me. No one will dare comment. Besides, you will look lovely no matter what you wear. If they snipe or whisper, it will be out of jealousy."

She didn't believe a word of it, but in desperate need of that kind of encouragement, she laughed. "You're good for my ego."

"And you laugh at my jokes." He turned her to the door. "We make a good pair. Go pack."

She quickly threw two sundresses, jeans and tops, undergarments and toiletries into her shabby bag. Trepidation nipped at her brain, but she stopped it. Antonio had left her alone with nothing to do and a staff that was afraid of her. At least with Constanzo, she'd be doing something.

With her suitcase packed, she took a quick shower, put on her taupe trousers and a crisp peach-colored blouse and headed downstairs.

She walked to the foyer, suitcase in hand, and was

met by Constanzo's driver, who took her bag and led her to the limo. When she slid onto the seat, Constanzo was talking on the phone. "Yes. The Barcelona penthouse, Bernice. And don't forget that other thing I told you." He disconnected the call. "Ready?"

She laughed. "Sure. Why not?"

Traveling with Constanzo, Laura Beth quickly learned that Antonio was right—his dad was a pain in the butt. His plane left on his timing. Cars had to be waiting for him, drivers ready to open the door and speed off, and his favorite bourbon had to be stocked everywhere.

They arrived in Barcelona late and went directly to the penthouse—a vision of modern art itself with its glass walls, high ceilings and shiny steel beams and trim.

She gasped as she entered. "Holy cow."

Constanzo laughed. "That's another reason I like you. You remind me not to take my good fortune for granted."

The limo driver set Laura Beth's bag on the marble floor and silently left in the private elevator.

Constanzo reached for the handle of her bag. "I will take this to your room."

"No. No! I'll do it." She picked it up. "See? It's light."

"Okay. Normally the gentleman in me wouldn't let you, but for some reason or another I'm very tired tonight." He plopped down on a white sofa. "Your room is the second door on the left. I'll check to see if the cook is here yet. We'll have a snack."

She almost told him she was more sleepy than hungry, but she finally realized he'd invited her along on this jaunt because he liked company too. So she headed for her room, intending to wash her face and comb her hair, then spend some time with him while he snacked.

Corridors with steel beams, skylights and glass walls took her to the second door on the left. She opened it and stepped inside.

She loved her room in Antonio's house, but this room was magnificent. Beiges, grays and whites flowed together to create a soothing space like a spa. She could almost hear the wind chimes and sitar music.

She put her suitcase on the bed and walked toward the bathroom, desperate to freshen up before her snack with Constanzo.

With a quick twist of the handle, she opened the door and there stood Antonio, wiping a white terry cloth towel down his chest, as if he'd just gotten out of the shower.

His eyes widened and he instantly rearranged the towel to cover as much of himself as possible.

But it was too late. She'd seen the dark swatches of hair covering his muscled chest, and—wrapped around the side of his neck—the black ink of the webbed wing of the rumored dragon tattoo.

He gaped at her. "What are you doing here!"

"Me?" Too shocked to monitor her responses, she yelled right back, "What are you doing here!"

"This is my dad's penthouse. Why would I not use it when I'm in Barcelona?"

She couldn't argue that, so she said, "Fine. Whatever." Lifting her chin, she began backing out of the marble-and-travertine bathroom, embarrassed not just by the fact that she'd walked in on him naked, but also because her mouth watered for a look at his tattoo. From his muscled arms, broad shoulders and defined pecs, she knew his back was probably every bit as spectacular. The right tattoo would make it sexy as hell. "I'm only here because your dad said this was my room."

"I always use this room when I stay here."

"Great. Peachy."

Her face hot, her mind reeling, she pivoted out of the bathroom and walked to the bed. Grabbing her suitcase, she headed for the main living area. Unfortunately, Antonio was right behind her.

Not about to be intimidated, she tossed her suitcase on a white sofa and made her way to the kitchen.

Constanzo sat on a stool at the center island, dipping bread into olive oil. "Come, *cara*. Eat."

Then Antonio walked in behind her and Constanzo's smile grew. "Antonio!"

He scowled at his dad. "What are you doing here?"

Constanzo laughed. "I live here."

"You live in a country house in Italy! This is a spare house."

He smiled. "It's still mine."

Antonio tossed up his hands in despair and walked to the center island. And there, on his back, was the glorious dragon.

Prickly heat crawled all over Laura Beth. The man was a god. Not only was the dragon perfect, crafted in reds, greens and blacks, but his shoulders were wide, and behind the ink of the dragon, well-defined muscles linked one to another. Every time he moved his arm, the dragon seemed to shift and shimmer as if alive.

Of course. What did she expect from an artist but a tattoo that was a work of art itself?

Oh, this was bad. Every time she learned something new about her boss, she liked him a little bit more. Deciding the best thing to do would be to pretend everything was fine, she strolled to the center island, sat on a stool and took a piece of the crusty bread.

Constanzo motioned for her to dip the bread in the olive oil. "So you and I, we go to see the sights tomorrow?"

She nodded as she slid the bread into her mouth. "Oh, this is wonderful."

From her peripheral vision, she watched Antonio's eyes narrow, as she and Constanzo behaved as if nothing was wrong, then he shook his head and stormed out.

When she was sure he was gone, she caught Constanzo's gaze. "I hope you have another bedroom for me."

He laughed. "There are five bedrooms. Suites, really. You don't even have to bump into him accidentally if you don't want to."

She sucked in a breath. Considering how much he didn't want to see her, she imagined Antonio would pack and move to a hotel the next morning, but she wasn't about to explain that to Constanzo. She sent him a smile. "Good."

But the next morning when she entered the dining room, Antonio and Constanzo sat at the long cherrywood table, as if nothing had happened. Both rose. "Good morning!"

Constanzo's greeting was a little cheerier than Antonio's, but at least he wasn't scowling. What was with these two that they could argue one minute and be best friends the next?

Was that why she couldn't get along with Antonio? Because she wanted resolutions to arguments, when he seemed perfectly happy to ignore conflict?

Antonio surreptitiously watched Laura Beth walk to her seat. She looked girl-next-door pretty in a coral-colored

T-shirt and jeans that were so worn she was either really, really poor or really, really in fashion.

He watched her all but devour a plate of French toast as his father rambled off a long list of places he wanted to show her that morning, including the Museum of Modern Art and the Picasso Museum.

His pulse thrummed. He never came to Barcelona without a trip to the Picasso Museum. But should he risk spending time with her when she pushed all his attraction buttons?

Without looking up from the morning paper, his father said, "Would you care to join us, Antonio?"

He wanted to, but he also didn't. He'd come on this trip to get away from the temptation of his assistant, the longing to paint, when he knew it was off, wrong somehow. She was a nice girl and he was a bleak, angry man who was as much attracted to the idea of painting again as he was attracted to her. No matter how he sliced it, he would be using her.

And, if nothing else, he knew *that* wasn't right.

"I'm thinking about—" He paused. His brain picked now to die on him? He was the king of excuses for getting out of things. Especially with his father. But he wasn't at home, where he could cite a million nitpicky things he could do. He was in his father's home, in a city he didn't visit often.

His father peered at him over his reading glasses. "Thinking about what? Going to the museum? Or something else?"

He couldn't make an excuse Constanzo would see right through. It would only make the old man more curious, and when he was curious, he hounded Antonio until he admitted things he didn't want to admit. If he gave his father even the slightest hint he was avoiding

Laura Beth, his dad would either get angry or he'd figure out Antonio was attracted to her.

Oh, Lord! With his nosy dad, *that* would be a disaster.

It was the lesser of two evils to just give in and join Laura Beth and Constanzo. He could always go his own way in the museum.

"Actually, I'd love to go to the museum with you."

Constanzo's face split into a wide grin. Laura Beth looked confused. Well, good. She certainly confused him enough.

An hour later, he strolled into the main room of the penthouse, where Laura Beth perched on one of the parallel white sofas, awaiting his father. Though Constanzo had said they'd leave at ten, his dad didn't really keep to a schedule.

"He might be a minute."

She laughed. "Really? I'm shocked."

Antonio lowered himself to the sofa across from her. He didn't want to be attracted to her, hated the fleeting longing to paint she inspired, if only because it always flitted away, but she was a guest and it was time to mend fences. Even if she returned to New York tomorrow, he'd see her at Olivia and Tucker's parties. They needed to get back to behaving normally around each other. Small talk to show he wanted to be friends was exactly what they needed.

"That's right, you flew here with him last night. You've experienced the joy of traveling with my dad when he doesn't fall asleep."

She winced. "He wasn't too bad. He just wants what he wants when he wants it."

"Precisely."

He tried a smile and she smiled back. But it was a

slow, awkward lift of her lips. Discomfort shimmied around them. And why not? He'd told her his thoughts. His desire to paint her. The fact that he thought she was classically beautiful. Right before he'd chased her out of his office and then arranged to be away from her. She probably thought he was just shy of insane and might never be comfortable around him again.

She rose from the sofa and walked to the wall of windows. "The ocean is pretty from up here."

He swallowed. Her little coral-colored top hugged her back. Her threadbare jeans caressed her bottom. In his mind's eye he didn't merely see her sensual curves; he saw the breakdown of lines and color.

Longing to paint swooped through him. But he answered as calmly as he could. "The ocean is always pretty."

She conceded that with a shrug and didn't say anything else, just gazed out at the sea, looking like a woman lost, with no home…because that's what she was. Lost. Alone. Homeless.

And pregnant.

Emptiness billowed through him, like the wind catching a sail, when he thought of the loss of his own child. But his conscience pricked. As much as he'd like to pretend everything between him and Laura Beth was okay—the way he and his dad always handled conflict—she was his friend. No matter that he couldn't paint her because he didn't trust the artistic urges she inspired; he'd treated her abysmally the night before.

Heat washed through him as he remembered her walking in on him in the bathroom. Her eyes had grown huge with surprise, but he'd seen the interest, too. And her interest had fed his. Two steps forward and he could have taken her into his arms, kissed her senseless.

That's why he'd gotten angry. It had been a defense mechanism against the temptation to take advantage of what he saw in her eyes.

He should say, "I'm sorry," and apologize for yelling. He nearly did, but that might take them into a discussion of his attraction, which would lead to a discussion of him wanting to paint her and they'd already gone that route. It didn't solve anything. It actually made things worse between them.

So maybe the just-gloss-over-what-happened-and-pretend-everything's-okay technique he and Constanzo used was the way to go? Some arguments didn't have conclusions, and some conflicts simply weren't meant to be faced.

He rose, walked beside her, and said the most non-romantic, nonconfrontational thing he could think of. "So how are you feeling today?"

She cast a quick glance at him. "I'm pretty good. No morning sickness, but I think that's because your dad keeps feeding me."

"Have you told him you're pregnant?"

She grimaced. "Still working on figuring out how to tell people."

"Well, my dad would be thrilled." He would have been even more thrilled with Antonio's child, but Gisella had stolen that from both of them. "I told you. He loves babies."

"Which is why he spends so much time with Tucker and Olivia?"

"Yes. That's part of it. But Olivia and Tucker also go out of their way to make sure he's a part of things. They think of him as family and he loves that."

"That's nice."

"It is, and it works for me, too. Because any week they're in Italy entertaining him is a week I don't have to."

"Oh, really?"

Antonio pivoted away from the window to see his dad standing in the entry to the main room.

Red blotches had risen to his cheeks. His eyes narrowed condemningly. "You think you have to entertain me?"

Antonio grimaced. "I didn't mean that the way it sounded, Dad."

"I'm perfectly clear on what you meant." His chin lifted. "And if I'm such a burden, then perhaps I'll just go back to my room and wait for the soccer game." He turned on his heel and headed down the hall.

"Dad, really!" Antonio started after him. "Wait!"

Constanzo spun around. "No, you wait. I'm tired today. Very tired. But I was happy to spend the day with you anyway. If you don't like having me around, then I'll do what *I* want to do—rest in my room with a good soccer game." He turned and headed down the hall. "It's not a big deal."

Antonio watched his father walk away and turn to the right to go to his room. Constanzo backing out of plans made no sense. His dad never turned down an opportunity to be out and about, doing things, seeing things, especially when he had somebody like Laura Beth to play tour guide for.

Antonio shoved his hands into his jeans pockets and walked back to the main room to see Laura Beth standing by the window, waiting for him.

"He isn't going. Says he wants to rest."

"Oh." Laura Beth hesitantly walked toward him. "Is he okay?"

"Yeah, he just seemed—" *Odd. Unusual. Confusing.* "Tired."

"I get that. He didn't sleep on the flight. We got in late. Then we stayed up another hour or so eating." She winced. "The man's going to make me huge."

He laughed. "He prides himself on being a good host."

She smiled, then glanced around. "So what now?"

He sucked in a breath. "I usually go to the Picasso Museum when I'm here."

She brightened. "Then let's go. I don't have anything else to do until the gallery opening tonight."

He wasn't surprised she and his father planned on going to the opening. When Constanzo butted in, he went full tilt. Maybe that was why he wanted to rest?

Antonio glanced back down the hall that led to his dad's suite. The gallery opening started late and ended in the wee hours of the morning. Constanzo wasn't as young as he used to be, and he might have realized he couldn't waste his energy today if he intended to be up until three. Maybe he knew he couldn't spend the day sightseeing and also go to the gallery opening? And maybe the whole nonargument they'd just had was his way of getting out of sightseeing so he didn't have to admit he needed the rest.

The crazy old coot hated admitting shortcomings. Even if they were a normal part of life.

With that settled in his mind, he glanced at Laura Beth, with her bright, expectant face. He should tell her no. He'd sort of gotten them back to being friends. Spending the day with her was like tempting fate—

Or he could turn it into a day to cement their friendship. He could show her around, acting like a friend, and maybe his attraction would go away.

Actually, that idea was perfect.

He hoped.

CHAPTER SEVEN

PRAYING HIS PLAN to get them back behaving like friends worked, Antonio pointed to the elevator and Laura Beth followed him into the plush car, through the ornate lobby and then to the street. The doorman tossed him a set of keys. He motioned to a shiny red sports car. Low and sleek, with the black top retracted, the Jaguar hit the sweet spot of luxury and fun.

"Oh, nice!"

"It's my dad's, of course." He paused halfway to the car as guilt unexpectedly nudged him. His dad shared everything he had, gave Antonio anything he asked for, and he shouldn't have made that remark about being glad that Tucker and Olivia sometimes entertained him. But as quickly as the thoughts came, Antonio shoved them aside. His dad hadn't been insulted by his comment as much as he'd been looking for a way to bail on a day of sightseeing. Antonio was positive he had nothing to feel guilty for.

Laura Beth ambled to the Jag. Her eyes lit with joy as she took in the stunning vehicle. "Your dad has the best taste."

"Yes. He does." He opened the car door for Laura Beth and motioned for her to step inside.

She slid in, immediately glancing behind her at the

nonexistent backseat. "Maybe it's a good thing Constanzo bailed. I'm not sure how we all would have fit in this."

Walking around the hood of the car, Antonio laughed. "No worries. My dad has a limo here. There could have been space for everybody if he'd really wanted to come along."

He jumped inside. As he slipped the key into the ignition, he could feel the heat of her gaze as she studied him. This was the closest they'd been since the day he'd explained why he wanted to paint her. Hot and sharp, his attraction to her tumbled back. The temptation to touch her was so strong, he fisted his hands.

"My mom does that, you know."

Expecting something totally different from her, he frowned and peered over at her. "Does what?"

"Tells me she isn't upset when I know she is. Especially when I'm home for a holiday and I want to go somewhere without her. It's not really passive-aggressive behavior. It's more like she sees I'm an adult, and, though it's hard, she has to give me some space. So she says she's not mad and lets me go alone." She caught his gaze. "Sometimes it makes me feel guilty. But I know it's her choice. Almost like a gift."

He frowned. If Laura Beth had picked up on his exchange with Constanzo, maybe it hadn't been so innocent after all. "A gift?"

"Yes. Time alone with my friends is a gift."

He scrunched his face in confusion. "Why would Constanzo think we needed alone time when we just spent several days together?"

She shrugged. "I don't know."

"Well, whatever he's doing, it's weird, because until today Constanzo's never dropped back."

"Maybe this morning he finally got the message that you don't want him around so much?"

The guilt rolled back. It tightened his chest and clenched his stomach. He looked out over the hood of the car, then faced her. "It's not like that. The only time I freak is when he meddles."

She shook her head. "No. You're pretty much always grouchy with him. But I get it." She put her hand on his forearm, as if what she had to say was supremely important and she wanted him to listen. "You're an adult who lives twenty minutes away from a retired wealthy man who adores you and has nothing to do but dote on you."

He laughed.

"When he first found you, all this attention was probably fun. Now you want to be yourself."

"I suppose." Except without painting he had no idea who he was. And maybe that's what made him the most angry with Constanzo's meddling. He wanted to be able to say, *Let me alone so I can paint, or feed the hungry, or gamble, or read, or sit on the beach*. But he couldn't. He had no interest in anything. And having Constanzo around always reminded him of that.

Not wanting to think about *that* anymore, he hit the gas and propelled them into the street, ending the discussion.

The wind ruffled through their hair, and Laura Beth laughed with glee. "This is great!"

He hit the clutch and shifted into the next gear, working up some speed before he shifted again, and again, each time sending the little car faster as he wove in and out of lanes, dodging traffic.

She laughed merrily, shoving her hands above her head to feel the air.

Something about her laugh soothed him. She hadn't

been right about Constanzo giving him space. Never in
their history together had his dad ever dropped back,
unless Antonio pushed him. But suddenly it didn't matter. With the wind in his face and the sun beating down
on him, it was just nice to be outside. To be away from
his dad. To be away from two years' worth of requests
for paintings. To be away from the studio that reminded
him he couldn't create.

He sucked in the spring air, let her laugh echo around
him and felt the tightness of his muscles loosen as he
drove to the Picasso Museum.

Laura Beth followed Antonio to a back entrance of the
pale stone museum. Glancing around, she said, "So,
are you a friend of the curator or is your dad a donor?"

He said, "Both," then pulled his cell phone from his
jeans pocket. "Carmen, we're here."

They waited only a few seconds before a short dark-
haired woman opened the door for them. Antonio said
something to her in Spanish, then she smiled and disappeared down a hallway.

The power of a billionaire would never cease to
amaze Laura Beth. "Nice."

"It is nice. I don't like having to work my way
through crowds or wait in lines."

"Nobody likes to work their way through a crowd
or wait in a line."

"Which makes me lucky that I can come in through
a back door."

She shook her head. "Right."

He led her through a maze of corridors until they
entered the museum proper. Paintings dominated the
space. Color and light flowed like honey. A true fan,
Antonio stopped, closed his eyes and inhaled.

Laura Beth stifled a laugh. Not because it wasn't funny, but because he was home. *This* was where he loved to be.

He didn't say anything, just walked up to a painting and stood in front of it. She ambled over, sidling up to him to see the picture. Her eyes narrowed as she looked at the odd shapes, the out-of-proportion dimensions, the unexpected colors.

"Isn't that something?"

She fought not to grimace. "Yeah, it's something, all right."

It took only ten minutes and two more paintings for her to realize she didn't just dislike the first piece of art. She didn't like Picasso. Still, she smiled and nodded in all the right places, if only because she didn't want to look like a bumpkin.

Finally, she couldn't take it anymore. "I'm sorry, but these paintings are weird."

He spared her a glance and said simply, "You don't like abstracts."

She winced. "I don't."

"Why didn't you say something sooner?"

"I thought you liked this museum."

"I do." He glanced around, as if the ten minutes had filled his desire and now he was fidgety. "But today I feel odd being here—"

She didn't think that was it. As casual and calm as he tried to be about his dad backing out of their plans, she knew it had upset him. Or maybe it nagged at him. If it really was the first time Constanzo had canceled plans with him, there was a reason. And Antonio was too smart of a guy not to know that.

So why did he keep pretending he didn't care?

He looked around. "Maybe I just don't want to be inside a building?"

"Maybe." And maybe he needed a little time in the good, old-fashioned outdoors to think things through. "We've got a pretty fancy car out there. If you wanna take a ride through the city, I'm game."

Antonio cast a longing look at a painting and another thought suddenly struck her. What if his edginess wasn't about his dad but about the paintings? Picasso might be his favorite artist and he might have visited this museum every time he came to Barcelona, but she'd bet he hadn't been here since he stopped painting.

He definitely needed to get out of here.

So she gave him an easy way out. "Please. I'd love to see the city."

"Then I will take you to see the sights."

She caught his arm. "Are you missing what I said about the fancy car? I don't want to walk through museums or cathedrals. I wanna ride. Besides, I think I could get a better feel for the city if we drove."

"Barcelona is beautiful." He sucked in a breath. "Actually, a drive might be a good idea."

They climbed into the little red sports car again. Within seconds Antonio eased them into traffic. Cool air and scenery—a mix of old buildings and new, leafy green trees standing beside palms, and a sea of pedestrians—whipped by as he shifted gears to go faster and faster and swung in and out of lanes.

Air ruffled her hair. The sun warmed her. But it was the power of the Jag that put a knot in her chest. For all her intentions to stop lusting after the wonderful toys and lives of her rich friends, she loved this car.

Longing rose up in her, teasing her, tempting her. Her fingers itched to wrap around the white leather steering wheel. Her toes longed to punch the gas to the floor. For twenty minutes, she constrained it. Then suddenly she couldn't take it anymore.

She leaned toward Antonio. Shouting so he could hear her above the wind and the noise of the city, she said, "Would you mind if I drove?"

He cast her a puzzled frown, as if he wasn't sure he'd heard correctly.

She smiled hopefully. "Please? Let me drive?"

"Oh!" His voice vibrated in the wind swirling around them. "Can you drive in a city you don't know?"

She nodded eagerly. "I've driven in New York."

He frowned. "Can you drive a stick?"

"Are you kidding? I was driving my granddad's old farm pickup when I was thirteen."

He eased the car over to a space on a side street between two tall stucco buildings with black wrought-iron balconies that looked to belong to apartments. "Thirteen was a long time ago for you. Are you sure you remember how to use a clutch?"

She playfully punched his arm.

"Okay, I get it." He shoved open his car door. "Let's see what you can do."

It took a minute for them to switch seats. When she got settled, she caressed the soft leather steering wheel before she turned the key in the ignition, depressed the clutch and punched the gas.

They jolted forward and he grabbed the dash for support. "Careful, now."

She laughed, hit the clutch and shifted to a better gear. "This car is like heaven." When the engine growled for release, she hit the clutch, shifting again. "Holy bananas. It's like driving the wind."

He laughed, but he still clung to the dash. "You're going to kill someone!"

She depressed the clutch and shifted a final time, reaching the speed she wanted, barreling through yellow lights, weaving in and out of traffic.

"I never knew you were a daredevil."

His eyes weren't exactly wide with fear. But they were close. Still, she was good. She knew she was good. Driving was in her blood. "I'm not. I just like a good car."

"Really? I'd have never guessed."

"What? You think women can't appreciate a powerful engine?"

"No, you just seem a little more tame than this."

She shook her head. Yet another person who thought she was dull Laura Beth. "Right. I guess we all have our secrets." She spared him a glance. "Our passions."

He tilted his head.

She shrugged. "You like to express yourself through art. I want to be free." She took her eyes off the road to catch his gaze. "And maybe a little wild."

He laughed. "You? Wild?"

"Thank you for underestimating me."

"I don't underestimate you."

"Right. That's why you refuse to paint me. You all but said you don't think I can handle it."

"I said *I* can't handle it."

"Oh, sure you could. I can see in your eyes that you could. You just don't want it to happen."

"Sitting for a portrait can be long and boring."

She shrugged. "So?"

Antonio shook his head, but didn't reply. Laura Beth suddenly didn't care. With the wind in her hair, the sun pouring down on her and the engine in her control, for once in her life she experienced the joy of total power. She soaked it up. Swam in it. She was so sick of everybody underestimating her, thinking they knew her, when all they knew was the shadow of the person she could be with no money, no opportunities.

She suddenly wondered if that's what Antonio saw when he thought of painting her. The longing to be something more. The hidden passion.

Hope spiked through her, then quickly disappeared. He might see it, but he didn't want it.

Saddened, she slowed the car. Palm trees and four-lane streets nestled into Old World architecture gave the city a timeless air but she barely noticed it. Something inside her ached for release. She didn't want people to pity her or dismiss her. She wanted to be herself. She wanted to be the woman Antonio saw when he looked at her.

And she honest to God didn't know how to make that happen.

The more she slowed down, the more Antonio relaxed in the passenger's seat. He forgot all about her little tantrum about him underestimating her when he realized how much she truly loved driving. A passenger on Laura Beth's journey of joy, he saw everything in squares and ovals of light that highlighted aspects of her face or body. The desire to paint her didn't swell inside him. Longing didn't torment him. Instead, his painter's mind clicked in, judging light and measuring shapes, as he watched the pure, unadulterated happiness that glowed from her eyes as she drove.

But something had happened as she slowed the car. Her expression had changed. Not softened, but shifted as if she were thinking. Pondering something she couldn't quite figure out.

He tapped her arm. "Maybe it's time to head back?"

She quietly said, "Yeah."

Curiosity rose in him. She was the second person that day to do a total one-hundred-eighty-degree turn on him. Happy one minute, unhappy the next. Still, he'd made a vow to himself not to get involved with her, and he intended to keep it.

He pointed at his watch. "We have a gallery opening tonight."

She nodded, and at the first chance, she turned the car around. He thought she'd stop and they'd switch places, but she kept driving, and he leaned back. Surreptitiously watching her, he let the images of light and lines swirl around in his brain. Normal images. Calculations of dimension and perspective. They might be pointless, but at least this afternoon they weren't painful. She was a passionate, innocent woman who wanted to love life but who really hadn't had a chance. And that's what he longed to capture. The myriad emotions that always showed on her face, in her eyes.

Eventually, she pulled into a side street and turned to him. "I'm a little bit lost."

He laughed. "I think you are."

"So you don't mind taking over?"

"No."

She fondled the steering wheel, then peeked at him. "Thanks."

The sudden urge to gift her the car almost overwhelmed him. Watching her drive might have been the first time he'd seen the real Laura Beth. And he knew that was the person she wanted to be all the time. The woman who wasn't afraid. The woman who grabbed life and ran with it.

"You looked like you enjoyed it."

Her gaze darted to his. "Maybe too much."

The desire to lean forward and kiss her crept up on him so swiftly it could have surprised him, but it didn't. The woman who'd pushed that gas pedal to the floor piqued his curiosity. Not just sexually, but personally. She was as complicated as his desire to paint her.

He moved closer, watching her eyes darken as she realized he was about to kiss her. His eyelids drifted shut as his lips met hers and everything inside him froze, then sprang to glorious life. She was soft, sweet and just innocent enough to fuel the fire of his need to learn more. His hands slid up her arms to her shoulders, pulling her closer as his mouth opened over hers and she answered. His lips parted. Her tongue darted out enough for him to recognize the invitation.

Raw male need flooded him. The powerful yearning to taste and touch every inch of her rose up. But when his hormones would have pushed him, his common sense slowed him down. It was as if kissing her made him believe they could have a real relationship. No painting seduction of an innocent, but a real relationship.

The thought rocked him to his core. Dear God, this woman was pregnant. A relationship meant watching her grow with another man's child, sadly realizing he'd lost his own.

Worse, the last woman he'd been in a relationship with had made a mockery of their marriage. She'd broken his heart. Stolen his ability to paint. He'd never, ever go there again. He'd never trust. He'd certainly never give his heart. And whether she knew it or not, that was what Laura Beth needed.

Someone to trust her. Someone to love her.

He broke the kiss. But he couldn't pull away. He stared into eyes that asked a million questions he couldn't answer.

"I'm sorry."

She blinked. "Sorry you kissed me?"

He stroked her hair as the truth tumbled out. "No."

Her voice a mere whisper, she said, "Then…what are you sorry for?"

"Sorry that this can't go any further. There can't be anything between us."

"Oh. Okay."

But she didn't move away and neither did he. Confusion buffeted him. If he knew it was a bad idea to get involved with her, why couldn't he move away from her?

"We should go."

"Yeah."

Grateful that she wasn't bombarding him with questions about why there couldn't be anything between them, he opened his door and got out, and she did the same. She rounded the trunk. He walked in front of the car to get to the driver's side. He slid behind the wheel, started the car, made a series of turns and headed toward Constanzo's penthouse.

Still rattled by their kiss, he wanted to speed up and get them the hell home so he could have a few minutes alone. But he slowed the car and let her admire the architecture, the town square, the street vendors and shops.

When they returned to the penthouse, she took one last look at the Jag before shoving open her door and stepping out onto the sidewalk.

Joining her, he tossed the keys to the doorman and led her to the elevator. Neither said a word. A strange kind of sadness had enveloped him. For the first time since he'd met Gisella, he found a woman attractive, stimulating. But he was so wounded by his marriage he knew it was wrong to pursue her.

He walked through the entry to the main room of Constanzo's penthouse, and saw a huge white sheet of paper propped up on a vase on the coffee table.

He ambled over, picked up the note written in Constanzo's wide-looped script and cursed.

"What?"

"My dad has gone."

Her brow wrinkled. "Gone?"

"He took the jet and went home." Realizing this ruined Laura Beth's trip, Antonio faced her. "I'm sorry."

She bit her lower lip. "I think that little tiff with your dad this morning was bigger than you thought."

"Seriously? Do you really believe he was angry that I said I was happy to have someone else entertain him every once in a while?" He tossed his hands in disgust. "I tell him that four times a week."

She shrugged. "That might be true, but he seemed a little more sensitive than usual this morning." When Antonio groaned, she added, "Why else would he leave?"

He crumpled the paper, annoyance skittering through him. What did his dad expect him to do? Race after him? Apologize, again? He'd apologized already and Constanzo had blown him off, told him he was tired. He'd given him more reason to believe he wasn't angry than to believe he was.

"Don't worry about it." He certainly refused to. If Constanzo wanted something, expected something, then maybe he needed to be forthright and not sulk like a sour old woman. "It's not a big deal. It just means you'll have to—" *Go to the gallery opening with me.* He almost said the words, but snapped his mouth shut as the truth finally hit him.

That meddling old man!

That's why he'd left him and Laura Beth alone that morning. He wasn't mad. He must have seen something pass between them, and he'd left so they'd be forced to interact.

No. They wouldn't just be forced to interact. They'd have fun, as they'd had driving that afternoon. And they'd connected. He *kissed her.*

Oh, Constanzo was devious.

Antonio shrugged out of his jacket and tossed it on the sofa, his blood boiling. As if making him feel guilty wasn't bad enough, matchmaking was the ultimate insult.

Still, just because Constanzo had played a few tricks, that didn't mean he had to roll over and be a victim.

His voice crisp, casual, he said, "The real bottom line to this is that he took the plane. But even that's not a big deal. If he doesn't send it back for us, I have a friend I can call."

She bit her lip again, took a few steps back. "I don't want to be a burden."

He sighed. When he saw Constanzo again he intended to let him have it with both barrels, if only for scaring Laura Beth. He'd left a shy, broke, single woman in a city where she didn't even speak the language.

"You're not a burden." But he also wasn't going to let Constanzo set them up this way. As much as he would like to take her to the gallery, to have her on his arm, to laugh with her he couldn't do it. It had been wrong for him to kiss her. Equally wrong for him to be interested in her. She deserved so much more than the broken man he was. He wouldn't be a bad host, but Constanzo's plan ground to a halt right here. They'd eat something, then he would retire to his room until it was time to dress for dinner and the gallery opening—for which he had plans with Olivia. Because this was business, he didn't even have to make an excuse for not inviting Laura Beth along. His plans were already set.

He glanced around. "So, lunch?"

"We're past lunch and jogging toward dinner."

"Oh, you want to wait for dinner?"

"Are you kidding? I'm pregnant and I haven't eaten since breakfast. I'm starving. I need something now."

"That's fine. We'll have Cook make whatever you want."

Antonio led her to the kitchen, but as soon as he opened the door, he knew Cook was also gone. The place wasn't just empty. It appeared to have been buttoned down, as if Cook had stowed everything away until Constanzo's next visit.

The prickle of anger with his dad heated his blood again. Now the old coot wanted him to take Laura Beth to dinner? Well, he had another thought coming, because Antonio had plans.

Strolling toward the pantry, Laura Beth said, "I can make something for us to eat. It'll be fun."

He winced. "I can't eat now. I have dinner plans with Olivia."

She stopped and faced him. "Oh."

"I'm sorry. We haven't had a real meeting in weeks, and she likes to give me pep talks…check in with me." He shrugged. "It's a working dinner."

She waved her hand in dismissal. "No. No. I get it. This is a business trip for you."

Feeling like a first-class heel, and not able to completely ditch her, even though he knew getting involved with her would only hurt hert, he halfheartedly said, "You can come—"

But Laura Beth knew she couldn't. It would be one thing to go to dinner and the gallery with Constanzo. People would look at her and assume she was his assistant. It wouldn't matter what she wore, how much she ate, if she laughed at all the wrong places. But with Antonio and Olivia and Tucker? They would look like a foursome. Olivia would be dressed to kill, and Laura Beth would be in an old sundress, looking foolish.

"No. Thanks." She caught his gaze. "I'm tired. It's better for me to stay in. I'll fix myself a little something to eat and probably go to bed."

"You're sure?"

The relief in his eyes rattled through her, confirming her worst suspicions, filling her with disappointment. He didn't want her to tag along. They'd been fine in the car, chatty even. She'd admitted things she normally didn't admit and he'd listened. But just as he didn't want to give in to the urge to paint her, he didn't want to like her, to get to know her. He'd made that clear after their kiss when he said there could be nothing between them.

And now here she was, like Cinderella, being told she couldn't go to the ball. Even though she knew damned well she didn't belong there, it still hurt.

So she smiled. "Sure. I'm fine."

He took a few steps backward. "If you're sure."

"Antonio, stop being so polite and go."

"Okay." He turned around and walked out of the kitchen.

She leaned against the center island, disappointment flooding her. She didn't know why she was upset. So what if he'd kissed her? The moment had been right. For all she knew she could have looked like a woman issuing an invitation. He'd taken it…but regretted it. And she was wise enough not to want a man who didn't want her. She'd already had a guy like that and she was smarter than to want to get involved with another. Her current overload of emotions had to be hormonal, brought on by her pregnancy.

So why did being left behind feel like such a huge insult?

Because, deep down, she knew he liked her. Damn it.

That's what had been simmering between them all along. Not her desperate need for a job or his unexpected desire to paint her. But attraction. Maybe even genuine affection.

She pulled away from the center island and straightened her shoulders. She had to stop thinking about this. She was hungry. She needed to rest. She also needed Antonio's plane or his friend's plane, or his help, at least, to get back to Italy. She couldn't get upset because he refused to admit he liked her.

She made herself some eggs and toast and ate them on the balcony, listening to the soothing sounds of the ocean. Finished eating, she set her plate on the table beside her outdoor chair and let herself drift off to sleep.

The sound of Antonio calling for her woke her. "Laura Beth?"

She snapped up on her seat. Her heart leaped, and for a second she let herself consider that he might have changed his mind about her coming along. Lord knew she could eat a second dinner. And though she hadn't liked Picasso, a gallery opening didn't usually showcase only one artist. She'd probably see lots of paintings she'd like.

Filled with hope, she pushed off the patio chair and slid the glass door aside to enter the main living area, and there stood Antonio, so gorgeous in a black tux that her breathing actually stuttered.

"Look at you!"

His hair tied back off his face highlighted the sharp angles and planes of his chin and cheeks and made his large brown eyes appear even larger. His crisp white shirt and sleek tux weren't just sexy. They made the statement of just how refined, how wealthy, he was. Even his shiny shoes spoke of pure elegance.

"It's the first time I'll be in a gallery in over two years. I figured I couldn't look like a slouch."

"Oh, trust me. You do not look like a slouch."

He laughed, but extended his right arm toward her. "I can't get this cuff link to close."

She walked over. "Let me see."

The cuff link in question was black onyx with a diamond stud.

"I can get it."

She smiled up at him and he gazed down at her, his beautiful dark eyes shiny with anticipation. Her heart tugged. He really wanted to be back in his world. Back with his peers. His people.

And here she stood in threadbare jeans, an old top and flip-flops. Her longing for him to ask her to come to dinner and the opening with him morphed into shame. Humiliation. Even if he begged, she had nothing to wear.

But he wasn't begging.

His phone rang and she quickly fastened his cuff link so he could grab it from the coffee table. "Olivia, what's up?"

She heard the sounds of her friend's voice, though she couldn't make out the words. But Antonio laughed.

"That's perfect. I love that restaurant." He headed for the elevator. "I've got my dad's limo. I can be at your hotel in twenty minutes." He pressed the button and the door magically opened. Listening to Olivia, he turned and waved goodbye to Laura Beth as the door closed behind him.

And she stood in the glamorous main room, alone, listening to the sounds of silence.

Tears threatened but she stopped them. She wasn't upset. She was angry. It didn't matter that she didn't have a dress to wear or shoes. Antonio hadn't been glad to ditch her because she was penniless. He'd been glad to leave her behind because they'd connected that afternoon. They'd talked about Constanzo. He'd let her drive. He'd kissed her, for heaven's sake. Then they came upstairs to the penthouse and he'd gotten—distant?

She glanced around.

Why would he suddenly become cold? The only thing that had happened was finding Constanzo's note—

No. He'd become cold when they'd discovered they were alone.

And he didn't want to be alone with her.

Part of her understood. She was a pregnant woman. What rich, eligible bachelor would want to be alone with a pregnant woman?

But he had no reason to fear her. She'd never made a pass at him. If anything, he'd made a pass at her. He'd kissed her—

She tossed her hands in the air in frustration. Why was she thinking about this!

To get her mind off it all, she took a shower and washed her hair. With nothing better to do, she heated the curling iron she found in a drawer and made huge, bouncy curls out of her long locks. Before she could comb them out and style her hair, her stomach growled.

With fat, uncombed curls and dressed in pajama pants and a huge T-shirt, she walked to the kitchen. Just as she opened the refrigerator, the building doorman rang up. Though she answered the phone, she winced when a bounty of Spanish bombarded her. With a grimace, not even sure she'd be understood, she said, "I don't speak Spanish."

He said something else, then disconnected the call.

Shaking her head, she headed back to the refrigerator to find a snack, but she heard the elevator doors open, and she walked to the main room.

There in the elevator was the doorman, package in hand, grinning at her.

She walked over. "Oh, a package. That's what you were saying. We had a package."

He nodded, handed it to her and left as quickly as he'd arrived, apparently deciding she was a poor candidate for a tip, and he was right, because she didn't have any of the local currency.

She started for the coffee table to leave the big box somewhere Antonio would see it, assuming it was something for him, only to see her name on the label.

She frowned. Who would send her something here? Who even knew she was here?

Slowly walking back to her room, she examined the label one more time to make sure it really was for her.

She closed her bedroom door behind her and opened the box to find a simple black dress and black spike heels.

Confused, she pulled the dress out of the box. The material was sinfully soft, rich in texture, like a chiffon or organza. A card sat in the crinkled tissue paper that had caressed the dress. She grabbed it, opened it and read, *"Cara, go to the opening. Constanzo."*

She stared at the card, then burst out laughing. This was just too weird. How did he know she wasn't going to the opening? Unless he'd realized that she'd refused to go to the opening with Antonio because she had nothing to wear? She had mentioned that to him—

What difference did it make? Antonio was gone. She didn't have money for a taxi. Antonio had taken the limo. And she couldn't get the doorman to bring the Jag around because she didn't speak Spanish. Constanzo might want her to go, but the dress had arrived an hour too late. Which was too bad. She'd really like to go to that opening and show vain, conceited, jumping-to-conclusions Antonio he had nothing to worry about from her.

She tapped the note against her palm, then glanced at it again and smiled. It was printed on Constanzo's stationery and had his cell number on it.

She glanced at the dress, glanced at the card, glanced at herself in the mirror with her hair curled but not combed. She might look like a street person right now, but Antonio had been the one to say he wanted to paint her. Considered her classically beautiful. Kissed her. She hadn't been the one to make passes at him. So why was he acting as if she were someone to be afraid of?

Anger bubbled in her stomach. How dare he behave as if *she* was the one with the crush on him and insultingly leave her behind when he was the one who'd kissed her?

The shy Kentucky girl in her filled with fire. She raced to the kitchen and picked up the phone the staff probably used to order groceries.

It took three rings before Constanzo answered. "Hello?"

"I need a coach."

"Excuse me."

"You sent me a Cinderella dress but it came too late for me to go to the opening. Antonio's long gone with the limo. I can't go with him to the gallery."

"I will call the driver and have him come back for you."

"I want the Jag."

Constanzo laughed. "Excuse me."

"I want the Jag. If I'm going to go to the trouble of getting all dolled up...I'm making an entrance."

Constanzo laughed with glee. "That's my girl. I'll call the doorman and tell him to have the keys waiting for you when you get downstairs."

"You better also get my name on the guest list for the opening. I'm pretty sure a fancy gathering like this one is by invitation only."

"I'll have Bernice call."

"Thanks."

"You're welcome. Go knock his socks off."

CHAPTER EIGHT

STANDING IN THE main room of the gallery, pressed in by art aficionados, Antonio glanced at his watch. His return to the world of art had been a subtle, almost disappointing, one. Olivia had other clients—working clients—she was schmoozing right now. Tucker had found two business acquaintances he was talking up. And Antonio stood by a gallery owner from Madrid who desperately wanted him to do a showing.

Half of him had gone breathless at the prospect. The other half wanted to run in terror.

The screech of a car grinding to a stop stabbed into the noise of the gallery. He looked up, past Juanita Santos to the wall of windows behind her. A red Jag had pulled up to the curb for valet parking. His eyes narrowed. That looked just like Constanzo's car.

The driver's door opened. A spike heel emerged, connected to one long, slim leg.

His eyebrows rose. The crowd outside the gallery turned to the newcomer. Men smiled. Women gave her the once-over.

Antonio's mouth fell open as Laura Beth tossed the keys to the valet.

With her hair pulled up, piled high on her head, and looking luscious in the slim black dress, she walked the cobblestone path like a model working the catwalk. The dress rode her curves, accenting her womanly figure, but the black color gave her a sleek, sophisticated air. In her worn jeans and goofy librarian work clothes, she was an all-American girl. In this dress, she was a woman.

And all eyes were on her.

His heart caught and his breathing faltered, but he ignored them. He wasn't in a position to get involved with her. Though looking at her in that dress, he was again tempted. Still, for all he knew, Constanzo had set this up. But even if he hadn't, his reasons for staying away from Laura Beth were sound. Responsible. He feared watching her belly swell with child, but his first marriage had also made him jaded, angry. She was absolutely too nice for him. And right now she was about to be rejected at the door.

A gentleman, he couldn't let that happen. He turned to Juanita. "If you'll excuse me."

"Of course."

He headed for the door, his heart thundering in his chest with fear that she'd be embarrassingly refused entrance. Instead, the young man smiled and motioned for her to enter.

She dipped her head in thanks and glided into the crowd.

He stopped and waited for her to see him. When she did, she approached him.

"Well, look at you."

She smiled slowly. "You've got to stop stealing my good lines."

He laughed. "I'm glad you're here, but I'm afraid I'm—"

He was about to say *busy*, when Olivia raced over. "Laura Beth?"

She raised her hands. "In the flesh."

Olivia squealed with joy. "What are you doing here?"

"I'm spending a few weeks with Antonio, helping him try to clear out his office."

One of Olivia's eyebrows rose as she looked at Antonio, who clearly hadn't mentioned that her best friend was living with him.

Laura Beth laughed. "Don't worry. Constanzo hired me. Antonio didn't. So he's not really cooperating."

Olivia tilted her head at him. "Pity."

Then Laura Beth totally surprised him by squeezing Olivia's hand and saying, "I'd love to chat. But Antonio was just telling me that he's busy. I'm assuming you've got people for him to meet, so I'm going to walk around the gallery and, you know, browse."

Olivia gave her a quick hug. "Have fun. I do have a few people I'd like Antonio to meet. But maybe we can catch up tomorrow."

Laura Beth smiled mysteriously. "Maybe."

Then she turned and walked away.

Antonio watched the slight sway of her hips, the long curve of her spine, as she moved away from him.

"Wow. She looked happy, huh?"

Antonio faced Olivia. "Happy?"

"Yeah. Lately she's been a little glum." She slid her hand into his elbow and turned him toward the crowd again. "I guessed she was a bit upset about being room-mateless, but she wouldn't talk about it. She won't take a thing from me or Tucker. Not even a job offer. She wants to make her own way in the world." She paused and frowned. "How'd Constanzo talk her into working for you?"

He blinked. Obviously, she didn't know Laura Beth was pregnant. So he shrugged. "I think losing her apartment really brought home the fact that she couldn't be choosy about who offered her a job."

"Yeah, well, if you really don't want her, Tucker does. He has an opening for an IT person who would work directly with him, somebody he can trust with his secrets."

"Sounds perfect for her."

"It is perfect for her. He was going to make the offer after the wedding, but she disappeared. Now at least we know where she went."

"Yes, you do." And Tucker wanting to hire Laura Beth was like a blessing from heaven. A relief.

Really.

There was no reason for the odd feeling in his stomach, the fear of losing her, the reminder of how empty his house was without her.

He peered around into the crowd but couldn't see Laura Beth. Then he caught a fleeting glimpse of her as she moved between two conversation circles. The men in each cluster smiled at her and she innocently smiled back.

Jealousy catapulted through him.

"Ready to mingle?"

Thanking God for a reason to take his eyes and his attention off Laura Beth, he smiled at Olivia. "Desperately."

He spent an hour with Olivia introducing him to gallery owners, art dealers and collectors. His former charm came back to him as if he hadn't lost it. If he'd had anything new to display or sell, he would have made a killing.

But he didn't have anything new to display or sell,

and he wasn't yet entertaining commissions, so everyone drifted away. The futility of his situation roared through him, frustrating him, making him wonder why the hell he was even here.

He faced Olivia. "I'm going to get a drink. Would you like one?"

"I think I better find Tucker."

Perfect. He could go to the bar, drink himself stupid with scotch and be driven back to the penthouse, where he could pass out and forget he was a has-been.

Shifting to the side, he slid through the throng of happy people and to the discreet glass-and-marble bar set up in a corner.

"Scotch." The bartender turned to go and he caught his arm. "Three of them."

The young man nodded, apparently thinking he was getting drinks for friends, and that was just fine with Antonio. He angled himself against the marble, but when he did he saw Laura Beth, standing alone, staring at a painting.

He studied the tilt of her head, the way it clearly displayed her interest in the picture, saw the light and shadows he'd use if he painted her, so everyone would see what he saw. A newcomer falling in love.

Damn it! What was he doing imagining painting her again!

"Here you are, sir."

The bartender set three crystal glasses of scotch on the bar. Antonio took the first one and downed it. He set the empty glass on the bar, then dug through his pockets for a good tip.

He walked away with a scotch in each hand, deliberately heading away from Laura Beth, but apparently she'd moved too, because there she stood, in front of another display. This one she seemed to like about as much as she liked the Picassos.

Watching her, he sipped the second scotch. The desire to capture her slithered through him again, just as Jason Ashbury stopped in front of him.

"I wanted to give you a card."

Antonio set his second scotch on an available tray with a wince. "Sorry."

Jason laughed. "Never apologize for enjoying a good scotch." He handed the card to Antonio. "I know you're accustomed to bigger galleries, but we'd love to have you in Arizona."

And he'd love to be in a gallery in Arizona. He'd love to have a showing anywhere. If he could just freaking paint again.

His gaze strolled to Laura Beth.

Jason shook his hand. "Come visit us. Maybe we'll inspire you."

He walked away and Antonio's eyes sought Laura Beth again. She all but shimmered in the sophisticated dress, but she couldn't hide that innocence. And maybe that's what drew him. She was his deceased wife's polar opposite. And if her innocence was the medicine he needed to paint again, maybe he shouldn't fight it.

He strolled over. "Are you okay?"

"What? You think a woman can't be on her own in a gallery?"

"No. You're pregnant and it's been a long night and you still have a bit of a drive home."

She winced. "Saw me in the car, did you?"

He took a step closer. "Saw you getting out of the car."

This time she laughed. "That was fun."

"You looked like you were enjoying it."

"Oh, I was." She took a long drink of air. "I'm going to miss this."

"Barcelona?"

"No. The dressing up tonight and playacting."

He raised one eyebrow in question. "Why? You've got a few more weeks in Italy. You can do all the dressing up and playacting you want."

She shook her head. "No. I can't. Walking around here tonight, I remembered something I'd thought at the wedding. I took what I believed was a real job because I'm not an executive or a trust-fund baby or even employable in New York City." She faced him. "But you don't want me and I don't really belong here. It's time for me to go home."

Panic swirled through him. "Home New York or home Kentucky?"

"Kentucky." She raised her gaze to meet his. "I know there's not much work for an IT person there, but I'm going to have a baby. I need my mom for moral support." She sucked in a breath. "But looking at one of the pictures, I also realized I had a pretty good childhood."

He frowned. "Which picture?"

She ambled to a picture a few feet away. "This one."

It was a painting of three dogs running through the dead brush around a pond in late fall. The colors were cool, dismal. The sky so dark it was almost charcoal gray.

"*This* reminds you of home?"

Gazing at the painting, she said, "Yes."

Hoping for the best, he said, "You had a dog?"

She laughed. "No. We had ugly Novembers. The cold sets in and lingers. But some of my best life things happened in fall."

She faced him with a light in her eyes that flicked

the switch of his longing to paint. But in a different way than the day he'd found her lying on her bed wrapped in a towel, a different way even than the technical visions of dimension and light that had overtaken him various times that day. This was a serious, quiet need, something that didn't hurt him or fill him with angry longing. This one was normal.

Breathlessly afraid to lose this feeling, he quietly said, "What sort of things?"

"Well, my birthday's in the fall, so there's the whole being born thing."

He laughed.

"And every fall we returned to school." She smiled at him but her eyes were distant, as if she were thinking back to the past. "Going to school meant seeing my friends, getting new clothes, football games, school play tryouts."

"Sounds like fun."

"It was."

"And that's why you're going home?"

She moved her eyes up to meet his gaze. "I just keep thinking I'd like to be around my mom when I actually have the baby. But I also had a great childhood. I want my baby to have that, too."

He whispered, "It makes sense," not sure why the moment felt so solemn, except it meant that their time together was ending. Or maybe because he knew he needed to at least try to paint her and if he didn't ask in the next few seconds he wouldn't get the chance.

"I still think about painting you."

"I know." She stepped away. "You told me it annoys you to think about painting me."

He laughed. "Tonight's feelings are different."

She faced him. "Really?"

"Yeah. Tonight it all feels real, doable."

"Well, that's…something."

He breached the space between them. "Actually, it is. The uncontrollable urge might have been a first step, but just as your feelings about becoming a mom are shifting, growing, so are my feelings about painting you."

Her breath caught. "You're serious?"

He glanced around. "Yes. But this feeling is so new and it's only cropped up around you." He caught her gaze. "Can you spend the next few weeks with me? Let me see if I can paint again?"

"Only if you also let me work as your assistant."

Her persistence made him laugh and long to kiss her. In that very second, the need was so strong he doubted his ability to resist it. Her face tipped up to him. Her earnest eyes held his. It would be so easy.

But he'd kissed her once and it had only reminded him that he couldn't have her.

Because he couldn't.

"I want the painting to be our focus."

"Can I earn my keep by answering the rest of your mail?"

He laughed. "No. I want to do this right."

She cocked her head. Understanding flitted across her face. "Okay."

And something wonderful sprinted through his blood. Acceptance. She had needs of her own. Troubles of her own. But instead of bargaining with him, she would simply help him.

"You know, Tucker wants to hire you when you get home."

Her eyes widened. "He does?"

"He needs someone to work directly with him."

"Oh my God. That might mean I could work from Kentucky."

Her eyes glittered with happiness and the lure of her lush mouth was as strong as an aphrodisiac. He wondered about his strength, his endurance, if he really could paint her without touching her.

But his fears melted away when he remembered he couldn't watch her pregnancy. And now he knew she was going home to her mom and a job from Tucker.

She would not be around forever. His endurance didn't have to last a lifetime. Only a few weeks. He had nothing to worry about.

CHAPTER NINE

WHEN THEY ARRIVED at Antonio's country home the next day, everything had a different feel to it. They were no longer adversaries. They were partners in his plan to paint again. The feeling of being on even ground was heady stuff for Laura Beth. She'd always been second-best, plain Laura Beth. Today they were equals.

Standing in the foyer, she faced him with a smile. "So? Ready to go to the studio?"

"It's Sunday."

"I thought artists had to work while they were inspired. Do you want to lose your momentum?"

She could tell from the expression that flitted across his handsome face that he didn't. Still, he said, "How about lunch first?"

She caught his hand and tugged him in the direction of the back door that led to his studio. "How about work first?"

He laughed. "Wow. I have never known you to turn down food."

"I had a peanut-butter-and-jelly sandwich while you took that catnap on the plane."

She turned the knob on the ratty door of the cottage and it gave easily. Surprise almost had her turning to ask why he didn't lock the door, then she realized he was totally comfortable here in the Italian countryside. Which was probably part of why it drove him so crazy not to be able to paint. This was his sanctuary, and it was letting him down. Since his wife's death, everybody and everything seemed to be letting him down. She would not.

Pride billowed through her. She might make nothing else of her life, but helping him to paint again would be her crowning accomplishment. Even if she never told another soul, to protect his pride, she would know simple Laura Beth Matthews had done something wonderful.

They wound their way through the maze of old paint cans, broken furniture and fabrics to the last room. His studio.

Happy, she faced him with a smile. "So where do I sit? What do I do?"

He ran his hand down his face. "We just got off a plane. Give me a minute to adjust."

His hesitancy filled the air. He wanted this so much and he'd tried and failed before. She knew that trying again, he faced disappointment again.

She stepped back, giving him space. "Sure."

He glanced around, then rummaged through stacks of paper in the drawer of a metal desk so old it didn't even have accommodations for a computer. He pulled out two tablets. One was huge. The other was the size of a spiral notebook. He set the large pad of paper on the top of the desk, and opened the smaller one.

"We'll do sketches first."

"What do you want me to do?"

"First, I just need to warm up, get the feel of your features, the shape of your body."

She nodded eagerly.

"So, I'll sit here." He leaned his hip on the corner of the desk. "And you sit there." He pointed at a ladder-back chair about ten feet away.

She frowned. "There?"

"Yes. These are preliminaries. Warm-ups. Something to get me accustomed to your shapes."

Her gaze involuntarily rippled to the chaise near the windows. That would have been more comfortable. She wanted to sit there.

But he pointed at the ladder-back chair again.

She smiled hesitantly. Though she understood what he was saying, something really drew her to that chaise. Still, she sat on the ladder-back chair. Antonio picked up a simple number-two pencil.

"Really? A pencil? You're not going to use charcoal or chalk or anything cool like that?"

He sighed and dropped the tablet to his lap. "I'm warming up!"

She waved her hand. "Okay. Okay. Whatever."

By the time Antonio had her seated on the chair, his anxiety about drawing had shimmied away. Praying that she would stop talking and especially stop second-guessing his choices, he picked up his pencil and began sketching quickly, easily, hoping to capture at least five minutes of her sitting still.

When she wrinkled her nose, as if it was itchy, he stopped and stretched. He'd drawn small sketches of her eyes, her nose, her lips, her neck, her eyebrows, the wrinkle in her forehead, the side view of her hair looping across her temple and one sketch of her entire face.

"If you need to scratch your nose, scratch."

She pulled in a breath and rubbed her palm across her nose. "Thank God."

"What? You were sitting for…" He glanced at his watch. "Wow. Ten minutes. I guess you do deserve a break. For someone unaccustomed to posing, ten minutes is a long time."

She popped off the chair. Shook out all her limbs. "I know I've sat perfectly still for more than ten minutes at a time, but sitting still without anything to think about or do? That's hard."

"I'd actually hoped to break you in with five-minute increments."

"Meaning?"

"You'd sit for five minutes a few times in our first two settings, then ten minutes in our third and fifteen in our fourth…that kind of thing."

"So we're skipping a step?"

"Which could be good."

"Can I see what you've done?"

He handed her the tablet.

She smiled. "These are great."

"That's just me messing around until I get a good feel for drawing your features. Then we move on to sketches of what I think a painting of you should look like."

She beamed at him and everything inside him lit up. He told himself he was happy that she was enjoying the process, happy that he hadn't yet had an anxiety attack, and motioned her back to the chair.

"If you can keep doing ten-minute sessions, we'll do two more, then break for the day."

"You're only working a half hour?"

He laughed. "Yes. I'm not just indoctrinating you into the process. I'm easing myself in too."

She sat on the chair, straightened her spine and lifted her face. "Okay."

He sketched for ten minutes, gave her a break,

sketched for ten more, then they had lunch. Later, while she sat by the pool, he paid his dad a visit. He expected them to argue like two overemotional Italians about Constanzo stranding them in Barcelona. Instead, his father quietly apologized, told Antonio he was tired and retired to his room.

The next day, Laura Beth easily graduated to sitting for fifteen minutes at a time. The day after that, she had a bit of trouble with sitting for twenty minutes, but eventually got it.

He drew her face over and over and over again. He sketched her arms, her feet, the slope of her shoulder. Feeling the rhythm of those shapes in his hand as it flowed over the paper, he felt little bits of himself returning. But he didn't push. Fearing he'd tumble into bad territory, he didn't let himself feel. He simply put pencil to paper.

On Sunday, with Ricky and Eloise in Italy on the last leg of their honeymoon, he forced Laura Beth to take the day off to visit with them.

Monday morning, though, she arrived in his studio, bright and eager to begin.

Trembling with equal parts of anticipation and terror over the next step of the process, he busied himself with organizing his pencils as he said, "This week we're doing potential poses for the painting."

"So now I don't just have to sit still? I have to sit still a certain way."

He glanced up. Her eyes were bright. Her smile brilliant. Enthusiasm virtually vibrated from her body.

"Basically, yes."

Knowing how uncomfortable the ladder-back chair had been, he walked her to the wall of windows in the back of the room. He posed her feet, positioned her shoulders, placed her hands together at her stomach and strode back to the old metal desk to get his pad and pencil.

He worked for twenty minutes, trying again and again to make her come to life in a sketch, but failing. He knew what he wanted. That faraway look. And though he saw snatches of it in her eyes, it didn't stay and he couldn't catch it when it was only a glimpse.

With a sigh, he said, "Let's take a break."

"Wow. Was that a half hour already?"

"Twenty minutes. I can't seem to get what I want from this pose, so I figured we'd stop, give me a bit of rest and try again."

After a bathroom break and a few sips of water, Laura Beth was ready to go again. Antonio picked up his pencil and tablet. She positioned herself and Antonio started drawing. After only a few seconds, he said, "The light is wrong."

She deflated from her pose. "Bummer."

He shook his head. "It is a bummer, but we can come back to this tomorrow morning. Right now..." He glanced around. "Let's try one with you sitting on the chaise."

She walked over and sat down. Without waiting for instructions, she angled herself on the chair with her back to him, then looked over her shoulder at him.

The vivid image of her lying wrapped in the towel on her bed popped into his head, quickly followed by the pose he'd so desperately wanted to paint. Her wrapped in silk, one shoulder and her entire back bare, the swell of her hip peeking out at him, her face a study of innocence.

His finger itched to capture that. But he was sure the urge was a leftover of an aberration. Watching her at the gallery, he'd envisioned several compelling poses, expressions, little bits of humanity that would result in a painting every bit as compelling. He did not need to go *there*.

"That's not how I want you."

"Okay."

"Let's try this." He wasn't entirely sure how to position her. He had facial expressions in his mind. Images of her hair falling just the right way. And he couldn't seem to get it right as he shifted her from one side to another, one pose to another.

"Okay. How about this? Lie down and pretend you're daydreaming."

"Oh! I get to lie down!"

He stopped in midstep toward the metal desk and faced her. "If you're tired or anything, I don't want you to overdo."

She stretched out on the sofa. "I'm fine."

Her inelegant movement struck a chord in him again and he eagerly grabbed the notebook. That was part of the essence he was trying to grasp. Beautiful yet impish. Troubled but still hopeful. With the image fresh in his mind, he began sketching. But after ten minutes he realized that pose didn't work either.

Neither surprised nor disappointed—today was all about trying and failing—he gave her a break, then sat her on a chair.

Backing away from her, he said, "Think deep thoughts."

Her face scrunched. "How deep?"

"I don't know." Remembering the feelings he'd had in the gallery and their subsequent conversation, he said, "Think about going home."

She nodded, and he watched the change come to her

eyes. Almost a sadness. Something tweaked inside him. But he didn't say anything. Though he wanted to comfort her, they weren't supposed to become friends from this. He wanted to paint her. She wanted to go home.

It made him sad. Almost angry. But he got the best sketches of the day.

After that they stopped for lunch. Rosina had prepared salads and bread, but Laura Beth skipped the bread, insisting she could *feel* herself getting fat.

He watched her single out and then dig in to her tomatoes with gusto and had to stifle a laugh. Feeling light and airy because he counted that morning as a success, he didn't want to upset her in any way, shape or form. But the look in her eyes as he'd sketched her haunted him.

Casually, as if it were the most natural question in the world, he asked, "Do you not want to go home?"

Her head popped up. Her gaze swung to his. "I need to go home."

"There's a wide gulf between need and want."

"I need my mother. Aside from Tucker and Olivia's kids, I've never been around a baby. And I can't really count Tucker and Olivia's kids because I've never changed their diapers, never fed one of them and most certainly never walked the floor."

"Ah. I get it. You need your mother's assistance."

"More her advice…her knowledge. Which means, since I need her so much, I *want* to go home."

He laughed. "That's convoluted at best."

She shrugged. "It is what it is."

But the faraway, sad expression came to her eyes again. He should have yearned to grab his pencil. Instead, that odd something tweaked inside him again.

Only this time, he recognized it. It wasn't a worry that they would get close. He hated to see her sad.

"What if you got a nanny?"

She gaped at him for a few seconds, then laughed out loud. "Right. I can't even afford an apartment. Hell, Tucker hasn't officially offered me a job yet, and you want me to hire a nanny?"

"But if he does offer you a job with a good enough salary, it would mean you could live where you want. That you wouldn't have to go back to a small town that clearly makes you sad."

"The town doesn't make me sad. I told you before. I want my child to be raised there."

He frowned. "So what makes you sad?"

Laura Beth fumbled with her napkin. For fifty cents she'd tell him the truth. She'd look him right in the eye and say, "I like being with you. I like the person I am with you. And I am going to be sad when I leave because I know I'll only ever see you at parties where we'll be polite like strangers."

But then he'd draw back. Then he wouldn't paint her. He might even put her in Constanzo's plane and ship her home so he didn't have to deal with her feelings.

So she'd handle them alone.

"I think it's just hormones."

"Ah." He nodded. "I seem to recall hearing a bit about them from Tucker when Olivia was pregnant."

And that was it. He totally believed her. He didn't even like her enough to say, "Are you sure?" He didn't dig deeper. Proof, again, that he didn't have the same kinds of feelings for her that she had for him.

In bed that night, she cautioned herself about getting so close to him—wouldn't let herself pretend there was any chance they'd be together—and the next morning she forced herself to be as chipper and happy as any woman posing for a portrait should be. She couldn't have him forever, but that didn't mean she couldn't enjoy what she had now. In fact, a wise woman would accept what she could get and make memories.

After breakfast, Antonio took her outside. She'd asked him a million times if there was anything special he wanted her to wear and every time he'd said, "Your jeans are fine."

But his attempts at capturing an outside pose failed. When the next day's poses also resulted in balled-up paper and strings of curses in Italian, Laura Beth had to hide several winces. On Friday, when his temper appeared—a real, live temper that went beyond curses and balled-up paper and resulted in explosions and tablets tossed into the trash—fear trembled through her.

Not fear of Antonio. She knew he would never hurt her. His anger was never directed at her, but always at himself. His lost focus. His inability to capture what he wanted. She also saw his volatility as part of his larger-than-life personality, very much like his dad's. What scared her was that he might quit trying and ask her to leave.

The very thought caused her chest to tighten. So Saturday after breakfast she suggested she meet him in the studio. He frowned and asked why, but she only smiled and raced off.

She styled her hair as it had been the night of the gallery opening, put on makeup and slipped into the black dress and the high heels Constanzo had bought her.

When she walked into the studio, Antonio had his back to her. She straightened her shoulders, lifted her chin and sashayed over to the wall of windows.

When he saw her, Antonio's face fell. He gaped at her for a good twenty seconds, then grabbed the tablet. Not knowing if the lighting was good or bad, she simply stood there. She thought deep thoughts, trying to get that faraway look he always talked about catching. She knew that the sooner the painting was done, the sooner she'd be going home, but she didn't care that dressing in the way that had inspired him would result in her going home. She longed to help him. This wasn't just about her doing something important with her life anymore. This was about him. About wanting him to get his life back.

And if the way he frantically scribbled was any indication, she was succeeding. Finally giving her man what he needed.

Her man.

She struggled with the urge to close her eyes. He was her man. She could feel it in her bones. And she was his muse. But he would let her go. Because he believed he'd had his woman, the love of his life, and even though Gisella was gone, he didn't want another love.

What she felt for him was pointless.

Antonio put down his pencil forty minutes later, belatedly realizing he'd made her stand stiff and silent way beyond her limitations.

"I'm sorry, *cara*."

She shook her shoulders loose, then smiled. "It's fine. Did you get what you wanted?"

"Yes." The desire to kiss her rose strong and sure. It wasn't just her pretty face and her bright personality that drew him. Her unselfish gestures never ceased to amaze him. For almost an hour, she'd stood stiff and straight, barely blinking. Even more, though, she'd realized what he needed when he didn't. The dress, the hair, even the shoes had brought back the feelings he'd had in the gallery, and his artistic instincts hadn't merely appeared. They'd jumped to full-blown life.

Because she'd made all the connections he couldn't seem to.

Still, he fought the urge to kiss her by turning away, puttering with his tablets, pretending interest in old sketches that had no value now that he'd found what he wanted. "Thank you for thinking of the dress."

She displayed her spike heels. "And let's not forget the shoes and hair."

She said it lightly, but an undercurrent of melancholy ran through her voice. All of this was about him. Nothing they'd done in the past ten days helped her. She still had her troubles.

He walked over and caught her hands. Fear of getting too close, of longing to kiss her, had to be shoved aside. He owed her. "You look so pretty. Let me take you to lunch."

She shook her head. "Nah. You don't have to."

"I insist. Give me ten minutes to clean up."

"It's okay. There's no need to thank me."

He smiled. "I'll let you drive."

Her eyes widened. "Do you have a Jag?"

"I have a Lamborghini."

"Oh, dear God." She pressed her hand to her chest. "How can I turn *that* down?"

He motioned for her to precede him out of the studio and up the cobblestone path, then headed to his room to change. Considering her attire, he slid into beige slacks and a short-sleeved white shirt, which he left open at the throat.

When she saw his car, she squealed with delight and

raced to get behind the wheel. He tossed the keys at her. She caught them like a left fielder for the Yankees. The engine rumbled to life and she shifted into reverse to get them out of the garage, then shoved the pedal to the floor when they reached the road.

The noise from the wind swirling around the open roof prevented conversation, so he pointed to give her directions to the nearest small town. He motioned with his hand to let her know she needed to slow down as they drew closer.

They entered the village and their speed decreased. The noise of the wind diminished. He heard the appreciative sigh that told him she was pleased with his choice of village, with its cobblestone streets, old houses, street vendors and sidewalk cafés.

"Park here."

She pulled the car into a little space. They both got out and he directed her to walk to the right.

The way she looked at his little town was like nothing he'd ever seen before. Her lips kicked upward into a smile of pure joy, but not like a person surprised by what she saw. More like a woman who'd found a place she loved.

Mesmerized by her excitement, he caught her hand and led her down the street to the outdoor seating of his favorite local restaurant.

They ordered salads and once again she refused bread. He shook his head. "You are supposed to gain weight."

"Yeah, but I'm not supposed to turn into a tub of lard."

He laughed. "The way you talk reminds me of my childhood."

Her gaze rose to meet his. "Really?"

"Yes. Everybody I know either speaks Italian or they're a bigwig in the art world or in one of Dad's former companies. You speak like a normal person."

"I am a normal person."

"And most of my foster parents were normal."

Her eyes softened. "Did you have a rough time?"

He shook his head. "Tucker had a rough time. I think that's because he was actually in New York City. I was in a quiet city in Pennsylvania. I had a bit of trouble with being angry about not knowing my dad, but my foster parents were always simple, normal people with big hearts."

She said, "Hmm," then cocked her head. "Pennsylvania's not so different from Kentucky."

He chuckled. "You have a twang that Pennsylvanians don't."

She frowned. "Hey, I worked really hard to get rid of that twang."

"And you've mostly succeeded."

Laughing, Laura Beth glanced across the table at Antonio. The blue sky smiled down on them. A light breeze kept everything cool. The hum of life, of street vendors, cars and chatting passersby, filled the place with life and energy. She totally understood why Tucker and Olivia spent several months a year in Italy. If she could, she would, too. But in a few days she'd be going home. Back to her blue-collar roots. Back where she belonged.

Emotion clogged her throat. She wouldn't just miss Antonio. She would miss his world. Italy. Art. Interesting people. Sun that warmed everything.

Still, she swallowed back her feelings. She'd already decided her future was in her small town with her parents. Because she loved that world, too. She loved crisp autumns. Sleigh rides and skating in the winter. The love of people she knew. A quiet, humble place to raise a child.

It just seemed so unfair that she had to choose. But, really, she didn't have a choice. She was broke. Longing to live in two worlds was the last resort of a foolish woman. And she knew it was time to get sensible. The best way to do that would be to take the focus of this conversation off herself and get it back on him.

"Tell me more about your childhood." Changing her mind, she waved her hand to stop his response. "No. Tell me about Constanzo finding you. I've only ever heard bits and pieces of that story from Olivia. I'd love to hear it from your perspective."

He grinned sheepishly and glanced down at his empty salad plate. A waitress strolled over and said something in Italian before she poured him a second glass of wine and took his empty plate.

He sucked in a breath. "Imagine being exactly where you are right now financially, taking your last pennies and getting on a plane to another continent and literally swapping a painting every month for your rent."

She sighed dreamily. "It sounds romantic."

"It was terrifying."

"Yes, but at least you had something to barter. You had paintings that your landlord obviously wanted."

He sniffed a laugh. "Don't think he was being altruistic. I'm sure he's made a bundle off me."

"Maybe. But you still had something to trade."

"Right. After I bought the canvases and paint." He shook his head. "I was always scrambling for odd jobs, in a country I didn't know, as I learned to speak the language."

The breeze lifted the hair around his shoulders and

she saw the tip of the webbed wing of his dragon tattoo, the sexy contrast to the quiet, calm man before her. Totally captivated by his smooth voice and his cool sophistication in the white shirt that accented his olive skin, she put her elbow on the table and her chin on her fist. "So what happened?"

He lifted his wineglass. "Constanzo bartered Tucker into paving the way for us to meet."

"So he'd already found you?"

Antonio nodded. "Yes. But he was clumsy about it. He'd chased my mom out of his office when she told him she was pregnant and she'd disappeared, gone to America without even telling her family where she was going. Humiliated, she clearly didn't want anyone to find her." He swirled the wine in his glass. "Her family didn't even know I existed. But Constanzo knew that somewhere in the world was a child he'd rejected and he knew our getting to know each other wasn't going to be easy."

"Wow."

"So Constanzo enlisted Tucker's help, but it was actually Olivia who brought me into the fold."

"I don't understand."

"Tucker is like a bull in a china shop. Very much like my dad. Olivia appealed to me as a person. We connected immediately."

She smiled. She could see Olivia and Antonio connecting. She saw signs of their closeness every time they were together. Until he'd stopped painting, they'd been totally in sync about his career. They connected like friends, not romantically, the way Laura Beth was drawn to him. But that was probably why it had been so easy for Antonio and Olivia. They were friends only, while she and Antonio had an attraction flipping back and forth between them, a longing to be close that actually somehow kept them separated.

"So how did they spring it on you that you were the long-lost son of a billionaire?"

"My cousin Maria had apparently figured everything out." He laughed. "Maria makes bulls in china shops look tame. So rather than risk that she'd bulldoze the information into a conversation, they told me at my first showing here in Italy."

She winced. "Yikes."

"It was weird. But Constanzo had been involved in the preparations for the showing right from the beginning as backer. So I'd gotten to know him a bit, and when they told me he was my dad, instead of that resulting in confusion, it just sort of pulled everything together."

The warm breeze ruffled past again, drawing her gaze to the square, the tourists and street vendors. "That's nice."

"What about you?"

Her gaze snapped over to his. Asking about his dad was supposed to keep the conversation off her. Now, here he was, bringing it back to her again. "Me?"

"Any odd stories in your life?"

"Unless you count the story of me getting pregnant, my life has been simple. Uncomplicated." She shrugged. "Which is why I'm simple, silly Laura Beth."

"Have you ever thought that being simple, being honest, being kind is a good thing?"

Her breath stuttered into her lungs. This was why she was falling head over heels in love with him. He didn't just like her as she was. He made her feel that who she was was more than enough. It was special. And she was so hungry to be special that she gobbled up his compliments like gelato.

"I used to."

"You should start believing it again." He took her hand and she froze. The way he touched her always sent a zing of excitement through her, but it also always felt right. Natural. As if the two of them had been created to touch and love and talk.

"To me, you are wonderful."

If she still had a sliver of her heart left, he took it with those words. And the horrible truth hit her. She wasn't falling in love with Antonio. She was already totally gone. So in love with him that when she had to leave, her heart would dissolve into a puddle of sadness.

CHAPTER TEN

GETTING READY FOR bed that night, she once again forced herself to face reality. She truly loved Antonio, and she believed he loved her too. Not the head-over-heels way she loved him, or the way he'd loved Gisella, but in a quieter, gentler way.

But he didn't *want* to love her. She saw the hesitation in his eyes every time he pulled his hands back, stepped away from her, turned away rather than kiss her. His wife might be dead, but she was very much alive in Antonio's heart. If he loved Laura Beth, and she believed he did, it wouldn't be the same way Tucker adored Olivia or Ricky worshipped Eloise. It would be a quiet, simple, you-are-second-best kind of love.

She let that realization wash over her because it would dictate every decision she made from now until she boarded a plane and left him…left this beautiful place.

Knowing that he had feelings for her, she could push him to admit them. She could promise him the one thing he truly wanted—his ability to paint. She could be his muse forever.

She would win him. Win a place in his life.

But even if he asked her to marry him, she would always be second-best.

Was winning the object of her love, getting to be with the man she loved, worth never being in first place in anyone's life?

She didn't know. Right now, just the thought of leaving him, or only seeing him at friends' functions, where he'd be distantly polite to her, shattered her heart. She wasn't even sure she could walk away. As much as she needed her mom's help, she also needed Antonio. She needed to hear him say she was special. She needed the feeling of purpose he'd inspired in her.

But she also needed to be someone's one true love.

And Antonio had had his one true love.

Antonio refused to work on Sunday, so it was Monday morning before they headed to the studio again. Knowing they would be working, she'd worn the black dress and spike heels, wound her hair into the fancy hairdo and put on makeup.

He raced down the cobblestone path. "Today is the day I get you on canvas."

She laughed. "Really? All in one day?"

"I'll do a slight pencil drawing today and from here on out you won't need to pose every day, just when I want to be reminded of something."

"Sounds good."

It really didn't sound good. It sounded like the beginning of the end. Still, she kept up the happy facade as he chose canvas, found pencils and went to work.

But he cursed at his first attempts to sketch her. He took digital pictures and studied the light, the angle of her head, shoulders and torso. But nothing pleased him. By noon, he was annoyed with himself, and they quit for the day.

Tuesday, he got angry. He'd drawn plenty of versions

of her, had captured the look he wanted in his initial drawings, but none of the sketches on canvas caught the look he wanted to show the world.

On Wednesday, she tried talking. So what if her face was moving? He wasn't getting anything he liked anyway. And when she talked, she usually calmed him or inspired him. But that day it didn't help.

As he ran an eraser over the shadowy pencil lines he'd made, her purpose shivered through her. The one thing she really wanted out of life—the one memory she wanted to hold in her heart to prove her time had meant something—was to pull him out of his anger, his funk, and get him painting again, and she was failing.

So she asked about Constanzo and let Antonio relax as he talked about his dad, about the success of his first showing and his rapid rise in the world of art. But he still sighed heavily and tossed that morning's canvas out the back door as if it were trash.

She wondered if sweet, wonderful Gisella had ever seen his little fits of temper, and had to hold back a gasp. They'd never spoken about his wife! They'd never even brushed against the real reason he didn't paint. And she suddenly saw the mistake in that. By ignoring that they were, in effect, trying to put a bandage on an open wound. She'd brought him this far by being someone he wanted to paint, but what if that was only half the battle? What if he needed to talk out some of his pain? What if he needed to face the sadness inside him before he could actually use his talent to the fullest?

As he set another canvas on the easel, she swallowed. Sucked in a breath. Prayed for strength. And finally said, "So is this what happened when you stopped painting?"

He peered over. "Excuse me?"

"Did you try canvas after canvas and toss them aside?"

He bristled. "Yes."

"So tell me about it."

"No."

She sighed. "Look, I get it that you can't paint because you lost the love of your life. I just lost a boyfriend who didn't really like me and it hurt like hell. But you lost the love of your life. You need to address that."

His expression shifted from angry to confused. Twice, he opened his mouth to say something. Twice, he stopped himself.

"What?"

He licked his lips and turned away. "Nothing."

Purpose rattled through her again. She needed to get him to admit he'd quit painting because without his wife his art had no meaning. He needed to say the words. Needed those words to come out into the open so he could face them. "It's not nothing. It's *something*. Tell me."

"I don't want to talk about it."

"Look, this…me posing for you…is all about you getting your mojo back. So we've hit an impasse." She glanced down at her black dress and heels, then smiled up at him. "I helped you through the last one by recreating the look that inspired you. Now I'm sensing that it's your wife—your love for your wife—that's holding you back. I don't think I'm wrong. You need to talk about it."

He tossed his pencil to the metal desk, massaged his forehead, then laughed slightly. "No."

A minute went by in complete silence, but eventually he picked up a pencil and began drawing a light outline on the canvas.

Desperation filled her, but so did a realization. In

falling for him so quickly, she'd forgotten his real pain. Maybe the first move was actually hers. "I don't think I ever told you I was sorry."

He peeked away from his work, across the room at her. "For what?"

"That you lost your wife." She paused a second. Though forcing him to talk about his wife was the right thing to do, it hurt. Gisella was the reason he would never love her. And she gave herself a space of time to acknowledge that pain before she said, "She was beautiful."

He turned his attention back to the canvas. "Yes. She was."

Laura Beth swallowed hard. "And special."

He said nothing.

"Please. I think you need to talk about her."

"No."

"My gram told me one of the hardest things about losing my pap was that after a few weeks people stopped talking about him. She longed to remember him, to keep his memory alive, and people seemed to forget him."

"Laura Beth, please. That's enough."

"I just want you to know that you can talk about her with me."

He stepped away from the canvas, his spine stiff, his eyes narrow. Irritation vibrated from him across the room to her. "Dear God! Will you just let it drop?"

She snapped her mouth shut. She knew he might not be eager to talk about Gisella, but she hadn't expected him to get angry. "I'm sorry. I just desperately want this for you. I want you to be able to paint again."

Antonio's fingers tightened on his pencil. He realized she was trying to help him relax by what she considered to be a logical method, but she had no way of knowing her comments about his wife were actually doing more harm than good.

Still, it wasn't her fault. No one knew the real story, his real pain, and though he would die before he would admit his failings, he could at least let Laura Beth know she wasn't at fault.

"Look, my wife wasn't exactly what everyone thought."

"Okay."

Again a soft word filled with regret. He shifted a bit, putting himself solidly behind the canvas. He hated the self-loathing in her voice. Hated that he was responsible for it. He might not be able to tell her the whole story, but he could tiptoe around enough facts that she'd stop feeling bad.

"I'm not angry with you. I've simply never spoken about my wife with anyone."

"I still think you should."

He sniffed a laugh. "Honestly, *carissima*, I don't know what I'd say."

"Why don't you just tell me the truth?"

The truth would probably scandalize her. But he suddenly noticed that his pencil was moving with easy efficiency. The image he captured was perfect. His vision. Exactly what he wanted.

He didn't know if it was the pose or the distraction of talking or even the power of the topic, but he was working...effortlessly. And he couldn't break the spell, ruin the moment or lose the opportunity.

"I wish I could tell you the truth." As the words spilled out and the picture before him began to take shape, something inside his chest loosened. A weird kind of excitement nudged his heart, and he wondered

if she was right. Did he need to talk about his wife to
let his anger with her go?

His pencil paused. He glanced over at Laura Beth.
He might need to talk, but was Laura Beth—was anyone—ready to hear what he had to say? "The story of
my marriage is not a happy one."

She frowned and the look he'd been trying to capture flitted over her features, filled her eyes. A longing
so intense it shifted every muscle in her face, darkened
her eyes.

His pencil began to move again, feverishly, desperate to get that expression.

"You weren't happy?"

"Is anybody ever really happy?"

"Don't talk in abstracts when you know the truth.
Olivia and Tucker are happy. Content. Eloise and Ricky
are happy. You know happy. You know what it looks
like. So you know if you were happy or not."

Absorbed in his work, more grateful that he was
succeeding than antsy about the conversation, he said,
"Then we were not."

"Then I'm sorry." She waited a beat before she said,
"Want to tell me what happened?"

As his pencil captured the fine details that made
Laura Beth who she was, he weighed his options. Sunlight pouring in from the wall of windows gave the
quiet room the feel of a sacred space. A time and place
he could be honest. Having been left by the father of
her child, if anyone could understand his situation, it
would be Laura Beth.

And if telling her the truth was what he needed to
do to rid himself of the demons that tormented him,
then so be it.

He cut right to the chase, didn't mince words, but

was as honest, as open, as she'd asked him to be. "My wife ran around on me and aborted my child."

The words that sounded so simple, so reasonable, in his head leveled him. His wife had gotten rid of his baby. Made a mockery of his naive love for her. Made him a fool. And now the words were out in the open, hanging on the air.

Behind the canvas, he squeezed his eyes shut, ran his angry fingers along his forehead. What was he doing?

He heard a soft swish, then saw Laura Beth's long legs approaching before she appeared at his side.

"I am so sorry."

A piece of her dark hair had fallen loose from its pins and framed her face. Her green eyes filled with sadness.

"I shouldn't have told you."

"What? That your marriage was a mess?"

"That my marriage was a lie. And I was a fool."

She stepped closer, examining his face. "All this time, I thought you were mourning her." She shook her head as if confused. "Everybody thought you'd been so sad these past years because you mourned her."

"Not her, my child. To the world she was an icon. But I lived the truth. She was a narcissist, who did everything she did not out of love or compassion but to make herself look important." He caught Laura Beth's gaze. "For two years I've been trapped. I couldn't tell the world who or what she was and yet I couldn't live the lie."

Her face softened. "Oh, Antonio."

Turning away from her, he grabbed a cloth and wiped his hands.

"You should talk about this with Olivia. She knows all about being forced to live a lie."

He shook his head. "I don't really want anyone to know."

"I know."

He sniffed a laugh.

"So maybe, since you started opening up, you should keep going." She paused, waited for him to look at her. "Get it off your shoulders."

Her honest eyes beckoned. The feeling of something loosening in his chest shuddered through him again and he knew she was right. He'd started the story. He needed to finish it.

"A year after we were married, she scheduled a trip for her charity. I'd lost her itinerary, so I went into her computer to find it and what I found was an identical itinerary for a man. She had an explanation, of course, so I felt foolish for accusing her."

He walked away from the easel. "Dear God, she held that first accusation over my head every time I questioned something she said or did. She'd remind me of how bad I felt over that mistake and I'd back off. For months, I believed lie after lie. Then she began to get careless. Her lies weren't as tight. Newspaper pictures of her with one man became commonplace. I saw the smiles that passed between them. I *saw* the intimacy. Until eventually I got so angry I went through the documents in her computer in earnest and that's when I found the abortion."

Laura Beth squeezed her eyes shut. "I'm so sorry, Antonio."

"She denied it. But I told her I had seen the appointment on her calendar, the check that paid the clinic. She told me that her life was her charity and she didn't want any time taken away from that for any reason. She said she wasn't cut out to be a mom. I exploded and told her

I wanted to be a dad and she laughed. That's when I knew our marriage was over." He tossed a rag to the table. "I don't believe she ever loved anyone as much as she loved herself. The fact that she didn't even give me an option with our child proved she never thought beyond herself."

"I'm so sorry."

"You needn't be. She taught me some valuable lessons. People change. Love doesn't last." He sniffed a laugh. "Trust no one."

The room grew quiet. Antonio heard the click of her heels again. When he turned she was right behind him.

"She didn't deserve you."

He sniffed a laugh.

"I'm serious."

"I have my faults."

"Oh, don't I know it. But I still think you're special." She caught his gaze. "Wonderful."

The magnetic pull of her innocent green eyes drew him to her. An inch. Then two. Then his hands were close enough that he could lay them on her warm shoulders. His mouth was close enough that he could touch his lips to hers.

As if thought gave birth to action, he closed the distance between them and brushed his lips across hers. Laura Beth edged closer too. Her lips were warm and sweet. The way she kissed him, answering the moves of his mouth slowly, hesitantly, then completely, spoke of submission. Honesty. A change in the way she felt about him, the way she related to him. She was taking the step that would shift them from friends to so much more.

He slid his tongue along the seam of her lips and when she opened to him he deepened the kiss.

CHAPTER ELEVEN

LAURA BETH SURRENDERED to the urgent prodding of Antonio's mouth. Desperate, shivering with need, she pressed into him as he pulled her closer.

He didn't mourn his wife.

He did want her.

She could be the love of his life.

Except he didn't trust.

The cell phone in his pocket began to chime out a happy beat. Antonio pulled away. Their gazes caught and held.

The phone rang again.

Antonio quietly said, "That ringtone is Bernice, my father's assistant. She never calls unless it's an emergency."

Laura Beth whispered, "You should take it."

As if in a trance, he nodded, retrieved the phone from his pocket and clicked the button to answer it. "Bernice? What's up?"

Because he'd put his phone on speaker, the voice of Constanzo's assistant erupted in the room. "Oh, Antonio! It's awful! Just awful!"

Laura Beth walked a few feet away. Her head spun—the truth about his life, his marriage, had shaken her to the core. It gave her a crazy kind of hope, even as it dashed her hopes. How could she expect to build a life with a man who couldn't trust?

Antonio said, "Hey. Calm down. Whatever my dad did, we can fix it."

"This isn't about a mistake." A sob escaped. "The ambulance just left. Your dad is on his way to the hospital. They think he had a heart attack."

Antonio stumbled to the chaise and collapsed on it. "A heart attack?"

Laura Beth gasped. "Oh, my God." All her other thoughts and troubles flitted away in a surge of worry about Constanzo.

"Yes! Hurry! Get to the hospital!"

He disconnected the call as Laura Beth walked to the door. "You give me directions and I'll drive."

Antonio raced out of the studio toward the house for keys. "*I'll* drive."

She didn't follow him, but ran to the garage. In less than a minute, Antonio joined her with his car keys. He jumped into the Lamborghini and Laura Beth climbed in too.

As he sped along the winding roads of the hills between his country house and Bogodehra, she wasn't sure it was wise for him to drive. But she was as desperate to get to the hospital as he was, and simply held onto the dashboard for support as they raced to the city.

When they finally arrived at the stucco building with loops of arches and fancy pillars, they jumped out and dashed inside.

Laura Beth's gaze winged from side to side as she took in the surroundings that were both familiar and unfamiliar. Department names were in Italian, but most of the words were close enough to English that she could translate. Still, the chatter of doctors, nurses, patients and patients' families in the area best described by an American as the emergency room was in Italian. Even Antonio spoke Italian when he reached a nurse's station.

Using the universal language of pointing, the nurse obviously told him to have a seat.

He sighed and faced Laura Beth. "We can't see him."

She caught his arm frantically. "We can't?"

He squeezed his eyes shut and Laura Beth realized she wasn't helping by panicking.

"They haven't yet gotten the word that he's stable."

Her heart dipped. Fear crept into her limbs and froze them. It was impossible for her to picture an event for one of Tucker and Olivia's kids without big, boisterous Constanzo Bartulocci, the man everyone thought of like a favorite uncle.

If she was this upset about Constanzo, she couldn't imagine Antonio's fright. Constanzo was his *father*. If her father was the one in this hospital right now, she'd be a basket case.

She tugged lightly on his arm and got him to a plastic seat. As if in a daze, he lowered himself to the chair. She sat beside him, but took his hand, keeping the connection, so he'd know he wasn't alone.

"My father and I haven't really spoken since we got back from Barcelona. When I did stop by, he said he was sorry for stranding us, but didn't want to talk about anything else. I never went over after that."

She smiled weakly, acknowledging that. "We've been busy."

He put his head back and rubbed his hand across his mouth. "I should have gone to see him again. I should have forced him to talk about that fight, or at least let him know I wasn't angry." He sighed. "Why are we always squabbling?"

She squeezed his hand and again her sense of purpose, of destiny, with Antonio filled her. All she had to do was listen to the easy way he confided in her, talked about such personal things, to know that he trusted her. He might not realize it, but she did.

"It's how you show love."

He sniffed a laugh. "Right. Either that or he hates me."

That admission further bolstered her belief that there was more between them than friendship, more between them than a few kisses. And she knew she was the person to help him through this crisis.

"He doesn't hate you. If he did, he wouldn't meddle."

Antonio shut his eyes. "He always meddles."

"Yeah, but I think his intentions are good. I'm sure Tucker and Olivia were glad he forced them to come to Italy together to find you."

He sniffed a laugh. "Such a matchmaker and a do-gooder."

"Lots of people would be glad their dad looks for ways to help other people."

"I am. Most days I'm proud of him." He sighed and closed his eyes. "I wish I'd told him that."

She tightened her hold on his hand. "I'm sure he knows."

"By my yelling at him?"

"By the fact that you're honest with each other." She thought of her parents back in Kentucky. "I wish I could be so open with my parents."

He turned his head and studied her. "You're not?"

"I haven't yet told them I'm pregnant." She shrugged. "I'm afraid of their reaction. I don't think you and Constanzo hold important things back. Even if you do sometimes get loud when you talk."

Antonio's eyes softened. "Have you even called your parents?"

Knowing the distraction of a different topic might be good for him, she said, "Yes. Once. I let them know I was here in Italy."

"Why haven't you told them?"

"I guess deep down I'm afraid of what they'll say. They'd wanted me to become a doctor or a lawyer and start a practice in our small town." She sighed. "But I wanted something more."

"Something more?"

Knowing she was doing a good job of keeping Antonio occupied, she decided to be honest, to continue the conversation that held his nerves at bay. "That's the bad part. I couldn't even give them a description of what I wanted. All I could tell them was I had this feeling in my soul that I was meant to do something wonderful with my life."

He winced. "But you couldn't tell them what."

"No. And now I'm returning educated but not employable." She shook her head.

"Hey, Olivia says Tucker has a job for you."

"But what if he doesn't? There aren't a lot of jobs for IT people in Starlight, Kentucky. So I'll end up being somebody's glorified secretary. I'll be coming back a failure and pregnant."

His gaze slowly met hers. "Some people would consider a child a blessing."

She swallowed. Caught in the fierce light in his dark eyes, she could almost read his thoughts. He had lost a child because his wife hadn't thought beyond her own needs. Antonio himself was born to an unmarried mother, the product of the same kind of mistake Laura

Beth had made. It was important that Antonio know she did not consider her baby a mistake.

"My child is a blessing. I don't know why I got pregnant, but I believe in destiny. This little boy or girl has a purpose."

"What if his or her purpose is only to sweep streets?"

She laughed. "Destiny is about more than a job."

"You should tell that to yourself some time."

She frowned.

"You're so concerned that without a law degree or medical license your parents will consider you're a failure. What if your destiny is to be the mother of the surgeon who makes the next great medical advancement or the architect who builds the next Sistine Chapel? What if your destiny is simply to be this child's mom?"

As she thought about that, a smile bloomed. "I get it."

"And even if his destiny isn't to be great—even if his destiny is to sweep streets—he's still important."

She squeezed Antonio's hand. "I know. All along there's been something inside me that happily responded to the idea of raising a child. I won't let him down."

Antonio ran his free hand down his face again. Though the conversation had distracted him for a few minutes, his nervousness had returned.

A doctor in green scrubs walked to the nurse's station. The same nurse who'd relegated Antonio to a plastic seat pointed at him again. The doctor walked over.

Still clinging to Laura Beth's hand, Antonio rose.

The doctor began to speak in Italian. Antonio quickly cut him off. "English for my friend?"

The doctor nodded. "My English not perfect." He

smiled at Laura Beth. "But good enough. Your father's heart attack was mild, but we'll be running some tests. If all goes well, in a few days he will go home with medicine."

"If all doesn't go well?"

"Probably a bypass." The doctor smiled. "And a diet."

Antonio shook his head. He said, "Lucky old coot," but Laura Beth could feel the tension draining from him. "Can we see him?"

Making some notes on a chart, the doctor said, "Yes. I'm sure it will be a few minutes before he's wheeled out for testing."

Laura Beth and Antonio walked to Constanzo's cubicle hand in hand. Even before they reached it, they could hear the rumble of Constanzo's deep voice as he barked out complaints that his bed was too hard and he wanted a sandwich.

Pushing open the privacy curtain, Antonio said, "Too many sandwiches are what got you here."

As if glad for the reprieve, the nurses scrambled out of the cubicle.

Constanzo's eyes lit. "Laura Beth," he said, turning his pleading gaze on her, "I almost died. Tell my son to be kind to me."

She laughed, but the oddest feelings poured through her. In what should be a very private moment between a father and son, she didn't feel out of place. In fact, she felt as if she belonged here. But more than that, it felt right, perfect, that Antonio held her hand. Turned to her for comfort. Gave her advice when she tried to distract him. Liked her.

Her heart stumbled a bit as he released her hand and walked to the head of Constanzo's bed. Even though neither of them had said it, she and Antonio loved each other. Not in the way they'd loved Bruce or Gisella. But in a deep, profound way.

She was the real love of his life and he was hers.

And as soon as Constanzo was better, she would prove it to him.

With Constanzo safe in the hospital, his private doctors on the scene and a battery of tests ordered, Antonio's stress level fell. By the time they left the hospital, the sun had set. The air had cooled, but not so much that they had to put the Lamborghini's top up. He and Laura Beth didn't talk, but they didn't need to. She'd pushed him to tell the truth about Gisella and he'd forced her to admit why she'd really run to Italy. She might want to return to Starlight to raise her child, but she wasn't looking forward to the conversation she had to have with her parents. She didn't want to return to her home-town a failure.

Still, they were both on the road to recovery in their respective life crises. Now they could get on with their lives.

Already he felt strong again. Having learned his lessons about weakness, about letting anyone get too close, he'd never go through that kind of pain again. Just as Laura Beth would never again let herself be taken in by a man. She'd raise her child in her hometown and be happy.

He could picture it. He could see her in a big house with a homey kitchen and a yard full of green grass for a growing child. He smiled at the vision, but his smile quickly faded. He should have a three-year-old right now. A toddler to teach and dote on. Someone to make Constanzo smile. Someone who might grow up to be a garbageman or doctor. It wouldn't matter. He would have been Antonio's heart.

The Lamborghini roared up the driveway and, filled with indescribable pain, Antonio drove it into the garage. He and Laura Beth piled out unceremoniously. Though it was late, Rosina met them at the door to the kitchen.

"How is Mr. Constanzo?"

"He's fine."

Antonio's usually calm and collected housekeeper all but collapsed with relief.

His eyes narrowed as he directed her back into the kitchen. Her reaction had been more than a little extreme and he almost cursed the stupidity, the fruitlessness of his life. Servants who got involved in their lives like family—because they saw more of their household staff than the real world. Money. Talent. Fame. None of it mattered! He wanted his child.

"I will make sandwiches and you will tell me everything?"

He almost told her he wasn't hungry. He wanted to be alone. To lick his wounds. To roar with anger. But a glance at Laura Beth reminded him he had responsibilities. Not just to feed his probably starving guest, but to his staff. Rosina wanted information. He needed to give it to her.

"Sandwiches would be good."

Laura Beth took the stool beside his at the center island. As Rosina cut bread and assembled cold cuts, they told her everything the doctors had said. Reassured, and her job done, Rosina shuffled off to her quarters behind the kitchen.

"She likes him."

Antonio glanced over at her. "Really?"

"When your dad came to the house the night he and I flew to Barcelona, I saw looks pass between them. I got the distinct impression she'd called him and told him I was bored with nothing to do. Now I wonder if it isn't more than that."

"So all this time I thought my dad was a meddler, I actually have two meddlers in my life?"

She playfully swatted his arm. "You're missing the big picture. I think your head housekeeper is in love with your dad!"

He shook his head. "Poor Rosina."

"Why? Your dad is great. I think he and Rosina would make a cute couple."

"I think she's wishing on a star if she thinks that's ever going to happen."

His negativity surprised Laura Beth. When she peeked over at him, she saw something in his eyes she'd never seen before. She'd always known he was wounded. She'd believed the loss of his beloved wife had leveled him. Now she knew it was more than that. That he'd fallen out of love with his wife long before her death, when he'd lost a child. And something about this situation seemed to be bringing it all back for him.

Carefully, quietly, she said, "He wouldn't want anything to do with her because of her class? Because she's the maid?"

"Because he's in his seventies and he's never even slowed down, let alone settled down. The one woman who might have caught him with her pregnancy—with me—he summarily dismissed from his life. If she's in love with him, Rosina will get her heart broken, because my dad can't settle down."

She tried to make the connection. Was there something about Constanzo deserting Antonio's mom and the loss of Antonio's own child that connected? What could have made him so angry?

They finished their sandwiches and a hush fell over the kitchen. Her mind skipped back to the studio, to how they'd been kissing when Antonio got the call. With Constanzo in no real danger, would they pick up where they'd left off?

Antonio caught her hand. "You must be tired."

She swallowed. "Truthfully, I haven't had enough time to think about it today."

Their gazes met. He smiled and she could almost hear the question he wanted to ask. *Will you come to my room with me?* They'd been on the verge of making love and everything inside her wanted to go with him, to give herself to him, to take away his pain.

She waited for him to ask the question.

His eyes darkened as he studied her face.

The urge rose up to bridge the gap between them and kiss him. To make the first move.

But that silly shy fear of hers filled her. She needed to know—it had to be *clear* that he wanted her.

He released her fingers and pulled back. "I'll see you in the morning."

Confusion filled her. For all the times and ways he'd confided, telling her what troubled him tonight should be easy. They should be heading for his room together, talking things out, making love. Instead, he was walking away.

He stopped at the kitchen door and faced her. "With Constanzo having tests in the morning, maybe we could get in a few hours in the studio before we go to the hospital?"

The studio. She'd gotten him to tell her about his wife

in the studio. Whatever the cause of this new sadness, she could get it out of him tomorrow.

They ate breakfast quietly. Clearly believing his father was in good hands, Antonio ate toast while reading the paper. Laura Beth took slow, measured breaths. He wasn't upset this morning. But his dad had also had a heart attack the day before. Maybe the sadness she was so sure she'd seen while they'd eaten sandwiches had been nothing more than sadness over nearly losing Constanzo? Maybe she'd made a mountain out of a molehill?

She slipped away while he finished his second cup of coffee and raced upstairs to slip into the black dress and spike heels. The dining room was empty when she returned, so she headed for the studio.

She found him assembling brushes and paints and simply headed for the chaise.

"Ready?" He peeked from behind the canvas and laughed. "Ah. Not just ready, ahead of me."

She smiled, but her lips wobbled. Something about the mood in the room didn't feel right. How could he have been so utterly sad the day before and be almost happy today?

"Is that bad?"

"I like eagerness in a woman."

He was trying to sound light and flippant, but having spent so much time with him Laura Beth noticed the strain in his voice. Her fears came crashing back. As any child would, he'd been upset about his father the day before, but something else had happened.

"Could you straighten the fabric at your back? There's a kink I don't like."

She nodded and reached behind her to find the unwanted fold in her dress, but couldn't reach it.

"Here. Let me."

He walked over. As he pushed her long hair out of the way, she could feel his fingers skim across her back. She drew in a quick breath. Pinpricks of excitement danced along her flesh.

Looking over her shoulder at him, she raised her eyes to meet his and his fingers stopped as their gazes met.

"You're very beautiful."

And here it was. The real truth between them. He found her beautiful. He saw her in a way no man ever had. And it didn't just thrill her. It seemed to set her free. To turn her into the woman she wanted to be.

"You're very handsome."

His fingers moved from the fabric and traced a line up her shoulder. Warm and sure, his hand flattened on her back as the other went to her waist to turn her to him.

Neither waited for the other to move. His head came down as she rose up a bit to meet him and their lips met in a reunion of delicious passion. Wave after wave of heavenly delight flooded her as their kiss went on and on.

When she would have thought he'd move away, he caught her by the shoulders and deepened the kiss. She met his fierce kiss with her own fierceness. When he pulled back, his mouth fell to her neck, skimming wet kisses along the line of her collarbone.

She shuddered as her eyes closed in ecstasy. "I love you."

The words came out naturally, easily. Still, she wasn't surprised when he stopped kissing her. This was momentous for them. They might have been tumbling to this point for weeks, but neither had ever said the words. She opened her eyes and smiled expectantly. But instead of the sheen of passion or the warmth of love, pain filled his eyes.

He gazed at her longingly, as if she held the secrets to his happiness, but he said, "I don't love you."

For thirty seconds, her ears rang with the silence, then as the reality of what he'd said sank in, her heart exploded in her chest. An indescribable ache radiated to every part of her body. The words *I don't believe you* sprang to her tongue, but she cursed them. When would she ever learn she was Laura Beth Matthews, simple girl? Not glamour girl like Eloise or earth mother like Olivia. But plain Laura Beth Matthews, IT person who couldn't find a job, and who was never going to be loved with passion.

She pulled away from him. "I see."

"I don't think you do."

He reached for her but she shook him off. Thank God for good, old-fashioned American pride. Her chin lifted. Her thoughts cleared.

"I understand very well." She caught his gaze, working to hide the pain that sliced through her, cutting her to the core, making her feel like the world's biggest idiot. "A lot more than you think." She drew in a calming breath, telling herself she could scream or cry or whatever she wanted to do as soon as he was gone. But right now she had to get him away from her. "Go see your father."

He stepped back. Confusion clouded his dark brown eyes.

So she smiled. Though it physically hurt to force her lips upward and to hold back her tears, she managed because she refused, absolutely refused to look like a fool in front of another man. "I think we both need a little time to cool off before we get back to the painting, and your dad's going to be griping at the nurses." She studied the lines of his aristocratic face, the wild black hair, the set of his jaw. He would say she was memorizing him, and maybe she was. Because she knew this would be the last time she saw him.

The pain of that sliced through her, but she ignored it. She took another step back. "You better go rescue them."

He ran his hand along the back of his neck as if confused. "What are we doing?"

She had no idea what he was doing, but she was leaving. He was a brilliant but broken man, and she'd walked right into the trap of loving him, thinking she could help him when clearly she couldn't.

"We need a cooling-off period and you should be checking up on your dad." She lifted her chin again and smiled shakily. "I need some time."

"I'm sorry—"

She cut him off. "Don't make this any weirder than it already is. I'm fine. I misinterpreted what was going on between us." She shrugged. "It happens all the time. No big deal. I just need a break. And you going to see your dad is the best way for me to get myself together."

Antonio's heart seized at the loss of her as she stormed out of the studio, but he let her go. Because it was for her good. He was an angry, bitter man, mourning the loss not of a deceitful wife but a child. And she was a naive young pregnant woman who'd already gotten involved with the wrong man once.

He wouldn't tie her to him, but more than that, he wouldn't taint the experience of her first child with his wounds, his regrets.

CHAPTER TWELVE

LAURA BETH CALLED Bernice and within an hour Constanzo's plane was ready for her at the private airstrip. She climbed the steps. At the top she paused, taking one final look at the beautiful Italian countryside.

Bernice had tried to talk her out of leaving, but she'd explained that her mind was made up. She said goodbye to Rosina and drove herself to the airstrip, leaving Antonio's car to be picked up by staff.

Strapping herself into the plane seat, she remembered flying to Italy, eating French toast, falling asleep beside Antonio, who'd put a cover over her. Her heart lurched, but the memory of his rejection poured through her. Dear God. She'd never been so surprised. She'd been so sure he'd say he loved her too.

Straightening in her seat, she scolded herself for letting herself remember even one minute of their time together. She'd had warning after warning that he wasn't ready for what she needed. Twice he'd stepped back rather than kiss her. He hadn't wanted her to go to Barcelona. Yet she'd ignored every signal he sent because he was a wounded man, so desperately in need of love that, of course, she'd longed to love him. Handsome, talented and desperate for love, he'd been just a little too much to resist.

Pain threatened to overwhelm her, but she shoved it down. She had responsibilities and realities of her own, and she'd come to her senses. After one quick pass of her hand over her tummy, she snuggled into a blanket, intending to fall asleep. But tears welled in her eyes. Her chest heaved. And sobs overtook her.

Alone on a plane with no one to see or hear her, she gave in and let herself weep.

On the ground in Kentucky, she rented a car. When she used her check card to pay for it, she discovered she didn't merely have the full salary Constanzo had promised her, but Antonio's father had also ponied up the promised severance pay.

She called Bernice to have it taken back, but Bernice laughed. "Are you kidding? Constanzo is happy to be alive. He's so generous right now that I'm surprised he didn't double it. He'll never take it back. Besides, he gave orders for the money to be given to you weeks ago, when you first arrived. No matter when you left that money was going to you…so it's yours."

Though Constanzo's generosity was a bit overboard, Laura Beth understood that he felt he owed her. Helping her set up her new life was probably how he'd deal with her leaving. He needed to know she'd be okay and money was his tool. So maybe it would be best to just take what he offered. She'd fulfilled at least part of her duties to Constanzo by helping Antonio clear out his office and getting him to a gallery opening. She'd also gotten him painting again—Constanzo's real goal. So, yeah. She could understand why Constanzo had been so generous.

Plus, the money meant she could move on. Never see Antonio again.

That filled her heart with pain. She let herself feel

it as a reminder that she never wanted to be so foolish again, but she didn't really need a reminder. In her heart, she knew she'd never love another man the way she loved Antonio.

She arrived at her parents' house a little before dawn. She made coffee and pancakes, and, as she expected, the scents woke her mom and dad and her two brothers.

As hugs were exchanged, she swallowed hard. She didn't want to ruin this reunion, but she knew it was time to accept her fate and do what needed to be done.

When everyone had a few pancakes on their plates, she smiled at the group. "I have some news."

Her tall, strapping construction worker dad laughed, and said, "You're staying in Italy," as if it were a foregone conclusion.

She shook her head. "No. No more Italy. I'm actually home for good. I got a huge severance from the gentleman who'd hired me. I can afford to buy a house here."

Her mom clutched her chest. "You're back?"

She nodded. "For good."

Then her mom surprised her. "Oh, sweetie, we love you and we love the idea of you living in town with us—" she caught Laura Beth's gaze "—but you wanted so much more for yourself. A big-time career. Are you going to be happy here?"

Laura Beth swallowed as unhappiness swelled in her. Still, it wasn't the big-time career she would miss. It was Antonio. The real love of her life. But how could she explain that to her parents when she was pregnant with another man's child? Worse, how could she explain that when Antonio didn't feel for her what she felt her him?

She couldn't. Her love for Antonio would have to stay her hidden secret. Another cross to bear.

For her parents' sake, she brightened when she said,

"Yes, I'll be very happy here, because I have a child to raise."

At her parents' confused look, she said, "I'm pregnant. Bruce doesn't want to marry me, but I'm okay with that. I don't love him either." An arrow pierced her heart again when she thought of the man she did love, but she ignored it. "And with the severance pay I got from Mr. Bartulocci, I can buy a house and support myself until after the baby's born. Then I may need to take some courses, like accounting, so I can find a job around here." She squeezed her mom's hand. "But it's all good."

Nothing was good. Antonio glanced around the private suite they'd given his dad, at the rows and rows of flowers that covered every flat surface in the room, and even parts of the floor. Still, his father grumbled.

"It's hot in here."

"It's almost June. It's supposed to be hot."

"I want to see Laura Beth."

Pain squeezed Antonio's heart, but he forced himself not to show it. When he'd returned to the house the day before, her room had been empty. Rosina knew nothing, though her crying suggested otherwise. He'd had to call Bernice before he got the news that she'd taken the plane and gone to Kentucky.

"She went home."

Constanzo kicked his covers around, trying to get comfortable, but obviously failing. "I can't believe she went home. What did you say? What did you do?"

"Interesting how you assume I somehow drove her off."

"Didn't you?"

He had. He knew he had. But this was none of his father's business. Plus, there were bigger issues in Laura Beth's life than a heartbreak from a guy who hadn't deserved her love.

He sucked in a breath and faced his father. "She's pregnant."

Constanzo stopped struggling. "Oh, my God! How did I raise you to let the mother of your child go? Did you learn nothing from my mistakes?"

Antonio shook his head. "It's not my baby."

Constanzo's eyes narrowed. "Is this why she was so eager to come to Italy?"

Antonio nodded. "She needed some time to think things through and a place she could gather herself while she figured out what to do. You provided it."

"I am good that way."

Oh, how the man could turn anything to his favor! "You're a crabby old man."

"I anticipate!" Constanzo yelled, then he sucked in a long, slow breath. Antonio tensed, worried something was wrong, but Constanzo quietly said, "You are going to make me pay until the end of time, aren't you?"

Confused, Antonio caught his father's gaze. "What? What am I making you pay for this time?"

"Leaving you." He brushed his hand in dismissal. "No. That is not correct. You aren't making me pay for leaving you. You are making me pay for everything wrong that happened in your life after your mother died."

Antonio bristled. He did nothing but ask, "How high?" when his dad said, "Jump." He catered to his whims and wishes. Canceled plans. Made plans. How could Constanzo even hint that Antonio was somehow making him pay?

"That's insanity."

"Is it? You always hold yourself away. You love me but you won't give me love."

Antonio gaped at him. "Are you lying in a hospital bed, recovering from a heart attack, splitting hairs with me?"

Constanzo fussed with the covers. "Yes."

"You have got to be kidding me."

"I almost died. It gives a man clarity."

"Right."

"I am right! I want my son to love me and respect me. Not give me bits and pieces of affection."

"Maybe you should have thought of that before you kicked my mom out of your office."

"And there we have it."

Antonio shook his head and turned away from his dad. "I'm not having this conversation. I'm tired, I'm stressed and you're pushing me into saying things I don't mean."

"And why are you stressed? I'm the one who almost died."

Antonio tossed his hands in disgust. "There's no winning with you."

"There could be. All you have to do is love me like a dad, not like an enemy you're forced to interact with." When Antonio said nothing, he sighed. "Forgive me for not believing your mom."

Antonio squeezed his eyes shut.

"Then forgive Gisella for being a slut."

His eyes popped open and he spun to face his dad. "What?"

Constanzo laughed. "You think I don't know? You think my own daughter-in-law could flaunt her affairs in my favorite cities and word would not get back to me?"

Antonio rubbed his hand down his face.

"You carry the weight of betrayal like a good-luck charm. Something you're afraid to set down for fear if you do bad luck will return. Because I didn't trust your mom, you're afraid to trust me. And because Gisella humiliated you, you won't trust Laura Beth."

"If it were that simple, I think I could get beyond it."

"Then tell me the part that's complicated."

He blew out a breath. "Gisella aborted our child."

His dad blinked. "Oh."

"And Laura Beth is pregnant. I have mourned the loss of my child for two long years. I wake up most days knowing I should have a son or daughter playing in my yard. I cannot handle having a pregnant woman under my roof, and it isn't fair to subject her to my anger when she's not at fault."

Constanzo closed his eyes and shook his head. "I am so sorry."

"Why? It's not like you understand. You very easily let my mother go...then forgot her. Forgot *me*. How could you possibly understand my loss?"

"I think it's time I tell you what really happened with your mom."

Antonio slowly lifted his gaze to meet his dad's. "I'm not in the mood, Dad."

"But this is finally the right time. The only time. If you don't change now, I fear you will be gone for good."

Gobsmacked, he only stared at his dad. "*I* need to change?"

"Yes. Just listen." Constanzo cleared his throat and quietly said, "Your mother was a rebound relationship."

Antonio frowned. "I thought you'd been dating?"

"We had. I'd lost the love of my life and one day your mother happened to be at a club where I was socializing. We struck up a conversation. One thing led to another and she came home with me."

Antonio shook his head, not sure how the hell this was supposed to help him. "She was a one-night stand?"

"She was a rebound. I'd been ridiculously in love with a woman I thought loved me too. But she hadn't. She hadn't been with me for my money or for love. A rich heiress, she was simply biding time. Waiting for a better guy to come around."

"So you did the same thing with my mom."

He winced. "Yes. And after a few weeks, I let her go." He fussed with the covers. "Then a few weeks after that she came to me with the pregnancy story and I thought it was a ruse. A way to get back with me or get back at me."

"So you kicked her out of your office and forgot her because you were busy?"

Constanzo nodded. "And though it seemed like the right thing at the time, ten years later I suddenly realized what I'd done. If she really had been pregnant, I'd tossed away a child."

Antonio sniffed a laugh.

"Oh, you think you're so superior. But my loss of you is not so much different than the loss of your child. Except in my case I had a hand in things. But when a person comes to his senses and realizes he's thrown away his one chance at real happiness..." He paused, caught Antonio's gaze. "It more than hurts. Sometimes, it stops a life."

Antonio swallowed hard.

"Did you love Gisella?"

"At one time."

"But the love died?"

He glanced up at his dad. "I'm not sure she had any love for me to die."

"So you feel a fool?"

He drew in a long breath and expelled it quickly. "That sort of gets lost in the grief I feel over my child."

"And you don't see the second chance you've been handed?"

He frowned.

"You love Laura Beth."

He shook his head. "She's a very nice woman. Far too good to be dragged into my pit."

"Oh, pit, schmit."

"Excuse me?"

"Now you are splitting hairs. Maybe because you're afraid."

"Afraid? Hell, yes, I'm afraid. How do I know I won't see my baby every time I look at hers? How do I know I can be a good husband when the only chance I got to try resulted in failure?"

"Do you love Laura Beth?"

He squeezed his eyes shut. "I have feelings for her that are beyond expression. Sometimes when she's around it's comfortable. Other days, she makes me think. I can't imagine anyplace I'd go, anything I'd do that wouldn't be more fun if she was there."

Constanzo laughed. "Oh, my son. You have it bad and it scares you."

Antonio licked his suddenly dry lips. "I failed with a woman who seemed to be tailor-made for me—"

"Men like you and me, Antonio, we're not made for princesses or supermodels. We're high maintenance ourselves."

Antonio laughed.

"We are made for the Laura Beths of the world. The

women who bring sunshine. The women who make us stop and enjoy life. If you let her go, you will regret it for the rest of your days. But more than that, if you can't finally learn to forgive, the regret you have over her leaving will be nothing compared to the sadness you will find when you wake up one day and discover you created your own prison."

Antonio looked over at his dad. "You want me to forgive you?"

"For real this time. And I want you to forgive Gisella."

He sniffed a laugh. "She doesn't need my forgiveness."

Constanzo shook his head sadly. "No. But your tired soul needs the rest forgiving will give you." He patted the bed, asking for Antonio's hand. Antonio slid his hand over to his dad, who caught it and squeezed. "You lost a family, but Laura Beth is offering you another. Sometimes fate is weird like that. It cannot give you back what you lost, but sometimes it finds a replacement."

The room was quiet for a second, then Constanzo said, "If you don't take this chance, another might come along. Fate is generous. But do you want to lose Laura Beth? The real love of your life? Now that you've met her, everyone will pale compared to her. You might find happiness. But you will never again find this joy."

Antonio rose. He walked to the head of the bed, reached down and hugged his father. "I forgive you, you old coot."

Constanzo patted his back. "For real this time?"

He sucked in a breath. "For real this time."

"Thank you. Now, go get Laura Beth. I want the sound of small feet in our big houses."

* * *

Antonio drove his Lamborghini back home. He understood what his father was saying about his mom. He also felt a swell of regret for withholding forgiveness from his father. But going to get Laura Beth?

Even though he knew in his heart she was the one true love of his life, going to her with his heart in his hand was risky. He wasn't just afraid. He was unworthy. Despite his ability to forgive his dad, he couldn't trust. He didn't want to trust.

Too wired to do anything, he headed for his studio. He unlocked the old wooden door and went to the back room.

There on the easel was Laura Beth.

He hesitated as he walked to the pencil drawing that would become a painting. Her laughing eyes beckoned. He ran his finger down the line of her cheek. The problem wasn't fear that she'd hurt him as Gisella had. The problem was he feared she'd hurt him worse. What he felt for her went beyond the surface, beyond a desire for her beauty. He loved her in a way he never could have loved Gisella. With his whole heart and soul. And that's why he feared her.

Gisella could never have held that kind of power over him, which was why it was suddenly easy to forgive her.

Feeling free for the first time in years, he made his way back to the house and stepped into quiet. The kind of quiet that became an early grave if a man wasn't careful.

He walked upstairs, to his room, letting himself imagine the sounds of a child, a soothing lullaby from Laura Beth, the click of computer keys as he arranged for something totally American—a Disney vacation—and he laughed.

Maybe his dad was right? Maybe fate was giving him a second chance, with a different child. His child might be gone, but Laura Beth's baby needed a daddy.

His life would be so different with her. Noisy. Complicated. Rich.

All he had to do was get on his father's jet and find her.

Laura Beth dragged her mother to the fourth real estate appointment in as many days.

"There's no sidewalk," her mother groused. "I'm not coming to visit you if I'm going to get mud on my shoes every time I walk to your back door." She stopped, crossed her arms on her chest stubbornly. "Take pictures with that fancy phone of yours. I'll be in the car."

"Mom!" Laura Beth called after her mother, who strode back to the little blue car Laura Beth had bought the day before.

"You don't need me for this one," her mom yelled back as she opened the car door and slipped inside. "I've got a key. I'll listen to the radio and be fine."

Laura Beth sighed and turned to walk to the back door of the brand-new house. Of course it didn't have sidewalks. The contractor hadn't poured them yet. And since when was her mom so picky? For Pete's sake. She'd eagerly seen the other three houses, but it had been like wrestling a bear to get her to come with her to see this house, and when push came to shove she wouldn't even go inside.

Whatever. She was an adult now. Able to make a decision about a house without her mommy.

She marched to the back door, pushed it open and called, "Hello? Anybody here?" It was a stupid question, since the Realtor's red Cadillac was in the driveway. Of course, he was here.

Still, before she could call again, the kitchen caught her attention. Happy green wood cabinets with creamy granite countertops filled a huge room that spilled out into a family room section. She let her purse slide to the floor and walked a little farther inside. She could put a table in the area with the bay window that would let in the morning sun, and decorate the family room area with sturdy furniture to accommodate her baby.

Her baby.

Her heart fluttered a bit. In the past four days of refusing to think about Antonio, she'd spent a lot of time wondering about her baby, thinking about whether it was a boy or girl, knowing she had to get a house set up before he or she was born.

"Hello?" she called again, heading for the big formal dining room. Seeing the high ceilings, she immediately pictured Antonio painting. Not green walls or white trim. But a mural. He'd love this space.

Pain pinged through her and she shook her head, reminding herself she wasn't allowed to think about him.

"Hello?" She walked out of the dining room and into a living room with a huge stone fireplace. Her first thought was of Antonio insisting they buy some kind of funky furniture for the room, or maybe artifacts from a dig in Mongolia. She laughed and this time reminded herself more sternly that she wasn't allowed to think about him. But that only caused her to realize the reason she kept thinking about him was that the house was probably out of her price range. Constanzo had been generous, but he wasn't an idiot. He hadn't given her enough to buy a mansion. And though Tucker had called and offered her a job, she fully intended to be wise with her money and not overspend.

As she walked up the sweeping stairway to the second floor, she knew beyond a shadow of a doubt that she couldn't afford this house. Searching for the real estate agent, she knew she had to tell him that she didn't want it. The place was huge. The master bedroom alone could fit two of the New York City apartment she'd shared with Eloise and Olivia.

She ambled into the bathroom, which had brown tiles, a travertine floor and a double-sink vanity.

"Hey."

Shé spun around. Expecting to see her Realtor, she gasped when she saw Antonio standing in front of the open stone shower. Because he was the last person she expected to see on the outskirts of tiny Starlight, Kentucky, she opened her mouth to ask him what he was doing there, but no words came out.

He looked crazy amazing. His hair was a mess, the way it was after a day of painting, her favorite time with him—which made her wonder if she was having some kind of sadness-related hallucination.

"What are you doing here?"

The best way to end a hallucination would be to force it to talk. If he said something impossible—like that he loved her—she would know she was imagining things.

"I heard you're in the market for a house."

Now, that was an illusion if she ever heard one. Her Antonio didn't talk about commonsense, normal stuff. Still, she answered, "Yes."

"Do you like this one?"

She laughed and glanced around. "Jeez, who wouldn't? Everything is gorgeous, but I think it's too big."

He pushed off the shower wall. "Of course it's big. You're looking at it because you're thinking down the line to when you have more kids. Anticipating, like Constanzo."

She laughed out loud. Good Lord, her imagination was powerful. "I'm going to have trouble enough raising one child."

"Your mother will help."

She sucked in a breath. "I know."

He stepped toward her. "I will help."

"Okay, time to end this hallucination."

He laughed. "I wondered why you were so calm. You think I'm a figment of your imagination?"

She winced and squeezed her eyes shut. Her time with him had seemed like a dream. The four days since she'd been here in Starlight she'd sort of vibrated with confusion. Was it any wonder she was having trouble with reality?

"Okay. I'm an idiot." Her eyes popped open. "What are you doing here?"

"Constanzo forced me to talk about our relationship and to forgive him."

"Oh."

"Weird, huh?"

Not half as weird as having the love of her life in the bathroom of the house she was looking at. Tears filled her eyes as she took in his handsome face. He was everything she'd ever wanted. Even things she didn't realize she wanted. But he didn't love her. He'd said it. And by damn, she wanted to be loved.

Passionately.

Men who told you they didn't love you did not fit that bill.

She took a step back, away from him. "So what does Constanzo forcing you to forgive him have to do with you being here?"

"I looked at your Realtor's offerings and I decided this is the best house for us."

Her heart stuttered, but absolutely positive she hadn't heard correctly, she said, "For us?"

"I've done some thinking in the past few days." He walked around the big bathroom. "And my dad forced me to do even more thinking. He made me realize my problem was that I couldn't trust anyone."

She bristled. She already knew that and so did he. So what the hell was he doing talking about a house for *them*? "Are you saying you don't trust me?"

"I thought I couldn't trust anyone. You could have been the woman in the moon and I would have held myself back." He caught her gaze. "I'm sorry about that, by the way."

She sniffed. "Right."

"I am."

"So you're asking me to accept second-best? You want us to live in this house together, but only if I can accept that you'll never trust me? Wow. You're a piece of work."

He laughed, but walked closer and stopped in front of her. "I'm not a piece of work." He tapped her nose. "And if you don't let me finish this in my own way, nothing's ever going to be right between us."

She frowned. But he put a finger over her lips to silence her. "I'm not asking you to live with me. I'm not saying that I don't trust you. I do trust you. I think I have for a while. It took weeks for me to tell you my story, but eventually you got the whole thing out of me."

Her heart lifted, but she couldn't let herself dare to believe. He'd hurt her because she allowed herself to fantasize that he might love her. She would not let him hurt her again. "I think the truth is you don't trust yourself."

He shrugged. "Maybe. You have to admit it takes a pretty stupid guy to marry a supermodel and not realize she's using him."

Because he said it lightly, she almost laughed, but this conversation was too important. "You loved her."

"Yeah. I did."

Her heart felt the pinch of that. This man had been married to the woman dubbed the most beautiful woman in the world three times. Laura Beth knew Gisella hadn't been as pure of heart as the rest of the world believed, but that couldn't take away from her beauty. How could Laura Beth ever think a man like Antonio would consider *her* beautiful?

"But, Laura Beth, I love you more."

Her head snapped up. "You do?"

"Yes." He ran his finger along the line of her jaw. "You are sweet and fun and funny. You are also beautiful. So beautiful that my memories of silly women like Gisella disappear."

Her breath caught. "You don't have to say things like that."

"I say only what's true." He slid his hands to her waist. "Now, will you live with me in this house?"

Her breath shivered. Live with him? In Starlight, Kentucky? Where her mom and all her friends would see that he liked her enough to live with her but not to marry her?

She stepped back. "No."

He blinked. "No?"

"I know you're scarred. I know it took moving mountains for you to trust." Her chin lifted. "But I deserve better than living with you."

He laughed. "Oh, that is all?"

She took another few steps back. "Don't belittle what I want." Her chin lifted even higher. "What I need."

He shook his head and removed a ring box from his back pocket. "I did this all wrong. I'm sorry." He opened the box to reveal a stunning diamond. "Will you marry me?"

She pressed her trembling lips together, met his gaze.

"You are my heart and soul. You are what I've been searching for forever. My father thought things between him and me were awkward because I couldn't forgive him. The truth was our relationship was awkward because it wasn't what I was searching for. Yes, I need him in my life. But what I really wanted was love. A true love. You are that love."

Tears filled her eyes. "Oh, Antonio." She fell into his arms.

And he breathed a sigh of relief. In those seconds with her arms around him and her body pressed against his, he felt his soul knit together. He felt his mother smiling down on him from heaven. He could see the family he and Laura Beth would create and that his place in the world wouldn't be secured because he was a great artist, but because he would be a part of something bigger than himself. A family.

And he could see his dad reveling in that.

EPILOGUE

ANTONIO AND LAURA Beth waited until baby Isabella was six months old before they had their wedding. With a huge white tent in the yard of Constanzo's country home, the old billionaire about burst with pride as he greeted guests, Rosina at his side. Not as Antonio's housekeeper or even a family friend. But as his fiancé.

Laura Beth watched from the second-floor window of the room she, Olivia and Eloise used to dress for the wedding.

"He is a crazy old man."

Pinning her veil into Laura Beth's fancy updo, Olivia laughed. "He might be crazy, but he brought at least two of us together with our perfect mates."

"So maybe he's wise," Eloise said from her position kneeling between Laura Beth and a centuries-old vanity said to have been used by Marie Antoinette, as she straightened Laura Beth's train. Eloise's boss, Artie Best, had designed the pale peach bridesmaids' dresses. But Eloise herself had created Laura Beth's gown.

With her hair up and her dress fastened, Laura Beth turned to look at herself in the full-length mirror. Strapless, her dress rode her curves and flared out a few inches below her hips to become a frothy skirt with lace trim. Sequins sparkled everywhere, including in the veil that flowed gracefully from her hair along her shoulders and to the floor.

Tears filled her eyes.

Eloise clutched her chest. "You don't like it?"

"I told you in all three fittings that I love it."

Olivia said, "Then what's wrong?"

Laura Beth faced her friends. "I'm beautiful."

As Eloise collapsed with relief, Olivia hugged Laura Beth. "Of course you are. Now let's get downstairs before Isabella starts crying for her mom."

The ceremony was a quiet but loving affair. Antonio looked amazing in his black tux, with her friends' husbands as his groomsmen. The sun shone down on the white tent filled with happy friends.

Just as the minister pronounced them man and wife, Isabella began to cry and Laura Beth took her from her mother, then Antonio took her from Laura Beth. She, Antonio and Isabella walked down the aisle to the sound of Constanzo sobbing loudly.

With joy.

They hoped.

As they greeted their guests, she watched Constanzo cast a quick look to heaven. Obviously believing no one saw or heard, he quietly said, "See, *carissima*. I finally did right by our boy."

Her eyes filled with tears, but she totally understood.

* * * * *

THE HEIRESS'S
SECRET BABY

JESSICA GILMORE

For Jo M

It seems pretty fitting that a book with a Parisian setting is dedicated to you just as we plan our girls' trip to Paris! I'm not sure how you have managed to be so positive and supportive and brilliant during the past five years; I am completely in awe of your strength. Thank you so much for being such a fantastic friend to me and an inspiration (and ever-patient hairstylist) to Abs.

Here's to Paris and most of all to medical advances and to a happy, healthy future xxx

CHAPTER ONE

My Secret Bucket List

~~Swim in the sea, naked~~
~~NB: in azure warm seas, not in the North Sea~~
~~Sleep out under the stars~~
~~Have sex on the beach~~
~~NB: the real deal, not the cocktail~~
~~Drink an authentic margarita~~
Fall in love in Paris

POLLY READ THE list through for the last time, feeling the carefree *joie de vivre* fall away and the old, familiar cloaks of respectability and responsibility settling back onto her shoulders. They were a little heavy, but maybe that was to be expected after three months away.

Three months, five wishes. And she'd achieved four out of the five, which wasn't bad going. The heaviness lifted for a second as the highlights of the last three months flashed through her mind and then it descended again.

What had she been thinking? She might as well have written the list in a silver pen and decorated it with pink love hearts and butterflies, pinning it on her wall next to a lipstick-kiss-covered poster of a pre-pubescent boy band.

Polly pulled the page out of her diary and, without allowing herself a second's pause to reconsider, tore it into pieces. It was time to reposition her three-month sabbatical into something more appropriate for the new CEO of a company with a multimillion-pound turnover.

She chewed on the end of her pen for a moment and then started a new list.

My Bucket List

~~Travel to the Galapagos Islands~~
See the Northern Lights
~~Walk the Inca Trail~~
Write a book
See tigers in the wild

There, two achieved, three to aspire to and all perfectly respectable. Not a grain of sand in any place it definitely shouldn't be…

The large luxurious town car drew to a smooth halt and jolted her back into the present day, away from dangerous memories. 'We're here, Miss Rafferty. Are you sure you don't want me to take you home first?'

Polly looked up from her diary and drew in a breath at the sight of the massive golden stone building stretching all the way down the block. She *was* home. Back at the famous department store founded by her great-grandfather. She hadn't expected to ever see it again, let alone to walk in as mistress of all that she surveyed.

She stared at the huge picture windows flanking the iconic marble steps, her heart swelling with a potent mixture of love and pride. Each window told a tale and sold a dream. Rafferty's could give you anything, make you anyone—if you had the money to pay for it.

'This will be fine, Petyr, thank you. But please arrange for my bags to be taken back to Hopeford and for the concierge service to collect and launder them.'

She didn't want to set foot in Rafferty's carrying her rucksack stuffed as it was with sarongs, bikinis and walking boots, no matter how prestigious the brand names on them. Polly had spent a productive night at a hotel in Miami turning herself back into Miss Polly Rafferty from Miss Carefree Backpacker—all it had taken was a little shopping, a manicure and a wash and blow-dry.

She was back and she was ready.

Petyr opened the car door for her and Polly slid out onto the pavement, breathing in deeply as she did so. Car fumes, perfume, hot concrete, fried food—London in the height of summer. How she'd missed it. She pulled down her skirt hem and wriggled her toes experimentally. The heels felt a little constrictive after three months of bare feet, flip-flops and walking boots but her feet would adjust back. She would adjust back. After all, this was her real dream; her time out had been nothing but a diversion along the way.

Polly lifted her new workbag onto her shoulder and headed straight for the main entrance. She was going in.

'Hello, Rachel.'

Oh, it had felt good walking through the hallowed halls, greeting the staff she knew by name and seeing the new ones jump as they realised just who was casting a quick, appraising eye over them. Good to see gossiping staff spring apart and how everyone suddenly seemed to find work to do.

Good that nobody dared to catch her eye. There must have been talk after her abrupt disappearance but it didn't seem to have affected her standing. She allowed herself a small sigh of relief.

But it was also good to go in through the Staff Only door, to be buzzed in by old Alf and see the welcome on his face. Alf had worked for Rafferty's since before Polly's father was born and had always had a bar of chocolate and a kind word for the small girl desperately trailing after her grandfather, wanting, *needing*, to be included.

And it was good to be here, back in the light-filled foyer where her assistant had her desk. Not that Rachel seemed to share her enthusiasm judging by her open-mouthed expression and panicked eyes, and the way her fingers shook as she gathered together a sheaf of papers.

'Miss Rafferty? We weren't expecting you back just yet.'

'I did let you know my flight details,' Polly said coolly. It wasn't like Rachel to be so disorganised. And at the very least a friendly 'welcome back' would have been polite.

Rachel threw an anxious glance towards the door to Polly's office. 'Well yes.' She got up out of her chair and walked around her desk to stand in front of the door, blocking Polly's path. 'But I thought you would go home first. I didn't expect to see you today.'

'I hope my early appearance isn't too much of an inconvenience.' What was the girl hiding? Perhaps Raff had decorated her office in high gloss and black leather during his brief sojourn as CEO. 'As you can see I decided to come straight here.' Polly gave her assistant a cool glance, waiting for her to move aside.

'You've come straight from the airport?' Rachel wouldn't—or couldn't—meet her eye but stood her ground. 'You must be tired and thirsty. Why don't you go to the staff canteen and I'll arrange for them to bring you coffee and something to eat?'

'Coffee does sound lovely,' Polly agreed. 'But I'd rather have it *in* my office if you don't mind. Please call and arrange it. Thank you, Rachel.'

Rachel stood there for a long second, indecision clear

on her face before she moved slowly to one side. 'Yes, Miss Rafferty.'

Polly nodded curtly at her still-hovering assistant. Things had obviously got slack under Raff's reign. She hoped it wouldn't take too long to get things back on track—or to get herself back on track; no more lie-ins, long walks on beaches where the sand was so fine it felt like silk underfoot, no more swimming in balmy seas or drinking rum cocktails under the light of so many stars it was like being in an alternate universe.

No. She was back to work, routine and normality, which was great. A girl couldn't relax for ever, right?

Slowly Polly turned the chrome handle and opened her office door, relishing the cool polished feel of the metal under her hand. Like much of the interior throughout the store the door handle was one of the original art deco fittings chosen by her great-grandfather back in the nineteen twenties. His legacy lived on in every fitting and fixture. She loved the weight of history that fell onto her shoulders as soon as she walked into the building. Her name, her blood, her legacy.

She stood on the threshold for a second and breathed in. It was finally hers. Everything she had worked for, everything she had dreamed of—this was her office, her store, her way.

And yet it had all felt so unachievable just three months ago. Despite four years as vice CEO and the last of those years as acting CEO while her grandfather stood back from the company he loved as fiercely as Polly herself did, she had walked away. After her grandfather had told her he was finally stepping down and installing Polly's twin brother Raff in his place she had dropped her swipe card on the desk, collected her bag and walked out.

The next day she had been on a plane to South America. She had left her home, her cat and her company—and replaced them with a frivolous bucket list.

Three months later that memory still had the power to wind her.

But here she was, back at the helm and nothing and no one was going to stand in her way.

The relief at seeing her office unchanged swept over her; the sunshine streaming in through the stained-glass floor-to-ceiling windows highlighting the wood panelling, tiled floors and her beautiful walnut desk—the very same one commissioned by her great-grandfather for this room in nineteen twenty-five—the bookshelves and photos, her chaise longue, her...

Hang on. Her eyes skittered back; that hadn't been there before.

Or rather *he* hadn't.

Nope, Polly was pretty sure she would have remembered if she'd left a half-naked sleeping beauty on her antique chaise longue when she'd stormed out.

Frankly, the mood she'd been in, she probably would have taken him with her.

She moved a little closer, uncomfortably aware of her heels tapping on the tiled floor, and contemplated the newest addition to her office.

He was lying on his front, his arm pillowing his head, just the curve of a sharply defined cheekbone and a shock of dark hair falling over his forehead visible. His jeans were snug, low, riding deep on his back exposing every vertebrae on his naked torso.

It was a tanned torso, a deep olive, and although slim, almost to the point of leanness, every muscle was clearly defined. On his lower back a tree blossomed, a silhouette whose branches reached up to his middle vertebrae. Polly fought an urge to reach out and trace one of the narrow lines with her fingers. She didn't normally like tattoos but this one was oddly beautiful, almost mesmerising in its intricacy.

What was she doing? She shouldn't be standing here admiring the interloper. He needed to wake up and get out. No matter how peaceful he looked.

Polly coughed, a short, polite noise. It was as effectual as an umbrella in a hurricane. She coughed again, louder, more irritated.

He didn't even stir.

'Excuse me.' Her voice was soft, polite. Polly shook her head in disgust; this was her office. Why was *she* the one pussyfooting around? 'Excuse me!'

This time there was some effect, just a little; a faint murmur and a shift in his position as he rolled onto his side. She couldn't help flickering a quick glance along the lean length. Yep, the front matched the back, a smattering of fine dark hair tangled on his upper chest, another silky patch emphasising the muscles on his abdomen before tapering into a line that ran down inside the low-slung jeans.

Polly swallowed, her mouth suddenly in need of some kind of moisture. No, she scolded herself, tearing her eyes away, heat flushing through her. Just because he was in her office she didn't have the right to stand here and objectify him. She gave the room a quick once-over relieved that no one was there to witness her behaviour; she was the CEO for goodness' sake, she had to set an example.

This had gone on long enough. This was a place of business, not a doss house for disreputable if attractive young men to slumber in, or a hidey-hole for her PA's latest boyfriend. Whoever he was she was going to have to shake him awake. Right *now*.

If only he were wearing a shirt. Or anything. Touching that bronzed skin felt intrusive, intimate.

'For goodness' sake, are you woman or wombat?' she muttered, balling her fingers into a fist.

'Hello.' She reached over and took a tentative hold of one firm shoulder, his skin warm and smooth against her hand. 'Wake up.' She gave a little shake but it was like shaking a statue.

All she wanted was to sit at her desk and start working. Alone. Was that too much to ask? Anger and adrenaline flooded through her system; it had been a long journey, she was jet-lagged and irritated and in need of a sit-down and a coffee. She'd had enough. Officially.

Polly turned and walked crisply towards her small en-suite cloakroom and bathroom, this time uncaring of the loud tap of her heels. The door swung open to reveal a wide, airy space with room for coats and shoes plus a walk-in wardrobe where Polly stored a selection of outfits for the frequent occasions where she went straight from work to a social function. She gave the room a quick glance, relieved to see no trace of Raff's presence. It was as if he had been wiped out of the store's memory.

That was fine by her. He had made it quite clear he wanted nothing to do with Rafferty's—and although they were twins they had never been good at sharing.

Another door led into the well-equipped bathroom. Polly allowed herself one longing glance at the walk-in shower before grabbing a glass from the shelf and filling it with water, making sure the cold tap ran for a few seconds first for maximum chill. Then, quickly so that she didn't lose her nerve, she swivelled on her heel and marched back over to the chaise longue, standing over the interloper.

He had moved again, lying supine, half on his back, half on his side revealing more of his features. Long, thick lashes lay peacefully on cheekbones so finely sculpted it looked as if a master stonemason had been at work, eyebrows arching arrogantly above.

His wide mouth was slightly parted. Sensual, a little voice whispered to Polly. A mouth made for sin.

She ignored the voice. And she ignored the slight jibe of her conscience; she needed him awake and leaving; if he wouldn't respond to gentler methods then what choice did she have?

Resolutely Polly held the glass up over the man's face and tipped it. For one long moment she held it still so that the water was perfectly balanced right at the rim, clear drops so very close to spilling over the thin edge.

And then she allowed her hand to move the glass over the tipping point, a perfect stream of cold water falling like rain onto the peacefully slumbering face below.

Polly didn't quite know what to expect; anger, shock, contrition or even no reaction at all. He was so very deeply asleep after all. But what she didn't expect was for one red-rimmed eye to lazily open, for a smile to play around the disturbingly well-cut mouth or for a hand to shoot out and grab her wrist.

Caught by surprise, she stumbled forward, falling against the chaise as the hand snuck around her waist, pulling her down, pulling her close.

'Bonjour, chérie.' His voice was low, gravelly with sleep and deeply, unmistakeably French. 'If you wanted me to wake up you only had to ask.'

It was the shock, that was all. Otherwise she would have moved, called for help, disentangled herself from the strong arm anchoring her firmly against the bare chest. And she would never, *ever* have allowed his other hand to slip around her neck in an oddly sweet caress while he angled his mouth towards hers—would have moved away long before the hard mouth claimed hers in a distinctly unsleepy way.

It was definitely the shock keeping her paralysed under his touch—and she was definitely *not* leaning into the kiss, opening herself up to the pressure of his mouth on hers, the touch of his hand moving up her back, slipping round her ribcage, brushing against the swell of her breast.

Hang on, his hand was where?

Polly pulled away, jumping up off the chaise, resisting the urge to scrub the kiss off her tingling mouth.

Or to lean back down and let him claim her again.

'What do you think you're doing?'

'Saying *au revoir* of course.' He had shifted position and was leaning against the back of the chaise, his eyes skimming every inch of her until she wanted to wrap her arms around her torso, shielding herself from his insolent gaze.

'*Au revoir?*' Was she going mad? Where were the panicked apologies and the scuttling out of her office?

'Of course.' He raised an eyebrow. 'As you are dressed to leave I thought you were saying goodbye. But if it was more of a good morning...' the smile widened '...even better.'

'I am not saying *au revoir* or good morning or anything but *what on earth are you doing in my office and where are your clothes*?'

She hadn't meant to tag on the last line but with the imprint of his hand still burning her back and the taste of him taunting her mouth she really needed to be looking at something other than what seemed like acres of taut, tanned bare flesh.

Surely now, now he would show some contrition, some shame. But no, he was what? Laughing? He was mad or drunk or both and she was going to call Security right now.

'Of course, your office! Polly, *bonjour*. I am charmed to meet you.'

What? He knew her name? She took an instinctive step backwards as he slid off the chaise, as graceful as a panther, and took a step towards her, hand held out.

'Who are you and what are you doing here?' She stepped back a little further, one hand groping for the phone ready to call for help.

'I am so very sorry.' He was smiling as if the whole situation were nothing but a huge joke. 'I fell asleep here, last night, and was confused when you woke me.' His eyes laughed at her, shamelessly. 'It's not the first time I've been awakened by a glass of water. I am Gabriel Beaufils, your new vice CEO. My friends call me Gabe. I hope you will too.'

No, that was no better, she was still looking at him as if he were an escaped convict. Not surprisingly, Gabe thought ruefully. What had he been thinking?

He hadn't. He'd been dreaming, stuck in that hazy world between sleep and wakefulness when he'd felt a warm hand on his shoulder followed by the chill shock of the water and, confused, had thought it some kind of game. After three weeks of eighteen-hour days, making sure he was fully and firmly ensconced at Rafferty's before the formidable Polly Rafferty returned, he wasn't as switched on as he should be.

Well, his wake-up call had been brutal. It was bad enough from Polly's point of view that he had been catapulted in without her say-so or knowledge—and a wake-up kiss probably wasn't the wisest way to make a good impression. He needed to make up the lost ground, and fast.

He smiled at her, pouring as much winning charm into the smile as he could.

There was no answering smile, not even in her darkly

shadowed eyes. The bruised circles were the only hint of tiredness even though she must have come straight here from the airport. Her dark gold hair was twisted up into a neat knot and her suit looked freshly laundered. Yet for all the business-style armour there was something oddly vulnerable in the blue eyes, the determined set of her almost too-slender frame.

'Gabriel Beaufils?' There was a hint of recognition in her voice. 'You were working for Desmoulins?'

'*Oui*, as Digital Director.' He debated mentioning the tripling of profits in the proud old Parisian store's web business but decided against it. Yet. That little but pertinent detail might come in handy and he didn't want to play his hand too soon.

'I don't recall hiring a new vice CEO.' There was nothing fragile in her voice. It was cold enough to freeze the water still dripping over his torso. 'Even if I had, that doesn't explain why you were sleeping in my office and appear to have mislaid your top.'

Nor why you kissed me. She might not have said the words but they were implied, hung accusingly in the air.

No, better to forget about the kiss, delightful as it had been. Strange to think that the huge-eyed, fragile-looking woman opposite had responded so openly, so ardently, that she would taste of sweetness and spice.

Damn it, he was supposed to be forgetting about the kiss.

'Polly, *je suis désolé*.' This situation was not irredeemable no matter how it seemed right now. It wasn't often that Gabe thought himself lucky to have three older sisters but right now they were a blessing; he was used to disapproving glares and turning the stickiest of situations right around.

'I have been using this office until you returned—we

didn't know if you would want to take over your grandfather's office or stay in here. But once again I was working too late and missed the last train back to Hopeford. It was easier to crash out on the couch rather than find a hotel so late. If I had known you were coming in this morning...'

He threw his hands out in a placatory gesture.

It didn't work. If anything she looked even more suspicious. 'Hopeford? Why would you be staying there?'

A sinking feeling hit Gabe. On a scale of one to ten this whole situation was hitting one hundred on the awkward chart. If she wasn't happy about having a vice CEO she hadn't handpicked then she was going to love having a strange houseguest!

'Cat-feeding. Raff was worried Mr Simpkins would get lonely.' He smiled as winningly as he could but there was no response from her.

Okay, charm wasn't working, businesslike might. 'I do have an apartment arranged,' he explained. 'But unfortunately, just before I was going to move in, the neighbour's basement extension caused a massive subsidence in the whole street. I can quite easily go to a hotel if it's a problem but as your house was empty and I was homeless...' He shrugged. It had made perfect sense at the time.

Apparently not to Polly. 'You're staying in my *house*? Where is Raff? Why isn't he there?'

'He was in Jordan, now I think he's in Australia but he should be back soon.' It had been hard to keep up with the other Rafferty twin's travels.

'Australia? What on earth is he doing there?' She sank down into the large chair behind her desk with an audible sigh of relief, probably worn out by the weight of all the questions she had fired at him. Gabe's head was spinning from them all.

'I thought Raff would wait until I got back before tak-

ing off again,' Polly murmured, her voice so low that Gabe
hardly caught her words.

If Gabriel had to narrow all his criticisms of his own
family down to just one thing it would be the complete lack
of respect for personal space—physically *and* mentally.
Every thought, every feeling, every pain, every movement
was up for general discussion, dissection and in the worst-
case scenario culminating in a family conference.

His middle sister, Celine, would even video call in from
New Zealand, unwilling to let a small matter like time
zones and distance prevent her from getting her two cen-
times' worth in.

The possibility of anybody in the Beaufils household
not knowing the exact whereabouts of any member of their
family at any given time was completely inconceivable.
Sometimes Gabe suspected they had all been microchipped
at birth. How could Polly Rafferty have no idea where her
own twin brother was or what he was doing?

She looked up at him, the navy-blue eyes dark. 'I think
I might be more jet-lagged than I realised,' she said slowly.
'Let me get this straight. You are working, here, at Raffer-
ty's, as the vice CEO and living at Hopeford. In my house.'

'Temporarily,' Gabe clarified. 'Your house, that is.'

She closed her eyes.

A knock at the door jolted her back to wakefulness, the
eyes snapping open.

'Yes?'

The door opened, followed a moment later by Rachel,
who was carrying a large tray. She flickered a sympathetic
glance over at Gabe and he couldn't resist winking back.

'Your coffee, Miss Rafferty.' Rachel set the tray onto the
desk and smiled at Gabe. 'I brought your usual smoothie,
Mr Beaufils,' she said in a much lighter tone. 'The chef
has your muesli ready. I said you might prefer to eat it in

the staff canteen this morning. Oh, and dry-cleaning has sent your clean shirt up. I'll just take it through for you.'

'*Merci*, Rachel.'

Polly had begun to pour her coffee but stopped mid flow, her eyes narrowed and fixed on her assistant.

'You were aware that Mr Beaufils was here? In my office?'

'Well, he often works late…' Rachel said.

'And you didn't think to warn me?'

'I…'

'Tell Building Services I need to see them this morning. Mr Beaufils obviously needs his own sleeping and breakfasting area. Oh, and his own assistant. Get on to HR. We'll discuss the rest later.'

'Yes, Miss Rafferty.' Rachel bobbed out with a sigh of relief, returning a second later with a crisply wrapped shirt, which she handed to Gabe before exiting the office and closing the door.

'Nice girl, very competent.' Gabe sauntered over to the tray and picked up his usual smoothie. It had taken a few days for the chef to get the mixture just right but it was pretty close to perfection now. He took it over to the chaise and sipped but could feel Polly's eyes on him and looked over at her with a faintly enquiring smile.

'Are you quite comfortable?' she asked. 'Are you sure you don't want to ask for your muesli in here? Take a shower before getting dressed? How about a massage?'

He bit back a smile at the sarcastic tone in her voice. 'A shower would be lovely, thank you.' He downed the shake, feeling the cool liquid hit the back of his throat, the vitamins working their way into his system. 'Don't worry about showing me the way. I know my way around.'

'Hold on.' But she was too late, Gabriel Beaufils had disappeared into the cloakroom.

Polly jumped to her feet but came to a stop. She was hardly going to follow him into the shower, was she?

Not that he would mind—he'd probably just ask her to pass him the towel! After all he had no compunction about parading around her office half naked. No wonder Rachel was smitten. Smoothies and muesli indeed.

The phone on her desk blared. It was probably the kitchen wondering if Gabe wanted a lightly poached egg with his breakfast. Polly glared at it before pressing the speakerphone button.

'Polly Rafferty.'

'You're home, then.' Familiar grizzled, curt tones.

'Hello, Grandfather. I hope you're feeling better.' He at least hadn't expected her to go back to Hopeford before returning to work. But then Charles Rafferty had never actually taken a holiday—*his* bucket list probably read 'spend more time in the office'.

Her grandfather merely grunted. 'Hope you're ready to get down to some serious work after your little holiday.' Polly bit back the obvious retorts; it hadn't been a holiday, she had left the company after barely taking a long weekend off in the last five years.

But what was the point? Words wouldn't change him.

'Have you met Beaufils yet?'

Polly couldn't stop her eyes flicking towards the cloakroom door. 'I've seen him,' she said drily. 'Confident young man.'

'He's Vincent's boy, Gabriel. You know Chateau Beaufils of course, we've been their exclusive UK stockist for decades. He's the only son.'

'That doesn't explain why he's here.' Her voice was sharper than she had intended.

She didn't want her grandfather to know how much Gabe's presence had shaken her.

'Oh, he's not here because of the vineyard although that's a good connection of course. Man did some great things at Desmoulins, which is why I snapped him up. Thought he'd be good balance for you.'

'Good balance for me?' Polly wasn't sure whether she wanted to laugh or cry. Balance or replacement? If he couldn't have Raff did her grandfather want this young man instead? Just how much did she have to do before he finally accepted her? 'I really think I should have been consulted.'

'No.' Her grandfather's answer was as sharp as it was unequivocal. 'Vice CEO is a board decision. We need someone with different strengths from you, not someone you can ride roughshod over.'

Talk about the pot and the kettle. Polly glared at the phone.

'He knows the European markets and is very, very strong digitally, so I want him in charge of all e-commerce. Oh, and Polly? It's going to take a few weeks before his apartment is sound again. It won't bother you to have him at yours until then? You barely spend any time there as it is.'

Despite her best intentions Polly found her attention wandering back to the moment she had first seen Gabe sprawled on her chaise. The line of his back, the strong leanness of him, the delicacy of that intricate tattoo spiralling up his spine.

Thank goodness her grandfather wasn't here to see the flush on her cheeks.

Her first instinct was to demand they find Gabriel Beaufils alternative accommodation a long, long way from her house and home. And yet…it might be useful to keep him close. What was that they said about friends and enemies?

'I can't imagine there's much to excite him in Hopeford,' she said sweetly. 'But of course he can stay.'

The more she could find out about Gabriel Beaufils, the easier it would be to outmanoeuvre him. She was in charge of Rafferty's at last and no smoothie-drinking, bare-chested, charming Frenchman was going to change that.

CHAPTER TWO

GABE FINISHED TOWEL-DRYING his hair and grabbed the clean shirt Rachel had brought him. Pulling it on, he began to button it up slowly, once again running the morning's unexpected events through his mind. What had he been thinking?

He hadn't been thinking, that was the problem, he'd been reacting. A sure sign he'd allowed himself to mix business and pleasure that bit too often. Not enough sleep and too many office flirtations.

What a first impression! Although he wasn't sure what had thrown her more—the kiss or the news of his appointment.

He couldn't blame her for being less than pleased with either but he was here and he was staying put. Unlike Polly Rafferty he didn't have the advantage of bearing the founder's name, but he was just twenty-eight, already the vice CEO of Rafferty's and his goal of running his own company by thirty was looking eminently doable.

Things were nicely on track to get the results he needed, to learn everything he could and in two years look for the opportunity he needed to achieve his goal. Because life was short. Nobody knew that better than Gabe.

He pushed the thought away as he strode out of the bathroom and along the passage that led to the office. It was time to eat some humble pie.

'Nice shower?'

Gabe came to a halt and stared at Polly Rafferty. Was that a smile on her face?

'Rachel tells me you've been working all hours,' she continued. 'I just want to thank you. Obviously it was less than ideal that I wasn't back before Raff left but it's such a relief that you were here to help out.'

'I was more than happy to step in.' Gabe leant against the door frame and watched her through narrow eyes.

Polly seemed oblivious to his gaze. She was leaning back in his chair—correction, her chair—completely at her ease. She had taken off her jacket and it hung on the hat stand in the corner, her bag tossed carelessly on the floor beneath it. Her laptop was plugged into the keyboard and monitor, his own laptop folded and put aside. Several sheets of paper were stacked on the gleaming mahogany desk, a red pen lying on top of one, the crossed-out lines and scribbled notes implying great industry. It was as if she had never been away.

As if he had never been there.

Polly looked up, pen in hand. 'You haven't had break-fast so I suggest you take an hour or so while I get to grips with a few things here, then we can discuss how it's going to work moving forward. Starting with a permanent office and an assistant for you.' She couldn't be more gracious.

In fact she was the perfect hostess. Gabe suppressed a smile; he couldn't help approving of her tactics. Polly was throwing down the gauntlet. Oh, politely and with some degree of charm but, still, she was making it clear that absence or no absence this was her company and he was the incomer.

'You don't want your grandfather's office?' he asked. 'I assumed that you would want to move in there.'

A flicker of sadness ran over her face disturbing the blandly pleasant mask. 'This room belonged to my great-grandfather. The furniture and décor is just as it was, just as he chose. I'm staying here.'

But she wasn't going to offer him the bigger room either; he'd stake his reputation on it.

'I don't need an hour.' He pushed off the door frame. 'I am quite happy to start in fifteen minutes.'

'That's very sweet of you, Gabe.' The smile was back. 'But please, take an hour. I'll see you then.'

The dismissal was clear. Round one to Polly Rafferty.

That was okay. Gabe didn't care about individual rounds. He cared about the final prize. He inclined his head as he moved towards the door. 'Of course, take as long as you need to settle back in. Oh and, Polly? Welcome back.'

Polly held onto the smile as long as it took for the door to close behind the tall Frenchman then slumped forward with a sigh. It had taken her just a few minutes to reclaim the office but it still didn't feel like hers. It smelt different, of soap and a fresh citrusy cologne, of leather and whatever was in that disgusting green drink Gabe had tossed down so easily. She'd sniffed the glass when he was in the shower and recoiled in horror—until then she didn't think anything could be as vile as the look of the smoothie, but she'd been wrong.

Her coffee smelt off too. It must be the jet lag and all the travelling she'd done in the last week—nothing smelt right at the moment. Her stomach had twisted with nausea at the mere thought of caffeine or alcohol and even the eggs she had tried to eat at the airport.

Polly pushed the thought away. Whining that she was tired and that she felt ill wouldn't get her anywhere. She needed to hit the ground running and not stop.

Walking over to the massive art deco windows that dominated the office, she peered through their tinted panes

at the street below. Coloured in red and green it looked like
a film maker's whimsical view of the vibrant West End.
Polly had always loved the strange slant the glass gave on
the world. It helped her think clearly, think differently—
helped her see problems in a new way.

And right now she needed all her wits about her.

'Gabriel Beaufils,' she said aloud, her mind conjuring
up unbidden the tall man lounging at his ease, jeans riding low, bare chested, the water still dripping from his wet
hair. What did that tell her?

That he was shameless. That he was beautiful.

Polly shook her head impatiently, replacing the image
in her mind with the man that had just left. Leaning in-
souciantly against the door, wet hair slicked back. Still in
jeans but now they were more sedately paired with a crisp
white linen shirt. No tie. Laughter in his eyes.

That was better. Now what could she deduce from that?
He didn't care what people thought about him, what she
thought about him. That he was confident and utterly secure in his charm. That he was underestimating her.

She could work with that.

What else? Polly pulled herself away from the view
and returned to her desk, running her fingers possessively
over the polished wood. *Okay, let's do this.* She pulled up a
search engine and typed in his name. 'Who are you, Monsieur Beaufils?' she murmured as she hit enter.

The page instantly filled with several engines. He had
left quite the digital trail.

Polly sat back and began to read. Some of it she knew.
He was from an affluent background, his family the proud
makers of a venerable brand of wine. However, Gabe had
left home in his late teens, gone to college in the States
and stayed on to do his MBA while working at one of the
biggest retail chains there.

'Good,' she muttered, returning to the results page and scanning the next paragraph, an article written about him just a few months ago. 'What else?'

Two years ago he had returned home to France, to Paris, to take charge of digital sales at Desmoulins. The young up-and-coming whizz-kid introducing innovation into one of Paris's most venerable *grande dames* had made quite a stir. Was that what he was planning to do here?

So much for his business history. Personal life? She moved through several lines of results. Nothing. Either he was very discreet or he didn't have a private life.

Polly's mouth tingled as if his lips were still hovering above hers. Despite herself she flicked her tongue over them as if she could still taste him. Discreet it was. That was a very practised kiss.

She took the cursor back to the top of the page and hit the images button. Instantly the page filled with photos of Gabe, smiling, serious, in a suit…in head-to-toe Lycra.

Hang on? He was wearing *what*?

She hovered over the image of Gabe walking out of a lake, wetsuit half undone, and Polly resisted the urge to zoom in on his chest. She checked the caption. He was a triathlete.

Gabriel Beaufils. Confident, charming, discreet and competitive.

She could handle that.

A smile curved her mouth. This was going to be almost too easy.

'I hope I didn't keep you waiting. I got caught up in something.'

As a matter of fact he was precisely on time—Polly would bet money that Gabe Beaufils had been standing outside the office watching a stopwatch to make sure he walked back in exactly one hour after she had dismissed him.

She would have done the same thing herself. Interesting.

Not that she was going to let him know that. She kept her eyes locked on her computer screen, giving every impression that she too was busy. 'I hope you had a nice breakfast.'

'Yes, thank you, most important meal of the day.' There was a dark hint of laughter in his voice.

'So they say.' She looked up and smiled. 'I'm usually too busy to remember to eat it.'

She had meant the glance and the smile to be brief, dismissive, but there was an intensity in his answering look that ensnared her. How could eyes be so dark, so knowing? Heat burned her cheeks, a shiver of awareness deep inside.

Reluctantly she pulled her gaze away, staring mindlessly at her computer screen, reading the same nonsensical sentence over and over again.

'You should take care of yourself, Polly.' His voice was low, caressing. 'Neglecting your body is not wise.'

'I don't neglect my body.' She wanted to pull the defensive words back as soon as she had uttered them.

'I exercise and eat well,' she clarified not entirely truthfully but she didn't want to admit to her snacking habits to him. Not when he was evidently so healthy. And fit. It took every ounce of willpower she had not to look up again, to sweep her eyes over him from head to toe, lingering on the muscles she knew were lurking under that crisp white shirt. 'I just don't make a big deal of it.'

She pushed her chair back and stood. 'I am going to do a walkabout,' she said. 'Would you care to accompany me?'

He stayed still for a moment, that curiously intent look still in his eyes, and then nodded courteously as he pulled the door open and held it for her.

Polly sensed his every movement as he followed her back out into the light, glass-walled foyer, awareness prickling her spine.

Rachel looked up as they walked by, curiosity clear on her face. Polly had no doubt that she was emailing all of her friends with a highly scurrilous account of her boss's encounter with a half-naked Frenchman. Let her; Polly would fill her PA's forthcoming days so completely that she wouldn't even be able to dream about gossiping.

It wasn't far from her office to one of the discreet doors that led out onto the shop floor. This was what Rafferty's was all about. No matter how essential the office functions were they existed for one purpose—to keep the iconic store in business. Polly ensured that every finance assistant, every marketing executive spent at least one week a year on the shop floor. Just as her great-grandfather had done. She herself spent most of December on the shop floor serving, restocking and assisting. The buzz and adrenaline rush were addictive.

'I've spoken to Building Services,' she said as she slid her pass through the door lock, turning with one hand on the handle to face Gabe. 'I am going to turn Grandfather's old office into the boardroom. It's bigger than any of the meeting rooms, far too big for one person—and I think he'll be pleased with the gesture. He is still President of the Board.'

Polly knew everyone expected her to move into the vast corner suite but couldn't face the thought of occupying her grandfather's chair, feeling him second-guessing her all the time, disapproving of every change she made.

'And me?' It was said with a self-deprecating and very Gallic shrug but Polly wasn't fooled. There was a sharpness in his eyes.

'The old boardroom.' It was a neat solution. Polly got to

keep her office, her grandfather would hopefully feel honoured and Gabe would get a brand-new office in keeping with his position. But not a Rafferty office, not one with history steeped in its walls.

'Building Services are confident they can create a room for your assistant with no major infrastructure changes and there's already a perfectly good cloakroom. You can start picking wallpaper and furniture this week and it should be ready end of next week.'

'And where do I work in the meantime?' His voice was still mild but Polly was aware of a stillness about him, a quiet confidence in his gaze. She didn't want to push too far, not yet. Reluctantly she discarded her plan that he sit in her foyer, with Rachel, or that she find him a spare desk in one of the bigger, open-plan offices where the rest of the backroom staff worked.

'We can fit a second desk in my room,' she said. 'Just until you're settled. But, Gabe? No more sleeping in the office, no more using my assistant to sort out your laundry and...' she swallowed but kept her gaze and voice firm '...you remain fully dressed and act appropriately at all times. Understood?'

Gabe's mouth quirked. 'Of course,' he murmured.

'Good.' She pushed the door open.

This was it, this was where the magic happened.

Polly blinked as she stepped out. They had entered the home furnishings department on the top floor and the lights were switched to full, purposely dazzling to best showcase the silks, cushions, throws, ceramics, silverware and all the other luxury items Rafferty's told their customers were essential for a comfortable home. Beneath them were floors and galleries devoted to technology, books, toys, food and, of course, fashion.

Polly's heart swelled and she clenched her fists. She was home.

And yet everything had changed. She had changed.

She had hoped that being back would ground her again but it was odd walking through the galleries with Gabe. If her staff greeted her with their usual respect, they greeted him with something warmer.

And how on earth did he know every name after what? Three or four weeks?

'*Bonjour*, Emily.' Polly narrowed her eyes at him as they entered the world-famous haberdashery room. Had his accent thickened as he greeted the attractive redhead who had turned the department into the must-go destination for a new generation of craft lovers?

'How is your cat? Did the operation go well?' He had moved nearer to Emily, smiling down at her intimately.

Polly's head snapped round. No way. He knew the names of every staff member and all about the health of their pets too?

'Yes, thank you, Mr Beaufils, she's desperate to go outside but she's doing really well.' Emily was smiling back, her voice a little breathy.

'They can be such a responsibility, *non*? I 'ave...'

Had he just dropped an aitch? *Really?* Polly had known him for what, an hour? And she already knew perfectly well that Gabe spoke perfect, almost accentless English. Unless, it seemed, he was talking to petite redheads. She coughed and could have sworn she saw a glimmer of laughter in the depths of his almost-black eyes as he continued.

'I 'ave been looking after Mademoiselle Rafferty's cat for the last few weeks. He is a rascal, that one. Such a huge responsibility.'

'They are,' Emily said earnestly, her huge eyes fixed on his. 'But worth it.'

'*Oui*, the way they purr. So trusting.'

That was it. Polly felt ill just listening. 'So greedy,' she said briskly. 'And so prone to eviscerating small mammals under the bed. If you're ready, Gabe, shall we continue? Nice work,' she said to Emily, unable to keep a sarcastic tone from her voice. 'Keep it up.' And without a backwards glance she swept from the department.

It had been an interesting morning. Gabe was well aware that he had been well and truly sized up, tested and judged. What the verdict was he had no idea.

Nor, truth be told, was he that interested. He had his own weighing up to do.

Tough, but not as tough as she thought. Surprisingly stylish for someone who lived and breathed work; the sharp little suit she was wearing would pass muster in the most exclusive streets in Paris—unusual for an Englishwoman. He liked how she wasn't afraid of her height, accentuating it with heels, the blonde hair swept up into a knot adding an extra couple of centimetres.

And she wasn't going to give him an inch. The solution to the offices was masterful. It was going to be fun working with her.

He loved a good game.

Gabe strode through the foyer, smiling at Rachel as she looked up with a blush. Maybe he should have gone a little easier on the flirting. He wouldn't make that mistake with his own assistant—he would request a guy or, even better, a motherly woman who would keep all unwanted callers away and feed him home-made cake. He made a note to keep an eye on the 'interests' section of any applicants' CVs.

He opened the door to Polly's office without knocking; after all they were sharing it.

'This is going to be fun,' he said as Polly looked up from her computer screen, trying unsuccessfully to hide her irritation at the interruption. 'Roomies, housemates. We should take a road trip too, complete the set.'

Bed mates would really make it a full hand but he wasn't going to suggest that. Totally inappropriate. But, despite himself, his eyes wandered over her face, skimming over the smattering of freckles high on her cheeks, the wide mouth, the pointed little chin. She kissed like she spoke—with passion and purpose—but there was none of the coolness and poise. No, there was heat simmering away behind that cool façade.

Heat he was better off pretending he knew nothing about.

'I'll let you have a lift in the company car. Will that do?' She looked unamused. 'Did you decide on office furniture? There's a temporary desk for you there.' She nodded over towards the wall where a second desk had already been set up, a monitor and phone installed on its gleaming surface.

'I'll be here a week or two at the most according to Building Services and then you're free of me.'

'Hardly,' she muttered so low he could barely make out her words then spoke out in her usual crisp tones. 'Are you available to talk now?'

'*Certainement*, if you need me to be.' He didn't mean to let his voice drop or to drawl the words out quite so suggestively but the colour rising swiftly in her cheeks showed their effect all too clearly. 'It would be good to start again, properly,' he clarified.

'Good.' Polly waited until he had taken his seat at his new desk. It wasn't quite as good a position as hers, which faced the incredible windows. When Gabe had sat there absorbed in his work he would look absently up every so

often, only to be struck anew by the light, the simple art-
istry of the stylised floral design.

Now his view was the bookshelves that lined the opposite wall—and Polly, her desk directly in his eyeline.
She swivelled her chair towards him, a notepad and pen
poised in her hand, her legs crossed.

The only way this was going to work was if he behaved
himself in thought and deed. But he was a mere man after
all and better souls than him would find it hard to stop
their gaze skimming over the long willowy figure and the
neatly crossed legs. Incredibly long, ridiculously shapely
legs. Of course they were.

'You've got a pretty impressive CV,' she said finally.
'Why Rafferty's?'

'That means a lot coming from you,' he said honestly.
'Oh, come on,' as her brows rose in surprise. 'Polly Rafferty, you set the standard, you must know that. I came
here to work with you.'

'With me?'

'Don't misunderstand me, there's a lot you can learn
from me as well. In some ways Rafferty's is stuck in the
Dark Ages, especially digitally. But, you have done some
great things here over the last few years. I have no problem admitting there are still things I need to learn if I am
going to be a CEO by the time I'm thirty...'

'Here?'

He raised an eyebrow. 'Would you let me?'

'You'd have to kill me first.' She shook her head, her
colour high.

'That's what I thought. No, maybe a start-up, or even
my own business. I'll see nearer the time.'

'You're ambitious. It took me until I was thirty-one to
make it.' Her eyes met his coolly, the blue of her eyes dark.

'I know.' He grinned. 'A little competition keeps me

focused.' He shrugged. 'Rafferty's is possibly the most famous store in Europe if not the world. It's the missing piece in my experience—and I have a lot to offer you as well. It's a win-win situation.'

She leant back. 'Prove it. What would you change?'

He grinned. 'Are you ready for it? You only just got back.'

The corners of her mouth turned up, the smallest of smiles. 'Don't pull your punches. I can take it.'

'Okay then.' He jumped out of the chair and began to pace up and down the room. It was always easier to think on his feet; those months of being confined to bed had left him with a horror of inaction.

'Your social media lacks identity and your online advertising is practically non-existent—it's untargeted and unplanned, effectively just a redesign of your print advertising. I suggest you employ a digital marketing consultant to train your existing staff. Emily is very capable. She just needs guidance and some confidence.'

He looked across for a reaction but she was busy scribbling notes. Gabe rolled his eyes. 'This is part of the problem. You're what? Writing longhand?'

'I think better with paper and pen. I'll type them up later.' Her voice was defensive.

'*Non*, the whole company needs to think digitally. The sales force need tablets so they can check sizes and styles at the touch of a button, mix and match styles.'

'We have a personal touch here. We don't need to rely on tablets…'

'You need both,' he said flatly. 'But what you really need is a new website.'

There was a long moment of incredulous silence. 'But it's only three years old. Do you *know* how much we spent on it?'

Polly was no longer leaning back. She was ramrod-straight, her eyes sparkling, more in anger than excitement, Gabe thought. 'Too much and it's obsolete. Come on, Polly.' His words tumbled over each other, his accent thickened in his effort to convince her.

'Do you want a website that's fine and gets the job done or do you want one that's a window into the very soul of Rafferty's? You have no other stores anywhere—this is it. Your Internet business *is* your worldwide business and that's where the expansion lies.'

'What do you have in mind?'

This was what made him tick, made his blood pump, the adrenaline flow—planning, innovating, creating. It was better than finishing a marathon, hell, sometimes it was better than sex. 'A site that is visually stunning, one that creates the feel and the look of the store as much as possible. Each department would be organised by gallery, exactly as you are laid out here so that customers get to experience the look, the feel of Rafferty's—but virtually. Online assistants would be available twenty-four hours to chat and advise and, most importantly, the chance to personalise the experience. Why should people buy from Rafferty's online when there are hundreds, thousands of alternatives?'

She didn't answer, probably couldn't.

'If we make it better than all the rest then Rafferty's is the store that customers will choose. They can upload their measurements, their photos and have virtual fittings—that way, they can order with certainty, knowing that the clothes will fit and suit them. Cut down on returns and make the whole shopping experience fun and interactive.'

'How much?'

'It won't be cheap,' he admitted. 'Not to build, maintain or staff. But it will be spectacular.'

She didn't speak for a minute or so, staring straight ahead at the window before nodding decisively. 'There's a board meeting next week. Can you have a researched and costed paper ready for then?'

Researched *and* costed? *'Oui.'* If he had to work all day and night. 'So, what about you?'

'What about me?'

'There must be something you want to do, something to stamp your identity firmly on the store.'

'I have been running the company for the last year,' she reminded him, her voice a little frosty.

'But now it's official…' If she wasn't itching to make some changes he had severely underestimated her.

She didn't answer for a moment, her eyes fixed unseeingly on the windows. 'We have never expanded,' she said after a while. 'We always wanted to keep Rafferty's as a destination store, somewhere people could aspire to visit. And it works, we're on so many tourist tick lists; they buy teddies or tea in branded jars, eat in the tea room and take their Rafferty's bag home. And with the Internet there isn't any real need for bricks-and-mortar shops elsewhere.'

'But?'

'But we've become a little staid,' Polly said. She rolled her shoulders as she spoke, stretching out her neck. Gabe tried not to stare, not to notice how graceful her movements were, as she turned her attention to her hair, unpinning it and letting the dark blonde tendrils fall free.

Polly sighed, running her fingers through her hair before beginning to twist it back into a looser, lower knot. It felt almost voyeuristic standing there watching her fingers busy themselves in the tangle of tresses.

'We were one of the first stores in London to stock bikinis. Can you imagine—amidst the post-war austerity, the rationing and a London still two decades and a generation from swinging…my great-grandfather brought several bikinis over from Paris. There were letters of outrage to *The Times*.

'We were the first to unveil the latest trends, to sell miniskirts. We were *always* cutting edge and now we're part of a tour that includes Buckingham Palace and Madame Tussauds.' The contempt was clear in her voice. 'We're doing well financially, really well, but we're no longer cutting edge. We're safe, steady, middle-aged.' Polly wrinkled her nose as she spoke.

It was true; Rafferty's was a byword for elegance, taste and design but not for innovation, not any more. Even Gabe's own digital vision could only sell the existing ranges. But it was fabulously profitable with a brand recognition that was through the roof; wasn't that enough? 'Can a store this size actually be cutting edge any more? Surely that's the Internet's role…'

'I disagree.' She shook her head vehemently. 'We have the space, the knowledge, the passion and the history. The problem is, it takes a lot for us to take on a new designer or a new range, to hand over valuable floor space to somebody little known and unproven—and if they have already established themselves then we're just following, not innovating.'

'So, what do you plan to do about it?' This was more like it. Her eyes were focused again, sharp.

'Pop-ups.'

'*Pardon?*'

'Pop-ups. Bright, fun and relatively low cost. We can create a pop-up area in store for new designers whether it's clothes, jewellery, shoes—we'll champion new talent right here at Rafferty's. Sponsor a graduate show during London fashion week in the main gallery.'

That made a lot of sense.

'But I don't just want to draw people here. I want to go out and find them—it could be a great opportunity to take Rafferty's out of the city as well. Where do we have the biggest footfall?'

It was a good thing he'd pulled those eighteen-hour days; he could answer with utter confidence. 'The food hall.'

'Exactly! The British are finally understanding food— no, don't pull a superior gourmet French face at me. They are and you know it. There are hundreds of food festivals throughout the country and I want us to start having a presence at the very best of them. And not just food festivals. I want us at Glyndebourne, Henley, the Edinburgh Festival Fringe. Anywhere there's a buzz I want Rafferty's. Exclusive invitation-only previews to create excitement, with takeaway afternoon teas and Rafferty's hampers—filled with a selection of our bestselling products as souvenirs.'

Gabe rubbed his chin. 'Will it make a profit?'

'Yes, but not a massive one,' she conceded. 'But it *will* revitalise us, introduce us to the younger market who may think we're too staid for them. Make us more current and more exciting. And that market will be your domestic digital users.'

Gabe could feel it, the roar of adrenaline, the tightening in his gut that meant something new, something exhilarating was in the air. 'It would create a great buzz on social media.'

She nodded, her whole face lit up. 'It all works together, doesn't it? I am presenting at the board meeting too. It's less investment up front than you will need—but this is something untried and untested and the current board are a little conservative. You support me and, once I've checked your finances and conclusions, I'll support your digital

paper. We'll have a lot more impact if we're united. Deal?'
She held out her hand.

Gabe worked alone. He preferred it that way. Sure, he
had good relationships with his colleagues, liked to make
sure they were all onside but he didn't want or brook interference.

Freedom at home and at work. That way he never had
to worry about letting anyone down.

But this was a great opportunity—to be part of the team
dragging Rafferty's into a new age. How could he refuse?
He took her hand, cool and elegant just like its owner.

'Deal.'

CHAPTER THREE

POLLY KICKED OFF her shoes with a sigh of relief. She was home, the sun was shining and it was Friday evening. This was exactly what she needed to get over this pesky jet lag. Surely the tiredness, the constant nausea and the lack of appetite should have gone by now?

It wasn't exactly a weekend break, she still had a lot of work to do if she was to wow the board in a week's time, but she could do it at home either in the little sunshine-drenched study at the back of the cottage or in the timber-beamed, book-lined sitting room. Away from the office.

Usually her office was a sanctuary but right now it felt alien. Gabe seemed to fill every corner of it. His gym gear in her cloakroom, a variety of equally disgusting smoothies on the table and, worst of all, Gabe himself.

He was so *active*, always on the phone, pacing round, chatting to every member of staff as if they were his long-lost best friend.

Even his typing was a loud, banging, flamboyant display. She couldn't think, couldn't concentrate when he was in the room.

But, although he had been living in Hopeford, in her house, for several weeks there was no trace of Gabe in the living areas of the cottage; his few possessions were kept neatly put away in the guest bedroom. Not that she'd snooped, obviously, but she had felt a need to reacquaint herself with her home, visiting every room, reminding herself of its quirks and corners.

It was odd being back after such a long absence. The cottage was clean, aired and well stocked, the rambling garden weeded and watered all thanks to the concierge service she employed to take care of her home. Mr Simpkins, the handsome ginger cat she'd inherited when she'd bought the house, was plump and sleek and bearing no discernible grudge after their time apart. But everything felt smaller, more claustrophobic.

For three months she had been someone else. Someone with no purpose, no expectations. It had been disconcerting and yet so freeing.

But that was over. She was home now and she had a lot to do. Friday night usually meant her laptop, a glass of wine and a takeaway. Polly put her hand to her stomach and swallowed hard; maybe she'd forego the latter two this week.

And think about a doctor's appointment if the tiredness and nausea didn't go away soon.

Hang on a second, what was that? Polly had visitors so rarely that it took another sharp decisive peal of the doorbell before she moved. Probably Gabe.

'If he can't keep hold of his keys how can I trust him with Rafferty's online strategy?' she asked Mr Simpkins. He merely yawned and turned over, stretching out in a patch of early evening sunshine.

Walking down the wide stairs towards the hallway, she took a moment to look around; at the polished, oiled beams, the old flagstoned floor, the gilt mirror by the hat stand, the fresh flowers on the antique table. It had all been chosen, placed and cared for by someone else. She lived here but was it really hers?

The doorbell rang again, impatiently. 'I'm coming,' she called, trying to keep the irritation out of her voice. It was hardly her fault that he had forgotten his keys. Unlocking the door, she pulled it open.

It wasn't Gabe.

Tall, broad, hair the same colour as hers and eyes the exact same shade of dark blue. A face she knew as well as she knew her own. A face she hadn't seen in four years. Polly clung onto the door frame, disbelief flooding through her. 'Raff?'

'I still have a key.' He held it up. 'But I didn't think you'd want me just walking in.'

'But, what are you doing here? I thought you were in Jordan. Or Australia?'

'Sorry to disappoint you. Can I come in?'

'Sorry?' Polly gaped at him as his words sank in. 'Yes, of course.'

She stepped back, her mind still grasping for a reason her twin brother was here in her sleepy home town, not trying to save the world, one war zone at a time.

Raff faced her, the love and warmth in his eyes bringing a lump to her throat. How on earth had four years gone by since she had last seen him? 'Come here.' He took her in his arms. It had been so long since he had held her, since she had allowed herself to lean on him.

'It's so good to see you,' he said into her hair. Polly tightened her grip.

It wasn't Raff's fault their grandfather had favoured him, wanted him to take over the store. Yet somehow it had been easier to hold him culpable.

'Hi, heavenly twin,' she murmured and took comfort in his low rumble of laughter. They had been named for the Heavenly Twins, Castor and Pollux, but Polly had escaped with a feminine version of her name. Her brother had been less lucky; nobody, apart from their grandparents, used it—Raff preferred a shorter version of their surname.

'Thanks for looking after everything.' She disentangled herself slowly, although the temptation to lean in and not let go was overwhelming. She led him down the wide hallway towards the kitchen. 'Looking after the house, Mr Simpkins.' She swallowed, hard and painful. 'Taking over at Rafferty's.'

'You needed my help, of course I stepped in.' He paused. 'I wish you'd called, Pol. Told me what was going on. I didn't mind but it would have been good if we had worked together, sorted it out together.'

'After four years? I couldn't,' she admitted, heading over to the fridge so that she didn't have to face him. 'You stayed away, Raff. You went away, left me behind and you didn't come back. Ever.' She swallowed painfully. 'I didn't even know whose side you were on—if you had spoken to Grandfather, knew what he was planning, if you wanted Rafferty's.' That had been her worst fear, that her twin had colluded with her grandfather.

Raff sounded incredulous. 'Surely you didn't think I would agree? That I would take Rafferty's away from you?'

'Grandfather made it very clear that nothing I had done, nothing I could do was enough to compete with your Y chromosome.' She turned, forced herself to meet the understanding in his eyes. 'It destroyed me.'

Raff winced. 'Polly, I spent three months running Rafferty's while you were gone and I hated every minute of it. How you manage I don't know. But even if I had come back and experienced an epiphany about the joys of retail I *still* wouldn't have agreed. I don't deserve it and you do. You've worked for it, you live it, love it. Even Grandfather had to admit in the end that his desire to see me in Father's place was wrong, that his fierce determination for a male heir was utterly crazy. I've agreed to join the board as a family member but that's it. You're CEO, you're in charge.'

Polly grabbed a cold beer and threw it to her twin, who caught it deftly with one hand, and pulled out a bottle of white wine for herself. She checked the label: Chateau Beaufils Chardonnay Semillon. One of Gabe's, then.

'So where have you been?' Raff was leaning against the kitchen counter. He raised the beer. 'Cheers.'

'Oh, here and there.' Polly's cheeks heated up and she busied herself with looking for a corkscrew. *Remember the new bucket list,* she told herself, ruthlessly pushing the more reprehensible details of her time away out of her mind. 'I went backpacking. In South America.' She flashed him a smile. 'Just like you always said I should.'

He smirked. 'When you say backpacking, you mean five-star hotels and air-conditioned tours?'

'Sometimes,' Polly admitted, breathing a sigh of relief as the stubborn cork finally began to give way. She eased it out carefully, wrinkling her nose as the aroma hit her. She held the bottle out to Raff. 'Is this corked?'

He took it and inhaled. 'I don't think so.'

She shrugged, and poured a small amount into a glass. She didn't sip it though; just the sight of the straw-coloured liquid caused her stomach to roll ominously. She put the glass down. 'But I did my fair share of rucksacks and walking boots too, along the Inca trail and other places.' She grinned across at him. 'You wouldn't have recognised me, braids in my hair, a sarong, all my worldly goods in one bag.'

'I had no idea where you were.' He didn't sound accusatory; he didn't need to. She had read his emails, listened to his voicemails. She knew how much worry she'd caused him.

'I didn't want you to. I didn't want pity or advice or

anything but time to figure out who I was, who I wanted to be if I wasn't going to run Rafferty's.'

'And?'

'I was still figuring it out when Clara emailed me telling me to come home. So, don't think I'm not glad to see you but why are you here? Did you miss Mr Simpkins?'

'My shirts don't look the same without a covering of ginger fur,' he agreed. 'Polly, there's something I need to tell you.' He turned his beer bottle round and round, his gaze fixed on it. 'I'm not going to be working in the field any more. I've accepted a job at the headquarters of Doctors Everywhere instead and I'm moving here, to Hopeford.'

Polly stared. 'But you love your job. Why on earth would you change it? And you're moving here? Hang on!' She looked at him suspiciously. 'Do you want to move back in? I'm not running a doss centre for young executive males who are quite capable of finding their own places, you know.'

'For who?' His face cleared. 'Oh, Gabe? He's still here? How are you getting on with him?'

'No.' She shook her head, unwilling to discuss her absent houseguest. 'No changing the subject. What's going on?'

Raff took a deep breath. 'You're not the only one who's been working things out recently. I have to admit I was pissed when you left with no word—I hotfooted it straight here, convinced that Clara knew where you were. I was determined to get it out of her, drag you back and get on with my life.'

'She didn't. I didn't even really know what my plans were.'

His mouth twisted into a smile. 'I know that now but things were a bit hostile for a while.' He shook his head. 'I can't believe it's only been a few months since I met her, that there was a time I didn't know her. Thing is, Pol, meeting Clara changed everything. I'm engaged. That's why I'm staying in the UK, that's why I'm moving to Hopeford. I'm marrying Clara.'

'*Bonsoir?*'

Polly should get off the sofa, should open her laptop, look as if she were working.

But she couldn't. Her appetite for the game, the competition had gone.

'Hi.' She looked up wearily as Gabe walked into the room. He was so tall his head nearly brushed the beams on the low ceiling.

'Nice run?' she continued. Small talk was good; it was easy. It stopped her having to think.

'*Oui.*' He stretched, seemingly unaware that his T-shirt was riding up and exposing an inch of flat, toned abdomen. 'A quick ten kilometres. It ruins the buzz though, getting the train after. I might try biking back to Hopeford one evening. What is it? Just fifty kilometres?'

'Just,' she echoed.

Gabe looked at her curiously. 'Are you okay?'

'Yes, no.' She gave a wry laugh. 'I don't really know. Raff's engaged.'

'Your brother? That's amazing. We should celebrate.'

'We should,' she agreed.

The dark eyes turned to her, their expression keen. 'You're not happy?'

'Of course I am,' Polly defended herself and then sighed. 'I am,' she repeated. 'It's just he's moving here, to Hopeford. He's marrying my closest friend and joining the board at Rafferty's.'

She shook her head. 'I feel like I am being a total cow,' she admitted. 'It's just, I have spent my whole life competing against him—and he wins without even taking part.

'And now…' she looked down at her hands '…now he's moving to my town, will be on the board of my company and is marrying the one person I can confide in. It feels like there's nowhere I am just me, not Raff's twin sister.'

The silence stretched out between them.

'I have three sisters,' he said after a while. 'I'm the youngest. It can be hard to find your place.'

Polly looked over at him. 'Is that why you're here? Not working at the vineyard?'

'Partly. And because I needed to prove some things to myself.' He walked over to Mr Simpkins, who was lying on the cushion-covered window seat set into the wall on the far side of the chimney breast.

Gabe should have been an incongruous presence in the white-walled, book-lined sitting room, the soft furnishings and details were so feminine, so English country cottage. He was too young, too indisputably French, too tall, too *male* for the low-beamed, cosy room. And yet he looked utterly at home reaching over to run one hand down Mr Simpkins' spine.

He was wearing jeans, his dark hair falling over his forehead, his pallor emphasised by the deep shadows under his dark eyes and the black stubble covering his jaw. He worked so late each night, rising at dawn to fit in yet another session in the gym—and the lack of sleep showed.

Polly watched the long, lean fingers' firm caress as her cat flattened himself in suppliant pleasure and felt a jolt in the pit of her stomach, a sudden insistent ache of desire as her nerve endings remembered the way his hand had settled in the curve of her waist, those same fingers moving up along her body, making her purr almost as loudly as Mr Simpkins.

'Is that why you went away?' he asked, all his attention seemingly on the writhing cat. 'Because of your brother?'

Polly flushed, partly in shame at having to admit her own second-class status to a relative stranger—and half in embarrassment at her reaction to the slow, sure strokes from Gabe's capable-looking hands.

'Partly,' she admitted. 'I had to get away, learn who I was without Rafferty's.'

'And did you?' He looked directly at her then, his eyes almost black and impossibly dark. 'Learn who you are?'

Polly thought back. To blisters and high altitudes. To the simple joy of a shower after a five-day trek. To long twilight walks on the beach. To lying back and watching the stars, the balmy breeze warm on her bare skin. To the lack of responsibility. To taking risks.

It had been fun but ultimately meaningless.

'No,' she said. 'I saw some amazing things, did amazing things and I had fun. But there was nothing to find out. Without Rafferty's I don't have anything…I'm no one.'

'That's not true.' His voice was low, intimate.

'It is,' she argued. 'But Raff? He is utterly and completely himself. I think I've always envied that. And now he has Clara—which is great, she's lovely and I'm sure they'll be very happy. But my brother and best friend getting married? It leaves me with no one.'

She heard her words echo as she said them and flushed. 'I am the most selfish beast, ignore me, Gabe. I'm tired and fluey and having a pathetic moment. It'll pass!'

He regarded her quietly. 'And you don't eat,' he said after a while. 'Come on, I'll cook.'

Polly was still protesting as Gabe rummaged through the fridge, trying to find something he could make into a meal a Frenchman could be proud of. It might have to be a simple omelette, he decided, pulling the eggs out of the fridge along with a courgette, some cheese and the end of some chorizo.

'You really don't have to cook for me,' she said. 'I'm quite happy with some bread and cheese.'

'Do you ever cook?' He looked at the gleaming range cooker, the beautiful copper saucepans hanging from their hooks looking as blemish free as the day they were bought.

'I butter bread and slice cheese. Occasionally I shred a lettuce.'

'That is some variety.'

'I know.'

He continued to chop onions as she watched.

'So you're a business whizz-kid, a gourmet chef, a tri-athlete. Is there anything you can't do?'

'I've never backpacked.'

'Didn't fancy the dirt and blisters?'

'I didn't have the time.' Gabe scraped the onions into the pan and tipped it expertly so they were evenly covered in oil. 'I went to university late and had a lot of time to make up. No chance to slack off.'

Polly was sitting at the counter, her chin propped in her hands. 'Is that why you set yourself such a punishing schedule now?'

Was it? All Gabe knew was that once you'd spent a year confined to bed, without the strength to get a glass of water, watching your classmates grow up without you, that once you knew just what losing someone meant then you had to make the most of every single second.

'You can sleep when you're dead,' he said. It was all too true; he'd thought about that long enough.

Now he just wanted to live every moment.

Polly continued to watch as he whisked the eggs. 'What do your parents think? Of you working away? Did they expect you to work with them?'

Ouch, that was direct. 'They found it hard to adjust.' He poured the eggs into the pan with a flourish. 'They wanted me to go to university nearby, stay in Provence. When I said I was going to Boston they were hurt. But they got over it.'

On the surface at least. The very worst part of being ill had been the despair in his parents' faces whenever they thought he wasn't watching. Or the forced positivity when they knew he was. It made it hard to say no to them.

'You're the son and heir.' There was no hiding the bitterness in her words. 'Of course they expect a lot.'

His mouth curved into a wry smile. 'Son? *Oui*. Heir? That remains to be seen. Celine is studying vineyard management in New Zealand and Claire is doing a very good job of opening the chateau up to guests and tourists while presenting them with a perfect trio of grandchildren.'

'Three!' She straightened up, pulling her hair back into a knot as she did so. He watched, fascinated, as she gathered up the silky golden strands and twisted them ruthlessly, tucking the end under. It wouldn't take much to make it spill free. Just one touch.

'Three in three years,' he confirmed. 'And Natalie is expecting her second. She takes care of all the advertising and marketing. So you see I have some formidable rivals for the vineyard. If I wanted it that is.'

'Isn't it funny? You and Raff could have it all on a plate. And you don't even want it.'

'We still have to work,' he argued. 'No one I work with cares what my parents do. Raff had to work his way up at Doctors Everywhere. It's exactly the same. Pass me a plate, will you?'

Polly got up and took two plates off the dresser, handing them over. Gabe shredded some lettuce and added a couple of tomatoes before cutting the omelette in half and sliding it onto a plate.

'*Voilà,*' he said, sliding it towards her.

'Thanks, Gabe, this looks great.' Her hair was coming loose and she gathered it up again, beginning the familiar twisting motion as she re-knotted it, before picking up her fork.

'I have worked at Rafferty's since I was legally allowed to get a job. Before that I spent every moment there.' Her voice was wistful, filled with love.

Gabe pictured the iconic store, its large dome and art deco façade dominating the expensive London street on which it was situated. It was always busy, exuding wealth and glamour and style. Exciting and as restless as its patrons, prowling in search of the bag, the outfit, the décor that would make them unique, special. It was easy to see why she loved it.

But then his mind turned to the chateau, to the acres and acres of vines, the scent of lavender and the scarlet flash of poppies. The old grey building, covered in ivy. He loved the buzz of retail but had to admit that no shop, no matter how magical, could match his home. The look in her eyes, the note in her voice spoke of the same deep connection.

'It's your home,' he said.

'Yes!' Polly pointed her fork at him. 'That's it. But only temporarily. It was made very clear to me that I could work there but it was never going to be mine. Grandfather even wanted me to study History of Art instead of business, not that I took any notice of him.'

So much dwelling on the past; if Gabe had done that he would still be in Provence, weeping in the graveyard. 'But now look at you. In charge of the whole store.'

Polly took a bite of the omelette, her face thoughtful. 'I told you I went away to find myself. The truth is I had no choice. Grandfather came to see me three months ago and told me he was signing Rafferty's over to Raff.' She laughed but there was no humour in the sound.

'My ex had just got engaged and Grandfather was concerned for me, or so he said. He thought I was leaving it too late, "letting the good ones get away".' She swallowed. 'He said it was for my own good—I should concentrate on marriage, have children before it's too late.'

'That was unkind.'

'It hurt me.' It obviously still did, her voice and her face full of pain. 'So I left my job, my home and I went away to try and work out who I was without Rafferty's. But then Raff walked away, for good this time, and I came back.'

She looked at Gabe, a gleam of speculation in her eyes. 'I have to admit I was thrown when I got back to find you already in place. At first I thought Grandfather was trying to replace Raff, but now?' She shook her head, once more dislodging the precarious knot of hair. 'I wonder what kind of game he's playing.'

'Maybe, he just knows I'm good at my job.'

'Oh, that will be part of it,' she agreed. 'But with Raff engaged I'll bet there's something else. It wouldn't be the first time he's played matchmaker. You've got to admit it's convenient, working together, living together.' Her voice trailed off.

'And I thought it was an over-ambitious developer tunnelling under my building. Your grandfather must have some extraordinary powers.'

'You have no idea,' Polly said darkly. 'He's pretty unscrupulous.' She shook her head. 'He just can't stop interfering.'

'You are just speculating. Besides, what does it matter? He can play all he wants.' Gabe made an effort to speak calmly but his heart was thudding so loudly he was surprised the kitchen wasn't shaking. Marriage? Children? If

Charles Rafferty was looking at Gabe to fulfil his dynastic dreams he had a long, long wait ahead. 'We don't have to join in. Not on his terms.'

Light, fun and short-lived. That was all he wanted, all he could cope with. Polly Rafferty was many impressive things but were light and fun part of her enticing package? She hid it well if so.

But getting under her skin *was* fun. He was pretty sure, by the way her gaze lingered on his mouth, by the sudden flush that highlighted her cheeks occasionally, that she hadn't forgotten about that kiss.

And he certainly hadn't—not for want of trying.

'Of course we don't.' She sounded more like her usual self. 'I've never allowed myself to follow the path Grandfather thinks suitable. I'm not going to start now he has finally retired. I'm still so tired, I'm probably imagining things. You're not my type at all. Even Grandfather must see that.'

This was where a wise man would stay silent. 'I'm not?'

The soft words caught her, echoing round and around her head.

'Of course not, you're an exercise-mad smoothie drinker who flirts inappropriately with half my staff.' Polly tried to keep her voice light but she could feel inappropriate heat rushing to her cheeks, a sweet insistent ache pulsing in her chest, reverberating all the way down to the pit of her stomach. She didn't want to look at him yet somehow she had turned, caught in his dark gaze. 'Not to mention that we work together.'

Had he leaned in closer? The dark eyes were even more intent than usual, black pools she was drawn to, the kind of bottomless depths girls could drown in. 'I won't tell if you don't.'

'Tell what?' But her tone lacked conviction even to herself. 'Gabe, I…' Polly wasn't entirely sure what she had been planning to say, whether she was going to lean in, close the distance between them and pull him in close—or turn away and tell him to grow up and stop with the innuendoes. She knew the sensible choice, the logical choice and yet she hesitated.

But the kitchen seemed to have shrunk, the space suddenly, suffocatingly small, the air so stuffy she could hardly breathe, the tumult in her stomach churning. She gasped for a breath, realising her mistake too late, pushing her stool back and running for the downstairs cloakroom horrifyingly aware that she wasn't going to make it.

'I am so humiliated.' Polly leant forward until her forehead touched the kitchen counter, grateful for the coolness of the granite. 'Thank you for taking care of me.'

That wasn't quite enough but she didn't want to articulate all the reasons for her gratitude. The gentle way he had rubbed her back, held her hair back from her face, waited with her until the last spasm had passed. 'You're good with sick people.' She looked up and smiled but he didn't return her admittedly pathetic attempt, his eyes filled with an unexpected pain.

'I have some experience.' His face was unreadable but his voice was gentle.

'I wasn't drunk.' Bad enough that it had happened; it would be far worse if he thought she was some kind of lush.

'You hadn't eaten. Even one glass could have that effect.' He looked at the glass she had poured earlier.

'I didn't even have one sip,' she protested. 'Just the smell made me feel ill. I must have picked up some kind of bug.'

He put a hand on her shoulder, just that one light touch sending shivers down her spine. 'You should eat something now, some crackers maybe.'

'No.' Not crackers. Her body was very insistent. 'I need…' She paused, thought. She *was* a little hungry, now the churning had stopped. 'Hang on.' She pushed herself to her feet and walked over to the stone pantry.

Polly opened the door that led to the old-fashioned, walk-in cold room and looked at the shelves that lined the walls, at the marble meat shelf at the far end.

'I know they're here somewhere. I saw them just the other day. I would never buy them. They must be Raff's, vile things. Aha!' Her hand closed triumphantly on a cardboard box. 'Got you.'

She hauled her prize triumphantly out, grabbing a bowl off the oak dresser and setting them both onto the counter. 'Cornflakes! Now I need sugar, lots of sugar. And milk, cold, rich milk. I never usually crave milk.' She pushed the thought away. 'Must be the bug. Maybe I need calcium?'

Raff hadn't said a word, just watched, eyes narrowed, as Polly poured a gigantic bowl of cornflakes, sprinkled them liberally with sugar and added almost a pint of milk to the already brimming bowl. 'This looks amazing,' she told him, almost purring with contentment.

'That looks disgusting. Like something my sister would eat when she's pregnant.'

The word hung there, echoing around the room. Polly put her spoon down and stared at him.

'It's just a bug.' But her voice was wobbling.

'Of course.' He sounded unsure, almost embarrassed, the accent thickening.

'Mixed with jet lag.'

'I know.'

'I'm not…'

'I didn't mean to infer that you were. I'm sorry.'

'But…what if I *am*?'

CHAPTER FOUR

WAS SHE? COULD she be? It should be impossible. It was impossible! Only technically…

Only technically it wasn't.

'Oh no,' she whispered. She looked up at Gabe. He was leaning against the kitchen counter, his face inscrutable. 'It was only once.'

His mouth twisted. 'That's all it takes, *ma chérie.*'

'How could I have been so stupid? What was I thinking?' She pushed the bowl of cornflakes back across the counter. They were rapidly going soggy and her nausea rose again at their mushy state. 'Obviously I wasn't thinking. I was trying not to, that was the point.'

But she had to think now; there was no point in giving into the rising panic swelling inside her. Her throat might be closing up in fear, her palms damp but she could override her body's signals. If only she'd done that ten weeks ago…

Ten weeks! And she hadn't even suspected, putting the nausea and the tiredness down to stress, jet lag, a bug.

It could still be! Two and two didn't always make four did it? Not in some obscure pure mathematical plane. Probably.

'I need a test.'

'Oui.' He was still expressionless. 'In the morning I'll…'

'Not in the morning!' Was he crazy? Did he think she was going to sit around and wait all night when liberation could be just around the corner? 'There's a twenty-four-hour supermarket in Dartingdon, I'll get one from there.'

She was on her feet as she said it. Thank goodness for modern twenty-four-seven life.

'You can't drive.'

She stopped still, swivelled and stared. 'I already said I didn't drink anything.'

'No.' He shook his head. 'But you're in shock. It isn't safe.'

So her hands were shaking a little, her legs slightly weak. She'd be fine. She'd driven the route a thousand times.

'And what if you throw up again?'

'Then I'll pull over. You don't have to take care of me, Gabe. I was big enough to get myself into this mess, I am certainly capable of sorting it out. I don't need anyone.'

His eyes bored into hers. 'If that's true then how did this happen?'

Ouch! That was well and truly below the belt. 'Want me to draw you a diagram?' She could hear the tremor of anger running through her voice and tried to rein it back.

'You fell out with your family here, went to find yourself, felt lost and lonely and so you what? Fell for the first smile and compliment?'

Polly stood stock-still, ice-cold anger running through her veins, her bones, every nerve and sinew. How dared he?

How dared he be so right?

'That wasn't what happened. Not that it has anything to do with you.' Shaking with a toxic mixture of righteous anger, adrenaline and nausea, she marched over to the counter to grab her car keys but before her hand could close on the fob it was whisked away in a decisive masculine hand.

'I'll go.'

'We drive on the left here. And do you even know where Dartingdon is?' she added slightly lamely. Polly wanted to prove a point but part of her knew he was right. Annoyingly. She was barely fit to run a bath let alone drive twisty country roads.

'I'm a big boy. I'll figure it out.'

'No.' All the anger had drained. Now she was just weary, utterly, achingly tired. 'You can drive but I'll navigate. And I'll scream if you take my beloved car even one centimetre over onto the wrong side.'

He regarded her levelly then nodded. 'Okay. I still think you would be better staying here.'

But she was adamant. Polly had never waited for things to be brought to her—she'd never have made it this far if she had. 'I can't wait that long,' she admitted. 'I need to know straight away.'

'And then what?'

That was the million-dollar question. 'Then I can plan. Everything's better with a plan.'

She was quiet. So quiet Gabe would almost swear that she was asleep except when he glanced over he could see the glare of her phone illuminating the whites of her eyes.

'Concentrate on the road,' she snapped but he could sense the worry under the anger. He had got used to that, with Marie. In the end when the pain had got too much, as the fear and anger and sheer bloody unfairness had overtaken her she had been cross all the time, barely able to be civil, even to those she loved.

Especially to those she loved.

'I am,' he said. He couldn't resist one little provocative grenade. 'If you drove a proper car...'

'This is a proper car!'

'It's a grown-up's toy,' he teased. It actually handled

pretty well, the small body taking the many twists and turns of the Oxfordshire country roads surprisingly well. 'Shame you'll have to get rid of it.'

He could feel her stiffen beside him. 'What do you mean?'

'It's a two-seater…' He didn't have to say any more. From the intake of breath he knew his point had hit home.

'Possibly not. We'll know soon enough.' But there wasn't any hope in her voice.

She didn't say anything for the next few miles. Despite his confidence earlier, this was the first time Gabe had actually driven a left-hand drive and it required most of his concentration to stay on the correct side of the road as he navigated the narrow curves. He wasn't helped by the car; low slung and powerful, she was absurdly responsive to his slightest touch, almost as if she were desperate to speed on.

Although there were no street lights in this country corner it wasn't too hard to see his way as he drove through hedge-lined lanes, fields almost at their ripest stretching out on both sides towards gently rolling hills. The summer solstice was nearly upon them and it was barely dark out, more of a gloomy dull grey. Like his mood.

There was no reason for him to feel so…so what? Slighted? Gabe sighed; he really needed to get over himself. One kiss did not equal any kind of relationship.

And if it did he would be headed the other way, right back to France.

It was just, if Polly Rafferty had really indulged in a night of meaningless, no-holds-barred, anonymous sex he wished she'd indulged with him.

He could be wrong, she might often go out prowling bars and clubs for one-night stands but he would bet the oldest bottle of wine in the vineyard's formidably stocked cellars that this had been a one-off occasion. And pregnant or not she was unlikely to indulge again.

'This doesn't have to change anything. It *doesn't* change anything.' Her voice penetrated his thoughts. Gabe risked a glance across at his reluctant passenger. Polly had pulled herself upright and was looking straight ahead, her jaw firmly set. 'The timing is awful but I could make it work.'

'Didn't you want children?'

There was another long pause. 'I don't *know* children,' she said after a while. 'I don't know how families work, normal ones. Raff and I were raised by our grandparents and they sent us away to school when we were small. It's not something I've ever thought about.' She huffed out a small laugh. 'Not every woman hits thirty and starts counting down her biological clock, you know.'

'But your house, it's begging for a family.' Five bedrooms, the large garden full of hidden corners and climbable trees. Despite the low ceilings and homely furnishings it felt too big, too echoey for just two people. And she had been living there alone for three years.

'It's just a building.' Her voice was dismissive.

Gabe shrugged. He was no psychologist but he had been through enough counselling—support groups, family therapy, grief counselling, chronic illness groups—to know a little bit about the subconscious. The cottage was a family-home wish come true.

'If you say so.'

She shifted, turned to look at him. 'How about you? Dreams of *petits enfants* clustering around your knee one day?'

'I'm a good uncle,' he said shortly.

'Guys can say that, can't they? No pressure to settle down, get married, churn out kids. You have all the time in the world.'

'None of us know how much time we have.' He meant to say it lightly but the words came out too quick, too bitter. He shot her a quick glance. 'I had cancer in my teens, a lymphoma. It teaches you to take nothing for granted.'

Polly gasped, a loud audible intake of breath as she put her hand to her mouth. 'Oh, Gabe. I am so sorry. I didn't mean…'

'It's fine.' This was why he hated people knowing. A brush with mortality and they never treated you the same way again. It was as if you were tainted with the mark of Death's scythe, a constant reminder that no one was safe.

'Besides, I can't.' The words were out before he knew it, the darkness beginning to shadow the car giving it the seal of a confessional, somewhere safe.

'Can't what?'

'Have children. Probably. Chemotherapy, stem-cell treatment…' His voice trailed off; he didn't need to add the rest.

'Oh.' Understanding dawned in the long drawn-out syllable. 'Didn't they freeze any?' Her hand was back over her mouth. 'I'm sorry. I didn't mean to intrude.'

'They didn't think it would have any long-term effects.' He smiled wryly. 'I was seventeen. To be honest it was the last thing I was thinking about—or my parents thought about. But it took longer, needed stronger drugs than they expected. It's okay. I'd rather be healthy.'

Her hand had crept to her stomach. 'Of course.'

'They did say it can change in time but I have never been tested. There's no point. I don't want them anyway,' he surprised himself by offering. 'The worst part of being ill was seeing my parents suffer. I'm not sure I'm strong enough to put myself through that.'

'I watched my father die.' Her voice was flat. 'That wasn't much fun either.'

They didn't speak the rest of the way there. Gabe was too absorbed in his thoughts and Polly had returned to jabbing furiously at her phone as if it could give her all the answers she needed.

Following the signs, he navigated his way around the roundabouts that ringed the old town, pulling off into an ugly development of warehouses and cavernous shops.

'We're here,' he said.

Polly didn't move, just looked out of the window at the neon orange streetlamps and the parking signs. 'Okay.'

'Why don't I go for you?' he suggested but she was already shaking her head.

'Thank you but I really need to do this by myself.'

'Are you sure you have enough?'

Polly bit her lip. Maybe two each of five different brands was slightly excessive but she had to make sure. If Gabe was potentially harbouring an alien life form inside him he would want to know one hundred per cent too.

'No.' She twisted the bag nervously. 'Do you think I should have got three of each?'

'I think you should leave at least one test on the shelves, just in case someone else is tearing through the night in need of answers.'

'Let's just get home.' She tugged impatiently at the car door, glaring at Gabe as he made no move to unlock it.

'Are you sure?'

She stared at him. 'What? You want to pop out for a nice meal first? Maybe go for a moonlight stroll? Of course I'm sure.'

He didn't react. 'I meant maybe you wanted to take the test now. Find out one way or another.'

'Oh.' How had he guessed?

Polly looked around the car park. There were several

chain restaurants but they were all showing signs of closing for the night. Or the supermarket toilets; they would
still be open.

She bit back a hysterical giggle. She had never actually imagined taking a pregnancy test, let alone taking it
in the strip-lit anonymity of a supermarket loo. It wasn't
the cosy scene depicted in the adverts.

But then she wasn't the hopeful woman on the advert
either.

'There's nowhere here.'

'Not here exactly.' Finally he clicked the button and the
doors unlocked. 'We can find somewhere a little more sa-
lubrious than this.'

It took him less than five minutes to exit the car park
and start back round the ring road, retracing their earlier
route.

'Don't worry,' he said as Polly looked worriedly at the
sign pointing the way back to Hopeford. 'I've got an idea.'

'I trust you.' And she did. Maybe because she had nobody else—not even herself.

At the Hopeford roundabout Gabe took a different exit,
driving into the car park of a large redbrick building. Polly
must have driven past it dozens of times but had never
registered it before. Why would she? Anonymous roadside hotels offering business deals and cheap weddings
weren't her usual style.

'Wait here.' He was gone before she could formulate a
reply. Resentment rose up inside her. Who was he to tell
her what to do? She half rose out of her seat, determined
to follow him, to regain control.

But no, she reminded herself, she had relinquished control, tonight at least. Polly sank back into her seat and tried
to control the panicked race of her heart.

The bag was on her lap, the sharp edges of the boxes an

uncomfortable fit against her thighs. Pulling out a handful, Polly turned them this way and that, reading the fine print on them curiously. Fancy being thirty-one and never having even properly seen a pregnancy test before!

But why would she have? She had been good to study with but she had never been the kind of friend others turned to. Not for panicked confidences and surreptitious tests in the school bathrooms or university toilets.

And she had never been the type to slip up herself. Not careful Polly Rafferty.

Not until now.

How could she have not known? Suspected that the bug she just couldn't shift might be something more? But she had continued with the pills her doctor had prescribed her for her trip, relieved to be spared the inconvenience of her monthly cycle, and missed nature's most glaring warning.

'Okay,' she muttered. How hard could taking one of these be? A blue line, two pink lines, a cross for yes. A positive sign? That was a little presumptuous. Another simply said 'pregnant'. She swallowed, hard, the lump in her throat making the simple act difficult. Painful.

She jumped as a knock sounded on her window, muttering as the packets fell to the floor. She hastily gathered them up. They felt wrong, like contraband. It was as if just being seen with them branded her in some unwanted way.

Looking up, she saw Gabe. He must have seen her reading the packets. Heat flooded through her and she took a deep breath, trying her best to summon her usual poise.

She opened the door. 'Hi.'

'They have a room we can use.' He stood aside as she got out of the car and waited while she gathered the dropped boxes, stuffing them into the carrier bag.

'Won't they wonder why we are checking in so late with no luggage?'

Gabe huffed out a short laugh. 'Polly. They will think we are illicit lovers looking for a bed for an hour, or travellers realising we need a bed for the night. Or, more likely, they won't think at all. Come on.'

He took the bag from her as if it were nothing, as if it didn't carry the key to her hopes and dreams. To the freedom she had never even appreciated until this moment.

'Come on.' He strode off towards the hotel.

Polly hesitated. Maybe she could wait until she got home after all. In fact maybe she could just wait, wait for this nightmare to be over.

Her hand crept to her abdomen and stayed there. What if? There was only one way to find out.

The hotel lobby was as anonymous as the outside, the floor tiled in a nondescript beige, the walls a coffee colour accented by meaningless abstract prints, the whole set off by fake oak fittings. Gabe led the way confidently past the desk and Polly noted how the receptionists' eyes followed him.

And how their eyes rested on her in jealous appraisal, making her all too aware of her old tracksuit, her lack of make-up. She lifted her head; let them speculate, let them judge.

They walked along a long corridor, doors at regular intervals on either side. 'Aha, *voici*,' Gabe muttered and stopped in front of one of the white wooden doors.

Number twenty-six. Such a random number, bland and meaningless. It didn't feel prophetic.

He opened the door with the key card and stood aside to let Polly enter. Her eyes swept around the room. The main part of the room was taken up by a large double bed made up in white linen with a crimson throw and matching pillows. The same tired abstracts were on the walls of the room; a TV and a sizeable desk completed the simple layout.

The door to her right stood open to reveal a white tiled bathroom.

The bathroom.

Panic whooshed through her and Polly put out a hand to steady herself against the wall. It was time.

What if she was pregnant?

What if she wasn't?

The thought froze her. That was what she wanted. Wasn't it?

'I'm going to order some food. I didn't manage more than a couple of forkfuls of that omelette. You should eat. What do you want?' Gabe's voice broke through her paralysis like a spoon stirring slowly through thick treacle.

Polly blinked at him, trying to make sense of the words. How could he even think of food at a time like this? 'I'm not hungry.'

'I'm ordering for you anyway. I'm going to have a beer. What do you want to drink?' He flashed a look at the bag on the bed. 'You're going to need a lot of liquid to get through that lot.'

As if the whole episode weren't mortifying enough. Why hadn't they invented tests you breathed on?

Gabe sat down on the bed and kicked off his shoes, one hand reaching for the menu, the other for the TV control. He looked like a man completely happy with his surroundings as he swung his legs onto the bed and reclined.

The bed.

The one and only.

'This is a double room.'

He grinned at her. 'I can see why they made you CEO.'

'You booked us a double?'

'I took the room they had available so that you—' he

cast a speaking glance at the bag next to him '—could get on and do what you have to do. I might as well be comfortable, fed and watered while I wait. Panic not, princess. Your virtue is safe with me.'

Or what was left of it, she silently filled in the rest of the sentence. What was she thinking anyway? She was potentially pregnant, definitely sick, had bags under her eyes big enough for a whole week's worth of groceries and was wearing an old tracksuit, her freshly washed hair pulled back into a knot. Clothes she had put on after puking over her outfit, floor and cloakroom. She wasn't exactly a catch.

To be honest she was surprised Gabe hadn't got them separate rooms, not a double. Anything less sexy than Polly Rafferty right now was hard to imagine.

'Right then.' She took a tremulous step forward, then another, leaning forward and grabbing the bag. 'Let's do this thing.'

He looked up from the menu, his eyes dark with concern. 'Do you want…I mean is there anything I can do?'

'You can hardly pee on a stick for me,' Polly snapped. She took a breath, her cheeks heating up. Great, she could add scarlet and sweaty to her long list of desirable attributes. 'No, really. I don't think either of us will ever recover if you come in there with me.'

The tiles were cold on her cheek and hands and beginning to chill the rest of her body. She should move, get up.

But getting up was a pretty tall order right now. In fact, Polly wasn't sure she was ever going to move again; she could spend the rest of her life curled up here, right?

Curled up in a foetal position. Now that was pretty damn ironic.

A bang on the hotel room door made her start. But of course, Gabe was there. He would take care of it.

She heard the mumbling of voices and the clink of crockery. If only they would shut up. Quiet was good. The bedroom door swung shut with a resounding *thunk*.

Good, peace again.

'Polly.'

Drat the man. If she didn't answer maybe he would go away.

'Polly, your food is here.'

The tiles had gone from cold to numbing. Polly liked numb. It was peaceful.

'Polly, if you don't answer me right now I am going to break down the door.'

He wouldn't, would he?

'Final warning, three, two…'

'Go away.' Was that her voice so clear and strong? She thought it would be croaky with years of misuse. But after all it had only been fifteen minutes since she had shut the door.

It just felt like centuries.

'Polly Rafferty, open the door this instant and come and eat some food.'

She pulled a face in the direction of the door.

'Now!'

Her peace had evaporated. He was evidently not going to give up.

'I'm coming.'

She rolled round and clambered painfully to her feet, hugging herself as the cold from the floor permeated every pore, and walked slowly to the door, twisted the lock and inched the door open. 'Satisfied?'

'I ordered you chips. And bread. Carbs are good for sore stomachs.'

'I thought you only ordered things full of vitamins.'

He didn't answer, just walked away to lift the silver covers off the plates on the desk.

'You're having chips as well?' Wonders would never cease. She'd bet half her trust fund that he would go on an extra run tomorrow and not stop until he had burnt off every calorie and gram of fat.

'I wasn't sure that you would cope with the smell of anything else.'

He hadn't asked about the test, not even with his eyes.

'They're positive.'

A flash of something then; sorrow, a hint of anger but both overshadowed with concern. 'They all agree?'

'I only managed to take six, even after drinking a gallon of water.'

She sank onto the bed. 'Oh, God, positive. What do I do?'

He handed her a plate. 'Tomorrow you plan. But now... now you eat.'

Polly was showing no sign of wanting to leave the hotel room. She had managed to eat a few chips and drink the tea he'd ordered. Now she was lying on the bed seemingly absorbed in the music videos playing on the TV.

But Gabe could tell she wasn't hearing a note.

He put the empty plates out into the corridor and walked back into the room. Polly hadn't moved, not even a centimetre. With one eye on her, as cautious as if she were a feral cat, Gabe sat back onto the bed and stretched out alongside her. Close but not touching.

He put his hands behind his head and stared at the ceiling. The plaster was perfectly smooth, as featureless as the rest of the hotel.

'I can't bake.'

He turned his head to look at her. She was still propped up on the pillows and staring at the TV.

'That's okay.'

'Of course it's not okay. You have to be able to bake. No one cares if a mother has an MBA or an amazing job. It's the cupcakes that count. I can't sew either.'

'No, but you work somewhere full of people who can do both those things so why care?'

She moved slowly until she was propped on her side looking at him. Her eyes were almost navy blue, matching the shadows deepening under them. Her skin pale under the rapidly fading tan. 'I bet your mother can bake and sew.'

'*Oui*, but she doesn't have an MBA.'

She didn't answer, just continued to look at him, her eyes searching his face as if he had all the answers.

'I don't know his surname.'

Cold rage swirled. How could anyone seduce this woman and just walk away? There were women who knew the game, who enjoyed playing, who wanted little more than a night or two. They were the ones you played with. 'We can find him.'

'You think?' The hope in her voice was killing. But then she shook her head. 'I don't see how. All I know is that he's Danish. What a mess. He probably wouldn't want to be involved, but he should know.'

'Who is he?'

'Markus. I met him in Mancora after I finished the Inca trail—he was about my age, recently divorced. A little lost.' She tried for a smile. 'Like me.'

'And I thought this was it, my life here, at Rafferty's, was over, that I needed to start again. I needed to be a new Polly.'

'That's a shame,' he said, keeping his voice level despite every trembling instinct. 'I kind of like the old Polly.'

'Me too,' she whispered as if it were a confession. 'But

old Polly had failed. No job, nobody who cared about me. Oh, I dated, had serious relationships but I always walked away. Relationships need compromise, you see. Only what they wanted was for *me* to compromise. For *me* to work less hours, to attend *their* work dos. To make the relationship work I had to be less. They could just keep on doing what they were doing.'

'Fools.'

Her mouth curved upwards. 'I thought so. I would leave and move on. But old Polly never learnt. She always went out with successful men, businessmen, suits and chauffeured cars and busy schedules and she always, always failed. So why not try someone new? Someone different?'

That had always been Gabe's philosophy. New, different, meaningless. It didn't sound so pretty on her lips.

'It makes sense.' In a warped way it did. He understood exactly why she had thrown caution to the wind.

'I had a list, of things I had never done, things most people did in their teens and early twenties. Swim naked, sleep under the stars.' She flushed. 'Have sex on a beach.' She shook her head. 'It sounds so childish.'

'No, it doesn't.' Gabe knew what it was like to miss out on things. He hadn't gone to teen parties, hadn't experimented with girls or beer or flirted with danger. Instead he'd hovered on the brink of death, he'd fallen in love, he'd lost everything.

'I've never done any of those things either,' he confided, trying to push away the image of Polly, tall and willowy, tanned bare skin glowing in the moonlight.

'It was supposed to mean nothing. Only now…' Her voice trailed off. 'I've messed up so badly. I finally have everything I always wanted but I don't know what to do.'

'You don't have to figure it out tonight.' Gabe was supposed to be keeping his distance, supposed to be the chauffeur, nothing more, but watching her tears spill out, hot and heavy, he couldn't not act. Without thought he edged closer, pulled her in, wrapped his arms around her and allowed her body to settle along his.

She fitted like a glove, her head on his shoulder, her chest against his, hip against hip.

'How could I mess up like this? I have never ever put a foot wrong. The one time I allow myself to just act, to not think and it explodes all over my dreams. I need to be a CEO, not a mother.'

'Who says you can't be both? When I was diagnosed I had so many plans. Plans to pull the hottest girl at school, to captain the rugby team. Plans to ace my exams. I had to rethink everything. In the end my plan was to live. And I did.'

'And the other things?' she asked softly.

'I didn't pull the hottest girl in school, but I fell in love with someone much better.' Gabe tightened his grip and tried not to remember Marie crying in his arms. 'I gave up rugby but took up marathons and triathlons—and I still aced my exams. Plans change, they adapt, you'll be fine.'

'How?'

Gabe sighed. It took time, adjustment, pain—but she wasn't ready to hear that. Not yet. 'We can figure it out tomorrow. It's all going to be okay. I promise, it's going to be okay.'

CHAPTER FIVE

IT WAS WARM, the mattress firm and comfortable but not quite as firm and comfortable as the bare chest she was nestled against. Polly sighed and rolled in a little closer, allowing her hand to slip round the firm midriff to trail along the smooth back.

Hang on. Skin? Muscle?

She snatched her hand back and rolled away, swallowing back the all too familiar nausea that hit her the moment she moved. And with it reality came crashing through the sleep fog, harsh, bitter. Terrifying.

She lay there trying to summon up enough strength to move, and doing her best to ignore the almost overwhelming temptation to move closer to Gabe, to put her arm back around him, snuggle in close and go back to sleep.

Getting into bed with strange men had got her into this situation. It looked as if she hadn't learned anything!

Not that the two cases were at all the same. She was still fully dressed in the tracksuit she had thrown on last night.

She was still pregnant.

An ache began to throb, squeezing the side of her temples, the sticky soreness of her eyes an unwelcome reminder of the tears she had shed the night before. The weakness she had displayed.

Polly put her hand over her mouth, stifling the groan that threatened to escape. What had she done? She had *cried*. Cried in front of Gabriel Beaufils of all people. She had just handed him the keys to utter humiliation. How could she spin this situation as a positive thing when he could expose her any second? Tell everyone that she had messed up.

That she was fallible.

But would he? Heat burned her cheeks as she remembered his gentleness, his words, his confidences.

No, somehow Polly knew deep down that he wouldn't expose her. But he would still *know*. Know that she wasn't strong, that she had allowed herself to lean on him.

It couldn't happen again.

'Morning.'

Polly turned her head slowly. Gabe was propped up on one elbow facing her. His expression was warm, radiating concern. Concern that she didn't need or want.

Polly slowly pulled herself up to a seating position, glad that the nausea seemed to have abated after that first rush.

'I thought we had a deal,' she said.

'A deal?' He looked surprised.

'That you were going to keep your shirt on.'

A slow appreciative smile spread over his face. It wasn't fair, Polly thought as the breath hitched in her throat. He already had soulful eyes and a well-cut jawline. Adding a smile that made you want to respond in kind, that sent a jolt of appreciation into the pit of your stomach, gave you a sudden urge to reach out and trace the firm mouth was too much.

'That agreement was only for the office,' he said. 'We are no longer in the office.'

'No.' Polly looked around at the generic bland furnishings. 'We certainly aren't. I'm sorry.'

'No need.'

'There's every need,' she corrected him. 'I dragged you out here. I'm pretty sure this isn't your usual style.'

Gabe's eyes swept over the room, coming to rest on Polly. She fought the urge to fidget, to straighten her mussed hair, pull at her baggy top.

'I don't know,' he said. 'I've had worse evenings.'

Polly stared at him, an unexpected bubble of laughter rising. 'Of course you have,' she said. 'What's more fun than a little vomit, a crazy late-night car ride and a night with a weeping woman in a downmarket hotel?'

'It was more than a little vomit. How are you feeling?'

Polly put a hand to her stomach, allowing it to linger there for a moment. Somewhere in there was the beginning of new life. A life she had created.

'Better,' she said, surprised that it was true. She thought for a moment, savouring the hollow feeling that had miraculously appeared. 'Hungry. Really hungry.'

'Room service?'

Polly shook her head. 'I need to get out,' she said. 'Although…' she looked at herself '…I'm not really fit to be seen.' But she didn't want to go home yet.

'How hungry are you?'

She was grateful that he didn't insult her intelligence by telling her that she looked fine. She had eyes and she still had the tattered remnants of her pride.

'Why?'

'If you can wait half an hour,' he suggested, 'I'll pop back to that supermarket and pick up a toothbrush and hairbrush and anything else you need. Then I think we should go out for the day.'

'Go out?' Polly leant back and eyed him suspiciously. 'To do what? We have papers to write, remember?'

'We've both put in a ridiculous amount of hours this week.' Gabe rolled off the bed unperturbed and picked up his T-shirt from the floor, shaking it out fastidiously before putting it back on. 'And it was an emotional evening.'

He smiled across at her as he said it, taking any possible sting out of the words. 'I need a walk, some fresh air and a change of scenery. Are you in?'

A vision of her laptop floated into Polly's mind. The half-written report. The statistics and recommendations and examples. The spreadsheet full of costings and projections and risk analysis. 'I should work,' she said, pulling her hair out of its ponytail and running her fingers through the tangled lengths.

Gabe didn't say anything, just regarded her levelly. Polly glared back.

'Last chance.'

She should work. She'd just had three months off, for goodness' sake. So what if she felt as if a steamroller had run her over physically and emotionally before reversing and finishing the job? She wasn't paid to have feelings or problems or illnesses.

She should work.

Polly glanced over at the window. The sun was peeping in around the blinds. Was that birds she could hear singing, their tuneful chirps not quite masked by the roar of passing traffic? She'd spent all of the previous summer indoors, working. The strangest part about travelling had been adjusting to being outdoors, the blissful heat as the sun soaked into her weary bones. She had missed out on so many summery weekends.

And next summer everything would be completely changed. There would be another person to take care of.

She glared at Gabe, who was still waiting, arms folded and an enquiring eyebrow raised.

'Oh, okay then. Let me write you a shopping list.'

Polly spent the entire half-hour of Gabe's absence in the hotel's surprisingly powerful shower, letting the hot jets

blast away the kinks in her shoulders and back, beat the
tangles out of her hair and massage the worry out of her
mind. By the time Gabe rapped softly on the door she felt
vaguely human again.

Wrapping the towel tightly around her, she took the
proffered carrier bag Gabe handed through the bathroom
door. Polly was conscious of an unprecedented intimacy.
Gabe had selected her clothes, underwear, her shoes.

It was disconcerting, made her feel vulnerable. Which
was ridiculous; she often ordered outfits or lingerie when
she needed a quick change for an unexpected meeting or
lunch. They were picked out and delivered by any one of
the many anonymous salesmen or women she employed
and she never felt a moment's hesitation about wearing
things they had handled.

She didn't even pick her own toothpaste; her concierge
service took care of all her household purchases.

But Polly couldn't help staring at the pretty lilac bra
and pants, the sleeveless, fifties-style summer dress in a
vibrant blue, the flared skirt ending just before her knees.
Had he just grabbed the first things he had seen—or were
they chosen especially for her?

Either way it was a choice between the dress or the
tracksuit she'd slept in.

Slowly Polly slipped on the underwear and buttoned up
the dress, her hands uncharacteristically clumsy. They fitted perfectly. Her figure was unchanged—for now.

Luckily she always carried a selection of miniatures
from her favourite make-up brands with her and in just
a few minutes she was ready, tinted moisturiser hiding
the last of the damage from the evening's tears, mascara
and some lip gloss an armour to help her through the day.
Slipping her feet into the flowered flip-flops Gabe had
provided, she stepped out of the bathroom strangely shy.

'Better?' she asked.

'That colour suits you. I thought it would.' There was a huskiness in his voice that reached deep inside her and tugged, a sweet sensual pull that made her sway towards him.

'Matches my eyes,' she said, aware what a lame comment it was but needing to say something, to try and break the hypnotic spell his words had cast.

'Non.' Gabe was still staring at her as if she were something deliciously edible. 'Your eyes are darker.'

Polly felt exposed before the hunger in his eyes. The dip of the dress suddenly seemed horribly low-cut, the hemline indecently short, her arms too bare. 'I've never worn a supermarket dress before,' she said.

'No.' He gave a quick bark of laughter and just like that the air of sensuality that had been swelling, filling the room, disappeared. 'Polly Rafferty in prêt-à-porter. There's a first for everything.'

'I wear ready-to-wear all the time,' she protested.

'Designer diffusion ranges?' He laughed again as she nodded. 'What about while you were away?'

'It pays to buy quality. It lasts longer,' she told him, unwilling to admit that even her travelling sarong had cost more than the entire outfit she was currently wearing. 'Now, I believe you promised me breakfast and then we need to decide what we're going to do.'

'We could just drive and see where we end up,' Gabe suggested.

'Oh, no, if I am taking a day off it needs to be well planned so I make the most of it,' Polly told him. 'And if you think I'm letting you drive my car one more time you're crazy. My nerves won't take the strain.'

Gabe grinned. 'We'll see,' was all he said. 'Come on, Polly. Let's go and organise a day of spontaneous fun.'

* * *

Of course it had begun to rain. Why had he given up the golden beaches of California or the flower-strewn meadows of his home for this grey, drizzly island?

Although Paris could be rainy too, Gabe conceded. But somehow in Paris even the rain had a certain style. In the English countryside it was just wet.

'Thoughts, Mr Spontaneity?'

Gabe sat back in his seat and considered. The prospects weren't appealing: a walk, a tour round a stately home, a visit to yet another of the exquisite market towns where the old houses were built from the golden stone with which the region abounded. If they were going to do that they might as well return to Hopeford—the most exquisite and golden and historic of the lot.

The sea? But they were in the middle of the country and the nearest coast was over one hundred miles away.

He could, if he hadn't been overcome with a ridiculous chivalry, have been on a train into the city right now. A visit to the gym, a couple of hours in the office and then a few beers in Kensington with some other émigrés. But there had been something vulnerable about the elegant Polly Rafferty slumped on a cheap hotel bed, that golden hair piled up into an untidy ponytail, red-eyed, white-faced. The circumstances couldn't have been more different, the women more different, but for one heart-stopping moment she had reminded him of Marie.

Of Marie as she began to give up.

The irony was that he had spent the last ten years turning away from women who provoked even the smallest reminder of his ex. One hint of vulnerability, of neediness and he was gone—so why was he sitting here watching the rain lash the windscreen on a magical mystery tour to nowhere?

Was it because he respected Polly? Knew that once she adjusted she would pick herself up and walk tall, head high, daring anyone to criticise her choices?

Or because he instinctively knew that she hid her weaknesses from the world. He might have been in the right place at the right time—or the wrong place at the wrong time—for her to collapse on him the way she had.

No matter why his usual 'turn tail and run' instincts weren't functioning normally. Not yet.

But they would. He didn't have to worry.

'What do you want to do?' He turned the question onto her.

'Not get wet?' Polly glared at the windscreen as if she could stop the rain with pure force of will. 'I took the day off to enjoy the sunshine. Besides, my new outfit doesn't include a cardigan or an umbrella.'

'It was warm just an hour ago. I forgot to factor in the crazy British weather.'

'Between May and September it's wise to carry an umbrella, a wrap and sunscreen at all times. Let that be your first lesson in British life. That and always have an indoor alternative.'

'I would suggest lunch but after that breakfast you just ate…' he said slyly.

'I'm eating for two!' The colour rose high in her cheeks. 'And I've barely eaten anything for the last week or two. I was in a major calorie deficit. Hang on, what does that sign say?'

Gabe peered through the slanting rain at the colourful poster, gamely flapping in the wet and cold. 'Probably some kind of fete,' he said. 'The British summer, always wet and cold and yet full of outdoor events. You're an optimistic isle, I'll give you that. Or crazy,' he added thoughtfully.

'No, it's not that. Oh!' With that squeal she put the indicator on and turned down the winding lane indicated by the poster. 'It's a Vintage Festival. Do you mind?'

'As long as it's dry and indoors.'

'What? Mr Triathlete scared of a little rain?'

'*Non*, just a man from the South of France who likes summer to be just that, summery.'

'Oh, boy, are you in the wrong country.'

The small country lane was long and winding and it took Polly a few moments to navigate its twists and turns before she followed another sign that took them through wrought-iron gates and up a sweeping, tree-lined driveway. Gabe caught a glimpse of large, graceful house before the road took them round to a busy car park.

'Wow.' Polly's voice was full of envy as she pulled to a stop, her eyes eagerly looking around. 'People have come in style.'

Hers was by no means the only modern car there but even her sporty two-seater was put firmly in the shade by the array of well-loved vintage cars from all eras. 'If I'd known we were coming I'd have brought Raff's Porsche,' Polly said sadly. 'It's a seventies car so not really vintage but older than this.'

The look she gave her own car was scathing, which, Gabe thought, was a little rich considering the fuss she had made over him driving it the night before.

'Aren't they gorgeous?' She had jumped out of the car, heedless of the rain, which had lightened to a drizzle, and was trailing her hand over a cream Austin Healey. 'And look at that Morris Minor, it's pristine. Wow, what great condition. Somebody loves you, don't they, baby?' she crooned.

Crooned. To a car. To an *old* car.

'They are very nice,' Gabe said politely as he joined her. 'For old cars.'

'Shh!' Polly threw him a scathing glance. 'They'll hear you. Don't listen to the nasty man,' she told the Austin consolingly. 'He's French.'

'We have old cars in France too,' Gabe said indignantly, stung by the slur to his country. 'I just prefer mine new.'

She patted his arm consolingly. 'This might not be the right place for you. Come on.'

It was a new side to Polly. Excited, eager, playful. It was a side he bet her staff never saw, that barely anybody saw.

'So, where are we?' Gabe asked as they walked along the chipping-strewn path that took them through a small wooded area and towards the house. Bunting was strung along the path, dripping wet yet defiantly cheerful.

'Geographically I'm not entirely sure, socially we're at a vintage festival.'

Clear as mud. 'Which is?'

Polly stopped and turned. 'Surely people go to them in France?'

'Possibly,' he said imperturbably. 'I, however, have not.'

'You are in for such a treat,' she said, grabbing his arm and pulling him along. 'There's usually stalls where you can buy anything old: clothes, furniture, jewellery. And tea and cakes, and makeovers and dancing. Loads of people come all dressed up in their favourite decade, mostly forties and fifties but you do get twenties and sixties as well.'

Gabe looked at her curiously. 'Do you go to these a lot?'

Her face fell. 'Not any more,' she said. 'Which is a shame because there are loads now, big affairs like this one looks to be. But I did go to a few vintage clubs and smaller affairs when I was at university. I've always loved the twenties; you know, flappers and jazz and the art deco style. Everything that was around when Rafferty's was founded.'

'Why don't you go any more?'

She sighed. 'The usual,' she said. 'Time—or lack of. I used to collect nineteen twenties accessories; costume jewellery, compacts, that kind of thing, but I haven't even wandered into an antique shop for a couple of years. Ooh.' Her face lit up. 'This is great timing. We could have a vintage pop-up at Rafferty's? Our centenary is in just a few years. We could have a whole series of twenties-inspired events leading up to that?'

Gabe had no intention of still being there in a few years but he could picture it perfectly. 'Is this just so you can dress up as a flapper?'

'Of course.' She looked down at her outfit. 'Although today I am loosely channelling the fifties. You must have known we were coming here when you picked out the dress.'

Gabe could see the house clearly now; they had ended up at a stately home after all. But this was a place gone back in time, to the middle of the last century if not back to its seventeenth-century roots.

The path had brought them out onto a large terrace at the back of the house overlooking lawns and ornamental gardens that seamlessly seemed to merge into the fields beyond. The furthest lawn was covered with an array of carnival rides, none of which was younger than Gabe, horses going round and round in a never-ending circle, helter-skelters and coconut shies.

Tables and chairs were dotted all around the terrace and lawns, served by a selection of vintage ice-cream vans parked in a row by the entrance gate, some selling the eponymous food, others cream teas, cakes or drinks.

'It's beautiful,' Polly breathed, still hanging onto his arm, her gaze transfixed on the scene before them. 'Doesn't everyone look fabulous? We're completely underdressed, especially you!'

Swing music was coming from the house, clearly audible through the parade of open doors. Parading in and out were people from another era: brightly lipsticked women with elaborate hair accompanied by men in old-fashioned military uniforms. Behind them girls with big skirts and ponytails were chatting to men with Brylcreemed hair and attitude to match. It was all pretty cool—if you were into fancy dress.

It had never been Gabe's kind of thing. Life was a mystery as it was; why complicate it by pretending to be someone you weren't? By emulating the lives of those long gone?

'It's a good thing the rain's stopped.'

Polly huffed. 'And people say the English are obsessed with the weather. Come on, Gabe. Let's go in.'

'What do you think?' Polly twirled around in front of Gabe, She hadn't been able to resist the opportunity to have her hair pin-curled and it hadn't taken much to persuade her into the accompanying makeover.

Or a new outfit. 'You look like you're from a film,' he said. Polly wasn't sure whether he meant it as a compliment or not but decided to go with it.

'That's the idea.' She looked down at the pink-flowered silk tea dress. 'It's not twenties but it will do. You need something too. A coat. Or a hat! We should get you a hat. This is so much fun. Why haven't I done this for so long?'

She led the protesting Gabe over to a stall specialising in military overcoats. 'I hope they have a French coat,' she said. 'Army, air force or navy?'

She knew she was chattering a bit too much, was being a little too impulsive, happily trying—and buying—anything that took her fancy.

It was better than thinking or worrying. She was almost fooling herself that everything was okay, that nothing had changed.

She wasn't fooling Gabe though. She could see it in his eyes.

'Lighten up.' She held a coat up against him. 'You're the one who wanted a day out, a change of scenery, remember?'

'Oui.' But his smile seemed forced, concern still radiating from him. Concern for her.

Unwanted, unneeded.

Suddenly the dress seemed shabby rather than chic, the lipstick heavy on her mouth. She had just wanted a day to forget about everything, a day with no responsibilities or decisions.

'I need some air.' She pushed past him, ignoring his surprised exclamation.

The swing band was still going strong in the ballroom and couples were engaging in gymnastics on the dance floor, a series of complicated lifts and kicks. At any other time Polly would have stopped to watch, to join in with the onlookers enthusiastically applauding each daring move, but she felt stifled, too hot, too enclosed. She wandered over to the terrace, stopping at one of the ice-cream vans to buy a sparkling water and took it over to a table where she examined her impulse purchases.

They were a mixed bag. A few old crime novels, a rather lovely, shell-shaped compact still with the wrist chain attached, two rose-covered side plates and a matching cake stand and some bunting made out of old dress material. It might look nice in the baby's room, she thought idly.

The baby's room.

Her breath whooshed out of her body and she held onto the iron table, glad of the cold metal beneath her palm, anchoring her to the world. She was pregnant. That was her reality and no amount of impromptu days out could change that.

But the expected panic, the gnawing pain in her stomach didn't materialise. Instead she felt light; it was okay. She didn't have a plan or any idea what to do next but it was okay.

For what must be the hundredth time that week Polly put her hand on her stomach but not in illness, or shock, or horror.

'Hello,' she whispered.

Nobody answered, there was no resulting flutter or any acknowledgement of her words, yet everything had changed.

She wasn't going to be alone any more.

'Would you like an ice cream?'

Polly pulled her hand away as if she had been caught doing something wrong.

'I'm okay,' she began, but the words died on her lips. 'What are you wearing?'

'They didn't have any French coats,' he said. 'So I got a hat instead.'

The trilby should have looked incongruous with the jeans and T-shirt, but somehow he made it look edgy.

Disturbingly sexy.

'It suits you.'

'What have you got there?' Gabe nodded at the bags spread over the table.

'Bits and bobs, bunting.' She looked up, met his eyes. 'For the baby's room.'

He tipped the trilby back; the gesture made him look almost heartbreakingly young, like a World War Two pilot heading back to base for a final mission.

'I hope he likes flowers, then,' he said doubtfully.

Polly gathered the bunting back up, stuffing it into the

bag. 'He might be a she, and either way no child of mine will be constrained by gender constructs.' She was aware that she sounded stuffy and that laughter was lurking in his watchful dark eyes.

For a moment she had a view of another path. One where the man teasing her wasn't a momentary diversion in her journey. One where the baby wasn't a shock to deal with but a welcome and much anticipated event.

A world where she might bicker playfully over the suitability of floral bunting, the colour of the paint, where to put the cot and the name of the first teddy bear. Where she wouldn't be doing this alone.

'So do you?' Gabe broke in on her thoughts.

She blinked, confused. Did she what? Want to take a different path? It was a little late for that.

'Polly? Ice cream?'

'Oh. No, no thank you. Actually, I think I want a walk. The grounds look spectacular.' Walk away from her thoughts and the sudden, unwanted regrets.

Gabe cast a doubtful look at the sky. 'Those clouds are pretty dark.'

Rolling her eyes, Polly got up and picked up her bags. 'You have a hat to keep you dry. Honestly, Gabe, you're not going to last five minutes in England if you can't cope with a bit of rain.'

'A bit? Not a problem. This nasty drizzle…' his accent elongated the word contemptuously '…it's not natural. I can't understand why the Normans didn't just turn straight around and go home as soon as they landed and saw the sky.'

'Exactly.' Polly began to walk away from the house, across the wet lawns and towards a small path covered in wood chippings that led through the cluster of trees. 'Romans, Vikings, Normans—rainy or not we're still quite the prize.'

Apart from a disbelieving snort Gabe didn't reply and they walked towards the woods in a companionable silence. After a moment Gabe reached across and took the carrier bags from her. Polly froze for a moment and then loosened her fingers and allowed him to relieve her of her load.

They wandered along for a few more moments, the air heavy with the promise of summer rain. Polly inhaled, enjoying the freshness of the countryside; the heady scent of wet leaves mixed with the damp earth and sawdust from the path.

They rounded a corner and the trees came to an abrupt end; in front of them a pretty ornamental lake stretched ahead, the path skirting the edge.

'Okay, Mr Spontaneity, right or left?'

'What is that?' Gabe sounded startled. 'Have we stumbled onto the set of a horror film?'

Polly followed his disbelieving gaze and saw a dark grey stone tower perched on the edge of the lake, the jagged edge of the spire reaching up into the sky.

'It's a folly. You know…' as he looked at her in query '…a couple of centuries ago it was the craze to build some kind of gothic ruin in a picturesque place. Around the time you were chopping aristocrats' heads off.'

'This is exactly why we were chopping off heads, if they squandered money on such crazy projects.'

'Hence the name. Want to take a look? There might be a princess for you to rescue at the top, or a prince in need of my knightly skills.'

It only took a few minutes to reach the base of the tower and Polly stood on tiptoe trying to get a look inside but the narrow slits that passed for ground-floor windows were set too high. 'Where's the door?'

Gabe had wandered off around to the other side. 'Here. Are you sure you want to risk it? You might disappear, never to be seen again, kidnapped to be the bride of a headless horseman.'

Polly joined him by the heavy oak door, the hinges exaggerated iron studs. 'Is it locked?'

'Only one way to find out.' Gabe grasped the heavy iron ring and turned it and, with a creak so loud Polly jumped, the door swung open.

'Ready? It looks dark in there.'

'So *you* are scared of ghosts?' she teased.

'*Non*, not ghosts. Spiders and rats on the other hand I am not so keen on.'

Rats? Polly shuddered, an involuntary movement of complete horror. She edged back. 'You think there are rats?'

'Hundreds. And cockroaches too,' he added helpfully.

Polly glared at him. 'Move aside, I'm going in.'

With an exaggerated bow Gabe stood aside, allowing her to precede him into the room.

'There are no stairs, how disappointing. Definitely no stranded royalty for us to rescue.' Polly swivelled slowly, taking in the large circular room paved in grey flagstones, the steep sides rising all the way up to the pointed tip of the tower. There were no other floors but it was mercifully dry. And free of any evidence of rat infestations.

'I still don't understand. What is it for?' Gabe had followed her in.

Polly flung her arms open as she turned. 'Probably somewhere for illicit trysts.'

'Ah, for the nobleman to meet the maid.' He leant back against the wall of the tower, arms crossed, face full of amusement, the hat still tilted back on his head giving him a rakish air.

Polly tilted her chin and stared up at the windows and considered. 'Or for the lady of the house to meet the game-keeper. Or maybe the stable boy.'

She looked across at Gabe to share the joke but he had gone still, his gaze focused intently on Polly. 'Is that what you would have done? Snuck out to meet the gamekeeper?'

Polly felt a jolt of heat hit the pit of her stomach as their eyes snagged and held, a flash of that first, unacknowledged attraction zipping between them.

'Or the stable boy.' Was that her voice? So husky.

'Of course. What would you have done with the stable boy in this room far away from everyone and everything?' His eyes were so dark, so intense it was hard to look into them, not to be swallowed up in their depths. Polly dropped her gaze to his mouth. Remembered how sure it had been. How demanding.

The heat spread.

'I don't know,' she lied, her mind filled with irresistible images of Gabe, those long legs clad in breeches, a shirt open at the neck. Her mouth dried. She could feel the heat of his gaze, scorching her where she stood, her whole body burning where it fell upon her.

But she couldn't move, desire humming deep in her veins, thrilling to the caress of his eyes.

'*Non?*' He pushed off the wall, walking towards her with sure, graceful strides. 'You came here to talk? To touch?' He raised one hand to her face, sliding a finger down her cheek, the lightest of embraces.

'Maybe,' she whispered.

The memory of their earlier kiss was throbbing through her. She could taste him, feel his arms around hers, the lean strength in his hold, the deftness of his touch. He was so close. She only had to step forward, lean against him, raise her face to his.

The desire pounded harder, her heart beating an insistent drum, every pulse point throbbing with her need to close in. To take the kiss further, explore him.

Just one step.

'What's this?'

'Cool, it's a castle!'

Excitable voices outside as sudden, as shocking as the cold water she had poured on Gabe just a few days ago. As shocking, as sobering. Polly took a step back.

'I think…' She took a breath, tried to get her ragged breathing under control. 'I'm tired. Maybe it's time to go home.'

Home. Sanity. Sense. There might be an undeniable attraction between them but now was not the time to act on it. Not while everything was changing, not while she was so vulnerable.

Polly walked across the room and picked up the bags Gabe had left by the wall. Without looking back she left the tower, and left the moment behind.

CHAPTER SIX

'Do you want to go over these papers before the meeting?'

Polly sat back in her chair and frowned as Gabe folded his long, lean frame into the chair opposite her desk. 'Now you have your own office it would be polite if you knocked.'

'Of course.' Not that he looked in the slightest bit put out, more amused. 'Do you?'

'Do I what?'

His eyebrows shot up. 'Want to go over the papers, of course. The board meeting *is* this afternoon.'

Oh, yes. That. In just a couple of hours her grandfather, Raff and the rest of the board would be sitting in Rafferty's renowned tearooms being suitably feasted before the meeting began.

She was expected to attend. Polly repressed a sigh. Normally she looked forward to these occasions, the buttering-up of contacts, starting to get her case across to the more swayable board members before the official business began, working out whose vote she could count on.

But today the usual thrill was missing; there was so much at stake; her return, Raff on the Board. Consolidating her position before she announced her news.

'We could have gone over the papers last night,' she pointed out, trying to prevent a waspish note from creeping into her voice.

Of course Gabe was free to do whatever he liked; she wasn't his landlady or wife. But surely it was plain good manners to let her know that he wasn't going to be back that night—or even that week.

Not that it was any of her business where he slept. As long as he looked refreshed, smart and in control for the meeting and was well prepared that was all that mattered. Whatever else he got up to—and who he got up to it with— was of no interest to Polly.

It wasn't jealousy that twisted her stomach as she watched him lean in that inch too close to Cordelia from Lingerie or to Amy from Accounts, those liquid brown eyes fixed soulfully on his unwitting victim, the way he murmured low and sweet. No, it was worry about an HR nightmare begging to happen. It was morning sickness.

'I was working late last night,' he said mildly. 'Some of my best contacts are in the U.S. West Coast so it was long past closing by the time I finished getting the information I needed. It was easier to stay here—sleeping in my own office, you'll be glad to hear.' His smile was fleeting but intimate and Polly's breath hitched in her throat.

Unbidden, a memory of her first sight of him flashed through her mind, the strength in that lean body, the tattoo whose lines and curves haunted her dreams.

'I don't think our insurance covers overnight stays. You should stay in a hotel or get the town car home.' She knew she sounded prim. That was fine; prim was good.

'Yes, ma'am.' Another amused look, as if they were sharing a joke only known to the two of them.

Polly inhaled, long and painful. Her heart *wasn't* picking up speed. For goodness' sake, one night of being held, of having her back rubbed and her hair stroked and she was a mushy wreck. It must be the hormones; the same ones that had her tearing up at life insurance adverts.

'So, are you ready now?' Gabe pulled out his smartphone and a USB stick.

'Ready?'

'To go over the papers,' he said patiently.

'Oh, yes. The papers.'

Yep. Hormones. Mush. And apparently turning her into Echo, which, she thought, looking over at the nonchalant man lounging opposite, made him Narcissus. Her eyes flickered over long legs outstretched, shirt collar unbuttoned, sleeves rolled up and day-old stubble; he looked more like an aftershave model than a Vice CEO.

Well, if the Greek allegory fitted…

Regardless, she was no sappy nymph, wafting around in hope of a smile.

'Are you okay?'

'Fine.' She summoned up as much poise as she could. 'Let's get on with this. We don't have much time.'

He looked at her critically, concern etched onto his face. 'Is it the baby? Do you need to lie down?'

'I'm pregnant, Gabe.' No, the ground didn't open up as she said the words out loud, nor did her grandfather appear in an accusatory puff of smoke. 'I'm not ill.'

If he heard the stiffness in her voice he didn't react, firing more questions at her like tiny, yet intensely irritating arrows pricking away at her conscience. 'Are you eating properly? Have you made a doctor's appointment yet?'

Oh, my goodness. It was like being stuck at a baby shower with no easy way of escape—only this time she hadn't primed Rachel to call her with a prefabricated crisis after twenty minutes as she did every time she couldn't get out of the sickly sweet events. If he even mentioned stretch marks or yoga or stitches then one of them would be headed straight out of the window. And she didn't much care which one it was.

'Look, I really appreciate what you did for me last weekend.' There, she said it quite normally despite her urge to grind the words out through gritted teeth. 'But this really isn't any of your business and I would appreciate it if you just…' She searched for a polite way to tell him to butt out. 'Just don't discuss it any more,' she said a little lamely.

He quirked an eyebrow. 'You seem very stressed, Polly. Have you considered yoga?'

Breathe, breathe again and again. It was no good. 'Butt out, Gabe!'

He put his hands up in surrender but his eyes were laughing. 'I'm sorry. Business first. Of course.'

'Good.' But she was unsettled. What if he was right? Should she see a doctor? It was probably the first thing most women did.

What if her independence hurt the baby? Polly clenched her fists; she wanted to reach down again, to cradle her stomach and make a silent vow to the baby that, unorthodox as its beginnings were, as much of a shock the whole thing was, she would do her best to keep it safe. Do her best to love it. But with those mocking eyes fixed on her she wouldn't allow herself to show any signs of softening.

'Hang on.' She couldn't look at Gabe. It felt like giving in. 'I'm just going to call my GP. I'll be with you as soon as I can'

She looked tired. Pale, drawn and thin. And vulnerable. It was a good thing he was hardened against vulnerable women.

'Thanks, yes. I will.' Her conversation at an end, Polly put down the phone and leant forward until her head touched the desk, her hands clasped in front of her. He could see the breaths shuddering through her. Slowly she straightened, pulling at the pins that held her hair in place, running her hands through the freed strands.

'I'm sorry, Gabe, but I need to go in right now.' She

smiled, a brief perfunctory smile that didn't go anywhere near her eyes. 'Perils of being a Rafferty. They like to see us early.'

'Sounds like a benefit to me.' It never ceased to amaze Gabe how those with good health took it for granted. He'd been like that once, heedless of his body and strength, unknowing what a miracle every breath, every step, every sensation was.

'Daddy was so young when he had his stroke, they worry about blood pressure.' She was gathering her papers and phone together to put into her bag. 'I tried to put them off until tomorrow but it was easier just to agree to go in. I know we need to talk about the papers. We'll just have to skip the board lunch.'

'I could come with you. We can talk on the way, better use of both our time.' His suggestion had nothing to do with seeing her reluctance to go, knowing how tough it must be to face so many changes alone.

She stopped dead and stared at him. 'You want to come to the doctor's with me? Why ever would you want to do that? I would have thought you of all people would have had enough of anything medical.'

'I'm not planning to come in with you and hold your hand, just to discuss business on the way.'

'I'm walking,' she said, almost defiantly. 'It's only a mile away and the sun's out. I could do with some fresh air.'

'Air sounds good,' he agreed. 'I missed out on a run yesterday. If you're good I might even buy you a frozen yogurt on the way back.'

Rafferty's was situated in the heart of London, not far from the bustle of Oxford Street, close to the rarefied boutiques of Bond Street. Tourists, commuters, shoppers and workers pounded the pavements in an endless throng of busy chatter and purposeful movement. There were times when Gabe would catch the scent of car exhausts, cigarettes, fried food and perfume and feel such a longing for the flower-filled air of Provence it almost choked him.

And there were times when these crowded streets felt like home. When knowing the shortcuts, the local shops, the alleyways, the cafés and bars off the tourist track, which tube stop was next, when it was quicker to walk was instinct. It gave him a certain satisfaction, a sense of belonging.

But Polly didn't need to belong. She might have moved to a quiet town miles from the capital but London ran through her veins, was in her blood. It was evident in her confidence, the way she moved through the crowd, never putting a foot out of place, seamlessly blending in.

And yet she'd chosen to leave. The city girl living in a sleepy rural town. The defiantly single woman living in a house made for an old-fashioned family with several children and a large golden dog. What was real? Did she even know?

'Do you miss London?'

'I'm here every day.'

'To work, not to play.' He grinned at her, but there was no responsive smile.

She didn't answer for a while. 'Everyone thought I was crazy when I moved to Hopeford—even though I bought my five-bedroom cottage for the same price as my two-bedroom flat,' she said eventually. 'People in their twenties *come* to London, they don't leave it—they only move out when they have children, or if they want to totally re-invent themselves.'

'People come to London for the same reason,' he said, but so quietly he wasn't sure whether or not she heard him.

'I went to Hopeford on a whim,' she said. She still wasn't

looking at him, almost talking to herself. 'It was Sunday. I was working as usual. I lived around here, in a beautiful flat, walking distance to Rafferty's. I worked all the time.'

'You still do.' Not that he could talk. But at least he had his training to break up the days, refresh his brain. Polly lived with her laptop switched on.

'That Sunday I was in by six a.m. I couldn't sleep. And by eleven I was done. No emails to send, no reports to read or write, no plans to check. And I didn't know what to do with myself. I had all this time and no way to fill it. It was terrifying.

'So I went for a walk. I was heading towards Regent's Park, I think, planning to go to the zoo. It's what we did as kids for a treat. Raff was already gone. Maybe I was missing him. Anyway I ended up at Marylebone. There was a train to Hopeford and I liked the name—*hope*. So I jumped on.' She shook her head. 'It felt so daring, just travelling to a strange place on a whim. And then I got there and it was like another world.'

'It's very pretty.'

'And very quiet. I couldn't believe it. No shops were open, nobody was working, people were just walking, or gardening or cooking. When you live and work in London you forget that people live like that. We sell the tools, you know, the sheets and the candles and the saucepans and the garden furniture but it feels a little like make-believe. I didn't want it to be make-believe any more. I wanted it to be real.

'So you moved?'

She laughed. 'No one could believe it; *I* didn't really believe it. It was the most impulsive thing I ever did. Well, until a few weeks ago anyway.'

'Are you happy there?'

There was a long pause. Nimbly she skirted a large

group of tourists taking photos of a mime artist and the window shoppers milling outside the many boutiques.

'Yes,' she said finally. 'I am.'

'Not everything needs to be planned out,' he said softly. 'Sometimes just going with your instinct is the right path.'

She stopped and stared at him. 'Are we still talking about Hopeford?' she asked.

He shrugged. 'Just making conversation.'

'Well, don't.' She gestured at a glass door, sober and discreet in a Georgian building. 'We're here. Meet me afterwards? We still have to talk about work, remember?'

'I'll come in with you.' The words were out before he had a chance to think them through. 'There's always a lot of hanging around at these places. We can talk inside.'

Polly knew she should be attending to everything that Dr Vishal was saying but it was so alien she couldn't get a grip on it.

Was this really her body? Her future? Now the nausea was dying down she looked and felt the same as always. Maybe she had made a really embarrassing mistake and it had been a bug after all?

'You're fine, but I want you to make sure you do everything I am recommending.' The doctor broke into Polly's thoughts. 'Vitamins and rest and midwife appointments. Careful blood-pressure monitoring, some light exercise and proper food,' she said, frowning at Polly. 'You're too thin, Polly. If you can't or won't cook then there are some good meal-delivery services. Lots of protein and vegetables.'

'I'll arrange it,' Polly promised. It was almost a shame Gabe was moving out; he took food seriously enough.

'Are you ready?'

'For what?'

'To see your baby of course. If you go with Sasha she'll

get you ready for your scan. We do them in house now although once your hospital referral goes through they'll want to scan again and sort out any extra blood tests.'

Polly followed Sasha, her brain whirling. A scan. Her hand fluttered to her stomach again. This was going to make the whole thing horribly real—unless it was a phantom-bug-baby after all.

Gabe was sitting on a chair in the corridor, his long legs sprawled out before him, frowning at the phone in his hand as he briskly typed out a message, but as Polly came close he shoved the phone into his pocket and got to his feet.

'Everything okay?'

'I think so. I have a long list of instructions. You'd like them; they use words like exercise and vitamins.'

'That's my language,' he agreed. 'Are you ready? We've still got an hour and a half until the meeting.'

'I've just…' Polly waved towards the nurse. 'A scan. To check everything is, you know, okay. I won't be long.'

'You're very welcome to come with us,' Sasha said with a bright smile. 'Ready to meet baby?'

Confused words of refusal rose to Polly's lips but when she started to speak nothing came out. Of course she didn't *need* company but it might be nice to have some backup, someone to reassure her that she wasn't imagining the whole thing.

Indecision was writ clearly on his face as he ran a hand over the dark stubble. 'Why not?' he said after a moment.

'No, don't worry,' she began but he was already on his feet.

'Come on,' he said. 'Let's go and see who's been causing you so much trouble.'

Gabe had seen more than his fair share of scan pictures. From the moment of his eldest niece's conception it felt as if he had been asked to admire thousands of fuzzy pictures of alien blobs. It wasn't just his family; more and more friends and colleagues were replacing their social media ID photos with what, he was fairly sure, was an identikit picture.

Secretly Gabe wondered if the whole thing was a scam, if there was just one photo that had been mocked up several years ago and was palmed off on every expectant couple. They probably made a fortune out of it.

The nurse led them into a small room. A chill shivered down Gabe's spine and his stomach clenched. The dull green walls, the blind at the window, the metal bed surrounded by machinery. It was a different country, a different patient and yet utterly, achingly familiar.

Old pains began to pulse in his limbs, scars to throb. He swallowed hard, trying to control his breathing. A cool hand touched his arm. Gabe braced himself for pity.

But all there was in the clear blue eyes was understanding. 'You can wait outside,' Polly said softly. 'It's fine.'

How did she know? How could she know?

He took a deep breath. 'I'm okay. Makes a nice change to not be the one on the bed.'

The hand lingered, squeezed. 'Thanks.' She didn't say anything else, just sat on the bed, her hands clasped, and waited for instructions.

Gabe folded himself into a chair while Polly was fussed over, the moment before frozen in his mind. He didn't often speak of his time in hospital, those days were over, but when it did come up there were usually two reactions: cloying pity or brisk heartiness.

It wasn't often anyone showed tact and understanding. He hadn't expected it from Polly; she was such a cat that walked alone. Why did she hide it? The sense of humour, the love of vintage accessories, her compassion? Did she feel that the human made her weak?

'Okay now, can you just lift your top?' The nurse's voice broke into his thoughts. The language was different but the tone exactly the same as the many, many nurses he had interacted with over the years: brisk, matter-of-fact.

Polly obediently rolled up the silk T-shirt, wincing as she did so, and Gabe tried not to laugh as he caught her expression—the carefully chosen top was going to get horribly creased. She was dressed for a board meeting not a doctor's appointment. Resolutely Gabe dragged his eyes away from the long legs lying supine on the bed, only to find himself staring at a flat stomach, the colour of warm honey.

It was a completely inappropriate time to stare but he couldn't help himself. She was on the thin side of slender, her ribs clearly visible. The cream fitted top set off the remains of her holiday tan; Gabe could hear her words echoing in his head: '*swimming naked in the sea*'. Just how much of her was honey brown?

He looked away quickly, trying to cleanse his mind of images of long limbs in clear waters, the hair floating languorously on the sea's surface. A lithe mermaid, dangerously desirable.

'This may be a little chilly,' the nurse warned her— '*it'll be utterly freezing*', Gabe translated mentally and by Polly's quick shudder as the gel touched her belly knew he was right. 'Okay.' The nurse was smiling at him. 'Ready to say hello?'

The language was cloying, the situation somewhat surreal and the nurse evidently under the assumption that he was responsible for Polly's situation but any embarrassment dissolved the second the nurse ran the scanner over

Polly's stomach. The screen wavered for a second and then there, in sharp focus, there it was.

Gabe stared at the screen. People used the word 'miracle' all the time until it lost any meaning but surely, *surely* this alien person floating around in Polly's body was a miracle?

He was so used to associating hospitals with pain and death he had completely forgotten what else they represented: life.

'It's still tiny,' the nurse told them. 'But perfect.'

Gabe looked over at Polly. Her head was turned to the screen; she was utterly transfixed. He didn't know if she had even heard the nurse.

'Is everything okay, as it should be?' he asked.

'It's still early days, you're what? Eleven weeks? But everything looks like it's right on track. The hospital will want to scan you again in about two to three weeks. All the details are in your pack. Do you want a photo?'

The ubiquitous photo. Suddenly Gabe could see the point of them after all. Why wouldn't you want to monitor every second?

He looked over at Polly but she didn't respond. But of course she would. Wouldn't she? '*Si*, I mean, please.'

Polly still hadn't spoken.

'Polly? Is everything okay?'

She blinked, once, twice as if released from a dream and then turned to him, her face transformed, lit up with an inner joy. It almost hurt to look at her.

'Oh yes,' she said. 'Everything is perfect.'

The contrast was completely surreal. One moment she was lying down, almost helpless as she deferred to the judgement and expertise of others, less than two hours later she had been on her feet, standing in front of a group of suited, booted, note-scribbling board members. Here she was the expert, the one in control, setting the pace and the agenda.

If she couldn't still feel the chill of the gel, sticky on her stomach, if she hadn't glanced down to see, with a shock of surprise, that she was no longer wearing the cream, fitted silk top but a sharply tailored pink shirt, she would think she had imagined her morning.

This was her future. A world of contrasts.

'That went well.' Her grandfather was sat at the head of the table. If his gaze lingered a little longingly on the bookcases that used to be filled with his belongings, if he eyed the pictures on the wall with barely hidden nostalgia then Polly couldn't blame him. The store was his life, his legacy.

As it was hers.

'Really interesting presentation, Pol,' Raff said. Her twin had spent his first meeting as a member of the Rafferty's board watching and listening intently but not jumping in. Not yet, although he had asked a few penetrating questions.

Polly knew him too well to think that he didn't have decided opinions—or that he wouldn't voice them—but he had been a supportive presence for her first official meeting as CEO.

She smiled at him, a rush of love for him flooding her. Despite their past disagreements and the long absences he was still part of her. And he would be part of her baby's life too, unconditionally, that went without saying. 'Thank you, Raff. For everything.'

'I love the pop-up idea—both in store and out. Where do you think you'll start?'

'In store,' she said, dragging her mind back to the matter at hand.

'We can use the centre of the Great Hall. It's mostly

used for themed displays anyway. I've found this great designer who uses vintage fabrics and jewellery and re-works them into a more modern design but still with a hint of history. They're something really special and tie in brilliantly with the building and best of all she's completely unknown. We would be a great launch pad for her and it's exactly the kind of thing I'm looking for. Unique and creative.'

'And start branching out with the food when?' Her grandfather might sound casual but his gaze was as sharp as ever.

Much as she wanted to get started, Polly knew this couldn't be rushed. 'Next year. We've left it too late in the season to start properly—all the best festivals are booked up and there's no point starting anywhere else. But we are investigating doing a few surprise pop-ups locally so that we can test some concepts—Hyde Park, South Bank, Hampstead Heath. Picnics and Pimms, that kind of thing. We're in the process of applying for licences.'

'Dip your toe in, eh? Not a bad plan.' Her grandfather shifted his gaze over to Gabe, who was busy packing up his laptop. 'That's all very well, but I still don't know about this digital strategy of yours. It's risky.'

'Not mine, Gabe's,' Polly corrected. 'I agree, it is a lot of money—but you were the one who told me to hand all digital concerns over to him.'

'What's your gut instinct?'

She hesitated as Gabe snapped his briefcase shut and turned his attention to the trio at the table, his eyes intent on her. 'Truth is I'm torn,' she admitted. 'I think it's innovative and brilliant, but the technology is untried at this scale and the outlay huge. My heart tells me to go for it but my head is a lot more cautious. But, if we wait, and someone else gets in first, then we lose both the competitive edge and the PR advantage. Gabe, what do you think? Honestly.'

Gabe leant back against the wall, arms folded, and regarded them intently. Polly willed him to dig deep, to find something that convinced her, convinced her family.

'My parents use something a little similar,' he said after a long moment. 'It's not as all singing and dancing as the concept I presented but their web and digital presence is very different from their competitors'—much more interactive, presenting the vineyard, restaurant and B&B virtually just as it is in reality. Why don't you come over and see? See how the physical matches up with the online and Natalie can talk you through click-through rates, bookings and the uplift in spend.'

Polly shifted nervously. 'Go to Provence?' Go to Gabe's home. Meet his parents and sisters, see the place he had grown up in?

A further blurring of the lines she kept trying to draw—and ended up rubbing out.

'That's an excellent idea,' Raff said warmly. 'I think that's exactly what we need, to see something similar and grasp just how it works in practice. You should go, Polly.' He looked at Gabe. 'If Pol agrees it's a goer then you have my vote.'

'I agree.' Her grandfather was looking at her thoughtfully. 'Take your time, look at every angle and then report back. If Raff and I are a yes then the rest will fall into line. But it needs your unequivocal approval, Polly. It's too much of a gamble for half-hearted efforts.'

'If we go this weekend the wine festival is on.' Gabe was checking his phone as he spoke. 'They have all kinds of stalls—wine, obviously, food, entertainment. Could be good research for planning just what the Rafferty pop-up brand will be.'

Polly nodded, to all intents and purposes solely focused on the matter at hand—but her mind was churning. This was all a little cosy.

She had spent the last week trying to re-establish much-needed boundaries—and so evidently had he. Now they had separate offices, now he spent so little time in Hopeford, she could convince herself that her evening of weakness was a one-off anomaly. A symptom of shock.

But if that *was* the case then what harm could a weekend do? It was just a working weekend like any other, she reminded herself. In fact it was probably a good thing, a chance to prove to herself that she was in control, in every way. 'It sounds perfect,' she said. 'Count me in.'

CHAPTER SEVEN

'WHAT A SHAME we didn't get to see some of Paris, but it was easier to fly in to Toulouse. I would have liked to have shown you around Desmoulins.' British retail royalty meeting the cream of Parisian style; it would have been an interesting introduction.

Now they were in his country, on his turf, Gabe was back behind the wheel, waving a protesting Polly into the passenger seat, refusing to listen to her attempts to direct him; no phone sat nav could possibly know the roads, the shortcuts better than the returning native.

'I've never been to Paris.' She was looking out of the window, seemingly absorbed in the scenery. It was worth looking at, the undulating hills and bright fields of lavender and sunflowers. At one point Provence had felt too rural, too stiflingly parochial to hold him. Now his blood thrilled to the scented air. He was home.

'You must have. A woman like you! Business, romance, shopping...'

She was shaking her head. 'Nope. Business I conduct in London. Romance?' She smiled wryly. 'I didn't really take time in my twenties for romantic breaks and the least said about this year, the better.' She rubbed her stomach. Gabe had noticed how often her hand crept there instinctively, unthinkingly, as if she had a primal need to connect with the life within.

'And I shop at Rafferty's of course. Or Milan or New York if I do want a busman's holiday.'

'But…' He was incredulous. Surely everyone came to Paris at some point in their lives. 'But what about fashion week?'

She shook her head. 'That's the buyers' job. I can't predict the next season's hits and I don't need to. I pay people with far more flair to do it.'

Oh, she had flair. It helped that she was almost model tall and model thin; it made it easy for her to wear clothes designed with willowy slenderness in mind. But she wore them with a panache that didn't come from the designer. It was innate. Even today, casual in a pair of skinny jeans and a yellow flowery top, she turned heads.

'But why? It takes what? Two and a half hours by train? It's a day trip.'

Polly smiled. A little self-consciously. 'It's silly.'

Gabe turned to look at her. Now he was intrigued; what on earth made Polly Rafferty blush in embarrassment?

'I can keep a secret.'

'I know.' She winced. 'You already know far too many of mine. I can't give you any more.'

She had a point. It was odd, knowing things not even her brother knew. Tied them together in a way that wasn't as unwelcome as it should be. He should even the score, make them equals.

Gabe turned his concentration back to the road ahead, navigating a tight bend before answering. 'That's fair. How about I tell you two of mine and then you answer?'

She leant back in her seat and considered. 'They have to be embarrassing secrets. Or deeply personal. Things you have never told anyone.'

'Okay.' He took a deep breath. Gabe was a businessman; he had always done what he needed to to get ahead. A little stretching of the truth here, taking a gamble on an assumption there. Nothing dishonest or illegal—more a prevarication.

But he couldn't prevaricate here; Polly was right. He did owe her a secret or two.

He just had so many to choose from. It might be nice to let one or two of them out, to lighten the load.

Gabe concentrated on the road ahead, his hands gripping the steering wheel so tightly his knuckles were white. 'When I was ill I hated my parents so much I couldn't even look at them when they came to visit.'

He heard her inhale, a long, shuddering breath. But she didn't protest or tell him he must be mistaken. 'Why?'

'Because they hurt so damn much. Every needle in my vein pierced them twice as hard, when I retched, they doubled over. My illness nearly killed them. They wanted me to live, to fight, so badly that when I slipped back I knew I was failing them. My illness failed them.'

He could feel it again: the shame of causing so much hurt, the anger that they needed him to be strong when it was almost too much. The responsibility of having to fight, to stay alive for them.

'They must love you a lot.' Her voice was a little wistful.

'They do. And I love them but it's a lot. You have to be strong for yourself in that situation, single-minded. Their need distracted me. Added too much pressure.'

'Is that why you don't want children?'

He thought back to her scan, to the life pulsing inside her, the unexpected protectiveness that had engulfed him and picked his words carefully.

'Our lives are so fragile, our happiness so dependent on others. I've been cancer free for nearly ten years, Polly. But it could come back. I don't want to put a wife or a child through the suffering I put my parents through. I don't want to suffer like that for someone else. Is it worth it?'

There was a pause and he knew without looking that her hand would be back at her midriff.

'I hope so,' she said after a while.

He continued driving while she busied herself with her phone. 'You still haven't told me your second secret.' She was looking away again. It was like being in the seal of the confessional: intimate and confidential.

Gabe didn't even consider before he answered. 'Ever since I kissed you in the office I've wanted to do it again.'

Another silence. This one more loaded. He was achingly aware of her proximity, of her bare arms, the blonde hair piled precariously in a loose knot, the hitch in her breath as he spoke.

His words had unlocked a desire he didn't even know he carried, one he had hidden, locked down. The kiss had been totally inappropriate. They were colleagues; she was his boss. He didn't want or need anything complicated—and nothing about Polly Rafferty was simple.

She was prickly and bossy. She didn't know the names of half her staff and was rude to and demanding of the ones she did know. She worked all the time. She was pregnant.

Sure, she was conventionally pretty with her mass of blonde silky hair, her dark blue eyes and legs that went on for ever but that was just the surface. It was the inappropriately intimate conversations with cars, that carefully hidden vulnerability and her way of looking into a man's soul and seeing just what it was that made him tick that made her dangerous.

It made her formidable. It made her utterly desirable.

'What does the tree mean?' Her words pierced the thickened atmosphere, the soft voice a little unsteady, her hands twisting on her lap.

'Pardon?'

'Your tattoo? What does it mean?'

His mouth twisted. 'My mother didn't cry once during any of my treatment but she wept when I showed her that tattoo. And not with pride.'

'I think it's beautiful.' Her voice was almost shy.

'It's life,' he told her. 'I wanted my body to reflect growth and hope, not death.'

'My mother told me you should visit Paris to fall in love.' Polly changed the subject abruptly. 'That's why I've never been.'

'You've never fallen in love?'

'I've been in "like",' she said. 'I've been in companionable comfort. I've desired.' Did her eyes flicker towards Gabe at the last word?

His chest tightened at the thought, the blood pulsing hot and thick around his body.

'But, no. I haven't been in love.' She bit her lip. 'That is rather shameful for a woman of thirty-one, isn't it?'

'Non.' The word was strong, vehement. 'Real love is rare, precious. Many of us will never experience it.' He'd thought he'd found it once. Had watched it slip away.

'My mother left home when I was eight. Our father died a couple of years later but he was in a home all that time.' Her voice faltered. 'We found him, Raff and I. He'd had a stroke. He needed full-time care and we were a mess. My mother just couldn't cope. People always took care of her, you see. She was one of those fragile women, all eyes and a way of looking at you as if you were all that mattered. She went away for a rest and just never returned, found someone else to take care of her.'

'I'm sorry.' The words were inadequate.

'Oh, it was a long time ago, and I think I always knew. Knew she couldn't be relied on. It was harder on Raff. He absolutely adored her. But for some reason I never forgot her words. She said she'd been to Paris before, with friends, boyfriends, but when she went with Daddy the city turned into a magical wonderland and she knew...'

'Knew what?'

'That she was in love,' she said simply. 'And she made me promise her, promise I would never go to Paris until I was sure I was ready to fall in love. It's funny, I have spent my whole life not being my mother, not relying on anyone else, always doing my duty. But I kept my promise.'

Her mouth curved into a reminiscent smile. 'She also told me to always wear lipstick, make sure my hair was brushed and to wear the best shoes I can afford. I never forgot that advice either.'

'Even on the Inca trail?'

She exhaled, an amused bubble of laughter. 'Especially then.'

'I hope you get to Paris one day.' She deserved it, deserved to have the trip of her dreams, to experience the world's most romantic city with somebody who loved her by her side.

But the thought of her strolling hand in hand through the city streets with some unknown other, cruising down the Seine, kissing on the Pont des Arts, made his whole body tense up, jealousy coursing through his veins.

It was ridiculous; he had no reason to be jealous.

Jealousy implied need. Implied caring. Sure he liked Polly, respected her, was attracted to her. But that was all.

If she worked somewhere else, if she weren't pregnant then she would be perfect—for a while. She was as busy as he was, as focused as he was, she wouldn't want him to take care of her, to text or call five times a day. She wouldn't care if he went away for a weekend's training or decided to pull an all-nighter at the office.

And when she talked about the likes, the companionable comforts and the desires of her past there was no hint of regret. She moved on without a second's thought. Just as he did.

But she *was* his boss and she *was* going to have a baby and there was no point dwelling on what-might-have-beens. Because the boss situation would change one day but the baby situation most definitely wouldn't. And that made her even more off-limits than ever. She deserved someone who would want a family, someone to take her to Paris.

'You may even fall in love there,' he added.

'Maybe.' She didn't sound convinced. 'It's a fairytale, though, isn't it? Not real life. Because, although Mummy had that perfect moment, it didn't mean enough in the end, didn't stop her bailing when things became rough.'

'No.' There was nothing else to say.

She took out a few pins and let her hair fall, before gathering it up and twisting it into a tighter knot, a few strands escaping in the breeze. 'It was a sharp lesson. If you rely on someone else you are vulnerable. You need to be self-sufficient, to protect yourself.' She sighed. 'It would be nice to meet someone who understood that, who didn't think being independent means not caring.'

She shook her head. 'One day I'll go to Paris, on my own. Or take the baby.'

'You could go to Disneyland.'

She grimaced. 'I am so not ready for this.'

Gabe glanced over. 'You will be,' he said. 'I think you are going to do just fine.'

There was something intimidating about meeting other people's families. Mingling, small talk, conferences, cocktail parties, those posed no fear at all for Polly. But the intimacy and warmth of family homes chilled her.

Even at school she'd hated the invites back to other girls'

houses for the holidays. It was all so alien: in-jokes and traditions, bickering, knowing your place was secure. So different from the formality of her grandparents' house, a place more like a museum than a home for two children.

Throw in a different language, a tangle of small children and in-laws and her arrival at the Beaufils chateau was a scene right out of her worst fears. She was seized upon, hugged, kissed and exclaimed over by what felt like an endless stream of people.

'It is lovely to meet you.' Madame Beaufils linked an arm through Polly's and whisked her through the imposing front door.

'Thank you so much for having me.' Polly did her best to relax. She wasn't really that comfortable with physicality, more of a handshake than a hug person, but she couldn't work out how to disentangle herself without causing offence. 'Your home is beautiful.'

No fakery needed here. Polly had grown up accustomed to a luxurious home; her grandfather still lived in the old Queen Anne manor house in the Berkshire countryside that she and Raff had been brought up in. But the weathered old chateau with its ivy-covered walls, surrounded by lovingly tended gardens that stretched into the vineyards beyond, had something her childhood home lacked.

It had heart.

There were pictures everywhere: photos, framed children's paintings, portraits and certificates. The furniture in the huge hall at the centre of the house was well chosen, chic but loved, the sofa a little frayed, the mirror spotted with age.

'It's a mess,' Gabe's mother said dismissively. 'We put our money into renovating the old barns for the B&B and wedding business, and for turning the wings of the house into apartments for Natalie and Claire and their families.

But I like it like this. It feels as if my children are still here with me.' She looked longingly at a large photo of a laughing, dark-eyed girl.'

'That's Celine,' she said with a sigh. 'My biggest fear is that she will meet someone in New Zealand and never return to us. It was worse when Gabe was in the States. Paris was better but at least he's just over the Channel. I can almost breathe again.'

It must be claustrophobic to be needed like that, Polly thought with a stab of sympathy for the absent Celine. But a small, irrepressible part of her couldn't help wondering what it would be like. Her grandmother was certainly miffed if Polly didn't meet her for tea and accompany her shopping when she was in town, and her grandfather liked updates on the store. But neither of them needed Polly for herself. Any granddaughter would have done.

'I've put you in the blue room.' Madame Beaufils led Polly up the grand circular staircase dominating the great hall. 'It has its own en-suite so you will be quite private. Why don't you take a moment to freshen up and then come back down for some lunch before we show you around?' She smiled. 'Natalie is very excited at the thought of showing off her website to you. She has been compiling numbers all week!'

The room she showed Polly to was lovely. It was very simple with high ceilings, dark polished floorboards and whitewashed walls with a huge wooden bedstead dominating one end of the room. The bed was made up with a blue throw and pillows; it looked so inviting Polly didn't dare sit down in case the fatigue pulsing away at her temples took over.

Instead she walked over to the large French windows and flung open the shutters to step out onto the narrow balcony. Her room was at the back of the house overlooking the peaceful-looking garden and the rows of vines beyond. She had never seen anything so vibrant, even on her travels—the green of the vines contrasting with the purple hues of the lavender in the distance, set off by an impossibly blue sky. Polly breathed in, feeling the rich air fill her lungs and, for the first time since that devastating conversation with her grandfather all those months ago, she felt at peace.

She reluctantly tore herself away from the view and took her toiletry bag into the pretty bathroom adjoining her room, emptying out her compact and lipgloss. It was time to apply her armour.

Or was it?

Polly stared at the deep berry red she favoured and then slowly set it back down.

She didn't need to hide. Not today. Instead she loosened her hair and brushed it out, allowing it to fall naturally down her back.

With one last longing glance at the inviting-looking bed, Polly took a deep breath and opened the door. She was ready.

She found the family in the garden, congregated around a large cast-iron table set under a large shady tree. It was already set for lunch and at the sight of the plates piled high with breads, salad, cheese and meat Polly's increasingly capricious appetite perked up.

Oh no, what if it was one of those days? It was all or nothing at the moment; mostly nothing, but when she did want to eat she had no stop mechanism. She hoped she didn't eat the Beaufils family out of house and home.

She could imagine them, gathered together in twenty years' time, telling tales of the Englishwoman who couldn't stop eating.

Polly leant on the corner of the house content just to

watch them for a moment. Everyone was talking, words tumbling out, interrupting each other with expansive hand gestures. Polly's French was pretty good but she was completely confused by the rapid crossfire of laughing conversation.

The laughter was loud and often. Each peal rang through her, making it harder and harder to take a step forward, to interrupt. Not wanting to break into the reunion, for the lively chatter to turn into the inevitable formal chitchat a stranger's presence would cause.

And the longer she stood there, the more impossible that step seemed.

She had never seen Gabe so utterly relaxed. Sitting at the head of the table, he had one plump toddler held firmly on his knee, another was crawling at his feet, attempting occasionally to climb up his denim-clad legs. His mother was pouring him wine, one sister showing him something on her iPad, his father grasping his arm as he made his point.

He was totally immersed, somehow paying attention to each member of his family. A smile of thanks, a nod of acknowledgement, a firm capturing of sticky fingers. Son, brother, uncle, the heart of his family. How could he want to escape this? If this was Polly's family she would never ever want to leave.

It was as if he could hear her thoughts. Gabe's head snapped up and he looked straight over at Polly, his dark gaze unwavering. She didn't want him to think her a coward, wanted to step out with her head held high but she was paralysed, held still by the understanding in his eyes.

She should have felt exposed, weak, but instead it was as if he was cloaking her in warmth, sending strength into suddenly aching limbs. It was almost painful when he dragged his eyes away, handing the toddler on his knee to his mother and scooping up the one by his feet as he rose gracefully out of his chair, walking over to Polly and expertly avoiding the small hands trying to grab his nose.

'*Bonjour*, Polly, this is Mathilde. She doesn't speak English yet but you must forgive her. Her French is terrible too.'

'Your French was terrible too when you were two, and it's not much better now,' interrupted a petite dark-haired woman with a vivacious grin as she came over to join them. She lifted the protesting small girl out of her uncle's arms, cuddling her close with a consoling kiss before turning to Polly.

'We must all be a bit much for you. It gets very loud when we are en masse. Especially when we have all the babies with us. I'm Natalie. I'm sure you didn't get a chance to work out who was who earlier.'

'It's lovely to meet you.' Polly couldn't help her gaze dropping to focus on the woman's large bump.

Natalie followed her gaze and grimaced. 'I know, I am enormous.' She shook her head ruefully. 'The doctor assures me it's not twins. I blame Maman's cooking. There's nothing like eating for two.'

'Not at all,' Polly said quickly. 'I was just thinking how well you look.'

Well. Happy and secure. Could that be her future?

'Come, sit and eat. Would you like some wine? *Non?* How about some grape juice made from our own vines? It's very refreshing.'

Polly allowed herself to be led to the table, to have her glass filled with the chilled juice, her plate filled with a tempting selection of breads, salads and meats, and did her best to join in with the conversation, which kept lapsing into French.

'*En anglais,*' Madame Beaufils said reprovingly. She

turned to Polly. 'I am so sorry, Polly. You must think us very rude.'

'Not at all. I think you are very happy to see Gabe. Please, don't speak English on my account. It will do me good to try and get along. My French is sadly rusty.'

'But so many of our hotel guests are English it does us good to speak it,' Claire said. Gabe's oldest sister was the quietest of the family, much of her time taken in attending to one of the two small children sitting by her side. A third slept quietly in a pram under the tree. 'I want these three to grow up with perfect English.'

Polly eyed the eldest child; he was no more than three, she thought, although children's ages were a mystery to her. One she would soon be solving. Despite many longing glances at a football in the middle of the lawn he was sitting upright on his chair eating daintily. 'He's very good,' she said. Maybe French children *did* have better manners.

Claire grinned. 'He's been bribed. Uncle Gabe will come and play trains with him if he eats all his lunch and behaves. Don't let him fool you. He's not usually this angelic.'

'How do you do it?' Polly looked from Claire to Natalie, both so laid-back, dressed simply but elegantly, not a hair out of place. 'Raise them and run this place?'

'With help!' Claire said emphatically and Natalie nodded in laughing agreement.

'I have an au pair, Maman is always on hand and my husband does a great deal.'

Polly smiled automatically but her mind was racing, calculating. She didn't have a mother or a husband—but she could buy in help. After all, she paid people to clean her house, buy her groceries, mow her lawn. Why not to raise her child?

Polly put the bread she was holding back on her plate

untasted. It sounded so cold. She looked over at the small boy trying so hard to be good and wished he were free to run free, to tear into his food with gusto. That her presence didn't constrain him.

She didn't want to recreate her childhood, to raise a perfectly behaved child painfully trying to live up to impossibly high expectations. She wanted...she wanted *this*. Loud, argumentative, affectionate and close. If she was going to have a child then she wanted a real family: wellies and mud and a big golden dog, the whole lot.

Well, maybe not a dog; Mr Simpkins would never cope.

Summoning up her best French, she leant over to the small boy. 'Bonjour, Jean. I love trains,' she said. 'When you've finished eating do you think you could show me?'

Jean put his bread down and regarded her with solemn dark eyes. 'I have cars too,' he said after a pause. 'Do you like cars too?'

'I adore cars,' Polly told him. 'Especially old ones.'

CHAPTER EIGHT

'YOUR FAMILY ARE lovely.'

It seemed odd to be alone with Gabe again after twenty-four hours of almost continuous company. After playing cars with Jean for a surprisingly enjoyable hour she had had a comprehensive tour of the vineyard and B&B accommodation followed by another long, laughter-filled family meal, this one enhanced by Claire and Natalie's charming husbands.

Visiting a vineyard and refusing to sample any of the products might seem eccentric but nobody had commented. Thank goodness she was past the sickness stage, otherwise she might have disgraced herself as soon as she entered the bottling room and storage cellars with their strong, distinct, alcoholic odour.

Gabe slid her a sidelong look. 'They like you.'

A glow spread through her at his words. She had been at the vineyard for such a short time, a stranger speaking a different language, but she felt a connection to the Beaufils family. It was nice to know it wasn't one-sided.

'Especially Jean,' he added. 'I think you've ousted me from number one. Luckily for me Mathilde still thinks I'm perfect.'

Polly rolled her eyes. 'They all seem very blinkered where you're concerned. Did I see your mother make your smoothie this morning?'

'She likes to,' he said with an annoying smirk, every inch the youngest child. 'I even managed to drag Papa out for a run. Well, more of a jog but it was a start. He eats too much—drinks too much. It's an occupational hazard.'

'How does your father feel about Claire and Natalie's innovations?' Polly asked. There were no traces of the power struggles she had experienced with her grandfather—but they could be good at putting on a public face. She knew all about that; public solidarity was part of the Rafferty code.

'He is overjoyed they are still at home, that they love the vineyard as much as he does.' Gabe pulled an expressive face. 'If he could keep us all there he would. I know he hopes Celine will come back and take over the wine production.'

'And you?'

'There's no place for me there, not now. My horizons are wider. I return home for holidays, weekends. I don't have the time to come back often.'

'I don't think there's any lack of ambition at the vineyard.' Polly had spent the morning with Natalie looking at all the digital innovations the Frenchwoman had introduced. It was impressive, a seamless interface between the physical world and the digital marketplace. 'Natalie is far ahead of much bigger businesses. There's an app for everything. And I think Claire plans to make it *the* premier events and hospitality venue in the country. She'll do it too, if she has the capital.'

'I can help out there.'

'I think they'd rather have your input than your money. Oh, I don't mean come back home to live. But they miss you.' She grinned at him. 'Talk about the prodigal son. If you get this kind of reaction after a few weeks in London I can't imagine what your mother feeds Celine when she comes home.'

'A full fatted calf.' He looked over at her. 'What did they say?'

A flush rose on her cheeks. She didn't want Gabe to think she'd been talking about him, probing for secrets and tales. But his family had been all too eager to share stories with her.

Almost as if she were his girlfriend, not his boss.

A wave of longing swept through her as unexpected as it was unwelcome. What would it be like to be welcomed into the bosom of a family such as this? To be part of a large, loving, chaotic throng? To have a place around the enormous scrubbed pine table that dominated the kitchen? To know your steps in the carefully choreographed dance of a family meal. Even Mathilde and Jean had gone straight to a drawer to collect and fold napkins. The sons-in-law were kept busy fetching and carrying.

Polly alone had had no role. The guest, set apart.

'They said you don't come home enough but they understand that you're busy.' Polly chose her words carefully. 'That as they look at expanding it would be good to have your input, only they know how it's hard for you to get away.'

Their eyes followed him everywhere, their need echoing out. They adored him, would absorb him back in if he gave them the chance. Polly could see how it smothered him, why he stayed away even as she wondered what it would be like, to be loved so comprehensively.

'Papa often talks about expanding.' Gabe was dismissive. 'Yet, he never does.'

'He might do if you were there to talk it through with him.' Polly could hear the tart note in her voice but didn't try to rein it in. 'Your sisters are specialists, great at what they do but very focused. You however are trained in managing the bigger picture. You should give him some time beyond a morning jog.'

There was a pained silence. 'One day here and you're the expert on my family.'

Words of apology rose to her lips but she swallowed them back. 'I don't need to be an expert. It's completely plain to anyone with eyes. I'm not saying move back home, but you could talk his plans through with him, advise him.'

'Maybe.'

'I know you needed to get away—and you did, you created a life away from them. Well…' she considered him '…you created a *career* away from them.'

Gabe's mouth was set tight, a muscle pulsing in his jaw. 'I don't see the distinction.'

'I know,' she said sadly. 'You and I are birds of a feather. We think success at work, achieving career goals is all that matters, all that defines us. But, Gabe, I *had* nothing else. The only approval I ever got was work-related—and I begrudged it. But you? You could announce you were giving it all up tomorrow to go back and, I don't know, create art out of vine leaves and they would still welcome you home and support you all the way.'

His mouth twitched. 'Art out of vine leaves?'

'It might be a thing.'

He didn't say anything for a few minutes, his eyes set on the road ahead. Polly sat back in her seat, losing herself in the vibrant scenery. What must it be like to grow up surrounded by so much colourful beauty?

'Why does it matter to you?' His words were so unexpected it took a moment for Polly to comprehend them.

'Why does what matter?' But she knew what he meant.

'My family, my place there.'

Her cheeks heated. 'It doesn't mean a thing to me personally,' she said. 'But I like your parents, your sisters. It seems a shame, that's all. I like you…' Her words hung there. Polly wanted to grab them, take them back.

But they *were* out there. So she might as well be completely honest. 'I like you,' she said again. *In for a penny,* she thought.

'I'm not keen on the workaholic who flirts with my assistant, the smell of those smoothies would turn my stomach even if I wasn't pregnant and I have very strong, negative views on people who turn up to work in Lycra cycling shorts.' Even if they did look as good as on Gabe. You had to have good legs to pull off the tightly fitting shorts. Gabe rocked them.

Some staff members had taken to standing near the staff entrance when he came back from his lunch time bike ride.

'Don't spare my feelings.' But there was a quirk at the side of his mouth as he tried to hide a reluctant smile.

'I really dislike the way you take one girl out for a drink and another the next day. I know you don't cross any lines or break promises, but it creates discord and I won't have that in my store. But...' she took a deep breath '...I do admire the way you remember everyone's name and what they do. I am a little envious of the rapport you have with my staff already. I don't doubt you'll be a CEO by thirty because you're focused and innovative and put the hours in.'

'Should I be blushing?'

'And I don't know what I would have done without you last week.' There, she had said it.

'Oh, Polly.' He shook his head, the smile gone. 'You would have been absolutely fine.'

'Maybe,' she agreed. 'I am used to doing things alone. I would have *coped.* I'd have had to. But it was nice not having to. Maybe it's the time I had away, maybe it's the hormones whooshing around turning everything upside down, but I am actually glad, glad that there is going to be something in my life apart from work. It may not be planned, the circumstances aren't ideal but I think the baby is a good thing for me.'

She smiled ruefully. 'Of course if you repeat that to anyone I will kill you.'

'I'd expect nothing less.'

'But you already have things outside work. Nieces and nephews and a family—and you keep yourself apart. I know why, I understand why. I just wonder…' She paused, trying to pick her words carefully. 'I just think maybe it's time you open yourself back up to them. Don't you think you've punished them enough?'

'I'm not punishing them.'

'Aren't you?' She pulled at her hair, twisting it round in her hand as she looked at him, at the set of his jaw, the line of his mouth. The dark chill in his eyes. 'Punishment? Atonement? Proving something? Whatever it is you're doing it's been ten years. I think it's time you gave them a break. I think you should give yourself a break. Before it's too late.'

Polly's words echoed round and round in Gabe's head despite his attempts to push them away, far away out of his subconscious.

Punishment.

She was right, damn her. But not as right as she thought she was. He wasn't punishing them.

He was punishing himself. For falling ill, for causing them such pain and anxiety.

For all the petty, nasty resentment he had allowed to build up during that long year of pain. Resentment towards his parents for their need and worry. Towards his sisters for their health.

He didn't speak for the rest of the journey. Polly didn't try to engage him in conversation, scribbling notes in her ever-present notebook instead but occasionally shooting him concerned glances.

Glances he pretended not to see. If he didn't engage

then he didn't need to speak and he could lock it all back up, deep inside.

Where it needed to be.

It took a while to find a parking space in the small riverside town of Vignonel. Sleepy for fifty weeks of the year, it was transformed into an international hub by the annual food and drink festival held there every summer. Over the years it had grown to include culture, local crafts and music, and every year thousands of people descended there from all over the world to dance, drink and eat.

They had all descended today, it seemed.

'This is where we've been going wrong,' Polly said after they were finally parked and had begun to thread their way through the main thoroughfare that led towards the main town square. 'We don't go out and find our suppliers any more. People come and pitch to us. Chris and the rest of his team should be here, searching out the best local producers and stocking them.'

'Yes.' But he barely heard her words, his attention snagged by the large church dominating the town square. His heart began to speed up and despite the heat of the day a cold sweat covered his hands.

He swallowed, a bitter taste coating his mouth. 'There's a lot to see,' he managed to say in as normal a tone as possible. 'We'll cover more ground if we split up.'

A fleeting expression flashed in Polly's blue eyes. For a moment Gabe wondered if he had hurt her feelings but dismissed the arrogant notion as her head snapped up and she became her usual focused self.

'Good idea.' She pulled out her notebook and pen. 'We'll compare notes when we meet up. Look out for suppliers but I am more interested in what makes a stall successful, what draws people in. The look, the branding, the offer.'

'The technology?' Gabe couldn't help giving the

leather-bound book a pointed look and Polly hugged it to
her chest protectively.

'What? I don't have to worry about the battery running
out or a system relapse wiping everything.'

'No, you just have to keep it dry and hope you don't lose
it.' They had reached an information point and he picked
up a map and guide, handing it to Polly. Her hand was cool,
soft. Comforting. A sudden urge to take it in his, to stroll
through the streets together, no notebooks, no reports, no
memories, hit him but he pushed it aside. It took more effort than he cared for to refocus.

'I promised Claire I'd call in at her tourism and marketing pavilion.' Was she really so oblivious to his momentary inner struggle? Evidently so. She was frowning
at the map in utter concentration. 'If I look at that part
of the market why don't you go into the wine quarter to
start? Your father's there on the regional wine stand this
afternoon. And no...' her eyes met his clearly '...I'm not
interfering, just being polite.'

She held his gaze, cool and self-possessed before in-
clining her head, a curiously old-fashioned gesture. 'I'll
see you back here, then.'

Gabe watched as she swivelled and walked away, her
head held high, the dark gold sweep of hair still loose, covering the slim line of her back. It was odd to see her hair
down, not in the customary loose knot, for her to leave it
unfettered. It made her seem younger, relaxed.

What would it be like to tangle his hand in that hair?
Let the silken tresses fold around his fingers?

She was wearing the pink dress she'd bought at the vintage fair and as Gabe followed the proud, straight figure
as she disappeared into the crowd he had a curious sense
of being out of time.

Okay, time to push such fanciful thoughts out of his

head, time to get on. To find his father, say hello, compliment him on the stall and the vintage just as Polly suggested.

As for the rest? It was ridiculous. He wasn't punishing them. He was protecting them.

Protecting himself.

If you had no ties then you couldn't get hurt. It was that simple.

The food and drink quarter was situated on one of the several windy streets that led off the square, opposite the church. Just a few minutes' walk up there and he would be among old friends and neighbours, watching his father do what he did best—enthusing about wine.

A smile curved his lips as he pictured the scene: a laughing group of tourists pulled in by his father's practised patter, sipping and tasting before parting with what would no doubt be a considerable amount of money.

Just a few minutes' walk. He should go, say hi.

He could even offer to help.

Gabe stood for a moment and then slowly turned to face the church.

A deep breath shuddered through him as if an icy fist had clenched his heart.

He hadn't set foot in that church for ten years and yet he could clearly picture the aged, wooden beams, see the sunlight dancing through the coloured glass in the ancient windows, the expression on the faces of the cold marble statues. He could smell the incense as it burned hot and heavy.

He could see the coffin.

Without conscious thought, without decision, he walked across the tree-lined square, away from the festival, past the church, to the narrow street that led out of town. Towards the old walled cemetery.

To Marie's grave.

Was it really ten years since he had stood by the open grave, pale faced and dry eyed as the white coffin had been slowly and solemnly lowered in?

White! She would have been horrified! Demanded black and velvet with silver clasps—or nothing at all, a quiet spot in a wooded glade. No X to mark the spot.

But burials weren't for the dead, they were for those left behind and her parents had needed every last trimming to get them through the day.

His mouth tightened. He hadn't written or contacted the Declors for years, unable to face another visit down memory lane. Not wanting to sit in the claustrophobic *salon*, sipping wine while looking through photo albums preserving the memory of a dead girl, pink cheeked and full of health. He had never known that girl. The Marie he had known had been like him, clad with a hospital pallor.

They were supposed to live or die together. He hadn't kept his part of the deal. Had she known, when she slipped away, that he wouldn't be joining her? Not yet.

Which was the worst betrayal? That he hadn't died with her or that she hadn't lived with him?

Had she forgiven him? He wasn't sure he had forgiven her yet. Or himself.

'Gabe?'

He jumped, a shiver running down his spine at the softly breathed words.

'Gabe!' No, not a ghost. Not unless Marie had developed a clipped English accent in the last ten years, had swapped the Converse low tops for high-heeled sandals that tapped smartly on the old cobbles.

He stopped and turned. Waited. Relieved to have the present intrude on the past.

'Claire was so busy I didn't like to disturb her.' Polly

stopped as she reached the tall figure, her hand automatically going up to nervously knot her hair, only to fall
away as she spoke. 'I wondered if maybe you wanted some
lunch, if I could buy you some lunch. I…er…I crossed a
line earlier. I need to apologise.'

She let a shuddering breath go and waited.

Lunch, work, an excuse not to face up to the past, to
push it away for another decade.

'That would be nice,' he said after a long moment. 'But
there's somewhere I need to go first. Polly, I'd really like
it if you came with me.'

The river rushed along, white-topped as it bubbled over
rocks and dropped over mini falls. The path along it was
flat, easy walking. Left the mind free to wander.

Polly wasn't entirely sure that this was a good thing.
She searched for something to say.

Nothing.

Now didn't seem appropriate to discuss work and she
had already ventured into personal territory once that day.
Look how well that had gone down, a clear indication to
mind her own business.

Only… It was just…

He had asked her to come along.

She hadn't gone all the way into the rather macabre
cemetery with its carved headstones, statues and family
vaults, as different from a tidy Church Of England graveyard as a Brie from Cheddar, rather she had waited by the
wall as Gabe had walked steadily to a white marble grave-
stone, topped with a carved cherub, and dropped to one
knee in front of it. He had stayed there for five minutes,
head bowed. Polly couldn't tell if he was weeping, praying
or just frozen in silent contemplation. Either way discom-
forting shivers had rippled down her spine.

She had witnessed something deeply personal.

So she should say something, right? Wasn't that the normal thing to do when someone allowed you to see a part of their soul?

Only it had never happened before. She had no compass for this kind of thing. No guidance.

Even at her very proper boarding school there hadn't been a lesson on how to handle this kind of situation.

How to greet an ambassador? Yes. Royal garden party etiquette? Of course.

But this? She was clueless. She was going to have to go in blind.

'Are you okay?'

Not the most insightful or original icebreaker in the world, but it was a start.

'Oui.' Gabe turned, looked at her, the dark eyes unreadable. 'Thank you.'

Polly stopped, tilting her head up to meet his gaze. 'What for? I didn't do anything.'

He shrugged. 'For being there. I needed a friend.'

Her eyes dropped; she was suddenly, oddly shy. 'I owe you.' Unable to resume looking at him, she started walking again and he fell into step beside her. 'Who was it?'

He sighed, low and deep. 'Who was your first love, Polly?'

'My what?' Flustered, she pushed her hair away from her face. 'I don't know. I thought we'd already covered that I don't really do love.'

'But there must have been someone, a crush, a passion. Someone who made your world that bit more exciting, your pulse beat that bit faster. Someone who made your blood heat up with just the thought of them.' His voice was low, his accent more pronounced than usual; each word hit her deep inside, burning.

You.

But she didn't say the word; she couldn't. That wasn't who she was, what they were. They might have crossed a line from colleagues to friends but the next line, from friends to lovers, was too far, too high, too unattainable.

And Polly didn't have many friends. She didn't want to screw this new understanding up.

First love? She dragged her mind back, to her lonely teenage years.

'I had a huge crush on my school friend's brother,' she admitted. 'I was sixteen and staying there one Christmas holidays. He kissed me on New Year and I went back to school convinced we were an item. When I next saw him he was with his girlfriend and barely acknowledged me.' She grimaced. 'I wept for a week. What a silly idiot I was.'

'*Non.*' To her surprise he reached over and took her hand. His long fingers laced through hers. Every millimetre where his skin touched hers was immediately sensitised, tiny electric shocks darting up her arm, piercing the core of her.

She shivered, all her attention on her hand, on her fingers, on the way he was touching her, the light caress.

It wasn't enough.

Just friends, remember? she told herself sternly. But who was she fooling? As *if* it were enough.

'That's how we learn, that complete single-mindedness of the teenage heart.'

'Learn what?'

His fingers tightened on hers. 'That feelings are not always worth the price.'

'Gabe.' Her voice was husky with the unexpected need. 'Who was she?'

'Marie.' The sound of loss and regret pulsed through her. 'She was sixteen.'

'Like I was,' she breathed, absurdly glad to find some tenuous link between her teenaged self and his ghostly lover.

'Same age as you were,' he agreed. 'Only I didn't find someone else. She left me.'

'You met in hospital?' It was all beginning to fall into place.

He nodded, his fingers almost painfully tight but Polly didn't care, welcomed his grip, anchoring him to her. 'It's not like anywhere else,' he said. 'Everything is distilled down. You're defined by your illness but underneath? Underneath you're still a person, a teenager desperate to act out and find yourself, and the steroid bloating and the hair loss and the bruising and burns? None of it changes that. Marie and I met and we knew each other. Instantly.'

A shocking, unwanted jolt of jealousy hit her and Polly swallowed it back. It was unworthy. Of her and of the story he was confiding in her.

'Tell me about her.' She wanted to know everything.

'She was understanding and acceptance. She was anger and rebellion and gallows humour. Just like me. It was…' he paused, searching for the right word '…intense. I don't know if we'd met in normal life if we'd have even liked each other. But then? Then she was all that I wanted, all that I needed. We were going to make it together or fail together.' He laughed softly, bitterly. 'The hubris of youth. But it didn't turn out the way we planned. I was so angry that she left me behind.'

'And now?'

'And now I am a decade older. That time is a memory, and Marie…' He swallowed. 'I don't even think of her day to day. I don't think of the boy I was. I took that time and I locked it away. I got well, I left Provence, left France, went away to college and I reinvented myself.'

'You're a survivor.'

She stopped and turned to face him. One hand was still held tightly in his; she allowed the other to drift up, to touch his cheek, to run along the defined line of his cheekbone and along the darkly stubbled jaw.

'You did what you had to do to survive. That makes you pretty darn amazing.'

He looked down at her, a pulse beating wildly in his cheek, the eyes almost black with pain. 'I forgot how to feel,' he said hoarsely. 'It hurt too much. Loss and pain and need. It was easier to smile and flirt and work and leave all that messy emotional stuff locked away. With Marie.'

'I know,' Polly whispered. She stared up at him. 'Emotions hurt.'

'Coming back, coming home, I can't forget. It's in every look, every word. My parents see me and they remember it all, all the hurt I caused them. And I see her, on every street corner, in every field. I see my broken promises.'

'You must have loved her very much.' Polly could hear the wistfulness in her voice and winced inwardly.

'Love?' He laughed softly. 'We were too young and fiery for love. I needed her, adored her, but love?' He looked right at her, gold flecks in his eyes mesmerising her. 'I don't know what love is either, Polly.'

She took a step towards him, eyes still fixed on his. The one small step had brought her into full contact, her chest pressed against his, hips against hips. She slid the hand cupping his face around his neck, allowing her fingers to run through the ends of his hair.

'Neither do I,' she said. 'I know want.' She stood on tiptoe and pressed a kiss on the pulse in his throat. He quivered. 'I know need.' Emboldened, she moved her mouth up and nipped his ear lobe. 'I know desire. Sometimes they're enough, they have to be enough.'

Her mouth moved to his, to drop a light butterfly kiss on

the firm lips. She had only meant to comfort him, to take his mind off the past but one small step, three small kisses, three dangerous words shifted the mood, charged the air.

'Are they?' he asked, his eyes burning a question.

Polly couldn't answer, couldn't speak, could only nod as he continued to look hard into her eyes, into her soul.

She had no idea what he saw reflected there, all she knew was that she was boneless with desire, burning up with the unexpected, unwanted, but very real need pulsing through her, his body branding her, claiming her at every point they touched.

She didn't want him to think, didn't want any regrets, she just wanted him to hold her tight, wanted to taste him. She pulled her hand out of his, the momentary loss of contact chilling her until she slid her arm around his waist, working her hand under his T-shirt to feel the firm skin underneath. There under her fingers was the tattoo. She traced it from memory feeling him shudder under her touch.

'Goddammit, Polly,' he groaned. 'I'm trying…'

'Don't.'

It was all he needed. With a smothered cry of frustration, of need, he gave in, his arms pulling her in tight, one hand on her back, the other tangling in her hair.

He looked one last time, searching her face and whatever he saw there was enough because he lowered his mouth to hers. Claimed her. And she allowed it. Allowed herself to lose herself in his mouth, his hands, his hard, strong body. Today at least, in this moment, it was all she could give him.

And she would give all that he could take.

CHAPTER NINE

'OH, NO!'

Polly had barely waited until the plane had landed and the seat-belt light was switched off before she had pulled her phone out and switched it on.

Keeping busy. Avoiding conversation. Just as she had done all last night, all morning. Chatting to his mother, going on yet another guided tour with Claire, bathing Mathilde.

Avoiding conversation. Avoiding physical contact. Avoiding Gabe.

Gabe closed his eyes. It wasn't as if he had been trying to get her alone either.

It was all too *real*. The taste of her, cinnamon spicy and sweet. The softness of her hair, the warmth and smoothness of her skin. The exquisite torture of her hands, roaming over him as if she could learn him by heart…

He took a long, deep breath, willing away the evocative memories. Willing away the urge to reach over, take her hands and draw her back to him. To lose himself in her again.

What had he been thinking? Necking like teenagers on a riverside path! Gabe couldn't remember the last time he had been content to hold and be held. To kiss, to touch with no expectation, no hurry to move on to the next stage. It wasn't just their admittedly exposed location. It was as if they were the teenage selves they had exhumed, armed with all that shy and explosive passion. No need to take it further. Content just to explore, to be.

No need to go further. Not then. And not since either.

It was probably all for the best. Every reason he had listed against getting involved with Polly still stood. Was valid. Even with the memory of the kiss thudding through him.

He opened his eyes and stared at the back of the airline seat. Yep, definitely all for the best.

'Honestly, does he never think?' Polly was still muttering as she glared at her phone as if it could answer her.

'Problems?' Gabe swung himself out of his seat and opened the overhead locker to collect their bags.

'Grandfather.' It was said expressively. 'He wants to meet us at the house when we get back. My house. He's asked Raff. It hasn't even occurred to him that we might be tired.'

'Why should it?' Gabe swung Polly's neat overnight bag down and set it onto his seat. 'It's not even three in the afternoon. It's the middle of your working day. Besides, have you ever put tiredness before business before? It's not like he knows that you're pregnant.'

'That's not the point…'

'Polly.' He put his own bag onto the floor and turned to face her, taking in the dark circles under her eyes. She looked as if she had slept as well as he had. Was it the heat or the baby keeping her awake—or was she, like him, taunted by the memory of soft lips and caressing hands? Had she got out of bed several times, determined to creep down the landing hall to tap at his door only to fall back onto the bed unsure what to say, what to do?

'You need to tell him.'

She turned the full force of her glare on him but Gabe simply shouldered her bag and collected his own. 'It's time, Polly. Everything's looking good. You've accepted it. You need your family.'

She blinked, the long dark lashes falling in confusion. 'My family isn't like yours. We don't do unconditional love.'

'Then it's time you changed that,' he said and walked off along the nearly empty aisle.

She didn't speak to him again as they exited the airport and found their way to her car and this time, when Gabe held out his hand for her keys, she didn't protest, handing them over almost absent-mindedly. He had expected her to spend the journey back to Hopeford as she had every other moment that day, tapping on her laptop or phone or scribbling in her notebook, but she simply laid her head back on the headrest and stared out of the window.

It didn't take them long; the small airport was conveniently close to Hopeford and it was less than an hour later when Gabe turned into the narrow lane and parked outside the cottage. An old red Porsche was already parked there along with a Mercedes saloon.

'Great, the cavalry are already here.'

Gabe shot her a concerned look. Where was the cool, collected Polly, in charge of everything and everyone? Where was the insistently questioning Polly, forcing him to face up to some unpalatable truths?

'Is that Raff's car? The vintage one?' Surely a mention of vintage cars would cheer her up.

'It was our father's. He got Daddy's car, I got Mummy's jewellery, the bits she left behind anyway. Never say that the Raffertys aren't conventional.'

She opened the door and slid out. 'Let's do this. Leave the bags, Gabe. We'll get them later.'

Gabe slowly exited the car and watched her. It was incredible seeing the way she breathed in, the mask slipping over her as she tilted her head up, straightened her back. She was every inch Polly Rafferty, CEO. On the outside at least.

He fell into step beside her but she didn't look at him as she marched up the small path that wound from the road through her flower-filled front garden to the wooden front door.

Twisting the handle, she made a face as the door opened with no need for a key. 'Hello,' she called as she pushed it open. 'If you're burglars then there isn't anything worth taking. If it's Raff how the hell did you get in?'

'Ah, that's my fault. I abused my position as your concierge service but I thought you would prefer to come home to a prepared dinner and a settled-in grandparent.' A woman with a heart-shaped face, wavy red-gold hair and the greenest eyes Gabe had ever seen came through from the kitchen, smiling a little shyly. 'Hi, Polly. I'm so sorry I haven't been round before today. Good trip?'

Polly stood stock-still for a moment and Gabe felt her take an audible deep breath as if steeling herself before she moved forward, her face wreathed in smiles. 'Clara! I should have known. It's so good to see you. Let me see…' She grabbed Clara's left hand and stared at the antique emerald ring on her third finger.

'I know it's customary to say congratulations but as Raff's twin I can't square it with my conscience if I don't first say *run*. I lived with him for eighteen years and you are far too good for him.'

Clara was glowing with happiness. 'It's too late. Summer would never forgive me. He's promised to take her to two theme parks in Florida this year.'

Polly shook her head. 'That's my brother. He always targets the weak spot! Congratulations, Clara. I hope you will be very happy. Have you met Gabe yet? Gabe, this is Clara, my brother's fiancée.'

'No, we haven't met but I know Raff, of course. Please accept my felicitations.' Gabe shook her hand warmly and smiled down into the green eyes.

'Polly, I am so sorry,' Clara whispered. 'I said you would probably be too tired for a meeting now, and the last thing you would want was your house invaded, but your grandfather was so insistent. I got Dad to make some food I can heat up, just a lasagne and salad, and Sue will clean it all up tomorrow so, really, all you have to do is eat.'

Polly didn't know how she would have managed without Clara's concierge service to manage her life over the last three years; she had never been more grateful for her friend's organisational powers.

'That's okay.' Polly gave Clara's hand a squeeze. 'But I hope you're sticking around. You're part of the family now. Where is everyone?'

Clara smiled back at her friend. 'Thanks, Polly. They're in the sitting room. Oh, and just to warn you before you go in, your grandmother is there as well.'

'What? With Grandfather? In the same room? Good God, thank goodness I don't have any priceless antiques.'

Polly led the way through the low-beamed door into the pretty sitting room. Gabe was so used to seeing the house empty it was a shock to find the room full of people. Charles Rafferty was ensconced on the straight-backed armchair by the unlit fire, his despised stick by his side. A white-haired, regal-looking woman with an unmistakeable look of the Rafferty twins in her straight nose and shrewd blue eyes was sitting on the sofa talking to Raff while a dark-haired girl of ten or so was lying on the floor whispering softly to Mr Simpkins as he purred around her hand.

'This is quite the welcoming committee.' Polly looked

calm and collected as she walked in. 'Hello, Grandmother.' She went over to the sofa and kissed the older lady's cheek. 'Raff.' A cool nod at her brother. 'Grandfather.' Another nod. 'Hi, Summer, how was Australia?'

'Polly!' The girl scrambled to her feet. 'Do you know you're going to be my aunt?'

'I do.' Polly stepped over and gave her a quick hug. 'My first niece. I'm looking forward to it.'

There was an ache at the back of Gabe's throat as he watched her dance so awkwardly around her family. She was right: he kept his at arm's length but it didn't matter. They would always be there, love him, have a space for him. Nothing he could do would provoke this kind of cold and formal reception.

He *should* go home more often. Talk to his papa about his future plans. Help out a little.

'Sorry for gatecrashing, Pol.' Raff was twinkling up at his sister. 'Grandfather insisted.'

'Clara explained. It's okay, of course you're all welcome but there's not much I can tell you today. Gabe and I haven't had an opportunity to pull our research together, although after seeing what Natalie is doing with the software on a smaller scale I have to say I'm very close to being completely convinced if we can make the numbers add up...'

'This isn't about Rafferty's,' her grandfather interrupted and Gabe could feel the shock reverberate through Polly as her cheeks whitened and she took a step closer to her grandfather's chair.

'Not about Rafferty's? Are you ill? I knew you should have stepped down earlier!'

'Charles isn't ill, at least, no worse than he was before the angina attack.' Polly's grandmother spoke calmly and Polly held her stare, looking for and apparently finding reassurance.

'Then what?'

'Polly dear, your grandfather and I are going to re-marry.'

Polly looked down the wooden table at her family and resisted the urge to rub her eyes. It was ironic, just last night she would have given anything to have her family congregated in her kitchen the way the Beaufils did, all eating together.

And here they were. Sure, it was a little more formal, a tad more awkward than in the Provence farmhouse. Summer was unusually tongue-tied and Gabe evidently embarrassed about being caught up in the family drama. Clara…

Clara only had eyes for Raff and he for her.

A hollow pit opened up in Polly's stomach. What would it be like for someone to look at her like that? As if she were the answer to every question? To every prayer.

Yesterday with Gabe she had come close. Close to letting him in. Colour flushed her cheeks as she remembered. She had almost begged him. No wonder he couldn't meet her eyes.

'Not hungry, Polly?' Clara looked pointedly at Polly's almost untouched plate.

'Sorry, Clara. Please don't tell your father. It was delicious as always. I'm just tired, I guess.' Without meaning to, Polly allowed her eyes to wander over to Gabe, somehow at the head of the table. Of *her* table. He looked completely at ease, mid-conversation with her grandfather, long fingers playing on the stem of his wine glass.

Fingers that just yesterday had been playing on her skin.

Polly shivered. How could a kiss be that sensual? More erotic than the most practised lovemaking?

What would it have been like if they had been somewhere more private? If they had gone further? If she had been able to explore that tattoo the way she had burned to, tracing it with the tip of her finger. With kisses. With her tongue, slick on salty skin.

She clenched her hands, allowing the nails to dig into her palms. She was at dinner, for goodness' sake. With her grandparents.

With her brother.

With Gabe...

He looked up, with that sixth sense he seemed to possess whenever she thought about him, eyes dark and intent.

'We should celebrate,' he said abruptly. 'Two engagements require champagne.'

'Yes, of course.' She should have thought of that. It was her house after all. And she was the only one without news to celebrate. Publicly at least. 'There's a couple of bottles out back.'

'I'll get them.' He pushed his chair back and disappeared into the pantry, reappearing with one of the bottles that had been chilling in the old stone cold room.

'Summer, *ma chérie*, could you go to the cupboard there and get me six of the long glasses? *Oui*, clever girl.' He flashed his warmest smile at the small girl as Summer proudly put the glasses on the table and Polly pushed her still-full wine glass to one side.

It had been easier to accept the glass and not touch it rather than face any questions. Gabe was right, she needed to say something. But how?

With an expert twist Gabe loosed the cork and began to pour the bubble-filled amber liquid into the first glass, handing the first to her grandmother and the second to Clara. When every glass had been filled and handed around every face turned expectantly to Polly.

Of course. This was her role. Head of the family firm.

She got to her feet, trying to drag her thoughts back to

the here and now, to the unexpected news that had greeted her return home.

'So there are two engagements to celebrate,' she said, keeping her voice as steady as she could. Raff and Clara were smiling up at her, her grandparents regarding her with more warmth than she had seen from them in a long time.

Her eyes flickered to Gabe. His eyes were fixed on her, expression inscrutable.

'I know my job involves looking for trends and seeing what lies ahead so all I can say is that thank goodness I don't run a dating agency because I didn't predict either of these. But that doesn't mean that I'm not truly happy for you all. Clara, you've been my closest friend in Hopeford.'

So close that I haven't seen you since I returned, a little voice whispered but Polly ignored it.

'I know how much Raff loves you and I know he will do everything he can to make you happy—and when Raff sets his mind to something he usually achieves it!

'And Grandfather, Grandmother. Thank you for raising Raff and me. I know it wasn't easy, that we weren't easy. I know it put a strain on you. I'm just glad you've found your way back together after thirteen years. You're the most formidable team I know. So.' She held her glass high. 'To the Raffertys. Congratulations.'

'The Raffertys,' they chorused, glasses held to hers before they sipped.

Polly put her glass down thankfully.

'Aunty Polly,' Summer's voice rang out clearly. 'Why aren't you drinking yours?'

Every eye turned to Polly and she sank back into her seat, instinctively looking over at Gabe for help.

But he just sat there.

'You didn't drink any wine either.' Raff sounded accusatory.

For goodness' sake, wasn't a girl allowed to not drink? It wasn't as if she were a lush!

But maybe Gabe was right. They had to know soon enough and although a big announcement hadn't been her plan maybe it would be better to tell them all in one fell swoop. Like ripping off a plaster.

Polly took a breath, feeling the air shudder through her.

'I have a little announcement of my own. This isn't quite how I wanted to do it…' she looked around the table, desperate for some reassurance '…but I suppose there isn't an easy way so I'm just going to say it. I'm pregnant.'

'That's great, Polly.' But Clara's voice was lost as both Raff and her grandfather sprang to their feet.

'Pregnant?'

'You'll marry her, of course!' Her grandfather was glaring at Gabe.

'What do you mean, pregnant?'

So much for extending the celebrations.

The noise levels rose. Polly couldn't think, didn't know which angry, accusatory face to answer first. 'Stop it!' She had risen to her feet as well, hands crashing down onto the table, rattling the crockery and silverware.

'Come on, Summer, let's go for a walk.' Clara threw her an apologetic glance as she shepherded her daughter from the table. 'We'll talk later, Polly. It's great news. Raff?' Her eyes bored into her fiancé, an implicit warning. 'I'll see you at home.'

Raff sank back into his seat. 'Sorry, Polly. It was just, it was a shock.'

Charles Rafferty wasn't so easily cowed. He was still on his feet and glaring over at Gabe. 'Well?' he demanded.

'Grandfather!' Polly said sharply. 'For goodness' sake. You are not some medieval knight, much as you might wish it, and I am *not* some dishonoured damsel to be married off to avoid a scandal. This is a good thing and it has *nothing* to do with Gabe.'

Maybe she had put too much emphasis on the 'nothing', she conceded as the Frenchman whitened, and added: 'I've only known him a few weeks.'

'Then whose is it?'

'Mine,' she said firmly. 'This is the twenty-first century, I am thirty-one and I am quite capable of doing this alone.'

'Yes, dear, we know how independent you are.' Her grandmother sounded like a dowager duchess from the turn of the last century. 'But what your grandfather means is who fathered it? Unless you went to one of those clinics,' she said a little doubtfully.

If only she had! That would be so much easier to admit.

'Someone I met travelling.' She held up her hand. 'I don't know his surname. Obviously if I had foreseen this I would have exchanged business cards but I didn't. So it's up to me. And you, if you want to be involved.'

'Of course we do, dear, don't be so melodramatic.'

But her grandmother's words were negated by her grandfather's expression. Shock, disapproval, horror, disgust passing over his face in rapid but sickening procession.

'A granddaughter of mine? Besmirching the family name with some dreadlocked backpacker? I told you to get married, Polly. I told you to settle down...'

'With respect, *monsieur*, that's enough.' Now Gabe was on his feet. 'Polly has done nothing wrong. It may not be your preferred path for her but she is going to be a great mother—and a great CEO.'

'A single mother in charge of Rafferty's?' Charles Rafferty huffed out a disparaging laugh. 'I thought you had more sense than that, Beaufils. As for you, Polly, I knew letting you take over was a mistake. I should have stuck with my gut instinct.'

The blood rushed from her cheeks and her knees weakened. He'd admitted it. He didn't want her. Her appointment, her career was nothing but a mistake in his eyes.

'Clara's a single mother,' Raff said. His voice was mild but there was a steely glint in his eyes. 'At least she was. Polly, I'm sorry, you…' He rubbed his jaw, the blue eyes rueful. 'You surprised me but you're not alone. I hope you know that. Clara and I are right here.' Polly nodded, numb inside, her eyes returning to her grandfather, still standing up, still glaring.

'You two always did stick together,' he said. 'It doesn't change anything. It's hard enough for any working mother to be at the top, impossible for a woman on her own. It's not old-fashioned, it's common sense.'

'There are plenty of single parents at Rafferty's, men and women.' Gabe's voice was soft but it cut through the tense air, drawing all the attention away from Polly, and she folded herself back into her chair, clasping her hands together to keep them from trembling.

'The only person, *monsieur*, who sees a problem here is you. Which is ironic because if you had seen her worth earlier, if you hadn't pushed her away, then maybe she wouldn't be in this position. You need to think very carefully about how you treat and value your granddaughter before you lose her for ever—and the great-grandchild she is carrying.'

Charles Rafferty paled and Polly and Raff exchanged a concerned glance as he sat down heavily in his chair. His tongue wasn't weakened though. 'I thought we had established that this has nothing to do with you.'

Gabe didn't quail under the withering tone. '*Non?* Who held her hair when she was sick? Who sat with her during the first scan? I didn't ask to be involved but she has no one else. You make it quite clear that she can't come to you.'

Charles Rafferty gasped, a shuddering intake of breath, and Polly was back on her feet. Before she could move round to him Raff had passed their grandfather a glass of water and her grandmother had moved round to him, her usually aloof expression one of concern.

This was all getting horribly out of hand. 'Gabe!' How dared he? How dared he try and explain away her actions? Interfere? 'A word? In private?'

Still trembling but now more with anger than with shock, she led him outside. Normally her garden was one of her favourite spots with shady, hidden spaces and a stream running across the bottom. Today it was just somewhere convenient.

'How dare you talk to my grandfather like that? What the hell do you think you're doing?'

His mouth hardened into a thin line. 'Standing up for you.'

The nerve of him! 'I didn't ask you to.'

His eyes narrowed contemptuously. '*Non?* I must have misunderstood the beseeching look you threw me when you sat there mute as your family shouted at you.'

'I didn't, at least I didn't mean for you to attack my grandfather! I don't need help. I am quite capable of standing up for myself.'

'*Oui*, keep telling yourself that.'

The words were thrown at her, sharp as arrows, and she quailed under them. 'What do you mean by that?'

'What I say. You tell me, you tell yourself that you don't need anything—anyone.' His eyes had darkened with an unbearable sympathy. 'But you're still just a little girl tugging at her grandfather's sleeve wanting attention. Without it, you allow yourself to be nothing.'

Polly hadn't known words could hurt before, not physically, but each of Gabe's words was like a sharp stab in her chest. 'How dare you…?'

'He rules the board, he rules you. He uses his health to keep you quiet and his disapproval to keep you tame. When he said you couldn't take over, did you stay to fight, to prove him wrong? No, you ran away.'

How had this happened? How had the passion and need of yesterday turned into these cruel words, ripping her apart?

'I couldn't stay. You know that.'

'You *chose* not to stay.' He laughed, not unkindly but the tone didn't matter. The unbearable sympathy on his face didn't matter. The words were all that mattered and they were harsh.

They were true. He had seen inside her and he was stripping her to the bone.

'You were quick enough to label me a coward, to judge me, but you know what, Polly? You were right when you said we were just the same. We define ourselves through work because without it? What is there? Who are we? Nothing.'

Polly stood there looking at him. She had thought that she knew him. Knew the feel of his mouth, the taste of him. The way the muscles on his shoulders moved, the play of them under her hands.

She'd thought that she understood him. That he might be coming to understand her. Maybe he did, all too well. She was defenceless.

'Get out,' she said, proud when her voice didn't waver. When the threatened tears didn't fall. 'Get out and leave me alone.'

He stood there for a long moment looking at her. She didn't move, didn't waver.

'You need people in your corner, Polly,' he said softly. 'People who will be there for you no matter what. Pick wisely.'

And he was gone.

Tears trembled behind her eyes but she blinked them back. *You don't cry, remember?*

She took a deep breath, almost doubling over at the unexpected ache in her chest, the raw, exposed pain and grief, like Prometheus torn open, awaiting the eagles. She had lost everything. Her grandfather. Gabe.

But no. She straightened, her hand splayed open on her still-flat stomach. Not everything.

She could do this. She could absolutely do this alone. Gabe was wrong. In every way.

Slowly she turned and walked back to the kitchen. Her family were at the table where she had left them and she was relieved to see colour in her grandfather's cheeks. Maybe she could fix this. She had to fix something.

'I'm sorry about what Gabe said.' She took her seat and picked up her water glass, relieved that her hands had stopped shaking enough for her to drink. 'He was out of line.'

She bowed her head and waited for more reproach and anger to be heaped on her.

'Charles.' Her grandmother spoke sharply and her grandfather leant forward, reaching for one of Polly's hands.

She couldn't remember the last time he had touched her first; she was usually the one bestowing a dutiful kiss on his cheek.

It felt comforting to have her hand in his. Unbidden, Gabe's words sprang into her mind. *'You're still just a little girl tugging at her grandfather's sleeve.'*

'I'm sorry, Polly.' Charles Rafferty's voice was a little wavery, his speech unusually slow and Polly's chest tightened with love and fear. 'I was shocked and I reacted badly. I said some terrible things and I hope you can forgive me, my dear.'

An apology? From the formidable Mr Rafferty? 'I'm sorry too,' she said, squeezing his fingers. When had they got so frail? 'I should have told you earlier. I needed time to process everything, to deal with it all, but I should have come to you.'

'You always were independent,' he said.

Was she? Polly wondered. Or did she just want to be thought that way? Was Gabe right?

'I didn't mean for this to happen.' She looked at her grandparents, pleading for them to understand. They might not be perfect but they were the only parental figures she had. She needed them. 'I was lost and met someone as lonely as me. He was nice, a teacher in Copenhagen and recently divorced. I *have* tried to track him down but with no picture or surname the private investigator wasn't hopeful. He gave it a week and then told me to save my money. You know how much I missed Daddy. I hate the fact that my baby will grow up not knowing his or her father.'

'Polly dearest.' Her grandmother was suspiciously bright eyed. 'Did Gabriel say something about a scan? I don't suppose there's a picture…'

A glimmer of something that felt a little like hope skimmed through Polly. 'There is a picture,' she said. 'Would you like to see it?'

CHAPTER TEN

'IT DIDN'T LOOK this dark on the tin.' Polly stood back from the wall and stared at the first splash of paint. 'I'm not intending to raise a baby Goth.'

'It'll be lighter when it dries.' Clara joined her and looked doubtfully at the wall. 'I hope. Are you sure you don't want me to find somebody to do it for you?'

'No, I am doing it all myself. My baby, my walls, my botch paint job in deepest purple.' Polly glanced at the tin. 'It's supposed to be lilac lace.'

'You *can* outsource some of the work, you know. To Raff or to me. I do special discounts for family…'

'I might consider outsourcing the actual birth part. That looks a little scary.' The books Clara had given her were piled high on the chest of drawers in the sunny room at the back of the house Polly had decided on for the nursery. After a quick flick through the graphic words and even more graphic pictures Polly had put them aside vowing not to go anywhere near them again.

There was some protection in ignorance.

'Sorry, Polly, there are some things even you can't delegate away.' Clara dipped her paintbrush in the deep colour and began to apply it to the walls in sweeping strokes. 'Talking of delegation, have you spoken to Gabe?' She sounded disinterested but the sly glance she slid Polly belied the light tone.

'I've sat in meetings with him.'

'Let me rephrase that. Have you had a conversation

with Gabe, just the two of you, that hasn't involved spread-sheets, budgets and forecasts?'

'That would be a negative.'

Clara added a bit more paint to her brush. 'Polly,' she said slowly. 'We've known each other for a while and I like to think that although we've never touched on anything really deep we're good friends.'

Polly bit her lip. Truth was Clara was her only friend. And yet she knew so little about the woman who was going to marry her twin. 'Of course we are, and I am delighted you're going to be my sister.'

'And the aunt of the lucky future possessor of these walls,' Clara agreed. 'So I hope you don't mind me prying a little bit but what is going on with you and Gabe?'

That was easy enough to answer. 'We're colleagues.'

'That's all?' Clara persisted.

Polly sighed and put her paintbrush down on the newspaper she'd spread over the furniture, before sliding onto the floor and hugging her knees. 'We kissed. Twice. Well, once was an accident.'

Not the other. No, the other had been wonderfully intentional.

'Don't you hate those accidental kisses?' Clara murmured, laughter in her voice.

Now she had started confiding Polly couldn't bear to stop. It was almost a relief to let the words spill out. 'We talked. Spent some time together.' It didn't sound much. Not the bare, bald facts. 'He was there when I needed him. And he was brilliant; patient and helpful and understanding. He's good to work with too, sparky and innovative and pushes me…' Her voice trailed off.

'Sounds good.' Clara was still painting. It was easier talking to her back than to have to face her, see concern or sympathy in her eyes.

'It was. I've only known him a couple of weeks but I thought maybe we had a connection.' Polly pulled at her ponytail. 'It's stupid, hormones playing up. I should have known better. Neither of us are looking for anything, want anything. In a different time or place maybe we could have had a thing. But the timing was off.'

And she didn't want a 'thing'. Not any more. Not with anyone. Especially not with Gabe.

She'd spent her twenties valuing her independence, her ability to walk away. It didn't seem such an achievement any more.

Clara painted another streak of colour onto the wall and stood back to assess the effect. Her voice was still light, conversational. 'You don't need to be looking to find it. I wasn't, Raff wasn't. We tried hard not to fall in love but it was too strong.'

Love? Polly swallowed hard, her heartbeat speeding up. 'Who said anything about love?'

'No one. Yet. But you said yourself there's a connection; he pushes you, understands you—and the kisses were good enough to make your voice go hazy just thinking about them. Even if one *was* an accident.'

Clara put her paintbrush down beside Polly's and slid into place beside her. 'It might not be love, Polly, not yet. But it sounds pretty close to me. I don't know why you've pushed him away, nor why he has let you. But isn't it worth trying swallowing your pride?'

'I miss him,' Polly admitted.

But it was more than that. She'd lived alone in this big old house for so long, had never felt lonely in it before. But now his absence was in every room.

It was ridiculous; he'd hardly spent any time there as it was.

It was the same at work. Sometimes she would look up

from her desk and glance over at the empty space where his desk had so briefly sat. It was so quiet without him typing loudly, his continuous conversations. The room so still without his pacing up and down. She would listen jealously for some mention of his name, to find out who he was flirting with this week.

But the staff grapevine was quiet.

And she *was* lonely. Raff and Clara were doing their best, almost overwhelming her with dinners and visits, trying to include her in everything. And she appreciated it, she really did. Only they were so very together.

It made her feel her solitary state even more.

She had never cared about being alone before. Or allowed herself to admit it.

'He took you to the hospital, helped when you were sick, what makes you think he doesn't want more? Have you asked him?' Clara was pushing but Polly didn't mind. The last few weeks, his last words had been going round and round in her head like an overactive carousel until she was so giddy she couldn't think. This was her opportunity to get it all straight.

To get over it.

'I don't need to. He's...' Polly searched for the right word. 'He's complex, Clara. He has this amazing family.' She could hear the wistfulness in her own voice and cringed. 'They're really supportive and loving, like yours if you multiplied your family by three, the noise level by ten, added in a host of toddlers and moved to France.'

'Just like my family, then.'

'Yours was the happiest, most together family I knew until I met the Beaufils,' Polly admitted.

'So he has the family you always wanted,' Clara said shrewdly. 'I still don't see the problem.'

'He was ill, really ill in his teens and it nearly killed his parents.' Polly winced as she pictured the pain in his dark eyes. 'I don't know whether he really blames them for caring so much or himself for causing so much pain. I think it's a mixture of both. Throw in a first love who died in her teens and you have one emotionally mixed-up man.'

'We all have our scars, but most of us are redeemable. For the right person.'

'That's just it.' Clara had got it. 'I'm *not* the right person, Clara. Gabe needs someone who understands him, someone with the patience to wait for him, to help him. Me? I have a business to run, a baby on the way. I have no idea how a functioning family works. I can't help him! He deserves better.'

Clara didn't say anything for a long moment and then she got up and picked up the paintbrush. 'It's a lot, I agree,' she said. 'But you've never backed down from anything daunting before. If you think you and he have a chance, if you think it might, could be love, then you should go for it. But, Polly, if you're backing down out of fear, then you're letting yourself down and you're letting Gabe down. Be sure before you let him walk away.'

He still had a key in his pocket but using it just didn't feel right. Not with her car parked outside and the windows flung open.

A part of Gabe had hoped that Polly was out, working maybe or with her brother, that he could have nipped in, gathered his stuff and left again leaving no trace.

Taking a deep breath, he pressed the doorbell. How hard could this be? After all, they saw each other every day at work. They sent emails, held meetings. It was all fine.

Polite. Formal. Fine.

There was a pause and then the sound of light footsteps running down the stairs before the door was pulled open.

'I left it open for you…oh!' Polly stepped back, her eyes huge with surprise. 'You're not Clara.'

'Non,' he agreed.

'She was just here, helping me paint and popped out for sandwiches so I thought, I assumed…' Her voice trailed off.

'Paint?' That made sense, he thought as his gaze travelled up her despite his best intentions to stay cool and focused. Bare feet, long tanned legs in a pair of cut-off denim shorts. Who would have thought the elegant Polly Rafferty even owned such disreputable-looking garments, fraying and paint splattered?

Her vest top was falling off one shoulder, revealing a delicate lilac bra strap.

Lilac. The colour he had bought her. It might even be the same set. His breath hitched, his heartbeat speeding up, blood pounding around his body in a relentless march.

No. He dragged his mind back to the matter at hand. They weren't on those kinds of terms, not any more.

They had almost got in too deep; he'd allowed her in too deep. Thank goodness Polly had seen sense.

Her hands tightened on the door. 'I'm decorating the baby's room purple, to go with the bunting. Only it's a little darker than I thought, more bordello than nursery.'

'It might lighten when it dries.' He shifted his weight onto the other foot. Such a non-conversation. As if they were mere acquaintances.

'That's the hope,' Polly said.

She still hadn't asked him in.

'I just wanted to return your key and get the last of my things.'

'Oh.' Her eyelashes dropped, veiling her eyes. 'Of course, come in.'

She opened the door fully, stepping aside as she did so. 'Is your flat fixed?'

Gabe grimaced. 'Unfortunately not. The underground cinema and gym is proving most expensive for my oligarch neighbour. He's still paying hotel bills for at least twenty people.'

'Including you?'

He shrugged. 'There's a gym. It's convenient for work. No more trains.'

'That's good.'

Gabe stepped over the threshold and stopped, unwanted regret and nostalgia twisting his stomach. The scent of fresh flowers mixed with beeswax and that spicy scent Polly favoured, a dark cinnamon, hit him. It smelled like home.

Only it wasn't. Not any more. It never really had been.

She was right to have pushed him away. What did he have to offer? Financial security? She had her own. No, what Polly needed was emotional security.

The one thing he couldn't offer.

She deserved it. Deserved more than a coward who spent his life hiding from his own family so that he didn't have to face up to the possibility of losing them. Of letting them down.

'I don't have much.' He needed to pack, to get out and leave the memories behind. Start afresh.

She turned to him, one hand twisting her ponytail, the other playing with the frayed cotton on her shorts. 'Gabe, I'm sorry,' she said.

What? 'No, I should apologise to you.' He squeezed his eyes shut. 'I was harsh. Unfair.'

'You were right.' She exhaled. 'You just gave me some home truths. I didn't want to hear them, to admit them. That doesn't stop them being true.' She huffed out a laugh.

'There doesn't seem to be a warning sign with us, does there? We just say whatever is in our heads and damn the consequences. I've never been so honest with anyone before.'

'No, me neither.'

'I'm not sure I like it.' She moved away towards the kitchen. 'Would you like a coffee?'

Gabe had intended to make a quick exit but he recognised the offer for what it was: a peace offering. 'Do you have decaf?'

'A month ago I would have laughed in your face but pregnancy does strange things to a woman. I have decaf and a whole selection of herbal teas, each more vile than the rest.'

'I could make you a smoothie,' he suggested and laughed, the tension broken by the horror in her eyes.

'Spinach and beetroot and those horrid seeds? I'm pregnant, not crazy.' She busied herself at the expensive coffee machine and Gabe leant on the counter, idly looking at the papers there. One letter caught his eye and he read a few lines before realising it was personal. He pushed it away just as she looked over.

Awkward, as if he had been caught purposely snooping, he gestured at the letter. 'You have a hospital appointment?'

'Yes. Clara's agreed to accompany me.'

His duties were well and truly over. He was free, to concentrate on work, to train for the Alpine triathlon in the autumn. To live his life the way he wanted it with no interruptions.

It was all going back to normal.

Polly walked back over, a steaming cup of coffee in her hand. 'Gabe.' She put the coffee down next to him. 'I really need to thank you. For everything.'

He shrugged. 'I was here. Anyone would have done the same.'

'Maybe, but you stepped up, more than once. You didn't have to. Not just with the practical stuff.'

She pulled up a stool and sank onto it, pulling the letter from the hospital over towards her, folding it over and over. 'I've been thinking a lot lately. About what I want from my life. I guess the pregnancy would have forced me to make some changes anyway but it's not just that. You *made* me think. About the kind of person, the kind of parent I want to be. My work, Rafferty's, is incredibly important, that won't change. But it's not enough. It shouldn't be enough. I don't want to turn into a female version of Grandfather, putting the business before family, before happiness.'

'I'm going to have a baby.' Her eyes were shining. Gabe had seen Polly experience a whole range of emotions about the pregnancy: shock, grief, acceptance. But not joy like this. Not before today. 'And I want that baby to have a family. I think, deep down, there's a bit of me that's always wanted your kind of family. Ironic, isn't it? When you find them too much?'

'Swap?' he offered.

'In a heartbeat.' She folded the paper again. 'I can't conjure up parents and a partner for the baby, but I want him or her to grow up with love and laughter and security. Clara and Raff will help, if I let them. And I will. I need to start letting people in. So thank you. For helping me realise that.'

'You're welcome.' The words almost stuck in his throat.

She smiled at him but there was sadness in her eyes. 'I just hope you find what you're looking for,' she said.

Gabe wanted to make some flippant comment but she was right. They *were* always honest with each other, no matter what the consequences. 'I'm not looking for much.

Another year healthy? Another goal achieved?' It didn't sound like much but it was all he had.

'I wish I could have helped you, the way you've helped me. It's not that I don't want to try, arrogant as that sounds, but I do. I like you, Gabe.' The colour flared on her cheeks.

Gabe wanted to speak out. To tell her that she had helped, that with her he had finally confronted memories locked away for too long.

To tell her how much he liked her too. That he lay awake at night replaying every single moment of that kiss, his skin heating where she had touched him.

But he didn't know how to.

Polly took a deep breath. 'I don't know what love is, not really. But I think we were close. At least, I was close. The closest I've ever been. But I have the baby to think of, the security I have promised it. Right now, it needs me to be putting it first, to be strong for it.'

She reached over and took his hand, her fingers soft in his. He curled his hand round hers, holding them tight and she raised his hand to her lips, dropping a kiss onto his knuckles. 'My mother didn't put us first. Or second or anywhere. Her need for love came before anything else. I guess I overcompensated, desperate to show the world that I didn't need anyone. That I wasn't like her. Now I wonder if maybe I took it too far. But now isn't the time to worry about that. I can't put myself first, not any more.'

'No.' What else was there to say?

'I do believe that there's someone out there who'll show you that life isn't a challenge or a goal, it's a blessing.' She closed her eyes, blinking back a tear. 'I have to admit I'm a little jealous of that someone.' Her voice was so low he hardly heard the words. 'Maybe you'll do it on your own. You're strong enough, goodness knows. The burdens you bear. The misplaced guilt.'

'I'm happy for you, really I am. But I'm fine.' He tried to smile. 'I don't need fixing.'

So much for honesty. He was utterly broken and they both knew it.

Breathe. Breathe. Breathe. It wasn't easy training for an Alpine triathlon in a busy, flat city like London. It was a particularly gruelling trial, a lake swim followed by a ninety-kilometre cycle-ride and a full marathon run. Although the trails didn't go too high up into the Tyrolean mountains it was a hilly course.

Just finishing wasn't an option. He wanted a winning time.

There was nothing better than pushing his body to its limits. Proving he was no longer at its mercy, that his mind was in control at all times.

Control. He'd lost it the past few weeks. It was time to regain it.

Gabe stopped, leaning against a tree, and took a swig of water. It didn't take long for fitness levels to drop. For an easy ten-kilometre jog to become a challenge.

He just needed to get his rhythm back, to regain that blissful state where all he knew was the thud of his feet, the beating of his heart.

Instead he ran to a soundtrack of Polly's voice, sad, resigned, defeated. *I like you.*

And he'd said? He'd said nothing. Because what could he say?

I wish I could have helped you, the way you've helped me.

Of course she did. She was an achiever. Polly Rafferty didn't like to leave tasks unfinished, a list unticked. She'd wanted to see him reconciled with his family, the past dealt with.

She was getting her happy ever after, she just wanted the same for him.

It was a shame life just wasn't that tidy.

Gabe set off again, wiping the perspiration off his forehead as he increased the tempo. He didn't need a happy ever after. He didn't deserve one.

But she did.

She deserved the whole damn fairy tale. Paris at her feet.

He just hoped that she would meet someone who recognised that.

The thought reverberated around his head, the echo getting louder and louder.

Someone else.

His stomach clenched and Gabe skidded to a stop, bending forward to alleviate the cramp, hand on his side.

No, he didn't want that for her at all.

Oh, how he wished he could be that altruistic, that selfless, that he could put her needs first. But he didn't think he could survive watching her laugh with another man, talking cars with another man, showing off vintage designs to another man, fired up as she planned business and strategy with another man.

Kissing another man.

Raising her child with another man.

And there would be someone else. For all her brave talk about going it alone, there would be. She might not have fallen in love in the past but she'd had partners whenever she needed them. How long before the new, softer Polly was snapped up? Opened up her heart to some lucky man?

They'd be queuing around the block.

And he was just going to let them?

Gabe straightened up, oblivious to the people walking around him, the sighs and tuts from commuters unwilling to step around a human being in their well-trodden path.

Of course he wasn't going to let them!

I like you, she had said. More than once. What must it have taken for the proud Polly Rafferty to say those words? And he hadn't reacted. Hadn't told her.

That he liked her too.

It was time he did.

If Polly wanted to have the whole white-picket-fence dream while running the world's most famous department store then she was going to need the best by her side.

And Gabe had always liked a challenge.

CHAPTER ELEVEN

'GOOD MORNING, RACHEL.'

Polly smiled at her assistant. Rachel had done her job beautifully. Unable to bear some big announcement of her pregnancy, Polly had, instead, confided in her PA. The news had spread around the store in less than a day, just as Polly had known it would.

At some point she would have to have a word with the gossip-loving woman about confidentiality and discretion. But not yet, not when she had just used Rachel to her advantage.

'Good morning, Miss Rafferty. There is a mint tea on your desk and Chef says that he has a summer fruit compote and a breakfast omelette for you this morning.'

It was surprising—and rather sweet—how many of her staff had taken the news of her pregnancy and turned it into a project. The kitchen sent up nutritious meals three times a day and were hopefully awaiting outlandish cravings so that they could rise to whatever challenge she set.

The make-up department manager had put together an entire basket of pre-natal oils, creams and bath salts and was sourcing and testing the very best in post-natal and baby unguents. As for the personal shoppers, not only were they putting aside more clothes than triplets could easily get through, they were also ensuring she would be the chicest mother-to-be in London.

Polly had always felt respected rather than liked—she had encouraged it. This new two-way process was a little disconcerting. But she was rather enjoying the interest and attention. It didn't feel as intrusive as she had feared, more warm and friendly.

Only Gabe was nowhere to be seen. He seemed to be constantly in meetings although he sent detailed emails and was obviously working as hard as ever. It wasn't hard to deduce that he was avoiding her.

She shouldn't have used words like love.

But somehow Polly couldn't bring herself to feel regret or embarrassment. She'd tried.

A little at least.

'Oh, Miss Rafferty, there's been a change to your afternoon appointment. The one with the web developer?'

'Has he postponed?'

Up to now Polly had left all the details about the possible new website with Gabe, but she wanted to check some final budgets and meet the developer herself before making the final recommendation.

Finding a mutually convenient date had been problematic—and now he couldn't make it? She hoped this wasn't a portent of his professional reliability.

'He's stuck in Paris and asked if you would mind going there instead?'

'To Paris?' Polly echoed. 'That's…'

'Less time to get to than Edinburgh,' Rachel said, putting a pile of papers onto the desk. 'I've booked you onto the noon Eurostar so a taxi will be here to take you to St Pancras for eleven. A car will collect you at the other end.'

Rachel looked a little anxious. 'I have done the right thing, haven't I? It's just you told me to use my initiative more and I know you want to talk to him yourself before making a final decision…'

'No, you did right. As you say it's quicker than Edinburgh.' Polly scooped up the pile of papers, including her passport, she kept it at work for just this reason, and re-treated into her office.

Sorry, Mummy, looks like I won't be keeping my word after all, she thought. But maybe this is a good thing. De-mystify Paris as part of her new start.

Baby steps.

It was so comfortable in Business Class that Polly realised with a jump that she had almost nodded off. *I think I pre-ferred the nausea to the tiredness,* she thought as she jolted back to awareness when the train braked, the papers still unread on the table in front of her, her laptop reverted to sleep mode. There were times when she eyed the couch in her office longingly, desperate to stretch out and just close her eyes.

Until she remembered Gabe sprawled out. The firm toned lines of his body, the tree spiralling up his back.

The couch seemed a lot less safe then.

Polly pulled her mind back to the present. She had enough to do without daydreaming and dwelling on the past, including finding her way around a totally strange city. Paris might be quicker to get to than Edinburgh but it felt a lot more alien.

Luckily she didn't have to think or organise herself at all; a driver was waiting for her as she stepped out of the bustling, light-filled Gare du Nord station with its impos-ing Gothic façade and, before she had a chance to take in the fact she was actually in Paris at last, he had pulled away into the heavy traffic.

It was only then that Polly realised she had no idea where the meeting was being held. He could be taking her anywhere. She shuffled through the papers Rachel had handed her, looking for some kind of clue.

Nothing. Budgets, technical specs, nothing of any use.

She felt so helpless, the annoyance itched away at her. The tiredness was bad enough; the effort it was taking to function at her usual level was soul destroying. Clara's reassurances that it wouldn't last, that she would be back to full capacity in just a couple of weeks, were little comfort. She couldn't afford to slack at any point.

Nobody had said it would be easy—and 'nobody' was right—but she couldn't let that derail her. Her grandfather might have apologised but she wasn't going to give him the slightest opportunity to think she couldn't cope.

The car drew up outside an imposing-looking hotel built of the golden stone Polly had already noticed in abundance as they drove down the wide boulevards. Each floor was populated with quaint balconies while colourful flower baskets softened the rather regal effect.

The driver had come around to open her door. *'Mademoiselle?'*

'I'm meeting him here?' she asked, puzzled. Polly knew a five-star hotel when she saw one and this looked top end. This kind of old-world luxury seemed a peculiar choice for a cutting-edge developer. Maybe it was a post-modern thing she wasn't cool enough to understand.

Either way she was here now—and the hotel certainly was Paris at its opulent best. The Eiffel Tower was clearly visible from the pavement and the foyer reminded her a little of Rafferty's with its art-deco-inspired floor and grand pillars. Polly looked around. How was she supposed to work out which particular bar, restaurant or café she was meeting her contact in—and what *was* his name again?

'Can I help you?' The intimidatingly chic receptionist spoke in perfect English. How did she know? Did they have a nationality detector at the door?

'Yes, I am Polly Rafferty and I am supposed…'

'Ah, Mademoiselle Rafferty. I have your key here. There is nothing to sign. It is all taken care of.'

'Key?' Polly took it in her hand. It was a key too, a heavy gold one, not an anonymous card. 'No, I'm not staying. I am meant to be meeting…' She thought hard. Nope. Nothing. Had Rachel ever told her the name? 'Someone,' she finished lamely.

'Yes, I know. Pierre will show you the way.'

It was a bit like being in a Hitchcock plot. Polly fully expected Cary Grant to walk past as the dapper porter showed her to the lift, not betraying by one eyebrow how odd it was for her to be checking in without as much as an overnight bag.

If checking in she was. Maybe he was merely showing her to a meeting room?

The lift went up. And up and up.

'Penthouse?' she queried. It was an odd place for a meeting room. Pierre merely motioned for her to follow and led her to a white door, the only one in a grand, formal-looking corridor richly papered in a gold and black oriental print.

I'm being kidnapped and I am far too English and polite to scream for help, Polly thought as she put the key into the lock and turned it. The door swung open and she found herself looking at quite the most perfect hotel suite she had ever seen.

The door opened into a large sitting room. Polly stepped in, her attention immediately captured by two floor-to-ceiling windows, both flung open and leading out onto one of the pretty balconies she had admired on the way in. Perfectly visible through both was a to-die-for view of the Eiffel Tower, majestically dominating the horizon.

Polly turned slowly, taking in her luxurious surroundings. The suite was decorated in shades of lavender and silver, the cool colours perfectly setting off the rich mahogany tones in the woodwork. Two sofas, lavishly heaped with cushions, surrounded the dark wooden coffee table and lavender silk curtains framed that perfect city view.

Polly stepped further in, looking back at Pierre for confirmation, but he had gone, closing the door behind him. She was alone.

If this was a kidnap then it was a luxuriously comfortable kidnapping. Her gaze stopped on a plate on the coffee table. A kidnapping complete with a plate of delicately coloured macaroons.

Polly had never stayed anywhere this beautiful. It wasn't that she couldn't afford to, but, her recent trip aside, she really only travelled for business and that was on Rafferty's budget. She stayed in good hotels, in comfortable, spacious rooms fully outfitted for the business traveller, but she would never charge a suite like this to her expense account.

And it had never occurred to her to book this kind of luxury for herself. What had she been thinking? From now on it was suites all the way.

She wandered around taking in each lavish detail. All the accessories from the light switches to the lamps, the vases to the mirrors, had a nineteen twenties art deco vibe to them. In fact, Polly narrowed her eyes, she was no expert but that fruit bowl looked pretty genuine to her.

If the bathroom had an enormous roll-top bath, vast, thick towels and an array of scented creams and bubbles then Polly had either died and entered her own personal heaven or was in some kind of weird reality show tailored to her every need.

She tiptoed through the large bedroom, noting with approval the terrace off it, complete with sun loungers, and entered the bathroom.

Oh! It was utterly perfect.

Would it be very wrong to have a bath when she was supposed to be prepping for the oddest business meeting she had experienced in ten years of work?

Reality asserted itself. A chill ran through her.

What kind of meeting was this? She should go back into the sitting room and take advantage of her solitude to complete the prep work she had neglected on the way here. More importantly she should phone Rachel and find out what on earth was going on.

Maybe, if this was all a mistake, she could book the suite anyway. After all, she was here now. She was finally in Paris. It would be a shame to just turn around and make her way tamely home now that her mother's spell was broken.

With a last longing glance at the bath Polly returned to the sitting room, resisting the urge to bounce on the bed as she passed it.

It was all just as gorgeous when she walked back into the main room but it just didn't have the same effect. The suite felt too big, too spacious. Too lonely.

This was why she had never stayed anywhere like this. This was a suite made for two. For lovers. From the massive bed to the double tub, the twin sun loungers to the sumptuous robes, it was a place heavy with romantic possibilities.

Polly walked over to the window and out onto the balcony, looking at the Eiffel Tower more like a set from a film than an actual view. What would it be like to be here with someone else? Sipping champagne—or, for her, right now, some kind of fruit cordial—and watching the city below?

What would it be like to stay here with Gabe?

Polly tried to push the thought away but it stuck there,

persistent. She had shared so much with him the last few weeks. If only she could share this too. Had she tried hard enough to get through to him? After all, she had pretty much told him that she was giving up and putting the baby first.

Had that been the right thing to do? It had certainly been the sensible thing, the logical thing.

But should she have fought harder?

Her hands clenched. In her desperation to prove that she wasn't her mother, had she thrown away her only chance at happiness?

A soft knock at the door pulled her out of her introspection and she gave the view one last, longing look. It was time to work.

She should have the meeting and then, maybe, she would think again. Make a final decision. Stick with it this time. She couldn't keep second-guessing her choices.

She didn't usually. Maybe this was a sign that she had got it wrong…

Another knock, a little louder this time.

'Yes, I'm coming…' If only she could remember his name!

She was going to have to wing it. Polly walked over to the darkly panelled door and opened it, words of apologetic welcome on her lips.

Only to falter back as she clocked the tall, dark-haired man on the threshold.

'Gabe? Are you in this meeting as well? Thank goodness. I am woefully ill prepared. I can't even remember the developer's name. Although I *will* deny it if you quote me on that.'

Gabe didn't say anything and she continued, the words tumbling out. 'Do you have any idea why he has arranged to meet us in such an odd place? Although it is completely beautiful. You should see it, it's like a slice of heaven. With macaroons *and* views.'

Okay, she was definitely gabbling.

But better gabbling than grabbing him by his lapels and dragging him in close. Better gabbling than flinging her arms around his neck and pressing her lips to his.

But, oh! How she wanted to. Especially now.

Her eyes took him in greedily. It was unfair. No man should look so good. It wasn't as if he were dressed any differently from his usual smart-casual style. Perfectly cut grey trousers, white linen shirt open at the neck, hair falling over his forehead, heavy stubble shadowing his sharply cut jaw. Standard Gabe.

Utterly irresistible.

How could she walk away?

She couldn't. She wouldn't.

She would try again, fight harder. Both she and the baby needed her to fight. Needed Gabe in their lives.

She stood aside as he strolled into the room. *'Bonjour*, Polly.'

She was going to make him see. If she could only figure out how.

She was biting her lip, looking thoroughly confused. It was kind of adorable seeing Polly off-kilter.

'I spent the last two years here in Paris,' he said, walking over to the window and looking out at the spectacular view.

It was like seeing the city for the first time, seeing it through her eyes. Golden, exciting, full of possibilities.

'I know, you were working at Desmoulins.'

'I had an apartment not far from here. I got up, jogged to work, worked, ate out, met friends, worked out. All in Paris.'

He took a step out onto the balcony and breathed in the city air. Car fumes, cooking smells, the river. It had always choked him before but today it was welcome. Felt fresher somehow.

Polly stood in the room for a moment and then came out to join him, looking around her in awe. 'It's even more beautiful than I thought it would be. It must have been hard to leave.'

Gabe shrugged. 'Not really. It was just a place. A place to climb up the ladder a little further. It didn't mean more to me than New York or San Francisco.'

'Oh.'

'I was hoping that if I came back to Paris with you, if I walked the streets with you, then that might change.'

'I was hoping it would become magical.'

The words hung there. Anxiously Gabe scanned her face but he couldn't read her expression.

'I don't understand,' she said finally. 'Is this a test? If I don't feel the pea through twenty mattresses I'm not a princess and we're not worth fighting for? Is that what you mean?'

'*Non.*' She hadn't understood. His heart speeded up; he could feel it thumping through his chest. 'Polly, you told me to go and like a coward, like a fool, I went.'

He grimaced. 'I told myself it was for the best, that I was doing it for you. But I don't think it can be for the best. I don't think anyone can feel the way I feel about you, love you the way I love you, and not be with you.'

He'd said it. Surely the sun should burn a little brighter, the birds sing louder. Some acknowledgement somewhere that he had finally cracked open his shell.

'I don't understand.' She turned to him, eyes huge and clouded with an emotion he couldn't identify. 'What about the meeting?'

Damn the meeting. What about his words? He'd rushed in, confused her. 'It's not until Monday. I asked Rachel to get you here early so we could have the weekend. The weekend for you to try and see the magic, see if I'm worthy.' He swallowed. Had he misjudged so badly?

'If you want to, that is. Your ticket will let you return today if you would rather, or you can have the room on your own. It's paid for, it's yours...'

He paused, waiting, heart thudding as the seconds passed.

Her voice was small. 'You arranged all this?'

'*Oui*. For you. Although,' he added fairly, 'Rachel helped.'

Her mouth turned up. A smile. It was like a medal awarding him hope. 'I had no idea. I guess she can be discreet after all.'

'I tried to plan it all. I looked up all the romantic things to do in Paris but they all seem to involve champagne or cocktails, which is no fun for you. And I thought, if we need a list to find the magic then something is wrong. So I tried again.'

'You did?' She took a step closer, the tilt on her mouth more pronounced, a gleam of hope in her eyes.

'I thought, what would Polly like? And I knew.' At least, he hoped he knew. 'Old Paris. Shopping at all the best vintage and antique shops, strolling around Montmartre paying our respects to the artists of the past. The Catacombs.'

It wasn't too exhaustive an itinerary, not for three days. Organised enough for Polly to have a sense of purpose, fluid enough for some spontaneity.

Her mouth trembled. 'What if there isn't any?'

'Any what?'

Her eyes closed briefly, the long lashes sweeping down. 'Any magic?'

Gabe's heart thudded, audibly, painfully. 'Polly,' he said, taking her hands in his. 'For me there is magic wherever you are. I don't need a walk around old streets to prove that. I can't wait to show Paris to you, can't wait to see you buy out the vintage shops or discover a new café with you, but I don't need to do these things. I just want to do them for you. With you.'

Her hands folded around his. 'Really?' she whispered. 'What about next week, next month, next year?'

He tightened his hold, drawing a caressing finger along her hands. 'I can't tell you I'm not afraid,' he said honestly. 'Your life is changing so quickly and if we do this, mine will too. I didn't want to cause my parents more pain. The thought of putting you through that…' He inhaled, a deep painful breath.

'I got given my life back but somewhere along the way I forgot to live it. It was easier not to care. I thought I was in control. I set goals. I worked, I ran, I didn't stop. The more I worked, the harder I pushed my body, the less I had to think. I thought I had found a way to conquer my demons, a way to take charge, but I was hiding. And then you came along and ripped my hiding place to shreds.'

'I'm sorry.' Tears were trembling on her lashes and he released one of her hands to capture the sparkling drop.

'Don't be. I've been more alive the last few weeks than I was in the last ten years. I worked away this week,' he confessed. 'Stayed at the vineyard, spent time with my parents.' He smiled at her. 'Trying to get my number one spot back with Jean. You're right, of course, there's a lot I can help them with even in England. Advice, contracts, that kind of thing.'

'I'm glad. They're so lovely.'

'That's funny, they say the same about you. I have to

admit there's a bit of me that thinks you'll agree just to spend more time with my parents.'

'Agree to what?'

'To marry me.'

Polly blinked. Had she heard him right? 'To what?'

Gabe squeezed her hands tighter. It was almost painful but she was glad of the contact. It was proof that she was actually here, on a balcony in Paris, being proposed to.

'I should be on one knee…'

'No,' she said quickly. 'Just say it again.'

'I don't have a ring. I hoped we might include some jewellers on our antique trail, find something vintage. Sapphires, like your eyes. I was going to wait till then but I can't,' he confessed, the dark eyes so full of love it almost hurt to keep looking into them. 'Polly Rafferty, *je t'aime*. And if you would do me the honour of letting me in, of being my wife, then I promise I will always love you. And the baby. I'll be the best husband, the best father I can be. I want to start living again, Polly. I want to start living with you by my side.'

Polly struggled to find the right words. She couldn't. She had no idea what to say. 'And Mr Simpkins?'

'He has always had my heart,' he assured her, his face lightening with hope, with love. 'Mr Simpkins, Rafferty's, Hopeford. Everything you love, I love too. And I hope you feel the same way about my home, my family. My heart belongs to you.'

'And you have mine.' It wasn't so hard to say the words after all. 'I know the future is utterly terrifying. But with you by my side I can face it, whatever it holds.'

Gabe let go of her hands, reaching up to cup her face, pushing her hair back, his hands tangling themselves in its lengths. 'Are you sure?'

Polly slipped her hands around his waist, pulled him in closer. 'I've never been surer of anything. I love you too, Gabe. I think I loved you from that very first day. I had never met anyone so infuriating, so annoying, so challenging.' She smiled up at him. 'Anyone I fancied more.'

'I thought you were going to slap my face.'

'The accidental kiss? I think it was meant to be.' She stood on her tiptoes and found his mouth at last, cool and firm and sure. 'I think we were meant to be. I think it was magic.'

EPILOGUE

POLLY DIDN'T THINK Rafferty's had ever looked more beautiful. Her talented window dressers had moved some of the make-up counters and beauty areas back, draping the rest in purple and cream fabric, and suspended huge intricate paper sculptures in the same colours from the ceiling. Upstairs, she knew the tearooms were decorated in similar colours ready to welcome her wedding guests.

A stage dominated the middle of the floor, right under the point of the iconic dome. Cream vases, the size of a small child, were filled with silver branches creating an ethereal woodland effect.

The chairs were set in a wide semi-circle around the stage, each row flanked with a massive altar candle, the flames casting a dancing light over the room, discreetly backed up with the store's lowlights.

They were usually open until nine in the evening on a Saturday but today, for her wedding, Rafferty's had done something even the Blitz had never forced them to do.

They had closed early.

Most of the seats were already filled. Suited men and elegantly dressed women in a bright assortment of colours whispered and snapped pictures of the fairy-tale scene. There were several overexcited children fidgeting beside their parents, tugging at their best clothes, and Polly breathed a sigh of relief knowing she had a room put aside for them, complete with films, toys and paid babysitters to watch over the younger guests.

Peeking over the balcony, Polly spotted her grandparents, regal in the front row, entertaining Monsieur and Madame Beaufils. Her heart gave a little squeeze of joy, her family. All together.

'Are you ready?' Clara touched her shoulder softly.

Polly shivered. 'I think so. I didn't expect to be nervous but now that we're here I'm beginning to wish that we'd run away and got married in secret.'

Clara laughed. 'Summer would never have forgiven you. This is her moment of glory. I wouldn't have forgiven you either and nor would Hope. It's not every three-month-old who gets to be a bridesmaid.' She dropped a kiss on her niece's's fuzzy head.

'She looks gorgeous,' Polly agreed, beaming at her small baby who was trying her best to eat the silk sleeve of her cream dress.

'Best dressed girl in the room.'

'For now.' Polly eyed her daughter darkly. 'I have three changes with me. I'm not sure that will be enough.'

'It's a good thing there's a whole baby department just one level up.'

'Clara…' Polly pulled at her skirt, her fingers nervous. '…will I do?'

The other woman smiled. 'You're beautiful,' she said.

Polly inhaled, a long deep breath. Her dress was simple, an ankle-length cream sheath, her loose hair held off her face with a beaded band. It was an utterly simple yet perfectly elegant outfit; a Rafferty's original, copied from one of the old designs Polly had found in the archives.

Clara smoothed down her own purple dress, a loose design that skimmed over her stomach, flattering the bump. There would be less than six months between the cousins and Polly couldn't wait to meet Raff's child. The smaller bridesmaids, Summer and Hope, were looking uncommonly neat and tidy in cream. For now. The chances of them ending the evening in their current outfits were pretty slim. Especially Hope, who was currently averaging four changes a day.

'I don't know.' Polly watched as Hope fiddled with the delicate platinum bangle she had given Clara as a bridesmaid gift. 'You were a pretty gorgeous bride.'

'I was marrying Raff,' Clara said simply, her green eyes glowing with love. 'I would have been happy with a sack and a takeaway.'

Polly grinned, she knew full well that Clara had adored every moment of her winter wedding to Raff. She would have preferred something smaller herself but Gabe wanted the world to see them become a family.

And she could deny him nothing.

They had started adoption proceedings as soon as they could but Gabe couldn't have adored Hope more if he had fathered her, and, Polly thought loyally, he had in every way that mattered—from holding Polly's hand through the long, arduous labour to night feeds and nappy changes.

The assembled guests had been talking quietly but when two tall men made their way to the front the murmuring ceased and heads craned to get a better look at the groom and his best man.

Dressed in identical morning suits, the two men couldn't have looked more different. Although they were of a similar height Raff was built on broad lines, his hair as blond as Polly's own, his brand of good looks deceptively boyish. Gabe was leaner, darker with a more dangerously attractive demeanour.

'They're there,' she told her friend shivering with anticipation as her grandfather climbed the sweeping stairs to join them, pride beaming in his face as he readied himself to escort his granddaughter down the makeshift aisle.

Polly gripped Clara's hand tightly and then took a deep breath, turning to greet her grandfather father with a kiss. She was ready.

Clara was poised, ready to go first, Hope in her arm, then Summer would follow on. Waiting out front, sprinkled throughout the congregation was her grandmother, her parents-in-law to be and all three of Gabe's sisters with assorted husbands and children. Waiting for her at the bottom of the aisle was her brother, tugging at his cravat.

And Gabe. Her fiancé, father of her child. His eyes were fixed on hers, a small, private smile just for her on those well-cut lips.

This time last year she had had no one. Now she was just ten minutes and a few words away from a huge, extended, noisy, chaotic, loving family. A challenging, questioning, adoring, supportive husband. She had a daughter, dependent on her for everything.

There was a time all this would have terrified her. But now?

Polly smiled back at Gabe. 'I love you,' she mouthed.

His sensual mouth curved. *Je t'aime,'* he mouthed back.

Polly Rafferty was completely and utterly happy.

* * * * *

BEST FRIEND TO
WIFE AND MOTHER?

CAROLINE ANDERSON

Huge thanks to Caroline and Adam, and Bryony and Owen, who inadvertently gave me wonderful wedding inspiration, and to Shirley and Roger, Mike and Trice, who invited us to share those days with them.

I love you all.

CHAPTER ONE

'ARE YOU READY?'

He eased a flyaway strand of hair from the corner of her eye, his touch as light as a butterfly's wing, his fingertips lingering for a moment as their eyes met and held. His voice, as familiar to her as her own, was steady and reassuring, but his words didn't reassure her. They sent her mind into free-fall.

They were such simple words, on the surface, but layered beneath were a million unasked and unanswered questions. Questions Leo probably didn't even know he'd asked her. Questions she'd needed to ask herself for months but somehow hadn't got round to.

Was she ready?

For the wedding, yes. The planning had been meticulous, nothing left to chance. Her mother, quietly and efficiently, had seen to that. But the marriage—the *lifetime*—with Nick?

Mingling with the birdsong and the voices of the people clustered outside the church gates were the familiar strains of the organ music.

The overture for her wedding.

No. Her *marriage*. Subtle difference, but hugely significant.

Amy glanced through the doorway of the church and caught the smiles on the row of faces in the back pew, all of them craning their necks to get a better look at her. The

villagers at the gate were mostly there for Leo, hoping to
catch a glimpse of their favourite son, but these people
in the church—her friends, Nick's—were here to see her
marry Nick.

Today.

Right now.

Her heart skittered under the fitted bodice that suddenly
seemed so tight she could hardly breathe.

I can't do this—!

No choice. Too late now for cold feet. If she'd been
going to change her mind she should have done it ages
ago, before the wheels of this massive train that was her
wedding had been set in motion. Or later, at a push—but
not now, so late it was about to hit the buffers.

The church was full, the food cooked, the champagne
on ice. And Nick would be standing at the altar, waiting
for her.

Dear, kind, lovely Nick, who'd been there for her when
her life had been in chaos, who'd just—been there, for the
last three years, her friend and companion and cheerleader.
Her lover. And she did love him. She did…

*Enough to marry him? Till death us do part, and all
that? Or is it just the easiest thing to do?*

You can *stop this,* the voice whispered in her head. *It's
not too late.*

But it was. Way too late. She was marrying Nick.

Today.

A curious calm settled over her, as if a switch had been
flicked, turning on the autopilot, steadying her fall into
oblivion. The voice in her head didn't care.

*Just because it's easy, because you know he'll be a
good husband and father and he's safe? Is that enough?*

Of course it was enough. It was just nerves unsettling
her. That was all. Last-minute nerves. Nick was—fine.

Fine? Like safe, steady, reliable, predictable—that kind

*of fine? No chemistry, no fireworks? And whatever hap-
pened to amazing?*

She tuned the voice out. There were more important
things than amazing. Trust, fidelity, respect—and chemistry was overrated—

How do you know that? You don't *know that. You
haven't got a clue, you've never felt it. And if you marry
Nick, you never will...*

She stifled the voice again, stuffing it firmly back in
its box; then, easing her death grip on the bouquet, she
straightened her shoulders, tilted up her chin and gave Leo
her most convincing and dazzling smile.

'Yes,' she said firmly. 'I'm ready.'

Leo felt his breath catch at that smile.

When had she grown up? Turned into this stunningly
lovely woman, instead of the slightly chubby, relentlessly
accident-prone girl who'd dogged his footsteps for ever?
He'd turned his back for what felt like five minutes, and
she'd been transformed.

More like five years, though, give or take, and a lot of
water under the bridge for both of them. Far too much, in
his case, and so much of it tainted by regret.

He cradled her pale cheek in his hand, and felt her
quiver. She was nervous. Of course she was. Who wouldn't
be, on their wedding day? It was a hell of a commitment.
Literally, in his case.

'You look beautiful, Amy,' he said gruffly, looking
down into the wide grey eyes of this lovely young woman
he'd known so well but now hardly knew at all. 'He's a
lucky man.'

'Thank you.'

Her eyes searched his, a flicker of uncertainty in them
echoing the tiny tremor in her cheek, the smile on her lush,
pink lips a little hesitant now, and he felt himself frown.

Second thoughts? About time. There was nothing wrong with the man she was marrying, from what little he'd seen of him—in fact, he'd liked him, a lot—but they just didn't seem *right* for each other.

There was no chemistry between them, no zing that he could see. Maybe she didn't want that? Maybe she just wanted safe and comfortable? And maybe that was a really, really good idea.

Or maybe not, not for Amy…

He hesitated another second, then took her hand in his, his thumb slowly stroking the back of it in a subconscious gesture of comfort. Her fingers were cold, trembling slightly in his, reinforcing his concern. He squeezed them gently.

'Amy, I'm going to ask you something. It's only what your father would have done, so please don't take it the wrong way, but—are you sure you want to do this? Because if not, you can still turn around and walk away. It's your life, no one else's, and nobody else can decide this for you.'

His voice dropped, his frown deepening as he struggled to get the importance of this across to her before it was too late. If only someone had done this for him…

'Don't do it unless it's right, Amy, unless you really, truly love him. Take it from me, marrying the wrong person for the wrong reasons is a recipe for disaster. You have to be absolutely, completely and utterly sure that it's the right thing to do and for the right reasons.'

A shadow flitted across her eyes, her fingers tightening on his, and after an infinitesimal pause that seemed to last an eternity, she nodded. 'Yes. Yes, of course I'm sure.'

But she didn't look sure, and he certainly wasn't, but it was nothing to do with him, was it? Not his decision to make. And the shadows in her eyes could just as easily be sadness because her much-loved father wasn't here to give her away. Nothing to do with her choice of groom...

Not your business who she chooses to love. God knows, you're no expert. And he could be a lot, lot worse.

He hauled in a breath.

'OK. Ready to go, then?'

She nodded, but he saw her swallow again, and for a moment he wondered if she'd changed her mind.

And then she straightened up and took a breath, hooked her hand through his arm and flashed a smile over her shoulder at her bridesmaids. 'OK, girls? Good to go?'

They both nodded, and he felt her hand tighten on his arm.

'OK, then. Let's do this.' Her eyes flicked up and met Leo's, her fake smile pinned in place by sheer determination, but it didn't waver and anybody else might have been convinced.

Not your business. He nodded to the usher, who nodded to the organist, and after a moment's silence, broken only by the shuffling of the congregation getting to their feet and the clearing of a few throats, the evocative strains of Pachelbel's *Canon in D Major* filled the church.

He laid his hand over hers, squeezed her fingers and felt them grip his. He glanced down, into those liquid grey eyes that seemed flooded with doubt despite the brave smile, and his gut clenched.

He'd known her for ever, rescued her from a million scrapes, both literal and otherwise; dammit, she was his best friend, or had been before the craziness that was his life had got in the way, and he couldn't bear to see her make the mistake of her life.

Don't do it, Amy. Please, don't do it!

'It's still not too late,' he said gruffly, his voice muted, his head tilted towards her so only she could hear.

'Yes, it is,' she said, so softly he barely heard her, then

she dredged up that expected smile again and took the
first step forward.

Damn.

He swallowed the lump in his throat and slowly, steadily,
walked her down the aisle.

With every step, her legs felt heavier and more reluctant,
her heart pounding, the sense of unease settling closer
around her, chilling her to the bone.

What are you doing?

Nick was there, watching her thoughtfully. Warily?

It's still not too late.

She felt Leo ease his arm out from under her hand and
step away, and she felt—abandoned?

It was her wedding day. She should feel a sense of joy,
of completeness, of utter, bone-deep rightness—but she
didn't.

Not at all.

And, as she glanced up at Nick, she realised that neither
did he. Either that, or he was paralysed by nerves, which
was unlikely. He wasn't remotely the nervous type.

He took her hand briefly, squeezed it in reassurance,
but it felt wrong. So wrong...

She eased it away, using the excuse of handing her bouquet to the waiting bridesmaid, and then the vicar spoke,
everyone started to sing 'Jerusalem', and she felt her mouth
move automatically while her mind whirled. *Her mind*, this
time, not the voice in her head giving her grief, or a moment of panic, stage fright, last-minute nerves or whatever.
This time it was really her, finally asking all the questions
Leo's 'Are you ready?' had prompted.

What are we doing? *And why? Who for?*

The last echoes of the hymn filtered away, and the
vicar did the just cause or impediment bit. *Was* there a
just cause? Was not loving him enough sufficient? And

then she saw the vicar's lips move as he began to speak the words of the marriage service, drowned out by her thudding heart and the whirlwind in her head.

Until he said, 'Who gives this woman to be married to this man?' and Leo stepped forward, took her hand with a tiny, barely perceptible squeeze, and gave it—gave her—to Nick.

Dear Nick. Lovely, kind, dependable Nick, ready to make her his wife, give her the babies they both longed for, grow old with her...

But Nick hesitated. When the vicar asked if he would take this woman to be his wife, he hesitated. And then— was that a shrug?—his mouth twisted in a wry smile and he said, 'I will.'

The vicar turned, spoke to her, but she wasn't really listening any more. She was staring into Nick's eyes, searching them for the truth, and all she could see was duty.

Duty from him, and duty from her? Because they'd come this far before either of them had realised it was bound to be—what were Leo's words?—a disaster?

She gripped his hands. 'Will you? Will you *really*?' she asked under her breath. 'Because I'm not sure I can.'

Behind her she heard the slight suck of Leo's indrawn breath, the rustle from the congregation, the whispered undertone of someone asking what she'd said.

And then Nick smiled—the first time he'd really smiled at her in weeks, she realised—and put his arms around her, and hugged her against his broad, solid chest. It shook with what could have been a huff of laughter, and he squeezed her tight.

His breath brushed her cheek, his words soft in her ear. 'You cut that a bit fine, my love.'

She felt the tension flow out of her like air out of a punctured balloon, and if he hadn't been holding her she would have crumpled.

'I did, didn't I? I'm sorry, Nick, but I just can't do this,' she murmured.

'I know; it doesn't feel right, does it? I thought it would, but…it just doesn't. And better now than later.' She felt his arms slacken as he raised his head and looked over her shoulder.

'Time to go, sweetheart,' he murmured, his mouth tugging into a wistful smile. 'Leo's waiting for you. He'll make sure you're all right.' He kissed her gently on the cheek and stepped back, his smile a little unsteady now. 'Be happy, Amy.'

She searched his eyes, and saw regret and relief, and her eyes welled with tears. 'You, too,' she said silently, and took a step back, then another one, and collided with Leo's solid warmth.

His hands cupped her elbows, supporting her as everything slowly righted itself. She turned to him, met those steady golden eyes and whispered, 'Thank you.'

And then she picked up her skirts and ran.

She'd done it. She'd actually done it. Walked—no, sprinted, or as close to it as she could in those ridiculous shoes—away from disaster.

Leo watched her go, her mother and bridesmaids hurrying after her, watched Nick turn to his best man and sit down on the pew behind him as if his strings had been cut, and realised it was all down to him. Appropriate, really, since in a way he was the cause of it.

He hauled in a deep breath, turned to the stunned congregation and gave them his best media smile.

'Ladies and gentlemen, it seems there isn't going to be a wedding today after all. I'm not sure of the protocol for this kind of thing, but there's food ready and waiting for you in the marquee, and any of you who'd like to come back and enjoy it will be more than welcome to do so before you head off. I gather the chef comes highly recommended,' he added drily, and there was a ripple of laughter that broke the tension.

He nodded to his father, who nodded back, pulling his mobile phone out of his pocket to set the ball rolling with their catering team, and with a brief nod to the vicar, Leo strode swiftly down the aisle and out of the church after Amy.

The sun warmed him, the gentle rays bringing the life back into his limbs, and he realised he'd been stone cold at the prospect of watching her make a disastrous mistake. He flexed his fingers as he walked over to the vintage Bentley and peered inside.

She was in there, perched on the seat in a billowing cloud of tulle and lace, surrounded by her mother and bridesmaids all clucking like mother hens, and the villagers gathered around the gate were agog. As well they might be.

He ducked his head inside the car.

'Amy?' he murmured, and she stared blankly up at him. She looked lost, shocked and confused and just a little crazy, and he could read the desperate appeal in her eyes.

'Take her home, I'll follow,' he instructed the driver tersely, and as the car whisked her away one of the crowd at the gate yelled, 'What's going on, Leo?'

He didn't answer. They could see what was going on, they just didn't know why, and he had better things to do than stand around and tittle-tattle. He turned to scan the throng of puzzled guests spilling out of the church, milling aimlessly around, unsure of what to do next, and in the midst of them he found his parents heading towards him.

'Is she all right?' his mother asked worriedly, and he nodded.

'I think so. She will be. Let's get out of here. We've got things to do.'

* * *

She'd done it.

Stopped the train and run away—from Nick, from the certainty of her carefully planned and mapped-out future, from everything that made up her life, and she felt lost. Cast adrift, swamped by a million conflicting emotions, unsure of what to do or think or feel.

Actually, she couldn't feel anything much. Just numbness, a sort of strange hollowness deep in her chest as if there was nothing there any more.

Better than the ice-cold dread of doing the wrong thing, but not much.

She tugged off her veil, handing it to her bridesmaids. If she could she would have taken the dress off, too, there and then. She couldn't get out of it fast enough. Couldn't get out of all of it fast enough, the church, the dress, the car—the country?

She almost laughed, but the hysteria bubbling in her throat threatened to turn to tears so she clamped her teeth shut and crushed it ruthlessly down. Not now. Not yet.

'Are you all right, darling?' Her mother's face was troubled but calm, and Amy heaved a shaky sigh of relief. At least she wasn't going off the deep end. Not that her mother was a deep-end kind of person, but you never knew. And her daughter hadn't ever jilted anyone at the altar before, so the situation wasn't exactly tried and tested.

'Yes, I'm fine. I'm really sorry, Mum.'

'Don't be. It's the first sensible thing you've done for months.'

Amy stared at her, astonished. 'I thought you liked him?'

'I do like him! He's lovely. I just don't think he's right for you. You don't have that spark.'

Not her, too, joining in with her alter ego and reminding her she'd been about to do the wrong thing for the wrong reasons and should have pulled out much, much earlier.

Or he should. Both of them, for everyone's sake. Oh, what a mess!

The car door opened, and she realised they'd come to rest on the drive. Gathering up her skirts, she climbed awkwardly out and headed for the front door. Her mother unlocked it and pushed it open and Amy was swept inside on the tide of her redundant bridesmaids, into the hallway of the house she'd left such a short time before as a bride on the brink of a nice, safe, sensible marriage. Now she was—she didn't know what she was.

A runaway bride?

Such a cliché. She gave a smothered laugh and shook her head.

'I need to get out of this dress,' she muttered, kicking off her shoes and heading for the stairs and the sanctuary of her bedroom.

'I'll come,' her mother said, and they all fell in behind her, threatening to suffocate her with kindness.

She paused on the third stair and turned back. 'No, Mum. Actually, none of you. I think I'd like to be alone for a moment.'

They ground to a halt, three pairs of worried eyes studying her. Checking to see if she'd lost her marbles, probably. Wrong. She'd just found them, at the absolutely last minute. *Oh, Nick, I'm sorry...*

'Are you sure you're all right?' her mother asked, her face creased with concern.

'Yes,' she said, more firmly this time. 'Yes, I'm sure.' Sure about everything except what her future held. 'Don't worry, I'm not going to do anything stupid.' Or at least, nothing as stupid as marrying the wrong man would have been. Not that she knew who the right one was, or how she'd recognise him. She seemed to have a gift for getting it wrong.

They were all still standing there as if they didn't know

what to do now their carefully planned schedule had been thrown out the window, but it was no good asking her. She didn't have a clue. She turned back to the stairs, putting one foot in front of the other, skirts bunched in her quivering hands.

'Shall I bring you up a cup of tea?' her mother asked, breaking the silence.

Tea. Of course. The universal panacea. And it would give her mother something to do. 'That would be lovely, Mum. Whenever you're ready. Don't rush.'

'I'll put the kettle on.'

Her mother disappeared into the kitchen, the bridesmaids trailing in her wake as one after the other they came out of their trances, and she made it to the safety of her bedroom and shut the door before the bubble burst and the first tears fell.

Odd, that she was crying when she felt so little. It was just a release of tension, but without the tension there was nothing, just a yawning chasm opening up in front of her, and she thought she was going to fall apart. Pressing her hand to her mouth to stifle the sobs, she slid down the door, crumpling to the floor in a billowing cloud of lace and petticoats, and let the floodgates open.

He had to get to her.

He could only imagine what state she was in, but that look in her eyes when she'd glanced up in the car—

He pulled up on the driveway of his family home, and after checking that the baby was all right and the catering was under control he headed through the gate in the fence into Amy's garden and tapped on the kitchen door.

Amy's mother let him in, her face troubled. 'Oh, Leo, I'm so glad you're here,' she said, and hugged him briefly, her composure wobbling for a second.

'How is she?' he asked.

'I don't know. She's gone upstairs. She wouldn't let us go—said she needed to be alone. I've made her a cup of tea, I was just about to take it up.'

'Give it to me. I'll go and talk to her. This is my fault.'

'Your fault?'

He gave her a wry smile. 'I asked her if she was sure.'

Jill smiled back at him and kissed his cheek. 'Well, thank God you did, Leo. I haven't had the guts. Here, take it. And get her out of here, can you? She doesn't need all this hoopla.'

He nodded, took the tea and headed for the stairs. Her bedroom was over the kitchen, with a perfect view of the marquee on his parents' lawn and the steady stream of guests who were arriving for the wedding reception that wasn't.

Damn.

He crossed the landing and tapped on her bedroom door.

Someone was knocking.

Her mother, probably. She dropped her head back against the door and sucked in a breath. She wasn't ready to face her. Wasn't ready to face anyone—

'Amy? Can I come in?'

Leo. Her mother must have sent him up. She heard the knob turn, could feel the door gently pushing her in the back, but she couldn't move. Didn't want to move. She wanted to stay there for ever, hiding from everyone, until she'd worked out what had happened and what she was going to do with the rest of her life.

His voice came through the door again, low and gentle. 'Amy? Let me in, sweetheart. I've got a cup of tea for you.'

It was the tea that made her move. That, and the reassuring normality of his voice. She shuffled over, hauling her voluminous skirts with her, and he pushed the door gently inwards until he could squeeze past it and shut it behind him.

She sniffed hard, and she heard him tutting softly. He crouched down, his face coming into view, his eyes scanning the mess her face must be. She scrubbed her cheeks with her hands and he held out a wad of tissues.

He'd even come prepared, she thought, and the tears began again.

She heard the soft click of his tongue as he tutted again, the gentle touch of his hand on her hair. 'Oh, Amy.'

He put the tea down, sat on the floor next to her and hauled her into his arms. 'Come here, you silly thing. You'll be OK. It'll all work out in the end.'

'Will it? How? What am I going to do?' she mumbled into his shoulder, busily shredding the sodden tissues in her lap. 'I've given up my job, I'd already given up my flat—we were about to move out of his flat and buy a family house and have babies, and I was going to try going freelance with my photography, and now…I don't have a life any more, Leo. It's all gone, every part of it. I just walked away from it and I feel as if I've stepped off a cliff. I must be mad!'

Leo's heart contracted.

Poor Amy. She sounded utterly lost, and it tugged at something deep inside him, some part of him that had spent years protecting her from the fallout of her impulsive nature. He hugged her closer, rocking her gently against his chest. 'I don't think you're mad. I think it's the first sensible thing you've done in ages,' he told her gently, echoing her mother's words.

She shifted so she could see his face. 'How come everybody else knew this except me?' she said plaintively. 'Why am I so stupid?'

'You aren't stupid. He's a nice guy. He's just not the right man for you. If he was, you wouldn't have hesitated for a moment, and nor would he. And it didn't seem to me as if you'd broken his heart. Quite the opposite.'

'No.' There'd been nothing heartbroken, she thought, about the flash of relief in his eyes in that fleeting moment. Sadness, yes, but no heartbreak. 'I suppose he was just doing the decent thing.'

Leo's eyes clouded and he turned away. 'Yeah. Trust me, it doesn't work.'

'Was that what you did?' she asked him, momentarily distracted from her own self-induced catastrophe. 'The decent thing? When you married the wrong person for the wrong reasons?'

A muscle bunched in his jaw. 'Something like that. Are you going to drink this tea or not?'

She took the mug that he was holding out to her, cradled it in both hands and sighed shakily.

'You OK now?'

She nodded. She was, she realised. Just about, so long as she didn't have to make any more decisions, because clearly she was unqualified in that department. She sipped her tea, lifted her head and rested it back against the wall with another shaky little sigh. 'I will be. I don't know; I just feel—I can't explain—as if I can't trust myself any more. I don't know who I am, and I thought I knew. Does that make sense, Leo?'

'Absolutely. Been there, done that, worn out the T-shirt.'

She turned to him, searching his face and finding only kindness and concern. No reproach. No disappointment in her. Just Leo, doing what he always did, getting her out of the mess she'd got herself into.

Again.

'Leo, will you get me out of here?' she asked unevenly. 'I can't stay here, not with all this…'

'Of course I will. That's what I'm here for.'

'To rescue me? Poor you. I bet you thought you were done with all that at last.'

'What, me? Change the habits of a lifetime?' he teased, and she had to laugh, even though it wasn't really remotely funny.

She glanced down at herself, then at him. He'd abandoned the tailcoat, loosened the rose-pink cravat which showed off his olive skin to perfection, and turned back the cuffs on his immaculate white shirt to reveal strong wrists above hands criss-crossed with fine white scars. Chef's hands, he called them, but the scars didn't detract from his appeal, not in any way. He'd been fighting girls off with a stick since he'd hit puberty, and the scars hadn't put them off at all.

She managed a small smile. 'We might have to change first, before we go.'

His lips quirked. 'You think? I thought I looked rather good like this.'

So did she, but then she thought he looked good in anything.

'You do, but if the press catch a glimpse of us, they'll think the nation's favourite celebrity chef's secretly tied the knot again,' she said, her mouth on autopilot, and his face clouded.

'Yeah, well, it'll be a cold day in hell before that ever happens,' he said tightly, and she could have kicked herself for blundering all over such a sensitive area. She closed her eyes and let out an anguished sigh.

'Oh, God, Leo, I'm so sorry. I can't believe I said that—'

'It's OK, it doesn't matter, and you're quite right. I don't need that sort of publicity, and neither do you.' He smiled fleetingly, then looked away again. 'So, anywhere in particular you want to go?'

'I don't know. Got any ideas?'

He shrugged. 'Not really. My house is still crawling

with builders, and I have to fly to Tuscany tomorrow on business.'

'Oh.' Her heart sank at the thought of him going, and she felt her smile slip. 'I don't suppose you want to smuggle me out there in your luggage?' she joked weakly, and propped up her wavering smile. 'I promise not to be a nuisance.'

'How many times have I heard you say that?' he murmured drily, and she felt a wash of guilt flood over her.

He was right—she was always imposing on him, getting him to extract her from one mess or another. Or she had done, back in the days when they really had been best friends. And that was years ago.

She forced herself to ease away from him, to stop leaning on him, both metaphorically and physically. Time to get out her big girl pants and put their friendship on a more equal and adult footing.

She scraped up the last smile in the bottom of the bucket and plastered it on her face.

'I'm sorry, I was only joking. I know you can't. Don't worry about me, Leo, I'll be all right. It's my mess, I'll clear it up.'

Somehow...

CHAPTER TWO

HE COULDN'T DO IT.

He couldn't desert her when her life had just turned upside down—and anyway, it might well be the perfect solution for both of them.

He'd been worrying about leaving tomorrow and abandoning her with the repercussions of all this, worrying about how he was going to juggle his tiny daughter and business meetings, and here was the answer, on a plate. Unless...

He studied her thoughtfully, searching her face for clues. '*Were* you joking about coming with me? Because if not, it could be a great idea. Not the smuggling, obviously, but if you did it could solve both our problems.'

A tiny frown appeared. 'You've got a problem?'

He nodded. 'Sort of. I've got meetings to go to, and business and babies don't mix. Normally I'd leave Ella behind with my parents, but this is going to be for several days and it's not fair on them at their age, especially on top of the wedding—and don't say it,' he added, pressing a finger lightly on her lips to stifle the apology he knew was coming.

She took hold of his hand and moved it away. 'Why not, since it's true? It *is* my fault, and they've gone to so much trouble—'

He pulled his hand back and placed it firmly over her mouth to silence her before she got back onto that again.

'I don't want to argue, Amy. Hear me out. Please?'

She nodded, and he lowered his hand and carried on. 'I like to be there for Ella every day, even if it's only for part of it, even if it means dragging her around with me. It's the only way I've been able to look after her and my business, and it's a precarious balance that so far seems to be working. I don't want to upset that balance, abandon her for days and nights on end—and anyway, shortly after I get back I start filming the next TV series for eight weeks or so, and I'm going to need my parents' goodwill for that. If you would come to Italy with us and look after her just while I'm in the meetings, it would be amazingly helpful.'

Amy eyed him thoughtfully. 'Really? You mean it? I *was* only joking, really. I didn't expect you to say yes. I was just trying to—I don't know. Make light of it, really. I don't want to be a burden to you.'

'Absolutely I mean it, and you wouldn't be a burden. Not at all. You'd be a real help. I'm trying to set up a contract with a family there to supply our restaurants. I tasted some of their products at a trade fair, and I was really impressed. I want to see how they operate, taste the whole range, negotiate the price and see if we can strike a deal. And doing all that with Ella on my hip *really* won't work.'

She laughed a little wryly. 'No, I can see that. Not exactly professional, and not really fair on her, either.'

'No, it isn't, and she's my top priority. If necessary, I'd cut the trip short rather than compromise my relationship with her, but I don't want to have to do that, because this is a really great business opportunity and it could be important for her future as well as mine.

'So—will you come? You'll have lots of free time to take photos, and it's beautiful at this time of year. You can chill out away from all this, get some thinking time, clear your head, work out what you're going to do next.

Maybe work on a portfolio of images, if that's where you think you're going.'

It sounded tempting. Very tempting, and she could see that he quite genuinely needed her help. He wasn't just making it up—and anyway, even if he was, did she have a better choice? No. And to stay here another minute was unthinkable.

She could hear the sounds of people thronging outside in the garden—not their garden, but his parents' garden next door, where the marquee had been set up for the reception.

Her hand flew to her mouth, her eyes locked on his. 'Oh, Leo! All that food…!'

She was swamped with guilt, but he shook his head briskly, brushing it aside as if it was nothing. Which it wasn't, far from it.

'It's not wasted. There are lots of people there to eat it, it's fine.'

'Fine?' It wasn't fine. Nothing was fine, and all of a sudden she was overwhelmed again. 'It was supposed to be a *wedding* present from you, and I didn't even *have* the wedding.'

'Oh, Amy,' he sighed, and pulled her head back down against his shoulder, soothing her as the tears spilled down her cheeks yet again and the enormity of what she'd done, the chaos she'd caused, the things she'd walked away from, gradually sank in and left her breathless with guilt and remorse.

'I can't even pay you back,' she choked out, but he tutted softly and cradled her head against that solid, familiar shoulder that felt so good she could have stayed there for ever.

'Hush. You don't need to. Forget it, Amy, it's the least important thing in the world right now. Don't worry about it.'

She pushed herself up, swiping the tears off her cheeks

with her palms. 'But I *am* worried about it! At least let me pay you back for it when I get a job.'

If she ever did. Publishing was in a state of flux, and she'd just walked away from a great career in a really good publishing house because she'd thought she'd have financial security with Nick and could afford to try freelancing with her photography, and now she had nothing! No job, no home, no husband, no future—and all because of some vague sense of unease? She must have been mad—

'OK, so here's the deal,' he said, cutting off her tumbling thoughts with a brisk, no-nonsense tone. 'Come to Tuscany with me. Look after Ella while I'm in meetings, so I can work all day with a clear conscience and still put her to bed every night, and we'll call it quits.'

'*Quits*? Are you *crazy*? I know what your outside catering costs, Leo!'

He gave her a wry grin. 'There's a substantial mark-up. The true cost is nothing like the tariff. And you know how precious my daughter is to me. Nothing could be more important than leaving her with someone I can trust while I'm over there.'

He gripped her hands, his eyes fixed on hers. 'Come with us, look after her while I'm in meetings, have a holiday, some time out while you work out what to do next. And take photos for me—pictures of me cooking, of the produce, the region, the markets—all of it. Your photos are brilliant, and I can use them for my blog. That would be really valuable to me, so much more professional, and certainly something I'd pay good money for. I usually do it myself and blag people into taking photos of me with chefs and market traders and artisans, and if I'm really stuck I get reduced to taking selfies, and that's *so* not a good look!'

She laughed, a funny little sound between a chuckle and a sob that she quickly stifled, and he hugged her again.

'Come on. Do this for me—please? It would be so help-ful I can't tell you, and it'll get you away from all this. You're exhausted and you need to get away, have a total change of scene. And I need you, Amy. I'm not making it up. Not for the photos, they're just a valuable added bonus, but for Ella, and I can't put a price on her safety and happiness.'

She searched his eyes again, and saw behind the reas-suringly calm exterior that he was telling her the truth. He wasn't just being kind to her, he really was in a jam, and he'd never ever asked her for help, although God knows he'd given her enough over the years, bailing her out of umpteen scrapes.

Not to mention the catering.

No. She had no choice—and she realised she didn't want a choice. She wanted to be with Leo. His sound common sense was exactly what she needed to get her through this, and let's face it, she thought, he's had enough practice at dealing with me and my appalling life choices.

She nodded. 'OK. I'll come—of course I'll come, and I'll help you with Ella and take photos and do whatever else I can while you're there. It'll be a pleasure to help you, and it's high time I gave you something back. On one condition, though.'

'Which is?' he asked warily.

'I help you with her care when the filming starts—take some of the burden off your parents. Then I'll call it quits.'

'That's a big commitment.'

'I know that, but that's the deal. Take it or leave it.'

His shoulders dropped, relief written all over him, and she felt some of the tension leave her, too.

'I'll take it. And thank you, Amy. Thank you so much.' His brow furrowed. 'Do you have a case packed ready to go?'

'Yes. I've got smart-casual, beach, jeans—will that do?'

He nodded and got to his feet. 'Sounds fine. I'll get Ella's stuff together and we'll go. I'm not sure, but we might even be able to fly out today.'

'Today!'

'Is that a problem?'

She shook her head vehemently. 'No. Not at all. The sooner the better. I was just surprised. I thought you said you were going tomorrow.'

'I was, but today would be better and I seem to be unexpectedly free now,' he added, that wry grin tugging at his mouth and making her want to hug him. 'I'll see what I can do. How soon can you be ready?'

She shrugged. 'Half an hour? Twenty minutes, maybe?'

'OK. I'll call if there's a problem. Don't forget your passport—and your camera.'

'In my bag. Just do one thing for me before you go. Get me out of this dress? I'd forgotten all the stupid buttons.'

She scrambled to her feet and turned her back to him, and he began undoing the million and one tiny satin buttons and loops that covered the zip underneath. And as he worked, button by button, he became suddenly, intensely aware of the smooth, creamy skin of her shoulders, the fine line of her neck, the slender column of her throat. He could see a pulse beating under the skin at the side, and feel the tension coming off her. Off him, too, but for an entirely different reason. Crazy. This was Amy, for goodness' sake! She was his childhood best friend, virtually his sister!

He finally freed the last button and slid the concealed zip down, and she caught the dress against her chest and turned to face him, a peep of cleavage above some transparent lacy undergarment taking him by surprise. He hauled his eyes up away from it, shocked by the sudden heat that flared through his body.

Really?

Amy?

He backed up a step. 'OK now?' he asked tersely, his throat tight.

'Yes. Thank you. I'll get changed and see you downstairs in a few minutes.'

'Good. Wear something comfortable for travelling.' Preferably something that covered her up. He backed away further, turning on his heel and reaching for the door handle, suddenly desperate to get out of there.

'Leo?'

Her voice checked him and he turned and looked at her over his shoulder, raising an eyebrow in question.

'I'm starving. Grab some food to take with us, would you?'

Food? He laughed, letting some of the tension go. Food was easy. Food he could do.

'Sure. See you in a bit.'

He called the catering manager on the way down the stairs, rang his mother to prime her and went into the kitchen.

Three pairs of eyes locked on him instantly. 'How is she?'

'She'll do. Jill, can you help her get ready? I'm taking her to Tuscany with me and we're leaving as soon as possible. I'm trying to get a flight this afternoon.'

'Tuscany? Brilliant, it's just what she needs.' She went up on tiptoe and kissed his cheek. 'Thank you, Leo. Bless you. She'll be ready.'

It was tight.

While he packed he rang the charter company he used from time to time, and found they had a small jet flying to Florence for a pick-up; he could hire the whole plane for the 'empty leg' rate, but it was leaving City Airport at three. And it was twelve forty already.

Tight, but doable, if she was ready to go. He rang to

warn her, loaded the car in no time flat and drove straight round there, reaching the front door as Amy opened it.

'I'm ready,' she said, her smile a little forced in her pale face, her eyes still red-rimmed, but there was life in them now, unlike the blank eyes of the woman he'd walked down the aisle less than an hour ago. Sure, she was hanging by a thread, but she'd make it, especially once he'd got her out of here, and he was suddenly fiercely glad that he'd managed to convince her to come with him.

'Got your passport?'

'Yes, I've got everything. What's the luggage limit?'

He smiled wryly. 'There isn't one. It's a private charter.'

Her jaw dropped slightly. 'Private—?'

He pushed her chin up gently with an index finger and smiled at her stunned expression. 'It's going on an empty leg to pick someone up—I'm only paying a fraction of the normal charge.' Which was still extortionate, but she didn't need to know that.

'Wow. Great. OK.' She turned to her mother, hugged her hard, hugged her bridesmaids and got in the car.

'Thank you, Leo,' Jill called, and he lifted a hand as he slid behind the wheel and closed the door.

'Did you get food?' Amy asked, and he leant over into the back and pulled out an insulated bag.

'Here. You can feed me en route.'

'Or I might just eat it all.'

'Piglet. Buckle up,' he instructed, but she was there already, her bottom lip caught between her teeth, the eyes that kept flicking to his filled with a welter of emotions that he couldn't begin to analyse. He didn't suppose she could, either, but there seemed to be a glimmer of something that could have been excitement.

He smiled at her, and she smiled back, but it was a fleeting parody of her usual open, happy smile, and he felt another sudden pang of guilt. What if it wasn't excitement?

What if it was hysteria? She was on a knife-edge, he knew that. Had he imposed his own feelings about marriage on her? Put doubts in her mind when they hadn't really been there at all? He hoped not—even if Nick hadn't been right for her, it wasn't his call to sabotage their wedding.

'You OK?'

She nodded. 'Yes—or I will be, just as soon as we get out of here.'

'Let's go, then,' he said, and starting the engine he pulled smoothly off the drive and headed for London.

Amy had never flown in such luxury.

From start to finish, boarding the little jet had been a breeze. They'd driven right up to the Jet Centre terminal, their luggage and the baby's car seat and buggy were handed over, and the car had been whisked away to secure parking. The security check-in was thorough but almost instant, and then they had a short walk to the plane.

At the top of the steps the pilot greeted them by name as he welcomed them aboard, gave them their ETA, a benign weather report and told them there was a car waiting for them at Florence. Then he disappeared through the galley area into the cockpit and closed the door, leaving them with the entire little jet to themselves, and for the first time she registered her surroundings.

'Wow.' She felt her jaw dropping slightly, and no wonder. It was like another world, a world she'd never entered before or even dreamed of.

There were no endless rows of seating, no central aisle barely wide enough to pass through, no hard-wearing gaudy seat fabric in a budget airline's colours. Instead, there were two small groups of pale leather seats, the ones at the rear bracketing tables large enough to set up a laptop, play games, eat a meal, or simply flick through a magazine and glance out of the window. And Ella's car seat was securely strapped in all ready for her.

Leo headed that way and she followed, the tight, dense pile of the carpet underfoot making her feel as if she was walking on air. Maybe she was? Maybe they'd already taken off and she just hadn't noticed? Or maybe it was all part of the weird, dreamlike state she'd been in ever since she'd turned her back on Nick and walked away.

A wave of dizziness washed over her, and she grabbed the back of one of the seats to steady herself and felt Leo's hand at her waist, steering her to a seat at the back of the plane across the aisle from Ella's.

'Sit. And don't argue,' he added firmly.

She didn't argue. She was beyond arguing. She just sat obediently like a well-trained Labrador, sinking into the butter-soft cream leather as her legs gave way, watching him while he strapped little Ella into her seat, his big hands gentle and competent as he assembled the buckle and clicked it firmly into place.

She hoped she never had to do it. It looked extraordinarily complicated for something so simple, and she was suddenly swamped with doubts about her ability to do this.

What on earth did she know about babies? Less than nothing. You could write it all in capitals on the head of a very small pin. He must be nuts to trust her with his child.

She heard voices as a man and woman in uniform came up the steps and into the plane, and moments later the door was shut and the woman was approaching them with a smile, her hand extended.

'Mr Zacharelli.'

Leo shook her hand and returned the smile. 'Julie, isn't it? We've flown together before.'

'We have, sir. It's a pleasure to welcome you and Ella on board again, and Miss Driver, I believe? I'm your cabin crew today, and if there's anything you need, don't hesitate to ask.'

She smiled at Amy as they shook hands, and turned her attention back to Leo.

'May I go through the pre-flight safety procedure with you?' she asked, and he delved into the baby's bag and handed Ella a crackly, brightly coloured dragonfly toy to distract her while Julie launched into the familiar spiel.

It took a few minutes, showing them the overhead oxygen, the emergency exit—all the usual things, but with the massive difference that she was talking only to them, and the smiles she gave were personal. Especially to Leo, Amy thought, and mentally rolled her eyes at yet another effortless conquest on his part. He probably wasn't even aware of it.

And then it was done, another smile flashed in his direction, and Julie took herself off and left them alone.

'Was that from me?' Amy asked, pointing at the dragonfly toy Ella was happily playing with.

Leo nodded, sending her a fleeting smile. 'You sent her it when she was born. She loves it. I have to take it everywhere with us.'

That made her smile. At least she'd done one thing right, then, in the last year or so. He zipped the bag up, stashed it in the baggage compartment, put her hand luggage in there, too, and sat down opposite Ella and across from Amy.

His tawny gold eyes searched hers thoughtfully.

'You OK now?'

If you don't count the butterflies stampeding around in my stomach like a herd of elephants, she thought, but she said nothing, just nodded, and he raised a brow a fraction but didn't comment.

'Do you always travel like this?' she asked, still slightly stunned by their surroundings but rapidly getting used to it.

He laughed softly. 'Only if I'm travelling with Ella or

if time's short. Usually I go business class. It's just much easier with a baby to travel somewhere private. I'm sure you've been in a plane when there's been a screaming baby—like this,' he added, as Ella caught sight of the bottle he'd tried to sneak out of his pocket so he could fasten his seat belt. She reached for it, little hands clenching and unclenching as she started to whimper, and Leo hid the bottle under the table.

'No, *mia bella,* not yet,' he said gently, and the whimper escalated to an indignant wail.

Amy laughed softly. 'Right on cue.'

She propped her elbows on the table and leant towards Ella, smiling at her and waggling her dragonfly in an attempt to distract her.

'Hi, sweet pea,' she crooned softly. 'You aren't really going to scream all the way there, are you? No, of course not!'

Finally distracted from the bottle, Ella beamed at her and squashed the toy. It made a lovely, satisfying noise, so she did it again, and Leo chuckled.

'Babies are refreshingly easy to please. Give them a toy and they're happy.'

'Like men, really. Fast car, big TV, fancy coffee maker… private jet—'

He gave a soft snort and shot her a look. 'Don't push it. And don't get lulled into a false sense of security because you managed to distract her this time. She can be a proper little tyrant if it suits her. You're a monster in disguise, aren't you, *mia bella*?'

He said it with such affection, and Amy's heart turned over. Poor little scrap, losing her mother so young and so tragically. Leo must have been devastated—although not for himself, from what he'd said. He'd told her that marrying the wrong person was a recipe for disaster and it would be a cold day in hell before he did it again, so it didn't sound as if his marriage had been a match made in heaven, by any means. But even so—

'I need to make a quick call to sort out where we're going to stay tonight. Can you entertain her, please, Amy? I won't be a moment.'

'Sure.' Amy shut the door on that avenue of thought and turned her attention to amusing Ella. She'd got enough mess of her own to deal with, without probing into Leo's.

But Ella didn't really need entertaining, not with her dragonfly to chew and crackle, so Amy was free to listen to what Leo was saying. Not that she could understand it, because he was talking in Italian, but it was lovely to listen to him anyway.

She always thought of him as English, like his mother, but then this amazing other side of him would come out, the Italian side that came from his father, and it did funny things to her insides.

Or maybe it was just the language doing that? That must be it. There was no way Leo talking Italian was sexy, that was just ridiculous. Not according to his numerous female fans, of course, but that didn't mean *she* had to fall under his spell. This was Leo, after all.

Yes, of course he was gorgeous, she knew that, and she'd had a serious case of hero-worship when she'd hit puberty, but she'd never felt whatever it was they all obviously felt—probably because she'd known him too long, knew all his weaknesses and irritating little habits as well as his strong points, like friendship and loyalty and generosity.

He was virtually a brother, a brother she loved to bits and would go to the end of the earth for. The best friend a girl could want. And no matter where she ended up, that would never change, but sexy? Nope—

'*Ciao. A dopo,*' he said in that delicious Italian of his, and her heart did a little back-flip to prove her wrong.

* * *

He put his phone away and smiled at Amy across the aisle.

'Well, that's our accommodation sorted,' he said with relief. 'I phoned Massimo Valtieri to tell him I'm bringing a friend to help with the baby so we'd make our own arrangements, but he wouldn't have any of it. He says there's plenty of room for you, too, and they're fine with us all staying at the *palazzo,* as from tonight. Problem solved.'

'*Palazzo*?' she squealed, and lowered her voice to a whisper. 'They live in a *palazzo?*'

Leo laughed softly at the awed expression on her face. 'Apparently. It's an old Medici villa. I've seen pictures of it, and it's very beautiful. It's been in the family for centuries, which is why I want to deal with them because it's not just a business, it's in their blood, it's who they are. The meetings will be there and they all live very close by, apparently, so it makes sense us being there, too, so if Ella kicks off and you can't cope, I won't be far away. And his wife's there, so you'll have company.'

'Oh, that's good,' she said, and a little worried crinkle in between her eyebrows smoothed away. She shook her head, her mouth kicking up in a wry smile. 'I still can't quite believe I'm going to be staying in a *palazzo.*'

She looked so flummoxed it made him chuckle. 'Well, you've got about four or five hours to get used to the idea,' he told her.

He was just relieved he'd be on hand; he didn't know what she knew about babies, but she knew almost nothing about Ella, so having a woman around who was a mother herself could only be a good thing, especially under the circumstances. He didn't want Amy feeling any more overwhelmed than she already was.

She was leaning over now and chatting to Ella, telling her what a lucky girl she was to stay in a *palazzo,* and he settled back in the seat and studied her. She was smiling, the haunted look in her eyes retreating as she fell under the spell of his tiny daughter, and for the briefest of fleeting seconds he wondered what life would have been like for all of them if she'd been Ella's mother.

It took his breath away.

CHAPTER THREE

AMY GLANCED ACROSS at Leo and frowned.

He was staring at her with the strangest expression on his face. 'Have I got a smut on my nose or something?'

'What? No. Sorry, I was miles away. Ah, here's Julie, we might be in business,' he added, and he sounded relieved, for some reason.

'We're about to take off now,' Julie said. 'Is there anything you need to ask before we're airborne?'

'I'm fine. Amy?' Leo said, raising an eyebrow at her.

'No, I'm fine, thank you.'

Julie left them, took herself off to her seat behind the cockpit, and then the pilot's voice came over the loudspeaker and they were off.

Leo strapped himself in, reached across with Ella's bottle and began to feed her as they turned at the end of the runway.

'It helps her ears to adjust to the pressure change,' he explained, but Amy didn't care right then. She leant back, gripped the armrests and closed her eyes. She hated this bit—

'Oh!' She gasped as she was forced back into the seat and the plane tipped up and catapulted itself into the sky.

'Bit quicker off the ground than a heavy commercial jet,' Leo said with a grin as they levelled out and settled into a gentle climb, banking out over the Thames estuary and towards the coast.

She looked away from him, staring blindly out of the window at the slightly tilted horizon as the reality of what she'd done kicked in. They were still climbing—climbing up, up and away from England. Away from the wedding that hadn't been, the redundant marquee on the lawn next door, the dress lying in a crumpled heap on her bedroom floor.

And she was going to Italy. Not on her honeymoon, but with Leo and Ella. Without a husband, without a wedding ring, without the engagement ring that was sitting on her dressing table at home where she'd left it.

She looked down at her hand. Nope, no ring. Just a faint, pale line where it had been.

Just to check, she ran her finger lightly over the empty space on her finger, and Leo reached out to her across the aisle, squeezing her hand.

'You OK?' he murmured, as if he could read her mind.

She flashed him a smile but it felt false, forced, and she looked away again. 'Just checking it's not a dream. It feels like I'm on drugs. Some weird, hallucinogenic stuff.'

'No drugs. No dream. You're just taking time to get used to it. It's a bit of a shock, such a drastic change of course.'

Shock? Probably. Drastic, certainly. It felt like she was falling, and she wasn't sure if the parachute would work. She met his eyes, worrying her lip with her teeth. 'I wish I'd been able to get hold of Nick. He wasn't answering his phone.'

'Did you leave a message?'

She shook her head. 'I didn't really know what to say. "Sorry I dumped you at the altar in front of all our family and friends" seems a bit inadequate, somehow.'

'He didn't look upset, Amy,' Leo reminded her softly. 'He looked relieved.'

'Yes, he did,' she agreed. 'Well, I guess he would do, wouldn't he, not being stuck with me?'

Leo frowned. 'Why should he be relieved about that?'

'Because clearly I'm an idiot!'

Leo laughed softly, his eyes full of teasing affection. 'You're not an idiot,' he said warmly. 'Well, not much. You just got swept along by the momentum. It's easily done.'

It was. And he was right, she had. They both had. Was that what had happened to Leo and Lisa when he'd done the decent thing and married her for the wrong reasons?

The seatbelt light went off with a little ping, and Leo undid his lap strap and swung his seat round slightly as Julie approached them with a smile.

'Fancy a drink, Amy?' Leo asked her. 'Something to eat?'

Amy laughed. 'Eat? I couldn't eat another thing! That picnic was absolutely amazing. I'm still stuffed.'

'Well, let's just hope everyone enjoyed it. I'll have a cappuccino, Julie, please. Amy?'

'That would be lovely, thank you.'

Julie smiled and nodded, disappeared to the galley area behind the cockpit and left Amy to her thoughts. They weren't comfortable. All those people who'd travelled miles to see her married, and here she was running away with Leo and leaving them all in the lurch when she should have been there apologising to them.

'I wonder if they're all still there having a post-mortem on the death of my common sense?' she murmured absently. 'At least a lot of them turned up to eat the food. It would have been a shame to waste it.'

'I imagine most of them will have left by now—and your common sense didn't die, it just woke up a bit late in the day.'

'Maybe.' She sighed, and smiled at him ruefully. 'The food really was amazing, you know. I'm glad I got to try it. Do you know how long it is since you cooked for me?' she added wistfully, and he gave a soft huff of laughter.

'Years.'

'It is. At least four. Five, probably. You did it a lot when my father died. I used to come and hang out in your restaurant while I was at uni and you'd throw something together for us when you'd finished, or test a recipe out on me. I've missed that.'

'Me, too. I'm sorry. My life's been a bit chaotic since the television series.'

Well, that was the understatement of the century. 'So I gather,' she said mildly. 'And you've opened the new restaurant. That can't have been easy with a new wife and a baby on the way.'

A shadow flitted through his eyes and he looked away, his smile suddenly strained. 'No. It took a lot of my time. Too much.'

So much that their marriage had fallen apart? If they'd even had a marriage in the real sense. It didn't sound like it, but she knew very little more than he'd just told her and the rest was rumours in the gutter press. They'd had a field day, but his parents didn't talk about it, and until today she'd hardly seen Leo since before his marriage.

All she knew was what had been in the paper, that Lisa had been knocked down by a car late one stormy night and had died of her injuries, and the coroner had returned a verdict of accidental death. Ella had been tiny—two months old? Maybe not even that. And Leo had been left with a motherless baby, a new business venture that demanded his attention and a television contract he'd had to put on hold. Small wonder she hadn't seen him.

'Your cappuccino, Miss Driver.'

The drink was set down in front of her, and she flashed a distracted smile at Julie and picked up her spoon, chasing the sprinkled chocolate flakes around in the froth absently.

His hand came out and rested lightly on her arm, stilling it. 'It'll be all right, Amy,' he murmured, which made her smile. Trust Leo to be concerned for her when actually she was worrying about him.

'I'm fine,' she assured him. And she was, she realised. A little stunned, a little bemused almost at the turn of events, but Leo was whisking her away from it all so fast she didn't have time to dwell on it, and that could only be a good thing.

She pulled out her little pocket camera and pointed it at him. 'Smile for the birdie!'

'Make sure you get my good side.'

She lowered the camera and cocked an eyebrow at him. 'You *have* a good side?'

He rolled his eyes, that lazy grin kicking up his mouth and dimpling his right cheek, and her heart turned over. She clicked the button, turned to get an interior shot while her heart settled, and clicked again.

'Day one of your Tuscan tour blog,' she said lightly, and he laughed.

She caught it, grinned at him and put the camera away.

They landed shortly before five o'clock, and by five thirty they'd picked up the hire car and were on their way to the *palazzo*. Ella was whingeing a little, so he pulled over in a roadside *caffè* and ordered them coffee and pastries while he fed her from a pouch of pureed baby food.

It galled him to do it, but it wouldn't kill her. It was organic, nutritionally balanced, and had the massive advantage that it was easy. He had enough fish to fry at the moment without worrying about Ella.

He glanced up and met Amy's eyes. She was watching him, a strange expression on her face, and he tipped his head questioningly.

'What?'

'Nothing. Just—I've never really got used to the thought of you as a father, but you seem very comfortable with her.'

He looked back at Ella, his heart filling with love. 'I am. I didn't know what it would be like, but I love it—love her, more than I could ever have imagined loving anyone. She's the most precious thing that's ever happened to me.'

Amy's smile grew wistful. 'It shows,' she murmured, and he thought of all the plans she'd mentioned that she'd walked away from, all the things she'd sacrificed. Like starting a family. And if he hadn't interfered…

She might have ended up in the same mess as him, he reminded himself, bringing up a child on her own after the disastrous end of a doomed relationship.

'Amy, it'll happen for you, when the time's right,' he told her softly, and she gave a wry little smile that twisted his heart.

'I know. But I have to warn you, I don't know anything about babies so it won't hurt to practise on Ella so I can make my mistakes first with someone else's child.'

He chuckled, ruffling Ella's dark curls gently. 'You won't make mistakes, and even if you do, you won't break her. She's pretty resilient.'

Her wry smile turned to a grimace. 'That's probably just as well. She might need to be.'

'Chill, Amy. She's just a little person. She'll let you know what she needs.'

'Yeah, if you can mind-read a ten-month-old baby,' she said drily, but the smile reached her eyes now and he let his breath out on a quiet sigh of relief. She'd been hanging by a thread ever since she'd turned her back on Nick, and it had taken till now before he'd felt absolutely sure that she'd done the right thing. Having a baby with the wrong person was a disaster, and that's what she could have done if everything had gone to plan.

Which let him off the hook a bit on the guilt front.

'Here, you can start practising now. Give her the rest of this so I can drink my coffee, could you, please?' he asked, handing her the pouch and spoon and sitting back to watch. Amy took it cautiously, offered it to Ella, and the baby obediently sucked the gloop from the spoon, to Amy's delight and his relief. Contrary to her predictions, they seemed to be getting on fine. 'There—see?' he said lightly. 'Easy.'

She threw him a cheeky grin and put the empty pouch down. 'Well, this end was easy, but I think she'll need her daddy for the other one. I can only master one skill at a time and there'll be plenty of time to learn about that later.'

He laughed, put his cup down and scooped up Ella and the changing bag. 'I'm sure there'll be lots of opportunities.'

'I don't doubt it,' she said drily, but her wry, affectionate smile warmed his heart and he was suddenly fiercely glad that she'd come with them.

By the time the sun was getting low on the western horizon, they were turning onto the broad gravelled drive leading up to the Palazzo Valtieri.

The track dipped and wound along the valley floor, and then rose up the hill through an avenue of poplars to a group of stone buildings on the top, flushed rose by the setting sun.

'I think that's the *palazzo*,' he told her, and Amy felt her jaw drop.

'What, all of it? It's enormous! It looks as big as some of the little hilltop towns!'

He chuckled softly. 'There'll be all sorts of other buildings there clustered around it. It won't just be the house.'

But it was. Well, pretty much, she realised as they approached the imposing edifice with its soaring stone walls and windows that she just knew would have the most amazing views. She couldn't wait to get her proper camera out.

They drove under a huge stone archway in the wall and into a large gravelled courtyard, triggering lights that flooded the area with gold. There were several vehicles there, and Leo brought the car to rest beside a big people-carrier.

They were facing a broad flight of steps flanked by olive trees in huge terracotta pots, and at the top of the steps was a pair of heavily studded wooden doors, totally in proportion to the building.

She felt her jaw sag again. 'Oh. Wow. Just—wow,' she breathed.

Leo's grin was wry. 'Yeah. Makes my house look a bit modest, doesn't it?'

'I haven't seen your house yet,' she reminded him, 'but it would have to be ridiculously impressive to compete with this.'

'Then it's a good job I'm not a sore loser. Unless you count a sea view? That's probably the only thing they don't have.'

She cocked her head on one side and grinned at him. 'That might just do it. You know me—I always wanted to be a mermaid.'

'I'd forgotten that.' His cheek creased, the dimple appearing as he punched the air. 'Ace. My house trumps the seat of the Valtieri dynasty.'

'I did say "might",' she pointed out, but she couldn't quite stifle her smile, and he laughed softly and opened the car door.

'You haven't seen my view yet.'

She met his smile over the top of the car. 'I haven't seen theirs, either. Don't count your chickens.'

'Would I?' He grinned again, that dimple making another unscheduled appearance, and her heart lurched.

'I guess we'd better tell them we're here,' she said, but it seemed they didn't need to.

One of the great wooden doors swung open, and a tall man in jeans and a blinding white shirt ran down the steps, smiling broadly, hand extended as he reached Leo.

'Massimo Valtieri,' he said. 'And you're Leo Zacharelli. It's good to meet you. Welcome to Palazzo Valtieri.'

He spoke in perfect English, to Amy's relief, faintly accented but absolutely fluent, and he turned to her with a welcoming smile. 'And you must be Miss Driver.'

'Amy, please,' she said, and he smiled again and shook her hand, his fingers warm and firm and capable.

'Amy. Welcome. My wife Lydia's so looking forward to meeting you both. She's just putting the children to bed and the others are in the kitchen. Come on in, let me show you to your rooms so you can settle the baby and freshen up before you meet them.'

Leo took Ella out of the car seat and picked up the changing bag, Massimo picked up Leo's bag and removed hers firmly from her grip, and they followed him up the steps and in through the great heavy door into a cloistered courtyard. The sheltered walls were decorated with intricate, faded murals that looked incredibly old, and more olive trees in huge pots were stationed at the corners of the open central area.

It was beautiful. Simple, almost monastic, but exquisite. And she couldn't wait to start capturing the images. She was already framing the shots in her mind, and most of them had Leo in them. For his blog, of course.

Their host led them around the walkway under the cloisters and through a door into a spacious, airy sitting room, simply but comfortably furnished, with French doors opening out onto a terrace. The sun had dipped below the horizon now, blurring the detail in the valley stretched out below them, but Amy was fairly sure the view would be amazing. Everything else about the place seemed to be, and she just knew it would be crammed with wonderful photo opportunities.

Massimo pushed open a couple of doors to reveal two generous bedrooms, both of them opening out onto the same terrace and sharing a well-equipped bathroom. There was a small kitchen area off the sitting room, as well, and for their purposes it couldn't have been better.

'If there's anything else you want, please ask, and Lydia said she hopes you're hungry. She's been cooking up a storm ever since you rang and we'd love you to join us once you've got the baby settled.'

'That would be great, but she shouldn't have gone to any trouble. We don't want to impose,' Leo said, but Massimo was having none of it.

'No way! She's a chef, too, and not offering you food would be an unforgivable sin,' he said with a laugh. 'Just as soon as the baby's settled, give me a call on my mobile and I'll come and get you. Both of my brothers and their wives are here as well tonight. And we don't in any way dress for dinner, so don't feel you have to change. We'll be eating in the kitchen as usual.'

The door closed behind him, and Leo turned to her with a faintly bemused smile.

'Are you OK with this? Because I'm well aware you've had a hell of a day and I don't want to push it, but it does sound as if they want to meet us, or me, at least. If you don't feel up to company, just say so and I'll bring something over to you and you can have a quiet evening on your own. Up to you.'

Her stomach rumbled, answering the question, and she smiled ruefully. 'Honestly? Yes, I'm tired, but I'm absolutely starving, too, and I'm not sure I want to spend the evening on my own. And anyway, as you say, it's you they all want to meet. I won't understand what you're all saying anyway, so I'll just sit in the corner and stuff myself and watch you all.'

'I think you will understand, at least some of it. His wife's English.'

'Really?' Another knot of tension slid away, and this time her smile felt a bit more spontaneous. 'That's good news. I might have someone to talk to while you're in meetings.'

Leo chuckled. 'I'm sure you will. I'll just bath Ella quickly and give her a bottle and pop her into bed, and then we can go and meet the rest of the family.'

Ella! She hadn't even given her duties a thought, but now she did. 'Will it be all right to leave her, or do you want me to stay with her? It's you they want to meet.'

He picked something up off a side table and waggled it at her.

'Baby monitor,' he said, by way of explanation. 'They really have thought of everything.'

They had. Absolutely everything. There were posh toiletries in the bathroom, the fridge was stocked with milk, juice, butter and fresh fruit, there was a bowl of brown, speckled eggs and a loaf of delicious-looking crunchy bread on the side, and a new packet of ground coffee next to a cafetière. And teabags. Amy was glad to see the teabags. Real English ones.

While Leo heated the baby's bottle and gave it to her, she made them both a cup of tea and curled up on the sofa to wait for him. Ella fussed a little as he was trying to put her down, but it didn't take long before she went quiet, and she heard a door close softly and Leo appeared.

'Is that for me?' he asked, tilting his head towards the mug on the table in front of her.

She nodded. 'I didn't know how long you were going to be, so it might be a bit cold. Would you like me to make you a fresh one?'

'No, it's fine, I'll drink it now. Thanks. I ought to ring Massimo anyway. I don't want to keep them waiting and Ella's gone out like a light.'

'Before you call him—did you say anything to them? About me, I mean? About the wedding?'

A frown flashed across his face. 'No, Amy, of course not. I didn't think you'd want to talk about it and it just puts an elephant in the room.'

'So—no elephants waiting for me?'

He gave a quiet grunt of laughter, the frown morphing into a sympathetic smile. 'No elephants, I promise.'

'Good,' she said, smiling back as the last knot of tension drained away, 'because I'm really, really hungry now!'

'When aren't you?' he muttered with a teasing grin, pulling out his phone, and moments later Massimo appeared and led them across the courtyard and into a bustling kitchen filled with laughter.

There were five people in there, two men and three women, all seated at a huge table with the exception of a pregnant woman—Lydia?—who was standing at the stove, brandishing a wooden spoon as she spoke.

Everyone stopped talking and turned to look at them expectantly, the men getting to their feet to greet them as Massimo made a quick round of introductions, ending with his wife. She'd abandoned her cooking, the wooden spoon quickly dumped on the worktop as she came towards them, hands outstretched in welcome.

'Oh, I'm so glad you've both decided to come over and join us. I hope you're hungry?'

'Absolutely! It smells so amazing in here,' she said with a laugh, and then was astonished when Lydia hugged her.

'Oh, bless you, I love compliments. And you're Leo,' she said, letting go of Amy and hugging him, too. 'I can't tell you how pleased I am to meet you. You've been my hero for years!'

To Amy's surprise, Leo coloured slightly and gave a soft, self-effacing chuckle. 'Thank you. That's a real compliment, coming from another chef.'

'Yeah, well, there are chefs and chefs!' Lydia said with a laugh. 'Darling, get them a glass of wine. I'm sure they're ready for it. Travelling with a baby is a nightmare.'

'I'm on it. Red or white?'

Leo chuckled and glanced over at Lydia. 'Judging by the gorgeous smell, I'd say a nice robust red?'

'Perfect with it. And it's one of your recipes,' Lydia told him with a wry grin. 'I've adapted it to showcase some of our ingredients, so I hope I've done them justice.'

They launched into chef mode, and Amy found a glass of iced water put in her hand by one of the other two women. It appeared she was also English and her smile was friendly and welcoming.

'I don't know about you, but travelling always makes me thirsty,' she said. 'I'm Isabelle, and I'm married to Luca. He's a doctor, so more of a sleeping partner in the business, really. And this is Anita, the only native Valtieri wife. She's married to Giovanni. He's a lawyer and he keeps us all on the straight and narrow.'

'Well, he tries,' Anita said, her laughing words heavily accented, and Amy found herself hugged again. 'Welcome to Tuscany. Have you had a good day so far? I thought Leo was supposed to be at a wedding today, but obviously not.'

Well, how on earth was she supposed to answer that? Except she didn't have to, because Leo appeared at her side and answered for her, fielding the question neatly.

'We managed to get away early,' he said, and she only just stifled a laugh. 'The journey was great, though. Seamless. And our accommodation is perfect. Thank you all so much. It'll make it very much easier for all three of us.'

'You're welcome,' Massimo said, glasses and a bottle in hand, and he and his two brothers immediately engaged

Leo in a conversation about the wine, so Amy turned back to the women and found herself seated at the table while they poured her a glass of wine and chatted about the business and the area and their children, and asked about Leo.

'So, how long have you known him?' Lydia asked, perching on the chair next to Amy in a break in her cooking.

'Oh—for ever. Our families have been neighbours since before I was born.'

'Gosh. Literally for ever! Lucky you!'

She laughed. 'I don't know about that. He used to test recipes on me when we were kids, but I was a willing victim.'

'Victim?'

She wrinkled her nose. 'He was a little adventurous, so there were a few interesting disasters along the way. I think his palate's refined a little bit since then.'

They all laughed, even Leo, and she realised he'd been standing right behind her, listening to every word.

'Damned by faint praise,' he said wryly, and she swivelled round and looked up at him with a grin.

'Well, I wouldn't like to swell your head.'

'God forbid.'

His mouth twitched, and she laughed and turned back and found Lydia, Anita and Isabelle watching her thoughtfully. Why? They'd always behaved in this playful way, she just hadn't thought about it, but—were the three women reading something else into it? Something that wasn't there? She felt herself colour slightly and dunked a bit of olive ciabatta into the bowl of oil and balsamic vinegar on the table in front of her.

Good move. The flavour exploded on her tongue and suddenly she understood why they were there. 'Wow. This is lovely. Is it yours?' she asked, and to her relief the conversation moved on as the food was put on the table and they all piled in, and the slightly awkward moment passed.

Then as the last plate was cleared away and it looked as if they'd split up into two groups again, Ella cried out, the monitor flashing right in front of Leo, and Amy seized the opportunity to escape before the women could ask any more searching questions.

'I'll go,' she said hastily to Leo, scraping back her chair and snatching up the baby monitor. 'You stay and talk.'

'Are you sure?'

His eyes searched hers, concern etched in them, and she found a smile.

'Absolutely. We'll be fine, and if we aren't, we'll come and find you.' She turned to the others. 'I hope you'll excuse me. It's been quite a…long and complicated day.'

'Of course. We'll see you tomorrow. If there's anything you need, just ask,' Lydia said, and she nodded.

'Thanks.'

Leo reached out a hand and stopped her briefly. 'I'll be with you in a minute. I won't be long.'

She nodded back, dug out the smile again for the others, thanked Lydia for the meal and made her escape. Long and complicated didn't even begin to scratch the surface of her day, and she was only too ready to head across the beautiful courtyard to their suite of rooms, let herself in and close the door with a shaky sigh of relief.

For some reason she could feel tears threatening, and frankly she'd done enough crying this morning—no, this afternoon. Whenever. The wedding was supposed to have been at noon. So still less than twelve hours since she'd turned her back on Nick and run away.

And she would be spending her wedding night alone in an ancient medieval *palazzo* in Tuscany, instead of with Nick in the honeymoon suite of an old manor house prior to heading off to a sun-soaked beach in the Indian Ocean for her honeymoon.

She gave a tiny laugh that turned into a hiccupping sob, and ramming her hand over her mouth she headed towards the bedrooms.

And stopped, registering for the first time that the room with the travel cot in it had twin beds, and the other room had a huge double. Not that the twin beds were in any way small, but it seemed wrong for her to take the double instead of Leo and she was, after all, supposed to be here to look after the baby, even though Leo had said he'd share with Ella.

She pushed the door open a little further and peered into the travel cot. The baby was fast asleep and breathing quietly and evenly, whatever had disturbed her clearly not enough to wake her properly, and Amy turned away from the bedrooms and headed for the kitchen.

She was tired beyond belief, her brain worn out from going over and over the repercussions of her impulsive behaviour, but she couldn't go to bed until she'd discussed their sleeping arrangements with Leo, so she put the kettle on, made herself a cup of tea and settled down to wait for him.

CHAPTER FOUR

LEO STAYED IN the kitchen for a while longer, deep in conversation with the Valtieri brothers. They were fascinating men, with a passion for what they produced, for the land, for their family ties and history and also for their future—a future he realised he wanted to share.

Their business was a part of them, utterly fundamental, their enthusiasm burning so intensely that it was infectious. It was how he felt about his own chosen path, his constant striving for perfection, for excellence, and it was wonderful to meet people who produced the raw ingredients of his craft with the same passion.

He'd missed this—missed talking to people who understood what drove him and shared it, missed immersing himself in the thing he loved most in the world apart from his family. Especially his daughter—

His gut clenched. Oh, hell. Amy was looking after her, and he'd totally forgotten!

What was he thinking about? He'd let her take the baby monitor so he had no idea how long it had taken Ella to settle, and Amy had enough to deal with tonight, of all nights, without a tired and fractious baby.

He shouldn't have taken her for granted, but he'd been so wrapped up in his own agenda, so busy enjoying himself, that she'd completely slipped his mind.

How *could* he have let that happen? Especially when he was so worried about her. She'd been quiet all day, so unlike her usually bubbly self, and although she seemed to have enjoyed the evening there'd been a distracted look in her eyes—and when Ella had cried, she'd grabbed the opportunity to escape with both hands.

And he'd let her do it. What kind of a friend was he?

'Sorry, guys, I lost track of the time, I'm going to have to go,' he said a little abruptly. 'It's been a long day and I need to check on Ella.' And Amy. *Dio*, how *could* he—?

'Sure. We'll see you in the morning. Nine o'clock?'

He nodded. 'That's fine. I'll look forward to it.'

'Tell Amy we'll be around,' Lydia chipped in with a smile. 'She and Ella are more than welcome to join us.'

'Thank you. I'll pass it on. I'm sure she'll appreciate the company. And thank you for a lovely meal. It was delicious. I'll have to return the favour one evening.'

Lydia laughed. 'Feel free. I'd love you to cook for us. It would be amazing. You can give me a master class, if you like.'

He gave a soft chuckle. 'No pressure, then.'

'I'm sure you can handle it, Chef,' she said with a grin, and he chuckled again and got to his feet, shook hands with all the men, said goodnight to the ladies and crossed the courtyard swiftly, letting himself quietly into the guest suite.

Silence. No screaming baby, no sound from Amy desperately trying to pacify her, and the tension drained out of him. She must have gone to bed and left a lamp on in the sitting room for him.

He turned towards it, and then he saw her in the soft glow, curled up in the far corner of a sofa, her hands cradling a mug and her face in shadow.

'You're still up,' he said unnecessarily. 'I'm sorry, I didn't mean to be so long. I take it Ella's OK?'

'She's fine.'

He frowned. Her voice sounded—odd. Disconnected.

'Amy?' he said softly. She turned her head and looked up at him, and his gut clenched. She'd been crying. He could see the dried tracks of tears on her cheeks, her eyes red-rimmed and swollen, and guilt rose up and swamped him.

Damn.

She hadn't meant him to find her like this, and now there was guilt written all over his face. She closed her eyes, biting her lip and kicking herself for not just going to bed.

The sofa dipped as he sat down next to her, his thigh warm against her hip, his arm around her shoulders solid and comforting. She felt his breath ease out on a weary sigh.

'I'm so sorry. I got caught up in conversation and I should have been here for you, not abandoning you on your own to deal with Ella. Was she a nightmare?'

She shook her head. 'No. She was still asleep. It's not that. I spoke to Nick,' she said, and her voice clogged with tears. She swallowed and tried again. 'He rang to find out if I was OK.'

'And are you?' he asked, although she knew he could see quite clearly that she wasn't.

She shrugged. 'I suppose. I don't know. It's my wedding night, Leo. I should have been married—'

Her voice cracked, and he took the mug out of her hands and pulled her gently into his arms.

'Oh, Amy, I'm so sorry. This is all my fault.'

'What's your fault?' she asked, tilting her head back and searching his eyes. 'That I left it so long to realise it was a mistake? Hardly.'

'That you're not married. Not on your honeymoon. That you've thrown away all your carefully laid plans.'

She shook her head and cradled his cheek in her hand. It felt rough, the stubble growing out now at the end of the

day, and there was something grounding about the feel of
it against her palm. Something warm and real and alive
that made it all make sense. Or complicated it all a whole
lot more. She dropped her hand back in her lap.

'That I'm not married to the wrong man,' she corrected,
her voice soft but emphatic, needing to convince him so
he didn't carry this guilt around like a burden for ever.
'You did the *right thing*, Leo. It was me who didn't, me
who ignored all the warnings going off in my head all the
time. I thought I was just stressing about the wedding, but
I wasn't, it was the marriage, the lifetime commitment to
him that was worrying me. I just didn't realise it. So for
goodness' sake don't beat yourself up over it, because it's
not your fault, OK?'

'So why are you crying?'

She gave a little shrug. 'Because the pressure's off?
Because I feel guilty because I'm glad I'm not married
to him when he's actually a really nice guy? Take your
pick.' She tried to smile, but it was a rubbish effort, so
she sniffed and swiped the tears off her cheeks and tried
again. 'There. Is that better?'

'Not much,' he said honestly, lifting a damp strand of
hair away from her eyes with gentle fingers.

'Well, it's the best I can do,' she said, her voice choked
again, and Leo closed his eyes and folded her close against
his chest and rested his cheek against her hair. It felt a little
stiff from the products she must have had put in it for the
updo, not as soft and sleek as usual. Not his Amy.

His Amy? What was he thinking? She hadn't ever been
his Amy, even in the old days. And now was not the time
to reinvent their relationship, when both of them were
an emotional mess. However appealing it might be. And
where the hell had that come from?

With a quiet sigh he loosened his hold and sat up a little,

putting some much-needed distance between them before
he did something stupid that he'd regret for ever.

'You'll feel better after you've had a good night's sleep.
Why don't you have a shower and go to bed?' he murmured, and she looked up at him, her eyes lost.

'Where? Which bed? The room Ella's in has only got
single beds and you can't possibly sleep in one of those, it
seems all wrong. You should have the double.'

'Don't be daft. They're not small beds. You take the
double, it's fine.'

'Are you sure?'

'Of course I'm sure, and I'm certainly not moving her
tonight. I'll sort the luggage out, and then you go and have
a shower and get off to bed. You'll feel better in the morning, honestly.'

'Is that a promise?'

She looked so forlorn that he laughed softly and hugged
her. 'Yes, it's a promise. New day, new life.'

It sounded great. He just hoped it didn't turn out to be
a false promise, because he was still waiting for that new
life after copious new days. New weeks. New months.
And there was no sign of it. He felt as if his life was on
hold, in limbo, and every dawn was just as bleak as the
one before...

Leo was right. She did feel better in the morning.

It shouldn't have surprised her; Leo was always right.
Why hadn't she asked him about Nick before? Except of
course it would have seemed disloyal, and even now it felt
wrong talking to him about Nick because there was nothing *wrong* with Nick.

It wasn't about Nick. It was about her, and the fact that
it had taken her such an unforgivably long time to realise
she wasn't going to settle for sensible.

She sighed softly. She'd never been sensible. She only

had to look at the mess she'd made of her other relationships to know that, so she might have realised it was never going to work with Nick. Except that was the very reason she'd thought it *might* work, because for once it *was* sensible, and it had taken her far too long to realise she was wrong.

Well, at least she hadn't left it until after they were married. That would have been worse.

She threw back the covers and climbed out of the ridiculously enormous bed that Leo really should have had. She wished he *had* had it, because lying alone in the vast expanse of immaculate white linen had just underlined all the things she'd walked away from.

Still, as Leo had said, new day, new life. That was yesterday. Today was a new day, a fresh start, and she needed to get out there and embrace it.

'Bring it on,' she muttered, staring at herself in the mirror and digging out a smile. There. See? She could do it.

She could hear Leo and Ella in the little sitting room of their suite and they seemed to be having a lot of fun, babyish giggles interspersed with the deeper, soft rumble of Leo's voice. She'd go and join them, bask in the warmth of their love for each other and see if it could drive out this aching loneliness.

She delved in her suitcase for her dressing gown, and frowned. Damn. She'd completely forgotten that she hadn't brought the ratty old towelling thing that she'd had for a hundred years but a slippery little scrap of silk deliberately chosen because it was beautiful and elegant and undeniably sexy. To inject some fireworks into their honeymoon?

Maybe. It was what the garment was designed for, like the camisole nightdress she'd worn last night, and she hadn't even thought about it when she'd said that she was packed ready to go, but she should have done, she realised in dismay. Not that she'd exactly had a lot of time to think about it in the hurry to leave.

She contemplated getting dressed rather than going out into the sitting room what felt like half-naked, but she needed a cup of tea and a shower before she could put on her clothes, and it covered her from head to toe. She tugged the belt tighter and opened the door. There. Perfectly respectable, if a little on the thin side, and it was only Leo, after all.

Only?

Scratch that. He was dressed in a battered old T-shirt and jeans, his feet bare, and he was sitting cross-legged on the floor with Ella, playing peep-bo from behind a cushion and making her giggle hysterically. And for some ridiculous reason he looked as sexy as sin. It must be the bare feet, she thought, and dragged her eyes off them. Or the tug of the T-shirt across those broad, solid shoulders—

He's not sexy! She swallowed and wrapped her arms defensively around her waist. 'Hi, guys. Are you having fun?' she asked, smiling at Ella and trying to avoid Leo's eye as he turned to look at her over his shoulder.

'My daughter likes to see the sun rise,' he said drily, and she chuckled and risked another glance at him.

Mistake. His eyes were scanning her body and he looked quickly away, a touch of colour brushing the back of his neck, and she wished she'd just got dressed because now she'd embarrassed him. Oh, God. Did he think she was flaunting herself in front of him? Idiot! She should have dragged on her clothes and changed them after her shower—

'Tea?' he asked, in a perfectly normal voice that didn't for some reason sound quite normal because there was a tension vibrating in it that she'd never heard before.

'That'd be great. I'll make it.'

But he'd already uncoiled from the floor in one lithe movement and headed for the kitchen, as if he was suddenly desperate for some space between them. 'I've had

two cups,' he said. 'I'll make yours, and you can sit and
come round slowly and play with Ella while I have a
shower, if that's OK. Deal?'

'Deal.'

He made it to the safety of the kitchen and let his breath
out on a long, silent sigh of relief.

'Thank you,' she called after him.

'Don't mention it.'

He flicked the switch on the kettle, then stuck his head
back round the corner while the kettle boiled, still managing to avoid her eyes by pretending to look at Ella. 'I've got
a meeting at nine that'll probably go on all morning—will
you be OK with her? She'll probably nap for a lot of it.'

'I'll be fine, I slept like a log. Were you OK in that single bed?' she asked.

Bed? Now she wanted to talk about the *bed*? He ducked
back into the kitchen and busied himself with her mug,
sending his unruly body a short, pithy reprimand. 'Fine,
thanks,' he lied. 'I told you it would be.'

It hadn't been fine, but he wasn't telling her that. Oh,
it had been perfectly comfortable, if he ignored the fact
that he was used to sleeping in a huge bed all to himself.
What wasn't fine was the fact that he'd been ridiculously
conscious of her just on the other side of the wall, and
swapping rooms wouldn't change that. It would also mean
sleeping in her sheets, and he'd had enough trouble getting her out of his thoughts as it was, without lying there
surrounded by the haunting scent of her.

He made her tea and went back through just as she was
trying to rearrange the dressing gown over her legs on the
floor, and he put the tea down out of Ella's reach and went
on walking, keeping his eyes firmly off the slim, shapely
thigh barely concealed by that slippery scrap of silk that
wouldn't stay where it was put.

'Back in a minute. Don't forget to drink it while it's hot.'

He closed the bathroom door with a frustrated sigh and shook his head. Where the hell had this crazy attraction come from? Not that she was helping, flitting about in that insubstantial little silk thing, but why should that affect him now? It never had before, and Amy frankly wasn't his type.

He liked sophisticated women, and there had been plenty to choose from, especially since the first television series. But he'd used discretion, or so he'd liked to think, until Lisa. Nothing discreet or sophisticated about that. They'd brought out the worst in each other, and the only good thing to come of it was Ella. Their entire relationship had been a disaster of epic proportions, and Lisa had paid for it with her life. He'd never forgive himself for that, and there was no way he was ready for another relationship, especially not one with someone as vulnerable and emotionally fragile as Amy.

Sure, she was a woman now, a beautiful, warm, caring woman, and without a shadow of doubt if she'd been anybody else he wouldn't have hesitated. But she wasn't, she was Amy, and she trusted him. It had taken a huge amount of courage to call a halt to her wedding the way she had, and she'd turned to him for help. The last thing he'd do was betray that trust.

However tempting she'd looked in that revealing bit of nonsense. Oh, well. Maybe Ella would be sick on it and she'd have to wear something else and everything would get back to normal.

He could only hope...

By the time she emerged from the shower, he'd had breakfast and was ready to leave.

'I have to go, I'm supposed to be meeting up with them at nine,' he said, fiddling with his phone. 'Are you sure you'll be all right? Lydia said they'll be around. They all stayed over last night so you should have some company.'

'Fine. Great. And of course I'll be all right,' she said, crossing her fingers behind her back. 'Just go. We're fine, aren't we, Ella?'

He flicked her a quick glance, nodded, kissed Ella good-bye, handed her to Amy and left.

Not popular. The baby gave a little wail, and it took all the skill Amy hadn't known she had to distract her from the loss of her beloved father.

'He'll be back soon,' she promised, and retrieved the dragonfly and squished it, making it crackle. It worked, thankfully, and she ended up sharing her toast with Ella before they went to find the others.

They were in the kitchen, the women chatting at the table while the younger children played on the floor and the two oldest, both girls, sat quietly reading at the table.

'Amy, hi,' Lydia said with a smile. 'Have you had breakfast?'

'Yes, thanks, we're done. Leo said I should come and find you, if that's OK?'

'Of course it's OK. Would you like a coffee?'

'Oh, that would be lovely, if you're having one. Thanks.'

'I'm not, but it's no problem to make you one. We're all on fruit teas—caffeine and pregnancy doesn't go well together,' she said with a wry smile. 'Black, white, latte, cappuccino?'

They were *all* pregnant?

'Um—cappuccino would be lovely. Thanks.'

'I'm sorry, I'll see you outside,' Isabelle said, getting to her feet with a grimace. 'I can't stand the smell of it.'

'No, don't let me drive you out, I'll have tea!' she protested, but Isabelle laughed.

'You're fine. It'll be OK outside and we were just going out there anyway. Max, Annamaria, come on.'

They all went, leaving Amy alone with Lydia while she made the coffee, and Amy took it with a rueful grimace.

'I really wouldn't have had one if I'd known. I feel so guilty.'

'Oh, don't,' Lydia said with a laugh. 'We're used to it, and the men still drink coffee. They just do it elsewhere. One of us always seems to be pregnant and they're well trained.'

That made her smile. She couldn't imagine anything making Leo give up coffee. 'So, is this your fifth baby, or have I lost count?' she asked as they headed for the doors.

'Gosh, no! It's only my second. Massimo was widowed just after Antonino was born,' she explained, 'and I didn't know when we met if he'd want any more, but he just loves children, so this is our second, which will be his fifth, and Anita's on her second, and it's Isabelle's third—her husband's an obstetrician, which is quite handy.'

'Keeping it in the family?'

She chuckled. 'Something like that,' she said and led Amy outside onto the terrace. It seemed to wrap all around the outside of the house, giving stunning views over the surrounding countryside, and Amy was blown away by it.

They settled in the shade of a pergola draped with sweetly scented jasmine, and she cradled her cup and stared out over the beautiful valley below them, taking the time to soak up the scents and sounds that drifted around them on the air.

'Gosh, it's so beautiful here, I could take a lot of this,' she murmured. 'And the *palazzo* is absolutely fabulous.'

'Not when you have to clean it,' Lydia said with a laugh, 'but at least we have some help. And, yes, of course it's beautiful. We all feel very privileged to be guardians of it for future generations.'

'Well, there'll be no shortage of them,' she said with a smile. 'Would you mind if I took some photos of it? Leo's asked me to take some for his blog while we're in Italy, and this would be fantastic. We'd let you vet them first, of course.'

'Of course we wouldn't mind,' Lydia said. 'I'm sure the guys would be thrilled if it appeared in his blog. Just make sure he gives us a plug!'

'Oh, I'm sure he will. I haven't seen him look as fired up and enthusiastic as this in ages. Not that I'm surprised. It's just amazing here.'

'It is,' Isabelle agreed softly. 'It's a wonderful place to live, and it really doesn't take very long to fly home, which is great for keeping in touch with our families. Well, you know how long it takes, you've just done it.'

'Yes, but it doesn't really count. Our trip was ridiculously easy because Leo wangled a private charter from City Airport—'

'No!' Lydia said, laughing. 'Really? That's where I met Massimo! I was in a truly awful wedding dress, trying to blag a flight to Italy for a runaway bride competition—'

Amy sucked in her breath sharply, and Lydia stopped and frowned at her, her expression appalled. 'Amy—what did I say?'

She laughed. She had to laugh, there was nothing else to do really under the circumstances apart from cry, and she'd done enough of that. Time to introduce the elephant.

She gave them a brief précis of her impulsive actions, and Isabelle reached out and rested a hand lightly on her arm, her eyes searching. 'Oh, Amy. Are you sure you're all right?'

'Yes, of course I am,' she said lightly. 'Or I will be once the dust has settled.'

'Much more all right than if you'd married the wrong man,' Anita put in wryly. 'I wish more people had the sense to pull out instead of making each other miserable and putting their children through hell.'

Just as she and Nick might have done. She felt sick, thinking how close she'd come to it, how devastating it would have been for all of them.

Then Ella toppled over trying to pull herself up, which gave Amy the perfect excuse to leave the conversation for a moment and regroup. Not that the women had been anything other than kindness itself, but she just didn't want to talk about her not-quite wedding or their relentlessly burgeoning happy families. The full extent of what she'd turned her back on was still sinking in, but, although the shock was receding, in its place was a terrifying emptiness that she wasn't ready to explore.

Was Nick feeling the same sense of loss? Maybe. Or maybe not. He'd asked if she minded if he went on their honeymoon alone, and of course she'd said no, but she wondered now if it was a good idea for him or if it would just be making it worse.

Not that it could be much worse than her running full tilt down the aisle away from him. God, the humiliation!

She groaned quietly, and Lydia shot her a thoughtful look and got to her feet.

'I need to make lunch. Are you two staying or going?'

'We're going,' Isabelle said briskly, standing up too. 'Anita and I are going to plan a shopping trip for baby stuff.'

Anita frowned. 'We are?'

'Yes, you know we are. We talked about it the other day.'

Or not, Amy thought, because Anita looked confused for a micro-second and then collected herself, scooped up her baby and went, leaving Amy alone with Lydia.

Two down, one to go, she thought with relief, and Lydia had to make lunch, so she could excuse herself—

'Come and talk to me while I cook.'

'Ella could do with a nap,' she said hastily, using the

now grizzling baby as an excuse to escape, but Lydia just shrugged.

'Put her down, then, and come back. Bring the baby monitor. She'll be fine.'

Of course she would, and she went down like a dream, so Amy had no justification for not going back to the kitchen and facing what she felt was going to be an inquisition.

It wasn't, of course. Lydia was far too sensible and sensitive to do something so crass, and her smile of welcome was just that. There was a jug of what looked like home-made lemonade in the middle of the table, alongside two glasses, and Lydia was sitting there chopping vegetables while her children played outside the doors.

'That was quick. She's a good baby, isn't she?' she said as Amy sat down. 'Have you had much to do with her, or is she just good with people?'

'She must be. I haven't really been around recently and nor has Leo, so I haven't seen either of them much. I've been busy planning the wedding and working in London, and since Leo's wife died...' She gave a little shrug. 'Well, he hasn't had a lot of time for anything but work and Ella,' she trailed off awkwardly.

Lydia slid a glass of lemonade towards her. 'Yes, I can imagine. It must have been awful for him, and it must be a nightmare juggling his work with Ella. I know what it's like running one restaurant, never mind a group like theirs, and raising a baby is a full-time job on its own. I'm surprised he hasn't got a nanny.'

'I don't think he needs one at the moment. His parents are close by and they've helped him a lot, but he likes to be hands on. Even so, I think it's been a real struggle.'

'It was good of you to offer to help him.'

She gave a little laugh that hitched in the middle. 'Well, I didn't have anything else to do, did I? And he didn't have to try hard to convince me. I love Italy, and I owe him big time. He's done a lot for me over the years.'

Lydia's eyes searched her face for a second before she turned her attention back to the vegetables. 'Like making sure you didn't marry the wrong man?

Her smile felt a little twisted. 'Absolutely. That's probably the biggest single thing he's ever done for me. He was giving me away—or not,' she said, trying to laugh it off, but the laugh turned into a sigh. 'My father died eight years ago, just after I went to uni, and I suppose I could have asked my uncle or his father or someone, but I wanted Leo, because he knows me better than anyone else on the planet. So I'm really rather glad I did or I might have ended up married to Nick and it would have been a disaster. Not that there's anything wrong with Nick, he's a lovely guy, it's just…'

'You weren't right for each other?' Lydia said wryly, meeting her eyes again.

She returned the understanding smile. 'Pretty much. Although why it took me so long to work out I have no idea. Probably because there *is* nothing wrong with him!' She gave a wry chuckle.

'And it's nothing to do with you and Leo?' 'No! Absolutely not!' she protested. 'I've known him all my life. It would be like marrying my brother.' Except it hadn't felt like that this morning, seeing him on the floor with Ella, when he hadn't been able to look at her, or her at him…

Lydia shrugged and gave a rueful smile. 'Sorry. It's not really any of my business, but—there just seems to be something, almost like some invisible connection, a natural rapport between you,' she said gently. 'Like with Anita and Gio. It took them years to work out what we could all see. And you seem to be so good together.'

Amy shrugged. 'He's just a really great friend. Or he was, but then Nick came along just after Leo's career took off, and then of course he got married, and Nick and I got engaged—and you know the rest. As I say, we've hardly seen each other recently, but he's still just Leo and I know if I ever need him I only have to ask. He's always got time for me, and he's still a really good friend. The sort you can lean on.'

Lydia nodded slowly. 'Well, I'm glad for you that you've got him. Going through something like this, you need a good friend to lean on. There's nothing like being with someone you don't have to explain yourself to, someone who knows you inside out and loves you anyway. I couldn't want a better friend than Massimo by my side.'

She threw the chopped vegetables in the pot, gave them a quick stir, put the lid on and turned back with a smile.

'So, tell me, what do you do when you're not running away from bridegrooms and being Leo's guinea pig?'

Amy laughed, as she was meant to, and the conversation moved on to safer, less turbulent waters, but Lydia's words echoed in Amy's head for the rest of the day.

Sure, she and Leo were the best of friends, but did that have to mean they couldn't be anything else to each other? Not now, of course. She was an emotional mess, and he was still dealing with the fallout of Lisa's death, but maybe, some time in the future…

…*someone who knows you inside out and loves you anyway*…

Like Leo?

And it suddenly occurred to her that for all these years, like Gio and Anita, they could have been missing something blindingly obvious that was right under their noses.

CHAPTER FIVE

THE MEN CAME back at lunchtime, and she found herself looking at Leo in a new light.

She could see just from the look on his face how much he'd enjoyed the morning, and their discussions continued for a few minutes, standing outside the kitchen door on the terrace with long, cold drinks in their hands, and they were all talking Italian.

It was the first time she'd heard them together like that, and it dawned on her with blinding clarity that, yes, it was a musical language but, no, they didn't *all* sound sexy. It wasn't the language, it was *Leo* talking the language.

Which changed everything.

They switched back to English as they came into the kitchen, but his voice still did things to her that no one else's did, and when he scooped Ella up in his arms and smiled the smile he reserved for her, Amy's heart melted all over again.

The conversation over lunch was very animated, but that didn't stop him juggling little Ella on his lap while he ate, and after lunch he handed her back to Amy reluctantly.

'I'm sorry. We're going out again to look at the olive oil processing plant this afternoon, if that's OK? Has she been all right?'

He looked a little worried, but Amy just smiled and shook her head slowly. 'She's been fine, Leo. Just go and do what you want to do. We're OK here. Lydia's been look-ing after us, haven't you, Lydia?'

Lydia smiled reassuringly. 'Leo, don't worry about us. Amy and I are getting on like a house on fire, and Ella seems perfectly happy. Just go. Shoo. We're fine.'

He frowned fleetingly, then gave a brisk nod, kissed the baby and left with the others, and to her relief the baby didn't cry this time.

'Have you got swimming things with you?' Lydia asked as the door closed behind them. 'We've got a heated pool, just in case you were wondering.'

Amy frowned. 'Yes, I have, but I don't know if Ella has.'

Lydia flapped a hand. 'She doesn't need one. I've got loads of swim nappies and arm bands and things. She'll be fine, and it'll only be us and the kids,' she said with a smile, and Amy felt herself relax.

'It sounds lovely. Really inviting.'

Lydia laughed. 'Oh, it is. I think we'd die without it when it gets really hot. At the end of a scorching day in the summer, it's just gorgeous to sink under that water in the evening when the kids are in bed and the stars are glit-tering overhead. So romantic.' She grinned mischievously. 'You and Leo should try it one night.'

She laughed awkwardly. 'I think the romance might be rather lost on us,' she said, trying not to picture herself and Leo alone under the stars.

Lydia found her a swim nappy, and they all changed and made their way to the pool set down below the terrace at a lower level. The water felt blissful on her hot skin, and Ella seemed to love it, so they spent hours playing in the pool, and it was lovely.

Ella, finally exhausted by all the fun, got a little grizzly, so Amy gave her a bottle and put her down to sleep in a travel cot strategically situated in the shade. She went out like a light, leaving nothing for Amy to do except chill out.

She should have brought a book with her, but she hadn't thought of it, so she settled herself on a sun lounger, arms wrapped round her knees, basking in the late afternoon sun and watching Lydia and the children playing in the water under the shade of a huge hanging parasol. Their squeals of delight washed over her as she gazed out over the beautiful valley below and soaked up the sun, and for the first time since the wedding that hadn't happened she felt herself relaxing.

Till the men appeared.

'The girls must be swimming,' Massimo said, and led Leo across the terrace to the railings. He could hear splashing and shrieking, and he leant on the railings beside Massimo and looked down at them.

Lydia was on the side with the youngest, wrapping him in a towel, and the other children were still in the water, but Amy was sitting on a sun lounger and he could see Ella sleeping in a travel cot in the shade just below them.

'Well, hi, there,' he said, and she looked up, her eyes shielded from him by her sunglasses.

'Hi,' she said, and wrapped her arms around her knees a little self-consciously. Not surprising. He could tell from here that her bikini was pretty insubstantial, and he felt himself willing her to unfurl her body so he could see it.

She smiled up at them, but it looked a little forced. Because of the bikini? Another honeymoon special, he thought, and his body cheered.

'Had a good time?' she asked, and he nodded.

'Great. Really interesting, but quite hot. That water looks very tempting.'

'Feel free, Leo. We've just finished,' Lydia said, gathering up the children's things and heading up the steps with the baby, the older children trailing in her wake, 'but help yourself. You're more than welcome to use it any time you like.'

'Yes, do,' Massimo agreed. 'I'd love to join you but I need to make a few calls before I can escape.' And taking the baby from her arms, he went inside with Lydia and the children, leaving Leo alone with Amy.

She didn't look any too thrilled. Because of the bikini? She would have worn it in public with Nick, he felt sure, so why did the fact that she was alone with him make any difference? Except of course it did. It certainly made a difference to him.

He went down the steps and crossed over to her, sitting on the edge of the sun lounger beside hers and pushing his sunglasses up onto his head so he could study her better. 'You've caught the sun,' he said with a slow smile. 'Just here.'

And because he couldn't resist it, he trailed a finger over her shoulder, and the heat that shot through him should have blistered his skin. Hers, too.

Why? It wasn't as if her skin was that hot. 'Mind if I join you for a swim?' he asked, and she shifted, straightening up so her shoulder was out of reach and giving him a perfect view of her cleavage.

'Actually, I'm going to go in, if you don't mind. I've been out here quite long enough,' she said, and swung away from him, getting to her feet on the other side of the sun lounger and wrapping the towel round herself quickly—but not before he'd been treated to the sight of her smoothly rounded bottom scarcely covered by a triangle of fabric, and his body reacted instantly.

She gathered up her things with indecent haste and turned to him, not quite meeting his eyes.

'Do you mind watching Ella till she wakes up? I could do with a shower.'

He swallowed. 'No, that's fine. How long's she been asleep?'

'I don't know. Half an hour? Bit more, maybe. She was pooped after the swimming. She's had a bottle.'

He nodded. 'OK. You go ahead, I'll take care of her.'

She walked slowly up the steps and across the terrace, resisting the urge to run away. She had been doing a lot of that recently, and look where it had got her, but the heat in his eyes had stirred something inside her that she couldn't trust herself not to act on, and she couldn't get away from him quick enough.

Because it echoed what she felt for him? Or because she feared it was just the knee-jerk reaction of a healthy adult male to a woman in about three square inches of fabric? In which case doing anything other than retreating could just embarrass them both.

She went in through the kitchen, across the courtyard and into their suite, closing the door behind her with relief. She didn't know how long he'd be before he followed her, but she wasn't going to hang around.

She showered quickly, opened her suitcase to look for some after-sun lotion and found the sheet of contraceptive pills that were part of her morning routine. She lifted them out slowly, staring at them without seeing while all thoughts of Leo drained away.

It was to have been her last course before she and Nick started trying for a baby, and she felt an aching sense of loss that had nothing to do with Nick and everything to do with the unfulfilled promise of motherhood.

Ironic that she'd never had much to do with babies before, and yet here she was now, surrounded by pregnant women and small children, so that just when it was suddenly out of reach she saw exactly what she'd be missing.

She hesitated for a moment, then popped the now purposeless pill out of the sheet and swallowed it, simply because she didn't want her cycle messed up.

She found the after-sun lotion, smeared it on her shoulders where she could still feel the tingle of Leo's fingertip, pulled on clean clothes and emerged from the bedroom just as he appeared, Ella grizzling unhappily and arching backwards in his arms.

'She's a bit grumpy, aren't you, sweetheart?' Leo murmured gently, his voice rich with the warmth of his love. He looked up from the baby and smiled at Amy, and the vague sense of loss she'd been feeling was overlaid with another, much more complex emotion that was much more troubling.

'I don't suppose you fancy putting the kettle on, do you?' he suggested. 'I could murder a cup of tea.'

'It was my next job,' she said lightly, and walked past them into the kitchen, wondering how on earth, when her world was steadily imploding, the scent of Leo's skin warmed by the sun could possibly be so intoxicating...

The next morning Lydia dropped the children off at school and ran a few errands, so Amy followed her suggestion and spent a while exploring the grounds with the baby in the buggy, taking photos either for Leo or possibly her own portfolio. Assuming she could find an outlet for them, which was by no means certain. Still, just to be on the safe side, she kept clicking, and she took lots of photos of Ella for Leo.

He checked in on his mobile from time to time, just to make sure that everything was OK, and then Lydia collected the children from school and the men came home for lunch, and after that they all went in the pool to cool off before the men went back to work.

It was stiflingly hot, so Amy joined them, but it didn't take very many minutes to realise that frolicking about in the water in her skimpy little honeymoon bikini in front of Leo wasn't clever. It had been bad enough yesterday when she'd just had to stand up and wrap herself in a towel, but in the water everything seemed to take on a life of its own and she'd had an embarrassing wardrobe malfunction when Ella had grabbed her bikini top. It was only by a miracle that no one else had noticed, but Leo had, and she vowed never to do it again, no matter how tempting the water was.

Then Ella started to fuss, so she grabbed the opportunity and climbed out of the pool, swathed herself in her towel and took the baby from Leo in the water, towelling her gently dry and putting a nappy on her before giving her a drink and settling her in the travel cot for a nap.

Leo swam to the side and folded his arms on the edge of the pool. 'Coming back in?'

'No, I don't think so,' she said without looking at him. 'I thought I could take some photos of you all for the blog.'

'Sure?'

'Sure.'

She forced herself to meet his searching gaze, then he shrugged and sank back under the water, leaving her to it.

She stayed resolutely on the side, wrapped in her towel and perched on a sun lounger, and spent the next hour capturing images of them all playing in the water with the children—ostensibly for Leo, since a disproportionate number of the photos were of him, but mostly so she didn't have to frolic about feeling hopelessly under-dressed.

Then Ella woke, so Leo swam to the side and vaulted out, water streaming off his lean, muscular frame and plastering his shorts to strong, straight thighs, and her heart somersaulted in her chest. She clicked the shutter, capturing the image for posterity, then put the camera away in its case, giving him time to grab a towel and knot it loosely round his hips.

'Your turn to swim, I'll look after Ella,' he said, but she shook her head and glanced back at him.

Not better. Not better at all. To her all too vivid imagination it just looked as if he had nothing on under the towel, and it was too much for her.

'I'm going to shower and get dressed, and then I'll download the photos,' she said, getting hastily to her feet, and with a smile and a wave to the others, she picked up her camera and headed for the sanctuary of the house.

She hardly saw him on Tuesday because the men didn't come back for lunch and then had a meeting after dinner, but then on Wednesday afternoon Massimo and Gio had a prior commitment and the women and children were at a birthday party, so they were left to their own devices.

'How about playing tourists?' Leo suggested, so they went out in the car with the baby and explored a nearby hill town Lydia had recommended for its food shops, and while he investigated them she clicked away on her camera, recording the day for Leo's blog.

It made her smile, watching him interacting with the shopkeepers. He went all Italian, of course, smiling and laughing and waving his hands all over the place, and she realised that he was always like that when he was fired up about something, and she just hadn't registered it until now, when it was slightly more exaggerated.

He'd always been just Leo, and she'd never really analysed him before, but she was doing it now, constantly, with every click of the shutter. Every move, every smile, every frown, every gesture, all logged and recorded in a little part of her brain labelled 'Leo', and her feelings were getting utterly confused.

Inappropriate? No, maybe not that, but certainly different, threatening the platonic status quo that she'd just realised was so fragile, and because of that, and because she wasn't going to repeat the fiasco with her bikini, when she spotted a likely-looking shop she took the opportunity to check it out.

'Can I have five minutes?' she asked him. 'I need another swimming costume if we're going to swim every day.'

A muscle twitched in his jaw and he nodded. 'Sure. I'll wait here for you.'

The shop was perfect, and she found a ludicrously expensive but utterly plain black one-piece swimsuit. She didn't bother to try it on. Whatever it was like, it had to be better than the bikini, and there was a limit to how many photos even she could take of Leo in and around the water. And anyway she wanted to swim; she just wasn't going to risk another disaster.

She picked up a pretty little pink swimsuit for Ella, as well, because it was irresistible, and she didn't even look at the price. She'd hardly given the baby anything, only the crackly dragonfly that was her constant companion, so she could easily justify it to herself.

She managed to pay without flinching, put her purse away, scooped up her shopping and went out into the sunshine to find Leo and Ella.

He wondered what she was looking for. Hopefully something that covered her up a little more successfully than that bikini, which had already given him two sleepless nights since Ella had grabbed it.

He was trying to keep an eye on the shop door, but an elderly matron who should have known better had cornered him and was flirting outrageously, so he was relieved to see Amy emerge.

'Got what you wanted?' he asked, and she nodded and waggled the bag at him.

'Yup. Are you done?'

'Definitely. We need to make a move.'

He turned to the woman to excuse himself, and she caught him by the shoulders and kissed his cheeks, laughing as she let him go with an outrageous parting shot and a cheeky pat on his behind.

He felt the colour run up his neck and walked hastily away, shaking his head in despair.

'What did she say to you?' Amy asked, eyeing him curiously as she struggled to keep up.

'Nothing,' he mumbled. 'Just goodbye.'

'I don't believe you. She was flirting—and she groped you.'

'No, she didn't. It was just a little pat. She recognised me, that's all.'

Amy rolled her eyes. 'I wasn't born yesterday, Leo. Most people don't pat you on the behind, and even I can tell a starstruck old biddy when I see one. She was hitting on you.'

He fought the rising tide of colour, and lost. 'OK, OK. She said if she was twenty years younger, she'd give you a run for your money. I didn't think it'd be wise to point out that we're not together. She might have dragged me off on her broomstick.'

Her chuckle was delicious, and he couldn't help but join in.

'You're such a babe magnet, Zacharelli,' she teased. 'They all hurl themselves at you, it doesn't matter how old they are.'

All except Amy.

The thought popped into his head without warning, but it was true. If he was such a babe magnet, how come she'd never even noticed him in that way? Well, not since she was fourteen and had come down with a serious case of hero-worship, and that didn't really count. Although God only knows he'd noticed *her* recently. Like Monday, with the bikini top that Ella had so helpfully dragged out of the way and that she'd now seen fit to replace. He'd certainly noticed that.

'Can we change the subject, please?' he muttered, to himself as much as Amy, and headed back to the car with Ella, leaving Amy to follow, still chuckling, in his wake.

The next day the men were out again, visiting the cousin who made the gorgeous balsamic vinegar that appeared with oil and bread at every delicious meal, and she and the three wives were left to their own devices for the whole day.

It seemed odd now, not seeing him at all for such a long time, and she seemed to miss him more than the baby did, which was a bit telling. They went to Isabelle's for lunch, for a change, and then retreated to the pool in the afternoon, and then at five, as they were just getting the children out of the water, Massimo, Gio and Leo reappeared, making her profoundly glad she'd bought the new one-piece.

Leo walked towards her, his eyes shielded by sunglasses, and she turned, the baby on her hip, to point him out.

'Hey, look, baby, it's your daddy!' she cooed to Ella, and Ella held her arms out to him, little starfish hands opening and closing as she jiggled with excitement.

Amy could identify with that. She watched Leo's face light up as he reached out for the baby, and felt a pang of envy. What would it be like, to have a little person so very pleased to see you?

Wonderful. Amazing.

He slid the sunglasses up onto his head and held his arms out, and she could see the wonder in his eyes.

'She's wet,' Amy warned him, but he just shrugged.

'I don't care. I need a shower anyway. Come here, *mia*

bellissima bambina,' Leo said, reaching for the baby, but his fingers brushed Amy's breast and she sucked in her breath. It was barely audible, but he heard it, and their eyes clashed and held, his darkening to midnight.

For a moment they both froze. She couldn't breathe, the air jammed solid in her lungs, and then with a muttered apology he lifted Ella out of her arms and turned away, laughing and kissing her all over her face, making her giggle deliciously and freeing Amy from his spell.

After a second of paralysing immobility, she grabbed a towel and wrapped it firmly round herself, then gathered up their things and headed for the steps, Leo falling in beside her at the top. They walked back together to their apartment, Ella perched on his shoulders with her little fists knotted in his hair, while he told her a little about his day and they both pretended that the moment by the pool hadn't happened.

'Sounds like it was worth going,' she said lightly as they went in and closed the door behind them, and he nodded.

'It was,' he said, prising the baby's fingers out of his hair and swinging her down into his arms. 'We had a lot to talk about, and we still have. And they're all off to visit their parents tomorrow. It's their mother's birthday and they can't reschedule, there isn't another time they're all available, which means we can't finalise the deal until after they're back on Sunday. Will that be a problem for you?'

A whole weekend alone with Leo? She felt a flicker of trepidation—anticipation? She didn't know. All she knew was that she couldn't refuse him and she didn't want to. 'No—why should it?'

He shrugged. 'I don't know. I said maybe a week, but we won't leave now until at least Monday or Tuesday and I don't know if you can give me that long or if there's something you need to get back for.'

She stared at him blankly. 'Leo, I can give you as long

as it takes. That's why I'm here. I owe you so much, for so many things—really, don't give it another thought. Do what you need to do. It's fine. I have nowhere else to be.'

'Sure?' he asked, but she could see the relief in his eyes and she wondered if he'd expected her to refuse.

She rolled her eyes. 'Of course I'm sure. Anyway, I'm having fun,' she said, keeping it light. 'So I'm going to be forced to spend a few more days in a medieval Medici palace with a beautiful swimming pool and a view to die for, playing with a cute baby and being fed by a celebrity chef. What a tragedy!'

He laughed softly, shrugged acknowledgement and put Ella on the floor on her towel, crouching down to peel off her costume. 'This is lovely, by the way. Really cute. Where did it come from? Did you borrow it?'

'No, I bought it yesterday in the shop while you were being chatted up by Methuselah's mother—and before you say anything, it's a present. So, are we going to be completely on our own, then, while they're away?' she asked, striving for casual while her hormones were having a field day.

'I believe so. They're going to give us keys and we'll have the run of the place till Sunday lunchtime, so we'll be able to just chill out, which is lovely. I really need that. It'll be like being on holiday, and I'll have a chance to try out some recipes using their ingredients. I'm actually really looking forward to it. I'm cooking for them all on Sunday so they don't have to do it when they get back, and I want to play around with some ideas for that.'

'Can I be your guinea pig?' she asked hopefully, latching onto the safe and familiar, and he tilted his head to look at her and grinned, suddenly looking like the old Leo.

'I'm relying on it. You have a terrifying gift for honesty where my food's concerned. And I'll try not to poison you.'

'You do that,' she said, secretly flattered by his back-handed compliment and relieved that the conversation had steered them seamlessly into safer waters.

'So how was your day?' he asked, straightening up with the naked baby in his arms. 'I felt I'd abandoned you. Were you both OK?'

'Leo, we were fine, and we've had a lovely day together. She's gorgeous. I didn't realise what fun a baby could be.'

His smile softened his features. 'Nor did I,' he murmured, brushing Ella's head with a gentle kiss, and the tender gesture turned her heart to mush.

Oh, Leo...

She showered and changed, then took herself outside, sitting on the bench in the cool shade of their east-facing terrace and leaving him to deal with Ella while she took advantage of a few moments to herself when she didn't have to pretend anything.

She'd tipped her head back and closed her eyes, but then she heard the gravel crunch, then the slight creak of the bench as he sat down beside her.

'Here. I've brought you a drink.'

She opened her eyes and sat up, taking the glass of sparkling water with a slice of lime floating in it, the outside beaded with moisture.

'Just what I wanted. Thank you. Is she asleep?'

'Yes, she's gone out like a light. The swimming must have tired her out. Look, I wanted to talk to you about this weekend. Are you OK with me doing all this cooking?'

Amy looked at him in astonishment, puzzled that he would even ask. 'Why wouldn't I be? You're the one doing all the work and it's not as if I won't get to eat it. It's not down to me.'

'It is in a way,' he pointed out. 'If I'm cooking, you'll need to look after Ella, and it's not really why you're here. I should have checked with you instead of just assuming.'

'Of course I don't mind,' she said, puzzled that he would even ask her. 'You know I don't. Ella's lovely, and, anyway, I am here to look after her.'

'Only when I'm in meetings. That was the deal.'

'Leo, it's fine, and, as you said, you need to play around with their produce, try out some recipes, and I'm more than happy to help you in any way I can. I owe you so much—'

'You owe me nothing,' he said softly, his eyes curiously intent. 'I've told you that.'

She shook her head briefly to free her from the magnetic hold of those mesmerising eyes. 'I do. Not just the catering. I'm OK with that now. That's just money, really, but—well, without you I would have married Nick, and it would have been a disaster. If you hadn't said what you did…'

His sigh sounded weary and dredged up from his boots. 'I had to, Amy. You just didn't seem happy enough for it to be right, and there was no way I could let you sleepwalk into a doomed marriage.'

'Like you did into yours?' she asked rashly, and then bit her lip and waited for his reply.

It was quiet on the shady terrace, the valley stretched out below them, the doors to his bedroom open so he could hear Ella if she woke. A light breeze whispered over Amy's skin, welcome after the heat of the day, and she pressed the cold glass to her face to cool it.

He glanced at her, then looked away. 'I didn't sleepwalk into it,' he said at last. 'Lisa did, to a certain extent, but I was railroaded into it by my own sense of decency. Lisa was pregnant, I was the father, I was responsible for her and the baby. I did, as they say, the decent thing. End of. Except that wasn't the end of it,' he added bleakly, 'and I don't know if it ever will be.'

He was staring out over the rolling hills, his eyes re-

mote and shuttered, and she reached out and laid a hand
on his shoulder.

'Oh, Leo, I'm so sorry,' she said softly. 'Want to talk
about it?'

He glanced briefly back at her, then away again. 'Not
really. Why would I? What's the point? It won't change
anything.'

It was a less than subtle hint to drop the subject, but
somehow she couldn't, so she pressed on. 'I know that, but
you always used to talk to me, get things off your chest.
I thought it might help you. You must be so sad, for Ella
if not for yourself.'

'Sad?' He gave a bitter little laugh that made her wince.
'I don't think sad even scratches the surface. Gutted?
Wracked with guilt? Ashamed?'

Ashamed...?

He turned his head to look at her, and in the depths of
those beautiful amber eyes she could see an unfathomable
despair. And then the shutters came down and he looked
away, glancing pointedly at his watch.

'It's time we went over for dinner,' he said, changing
the subject so emphatically now that there was no way she
was about to argue with him. And that was that—the end
of anything deep and meaningful, at least for now.

Just as well. She was getting altogether too interested
in Leo and his thoughts and feelings, and it was time she
remembered that it was none of her business, and that he
was just a friend.

*It's not wrong to take an interest in your friends. You
were only asking because you care.*

No, she wasn't. She was being nosy, delving into parts
of his psyche that were absolutely none of her business,
friend or not. If he wanted to tell her about his disastrous
marriage, no doubt he'd do it in his own time, but it wasn't
down to her to ask.

He got up and went inside, leaving her sitting alone on the terrace. She closed her eyes, tilted her head back against the worn old stone and sighed softly.

There had been a time, not all that long ago, when he'd told her everything. He'd poured his heart out to her on numerous occasions; break-ups with his girlfriends, rows with his parents—all manner of things. She'd done the same with him, and there'd never been anything they couldn't talk about.

And there'd been the good things, too, like the time he'd won the TV cookery competition when he was only nineteen, and his first job as a head chef when he'd scarcely finished his training, and his meteoric rise to success as a TV celebrity chef.

That was when his ageing father had handed over the reins of the company restaurant business, and he'd raised his game and gone from strength to strength.

But all the time he'd talked to her. She'd been part of all his ups and downs, but not any more, apparently. Not since Lisa, and the marriage that had left him, of all things, ashamed.

Why? Why *ashamed*? Of his choice of bride? His behaviour towards her? Because she'd died in such tragic circumstances? Hardly his fault—unless there was something about her death that she didn't know. And she wasn't likely to now, because apparently he wasn't prepared to share anything more intimate than a menu, and she couldn't believe how much it hurt.

CHAPTER SIX

As THEY WERE seeing the others off the following morning, Massimo apologised for abandoning them.

'Don't worry about it, we'll be fine,' Leo said. 'Can I raid your vegetable garden, Lydia?'

'Oh, feel free, you don't have to ask,' she said whole-heartedly. 'Use anything you want, there or in the kitchen. Are you sure you don't mind doing lunch for us all? I don't want you to feel you have to.'

He laughed. 'Don't be silly, it'll be a pleasure and I love a family party. It'll be fun. And don't worry about us, we'll be fine, won't we, Amy?'

'Of course we will,' Amy said, but the butterflies were at it again at the thought of forty-eight hours alone with him. His accidental touch yesterday by the pool was still fresh in her mind, and they'd been surrounded then. What would have happened if they'd been alone?

Nothing, probably, and if there was another awkward moment like that she'd only have to mention Lisa and he'd back off at the speed of light. She let out a quiet sigh and waved goodbye to the family.

'Right,' he said, watching the dust trail thrown up by their car as they drove away. 'I need to do some food shopping. There's a market on where we went the other day. Want to come?'

'Sure.' She flashed him a cheeky smile. 'I can defend you from all the old women who want to grope you.'

He chuckled and rolled his eyes. 'Oh, Amy, how would I cope without you?' he said softly.

'Well, aren't you lucky you don't have to?' she quipped straight back at him, and turned away so he didn't see the yearning in her eyes.

Ella fell asleep in the car, so he put her carefully in the buggy and plundered the produce stalls while Amy followed with Ella and captured the atmosphere on her ever-present camera. He found the butcher Lydia had recommended and got into an earnest conversation, which as usual brought out his lovely Italian side that was so irresistibly sexy.

He bought a shoulder of mutton, not something readily available in England, and three racks of lamb. 'I'm going to do lamb two ways for Sunday lunch,' he told her when he finally got away. 'Easy for the numbers, and tender enough for the kids to eat.'

'Yummy.'

'It will be. Even though you have no faith in me.'

She laughed. 'I never said that.'

His mouth twitched but he said nothing, just hung the bag on the back of the buggy and carried on, wandering along the stalls, chatting to people and picking up this and that as they went, and she strolled along behind him with Ella in the buggy, taking photos and pretended to herself that they were a couple.

'Right, I'm done here. Anything else you want to do before we go back?'

She shook her head, so they walked back to the car, him laden with bags, her pushing the buggy with that surreal sensation that somehow it was her place to do it. If only...

'It's getting hot,' he said, tilting his head back and looking up at the sun. 'It'll be a scorcher later.'

'It's hot enough now,' she said, happy to walk in the

shade and wondering if everyone was looking at them and speculating, because everywhere they went he was recognised, and not just by women old enough to be his grandmother. She hadn't realised his fame was so widespread in Italy, but apparently it was.

And mostly he tolerated it with good grace, but she could tell that for once he would have liked to be able to walk around without people saying something to him, or nudging each other and staring. At him, or them together? Would it spark a whole lot of media speculation about his private life? She hoped not, for his sake, and she was glad to get back to the car and away from prying eyes.

He stashed everything in the boot, strapped Ella into her seat and drove home.

No. Not home. They didn't have a home, and there was no 'they', either. Just him and Ella, and her.

'I fancy a dip,' he announced, putting the last things away in the kitchen. 'Want to swim, baby?'

She opened her mouth to answer and then realised he was talking to Ella. Well, of course he was! Why wouldn't he be? He'd never called her baby. Never called her anything except Amy. And brat, on occasions, when she had been, which had been quite often all those years ago.

'Going to join us?'

Was she? She turned her head and met his eyes. They told her nothing. 'Do you want me to?'

He shrugged. 'Only if you want to. It's easier with Ella if there are two of us, but it's not strictly necessary if you'd rather not.'

Of course. He just wanted help with the baby, and put like that it was hard to refuse. Besides, she couldn't think of anything she'd rather do than dive into the cool, refreshing water, so they changed and went over to the pool, and he rigged up the tilting parasol so it hung across the water and they played in the shade with Ella until it was time for her lunch.

'Stay here a bit longer if you like. I'll get her dressed and feed her and then I might put her down for a bit,' he said, handing the baby to her for a moment while he vaulted out of the water, rubbed himself down roughly with a towel and then bent and took Ella from her and walked away.

She let out a long, slow, silent sigh of relief as he went up the steps and disappeared from sight onto the terrace. She'd put on the one-piece again that she'd bought on Wednesday, but she'd felt every bit as naked and as aware of him in that as she had in the bikini.

Because his hand had brushed her breast yesterday afternoon? It meant nothing, she told herself, just an accidental touch.

So why couldn't she forget it, and why couldn't he look at her straight in the eye any more? Or, at least, he hadn't in the past hour or so, since she'd been wearing it.

Stupid. So, so stupid. And it was changing the dynamics of their relationship.

She kicked away from the end of the pool, gliding under the surface with her arms stretched out in front of her until her fingertips hit the other end, and then she tumble-turned and swam back again, up and down, up and down, pushing herself harder and harder until her arms and legs were shaking with the effort.

Even Leo hadn't worked her that hard the summer he'd coached her to swim for the school relay team. And she was thinking about him *again!*

She swam two more lengths to get him out of her mind, then gave up and rolled onto her back and kicked lazily into the centre of the pool, floating with her face turned up to the sun and her arms and legs outstretched like a star.

It was gorgeous. The heat of the sun warmed her where the water had cooled her skin, and she felt all the tension of the last few days soaking out of her body and drifting away across the surface of the pool.

Bliss. Utter, utter bliss—

Something cold splashed onto her face, and she gave a startled shriek and jack-knifed up, frantically treading water while she looked up into Leo's laughing eyes.

'How long have you been there?' she asked indignantly, righting herself and glowering at him.

'Only a moment or two. You looked so peaceful it seemed a shame to disturb you, but I've brought you a nice cold drink.'

'Yes, I rather got the *cold* when you tipped it on me.'

'Drizzled. Not tipped.'

'Semantics,' she muttered. She stood up, cupping a handful of water and hurling it at him. It hit him right in the middle of his chest, and he folded in half and backed away, laughing as he tugged the wet material away from his midriff.

Oh, for the camera...

'I've only just put this shirt on!'

'You should have thought of that before you tipped my drink all over my face. At least I threw warm water at you.' She folded her arms on the side of the pool and grinned up at him cheekily. 'Well, come on, then, let me have it.'

He gave a soft huff of laughter and dangled the glass just out of reach. She stretched up, and just too late she caught the mischief in his eyes.

She should have seen it coming. She knew Leo well enough to know he wouldn't let her get away with soaking him. Even so, the icy flood down her arm and over her chest caught her by surprise, and she gave a strangled shriek and ducked back under the warm water for a second, coming up further away, out of reach.

She swiped the wet hair back off her face and tried to glare at him. 'That was so mean!'

Leo just smiled, set the glass down on the edge of the pool and retreated to a sun lounger a safe distance away. Wise. She swam over to the half empty glass and sipped cautiously.

Gorgeous. Ice-cold sparkling water with a dash of lime. Pity it was only half a glass now, but she wasn't going to pick a fight with him over it. She knew she'd never win. Leo always, always had the last word. She drained the glass and set it down.

'Where's Ella?'

'Napping. She was pooped after the swimming so I stuck her in the travel cot the second she'd finished eating and she went out like a light.' He tipped his head on one side and eyed her thoughtfully. 'Your shoulders have caught the sun again. Are you going to stay in there until you look like a fried prune?' he asked mildly.

It was tempting. The alternative was to get out of the pool in front of him, and she felt curiously, ridiculously naked, even in the one-piece, but she couldn't stay in there for ever, so she swam over to the steps where her towel was waiting, climbed out and wrapped herself in it before she turned round to face him.

'Happy now?'

'I was quite happy before,' he said deadpan. 'It was you I was worried about.'

'You don't need to worry about me, Leo. I'm a big girl now. I can take care of myself. And don't worry about Ella. I'll look after her, if you want to play in the kitchen. I could do with downloading today's photos and sorting through them.'

Anything to keep herself out of his way.

Picking up her empty glass and the baby monitor, she headed up the stone steps to the top of the terrace and left him sitting there alone, hopefully oblivious of the trembling in her legs and her pounding heart and this crazy, absurd awareness of him, which seemed to have sprung out of nowhere in the last few days…

Leo let her go.

Not that there was anything else he could do, short of grabbing her and hanging on, and that didn't seem like an immensely good idea right now. So he settled for watching the slight sway of her hips as she went up the steps, the beads of water on her shoulders sparkling in the sun.

His eyes tracked down to linger on those slender ankles below the smooth, gleaming curve of her calves. Her legs were browner. Even in the last few days she'd acquired a delicate tan from the glorious Tuscan weather. It was early June, hot yet still bearable, and Amy was flourishing, like a flower turning its face up to the sun.

And he was getting obsessed. He had ingredients to experiment with, the Sunday lunch menu to finalise, and he was wasting the precious time he had while Ella was asleep. He should be using that time wisely, not staring at Amy's legs as they disappeared up the steps and behind the parapet wall and imagining them wrapped around him.

And he should *so* not be thinking about her like that!

He groaned. He wasn't interested in Amy.

At all.

So why was he still watching her?

She vanished from sight and he closed his eyes and dragged his hand down over his face as if he could wipe away the image from his mind.

Not a chance. With a sigh dredged up from his boots, he picked up his glass, got to his feet and took her advice. Time to go and have a look at the vegetable garden, and then do something useful in the kitchen, instead of fantasising the day away. And from now on he was going to keep his distance and hope that also meant he could keep his sanity.

* * *

'So, my little guinea pig, are you ready for this?' Leo asked.

He was lolling against the kitchen cupboards, lean hips propped on the edge of the worktop, arms folded, a slight smile playing around the sides of his mouth, and he looked good enough to eat. He also looked more like the old Leo, to her relief, so she played along, trying hard not to be distracted by how downright gorgeous he looked.

Not your business! Nothing about him is your business, especially not that. Only Ella, and her care, and taking photos for his blog. Nothing else. He couldn't have made it clearer if he'd tattooed 'Back Off' all over himself...

'Are you ready for my honesty?' she said drily.

His warm chuckle filled the kitchen and made her insides melt. 'Oh, ye of little faith,' he teased, eyes crinkling at the corners and making her heart turn over. 'I just fancied playing around with some ideas and I didn't know if you were up for it.'

She shook her head slowly. 'Leo!' she said reproachfully, trying not to think about playing around with him or what she might be up for. 'When have I ever said no to you?'

'Oh, now, let me think—when I tried to kiss you?'

A distant memory stirred, and she laughed. 'I was eight!'

'I think you were nine, actually, and I was nearly thirteen—and as I recall, you told me not to be gross.'

She bit her lips to stop the smile. 'I remember. I also remember when I was fourteen and wanted you to try again, but you never did.'

His eyes changed, becoming curiously intent. 'You were a child, Amy, a minor, and I was an adult by then, so, no, I never did,' he said.

'I'm not a child now,' she said, her mouth on autopilot.

The soft caramel of his eyes darkened, the pupils flaring as he gave her a slow, slightly wry smile.

'I had noticed,' he murmured slowly, and pushed himself away from the worktop, heading towards the fridge. 'So—are you up for this, then? I promise not to poison you.'

She let her breath ease out on a sigh. 'You've tried before.'

'I have not!' he said indignantly, but it didn't work because she could hear the laughter underlying it and her lips twitched.

His laughter was so infectious she gave up the struggle and joined in, the sensual moment pushed into the background as their old banter resumed. 'Oh, all right, if you insist,' she relented.

'Ah, see? You still love me, really.'

Her heart crashed against her ribs. Love him? *Really?* She *loved* him? *Like that?*

'In your dreams,' she said drily, and wondered if he could see her heart pounding in her chest.

She couldn't—could she?

Still grinning, he wandered over to her and hugged her briefly, swamping her in that brief moment with a welter of scents and sensations that sent her emotions into a tailspin, before letting go all too soon to open the fridge and examine the contents.

'Do you fancy a glass of fizz while I cook?'

'Now you're trying to get me drunk and kill my taste buds,' she said, her heart still jiggling after the hug, the word *love* echoing in her head like the aftermath of a thunderclap.

He just rolled his eyes and plonked a bottle down on the table. 'Some people are never satisfied,' he said, then set two flutes down in front of her. A quick twist, a soft pop and he filled the glasses with pale, delicately foaming Prosecco, put the bottle back in the fridge and starting pulling out ingredients.

She sat back in her chair, twiddling the glass, watching condensation bead on the outside as the bubbles rose and popped on the surface.

Did she love him? As in, *in love* with him?

Well, at last! You've taken your time to work that one out.

She ignored her inner voice, took a slurp of the Prosecco and tried not to sneeze when the bubbles went up her nose, then swivelled round to look at him, camera in hand.

'So, what exactly are you planning to experiment with?'

He shrugged, his broad shoulders rising and falling and grabbing her attention. How had she never noticed them before this week? Had she been utterly blind? Evidently. But not any more. She clicked the shutter for posterity. Or her private collection, which was growing at an embarrassing rate.

'I'm not really sure. I haven't come up with anything concrete yet.'

'Concrete? How about your rock buns?' she added to get a rise out of him.

He rolled his eyes. 'They were fine.'

'They were rocks, and you know it.'

He sighed softly, but his eyes were brimming with laughter. 'So they were a little over-baked. I was—what? Nine? And you've never let me forget it.'

'You must have been more than that.'

'Not much. Ten at the most. And you had trouble biting into them because you didn't have any front teeth, I remember that.'

'Yes, and you teased me constantly about it.'

'And you rose to the bait without fail. You always did. Still do.' He stopped teasing her and shook his head slowly, a soft smile playing around his mouth. 'That was a long time ago.'

'It was. It feels like another lifetime.'

'Maybe it was.' The smile faded, a fleeting sadness in his eyes, and he turned his attention back to the fridge, effectively changing the subject.

'So, what are you going to kill me with tonight, then?' she asked lightly, swirling her Prosecco in the flute and following his lead.

He shrugged away from the worktop and shoved his hands into the back pockets of his jeans, drawing her attention in a way that did nothing for her peace of mind. She captured the image. Not that she needed to. It was burned onto her brain, alongside all the others.

'I don't know. I just want to play around and get a feel for their oil and cheese, amongst other things. I've had a look at Lydia's vegetable garden, which has given me some ideas. I think tonight's going to be pretty tame, though, so you're safe.'

She didn't feel safe. She felt—confused. As if her world had slipped on its axis, even though, in reality, nothing had changed.

Nothing? You ran away from your bridegroom at the altar! This is not nothing!

But it was nothing to do with Leo.

Or was it? Was that why she hadn't married Nick? Because of Leo?

The thought held her transfixed, and she watched him blindly while her thoughts cartwheeled in the background.

He diced an onion at the speed of light, pulled cupboards open, inspected spices and herbs, chose some, rejected others. She could almost hear him thinking on his feet. A slab of bacon appeared out of the fridge, and he cut a thick slice and diced it rapidly into lardons and tossed them into a sizzling pan with the onion.

The aroma of frying bacon began to fill the kitchen, and her mouth was watering. Rice appeared, a glug of wine, some stock—

'Are we having risotto?' she asked hopefully.

'Looks like it,' he said with a grin.

Her stomach grumbled. 'Sorry. Smells good.'

'Twenty minutes,' he said, and while he stirred and added a glug of this and a drop of that, he pressed thin slices of ciabatta onto a griddle and stirred something else in another little pan that he piled onto the crispy bread.

'Here, try this,' he said, sliding a plate across to her. 'Tell me what you think. I've used their oil and olives.'

'Gorgeous,' she mumbled, and had to say it again because he didn't understand her first attempt.

'Didn't your mother ever tell you it's rude to speak with your mouth full?' he said, laughing at her, and she poked her tongue out at him.

'Is this all for me?' she asked, and he leant over and snatched the plate back.

'No, it's not!'

'Pity,' she said, watching as his almost perfect white teeth bit through a slice of the delicious *bruschetta* topped with some gorgeous sundried tomato and olive concoction topped with anchovies. She didn't know what she wanted more, the *bruschetta* or the man.

She stifled a laugh and picked up the camera again. If she had the *bruschetta*, she'd eat it this once and that would be the end of it. If she had the man, she could have the *bruschetta* any time she asked for it. And not just the *bruschetta*—

Heat shot through her, stealing her breath and leaving her gasping.

There was a squeak from Ella over the baby monitor, and she shot back her chair and got to her feet. 'I'll go, you're busy,' she said, and left the kitchen hastily, glad of an excuse to get away from him while she reassembled her jumbled thoughts.

Closing the door of their apartment softly behind her, she leant back against it with a quiet sigh.

Whatever the change in direction of her feelings, and probably his, it was perfectly obvious that Leo wasn't in the slightest bit interested in a relationship with her other than the one they already had, a friend helping him out by looking after his daughter. That was all she was here for, and she had to remember it and keep her overactive imagination under control before it got them both into a whole heap of trouble and embarrassment.

Or her, at least, because for all the banter Leo wouldn't even talk to her any longer about anything personal, far less take advantage of her shaky emotional state. Which, she was beginning to realise, was more to do with Leo than it was with Nick and the abandoned wedding.

She pushed away from the door and crept over to the bedroom, but all was quiet. Ella was lying on her front with her bottom stuck up in the air, and she was fast asleep.

And Leo would know this, because the monitor had gone silent. She closed her eyes briefly, sucked in a deep breath and made herself go back to the kitchen. Nothing had changed, nothing was any different, and it wouldn't be if she kept a lid on it. Yes, she loved him, but just in the way she always had. Nothing more, nothing less, and certainly not like *that*—

Liar!

'Gosh, that smells lovely,' she said brightly, walking back into the kitchen and ignoring the nagging voice that had far too much to say for itself. 'Really yummy.'

'Is she okay?'

'Yes, she's fine. Fast asleep.' She picked up her glass and peered at the dribble in the bottom. 'Any more Prosecco in the fridge?'

He glanced over his shoulder. 'There should be, unless you've already drunk it all. You can top me up while you're at it. I've been working hard.'

She arched a brow at him and chuckled. 'Don't give me that. You could make that risotto in your sleep.'

His lips twitched, drawing her attention to their soft, ripe fullness, and she had an overwhelming urge to get up and walk over to him and kiss them.

No! What was she *thinking* about?

She did get up, and she did walk over to him, but only so she could top up their glasses. Then she retreated back to the table, sat herself down and concentrated on the power of mind over matter. Or head over heart, more likely. The last thing she needed was to allow herself to fantasise about being in love with Leo. Not that she was even thinking about love. Nothing so ethereal. Just at the moment, she was quite preoccupied enough with thinking about kissing him senseless.

She stifled a groan of frustration and impatience at herself, chewed her way thoughtfully through another slice of the delicious *bruschetta* and tried not to down the wine so fast that she fell off her chair. Getting drunk would *not* be an asset to the situation!

In the nick of time a wide, flat bowl appeared in front of her, heaped with risotto drizzled with green-gold oil and scattered with torn basil leaves, and Leo leant across her and shaved some slender curls of a wonderful hard pecorino cheese over it. She sniffed appreciatively, and got a touch of Leo in the fragrant mix.

'Wow, that smells amazing,' she said, bending down to hide the sudden flush of colour that swept her cheeks. 'Utterly gorgeous.'

Leo, sitting down opposite her in front of his own plate, couldn't agree more. She was. Utterly gorgeous, and he'd never really noticed it before the last few days. When it had happened, he couldn't work out, but it had, and he was finding it quite difficult to ignore—especially since the incident with her bikini top earlier in the week.

He frowned, picked up his fork and plunged it into the steaming pile of creamy rice and tried to blank the image of the pale swell of her breast out of his mind, but the delicate rose pink of her nipple, puckered with the cold, was seared on his retina, and he could still feel the soft jut of it on the back of his hand when he'd brushed against her yesterday, taking Ella from her.

Spending time with her was awakening something that had been dormant for months—years, maybe. Something hungry and a little wild and beyond his control that was flaring to life between them. Maybe he didn't need to ignore it. Maybe he needed to talk to her about it?

But not now, if ever. She was a friend, a good friend, helping him out when he was in a bad place and so was she. The last thing either of them needed was him muddying the waters at this point in their lives, but his body had gone stone deaf to the pleading from his mind.

'So what do you think of it?' he asked, watching her demolish the risotto. 'I like the pea and mint with the bacon, and I think their oil and cheese really lend something interesting.'

'Mmm. Not going to argue,' she said, scraping the bowl. 'Is there any more?'

CHAPTER SEVEN

WELL, HE'D MANAGED to keep the conversation on track, he thought with relief as the door closed behind her.

They'd finished their meal, and then he'd told her he needed more time to play with the flavours so she'd gone to do some more work with the photos, which didn't surprise him because every time he'd looked up for the past few days she'd had that wretched camera in her hands.

But at least she was taking his request seriously, he thought as he worked. She must have recorded every last breath he'd taken, but he wasn't going to complain because the results that he'd seen so far were far better than anything he'd ever managed.

He fiddled around in the kitchen for another hour or two before it dawned on him that he was just keeping out of the way until he was sure she was asleep. Then he cleared up the kitchen, which meant there was nothing else for him to do tonight apart from test every type of wine they produced.

Which would be a waste, he thought morosely, staring at the opened bottle on the table in front of him. It was far too good to use as anaesthetic, and the last thing he needed was a hangover in the morning. He folded his arms on the table, dropped his head down and growled with frustration.

He should have been tired—not tired as in just finished a nineteen-hour shift in one of his restaurants, but tired enough to sleep, at least. Instead, he felt restless. Edgy.

He glanced at the baby monitor. She'd left it behind when she'd gone, and he'd heard her go in to check Ella, heard the gentle murmur of her voice when Ella had cried out once, but now there was nothing. He could let himself back in there, pick up his shorts and a towel and have a swim without disturbing them. That was what he needed. A long, hard swim, to burn off that excess restless energy. And maybe then he'd be able to sleep.

Something had woken her. She wasn't sure what, but she realised she was hot and thirsty. Maybe it had just been that?

But her bedroom door was still wide open. She'd left it open so she'd hear Ella, as Leo had the baby monitor in the kitchen, but she would have expected him to close it, or at least pull it to.

She lay for a while and listened, but there was nothing, no creaks or snores, not a sound even from Ella. She slid her legs over the edge of the bed and picked up her phone, checking the time. Twelve thirty-four. He must be back, she just hadn't heard him.

She tiptoed out into the hall and peered into Ella's room, but his bed was undisturbed, and there were no lights on anywhere except the dim glow of Ella's nightlight and the slanting moonlight through the French windows. The baby was sleeping peacefully, bottom in the air as usual, one little arm flung out to the side, and otherwise the apartment was deserted.

Surely he wasn't still cooking?

Tugging on her robe, Amy walked barefoot across the moonlit courtyard to the kitchen and found it empty, the room in darkness. She switched the light on and looked around.

It was spotlessly clean, everything cleared away, the

fridge humming quietly in the background. And the doors to the terrace were open.

She stood in the open doorway and listened. There. A rhythmic splash, barely a whisper, but continuous.

He was swimming.

And suddenly there was nothing in the world she wanted more than a swim. She went back to her room and realised the more modest black costume was still wet, so she put the bikini on, grabbed her towel and the baby monitor, and crossed the terrace.

She could see him now in the moonlight, every stroke leaving a sparkling trail of ripples on the surface, and she picked her way carefully down the steps, dropped her towel on a sun lounger and slipped silently into the water.

It was cool, the air around sweetly scented with jasmine, and she let her breath out on a quiet sigh of pleasure. There was something magical about it, about swimming in the moonlight with Leo, the soft water lapping gently around her, the drift of jasmine in the air. Beautiful.

Romantic.

That was what Lydia had said to her. *'It's just gorgeous to sink under that water in the evening when the kids are in bed and the stars are glittering overhead. So romantic...you and Leo should try it.'*

Her heart hitched a little in her throat. It wasn't meant to be romantic. She'd just wanted to join him for a swim, but suddenly it didn't feel like that, with the moonlight and the silence. She was playing with fire, crossing a boundary into dangerous territory, and she had to go. Once he'd turned and was swimming away from her, she'd make her escape and he need never know she'd been there.

Except, of course, he didn't turn.

The best-laid plans and all that, she thought as he slowed his pace and coasted in right beside her, standing up as he reached the end, sluicing water off his face and hair and knuckling the water out of his eyes.

The water streamed off his shoulders, turning to ribbons of silver in the moonlight, and she wanted to reach out and touch them.

Touch him.

No! Why hadn't she stayed inside, left him alone, kept out of his way, instead of surrendering to this magnetic attraction that had sprung out of nowhere in the last few days and taken her completely by surprise?

She must have moved or taken a breath, done something, because he turned his head towards her, his eyes black in the moonlight, a frown creasing his brow.

'Amy?'

'Hi,' she said awkwardly, the word a little breathless and utterly inadequate somehow in these odd circumstances.

His head tilted slightly. 'What's the matter?'

'Nothing. Ella's fine, she's fast asleep. I came to find you,' she explained, hoping it sounded more plausible than it felt at that moment. 'It was late, and I woke up and wondered where you were, but then I realised you were swimming and I thought it seemed like a good idea. You know, as it's a hot night...'

She floundered to a halt, trying to bluff it out when all she wanted to do was run away. Or throw herself into his arms. Neither exactly brilliant options. Oh, why on earth had she been so stupid?

Leo let out a quiet sigh and sank back into the water, stretching his arms out to grasp the edges of the pool as he faced her from his position in the corner.

What sneaky twist of fate had made her wake and come down here to torment him? His fault, most likely, going in there to pick up his shorts and towel. Damn. Well, thank God he'd got the shorts on and hadn't decided to skinny-dip. At least this way he could hide his reaction.

'Sorry, I didn't mean to disturb you. I just didn't feel tired enough to sleep, and I was hot and sticky, and the thought of the water just tempted me.'

That, and the fact that he hadn't trusted himself to go back into their apartment until he was too tired to act on the physical ache that had lingered long after she'd left the kitchen. And he'd just about done it, and now here she was to undo it all over again.

'It's the middle of the night, Leo,' she said, her voice troubled. 'You must be exhausted.'

Apparently not. Not nearly exhausted enough if his body's reaction was anything to go by. 'And you're not? Why are you here, Amy?' he asked, a trifle desperately. It was a rhetorical question, since she'd already told him, but she answered it anyway and perhaps a bit more truthfully.

'I was concerned about you. You just seemed—I don't know. Not you. Sometimes it's fine and then all of a sudden there's this great gulf that opens up between us and it's as if I don't know you at all.'

She gave a soft, disbelieving laugh. 'And I don't know why. All the time I feel as if I'm walking on eggshells with you, as if anything I say can upset you, and you just won't talk to me. It's like you're avoiding me or something and I don't know why.'

Because I want you. Because it's inappropriate, messy, and I'm not going there—

'I'm not,' he lied. 'I do talk to you. I've been talking to you all day.'

'Not about anything that matters. And that's not like you. You've always told me what's wrong, and now you won't. So what is it? Is it me? And if so, why? What have I done to hurt or upset you, Leo? Just tell me.'

He sighed softly. 'You haven't done anything, Amy. It's nothing to do with you.'

'So why won't you talk to me? You always used to; you

said it helped you sort through things, cleared your mind. I only want to help you...'

Her hand reached out and rested on his arm, her cool fingers burning him with a river of fire that scorched through his veins and threatened all his hard-won control. His eyes closed, shutting out the image of her fingers pale on his skin. 'You can't help me, Amy. You're just adding another complication.'

She whisked her hand away, her voice puzzled. 'I'm a *complication*?'

'That wasn't what I meant—'

'So what did you mean? What's going on, Leo? What's changed? Because it's not just me, is it?'

He let his breath out, a long, silent exhalation, and dragged a hand through his hair.

'No. No, Amy, it's not just you, and I don't know where it's come from or why, but I can't let it happen. I *won't* let it. You're emotionally fragile at the moment, and I'm a complete mess, but we're both adults, we've got needs, and what we're feeling is just a knee-jerk response. We feel safe with each other, we can trust each other, but it isn't safe, not for either of us.'

He gentled his voice, not sure how to handle this situation and desperate not to make it any worse. 'I'm sorry it's all gone wrong for you, and I know it should have been your honeymoon, but I'm not the guy you need to choose for your rebound affair, Amy, so don't humiliate either of us by asking me, please.'

Rebound affair? For a moment she was so shocked she could hardly reply. 'I don't want—'

'No? So why are you *really* here now, then?' He shook his head, his harsh sigh slicing through the air. 'I'm not doing this, Amy. There's no way I'm adding you to the list of things in my life that I'm ashamed of.'

Pain ripped through her, making her gasp. *He was ashamed of her?*

Like he'd been ashamed of Lisa?

He turned and vaulted lightly out of the pool, the water streaming off him in ribbons as he picked up his towel and the baby monitor and walked away towards the steps, leaving her standing there, her lips pressed tightly together, her eyes stinging with tears as she watched him walk away.

They scalded her cheeks, searing their way down, and she closed her eyes, turning away from him and holding her breath until the heavy silence told her he'd gone. Then she folded her arms on the side of the pool, rested her head on them and sobbed her heart out.

It was a good hour—no, scratch that, a lousy hour—before he heard her enter the apartment.

He'd towelled himself roughly dry and pulled on his boxers and a T-shirt, then gone out onto the terrace, sitting on the bench against the wall and staring out over the moonlit landscape while he drank the wine he'd picked up on the way over. Not a wise move, but he didn't care any more. He was over being wise. It didn't seem to be working, not for either of them.

The valley was flooded with a cold, eerie light, and he felt oddly chilled. Not that it was cold, it was just that the moon drained all colour from the surroundings and turned it into a mass of stark white, interspersed with menacing black shadows.

Under other circumstances, it would have been romantic. Not tonight, when he was sitting here waiting for Amy and wondering how long he could leave it before he went to find her. Because he would have to, he knew that.

Oh, Amy. What a mess.

What was she doing? What was she thinking? He

shouldn't have left her like that, but he hadn't trusted himself to get closer to her, to reach out to her, because if he once let himself touch her, that one touch would never be enough and there was no way—*no way*—that he was going there. Not with Amy. He was a mess, his life in tatters, the last thing she needed when she was so emotionally fragile. Not even he with his appalling track record could betray her trust to that extent.

He heard a door creak slightly, the click of a latch, water running, the muffled sound of her bedclothes as she got into bed a few moments later. The doors of her room were open to the terrace, as were his, and he listened for any further sound.

Nothing. Then a soft, shaky sigh, followed by a dull thump—punching her pillow into shape?

He put his glass down, got up and crossed the gravel, standing silently in the open doorway. She was lying on her side, facing him. Her eyes were open, watching him, waiting for him to move or speak, to do something, but he couldn't. He had no idea what to say to her in these circumstances, so he just stood there and ached with regret. He couldn't bear to lose her friendship, and he was horribly afraid that was the way it was heading.

'What have I ever done to make you ashamed of me?'

Her voice was soft, barely a whisper, but it shocked him to the core.

'I'm not ashamed of you,' he said, appalled that that was what she'd been thinking. 'Amy, no! Don't ever think that! I'm not ashamed of you, not in the slightest, and I never have been.'

'But—you said...'

She trailed off, sitting up in the bed, arms wrapped around her knees defensively, and in the good old days he would have thought nothing of climbing on the bed and hugging her. Not now. Not with this demon of desire stalking them both. He rammed his hands through his hair and gave a ragged sigh.

'I didn't mean it like that. Really. Believe me. I'm sorry—I'm really so sorry—if you misunderstood, but it isn't, and it never has been, and it never will be you that I'm ashamed of. It's me, the things I've done, the people I've hurt.' He sighed wearily. 'I need to tell you about Lisa, don't I?'

'Yes, you do,' she said, her voice stronger now, making his guilt twinge, 'because I don't know who you are any more and I can't help you like this. Not really. Sometimes I think I understand you, but then you say something, and— it just confuses me, Leo. Tell me what it is that's happened that's destroying you,' she pleaded, her eyes dark holes, featureless in the faint light, unreadable. 'Help me to understand what's hurting you.'

He hesitated for a moment, then gave another quiet sigh. 'OK. But not here, like this. Come outside. Have some wine with me. I picked up a bottle from the kitchen on the way back and I need help drinking it or I'm going to have a killer hangover. I'll get you a glass.'

He checked Ella as he passed, fetched another glass from the kitchen and went back out to the terrace and found her waiting for him.

She was curled into one corner of the bench, her arms wrapped round her legs. He recognised it, that defensive posture, shielding herself from hurt, the wide, wary eyes and wounded mouth making her look like a child again. A hurt and frightened child, but she wasn't a child. Not any more. And that just made it all the more complicated.

He sat down at the other end of the bench at a nice, safe distance, put the wine glass down between them next to his and filled them both.

'Here.'

She reached out and took it from him, her fingers brush-

ing his, and he felt them tremble. 'So—Lisa,' she said, retreating back into the corner with her wine glass. 'What
happened between you that's changed you so much, Leo?'

'It hasn't changed me.'

'It has. Of course it has. It's taken the life out of you.
Most of the time you're fine, and then, bang, the shutters
come down and you retreat. The only time you really relax
is when you're with Ella, and even then there's something
wrong. I thought at first it was grief, but it isn't, is it? It's
regret, but why? What happened that you regret so much,
that you're so ashamed of?'

How had he thought she looked like a child? She was
looking at him now with the eyes of a sage, coaxing him
to unburden himself, and once he started, he found he
couldn't stop.

'I didn't love her,' he began. 'It was just a casual fling.
She was part of the team on the last TV series. I'd never
spoken to her, but she must have decided she'd like a piece
of me as a trophy so she engineered an invitation to the
party to celebrate finishing the filming, cosied up to me
and—well, she got pregnant. I thought I'd taken care of
that, but she told me much later she'd sabotaged it, and she
didn't show a shred of remorse. And at the time she didn't
seem shocked or upset by the surprise pregnancy. Far from
it. Not until the whole situation became much more of a
reality, and then she just went into meltdown.'

'So you didn't love her? You married her just because
she was pregnant?'

He gave her a wintry smile. *Just because?*

Amy found herself smiling back, but she wanted to cry
for him, for what she'd heard in his voice. 'You could have
said no to her instead of doing the decent thing.'

'Except that it was my fault. She'd had too much to
drink, I shouldn't have done it.'

'Was she very drunk?' she probed.

'I thought so, but she might have been acting. But then, to be fair, I wasn't exactly sober so it's hard to tell. It was quite a party, and I suspect my drink was being well and truly spiked by her. And that was only the first time. She stayed all weekend—'

'You took her back to yours?' To his flat over the restaurant? The place they'd sat and talked long into the night, over and over again? She knew it was ridiculous, knew he must have taken countless women there, but still she felt betrayed.

'The party was at the London restaurant. I lived above it. Where else would I take her?'

'Anywhere in the world?' she suggested, and he gave a rueful laugh.

'Yeah. Hindsight's a wonderful thing. But after the weekend I told her I wasn't interested in a relationship. I had the new restaurant opening coming up in Yoxburgh in a few months, so much to do to prepare for that, and I was trying to consolidate the business so I could afford to abandon it for a while to get the new restaurant up and running smoothly before the next TV series kicked off, and a relationship was the last thing I needed.'

'So—she left you alone?'

'Yes, she left me alone, sort of, for a few weeks, anyway. And then she turned up at the restaurant late one night and said she needed to speak to me, and she told me she was pregnant. I didn't believe her at first, but she had a scan six weeks later and the dates fitted, and she was adamant it was mine. And she was delighted. Of course.'

'What did your family say?'

He snorted softly. 'Have you never met my grandmother?' he asked unnecessarily, and Amy smiled wryly.

'Nonna told you to marry her?'

'She didn't need to. She listened to my side of the story, told me I'd been a fool to let it happen, but that I owed my

child the right to have its father in its life. And she was
right, of course. I already knew that. I also knew that the
business didn't need the media circus that would follow
if I walked away from a pregnant woman, and I knew she
wouldn't keep it quiet. So we had a quiet wedding and
moved up to Suffolk, into a rented house, so I could concentrate on the new restaurant.'

'Don't tell me. She didn't like it?'

'She didn't like it one bit. She'd thought we'd have a
glamorous life in London, and she didn't take kindly to
being imprisoned in a tinpot little backwater like Yoxburgh. Her words, not mine. And then Ella was born, and
she was even more trapped, and she started drinking.'

'Drinking? As in—?'

'Heavy drinking. Getting utterly bat-faced. Night after
night. I told her to stop, promised her a new house, said we
could go back to London, split our time between the two,
but that wasn't enough. To be honest, I think the reality of
the whole thing—the pregnancy and birth, the move, the
amount of time I was giving to the restaurant—it was all
too much. It would have been too much for anyone, but
she was so far out of her comfort zone that it was just impossible. And then...'

He broke off, the words choking him, and Amy shifted,
moving the glasses out of the way and snuggling up against
his side, one hand lying lightly over his heart. He wondered if she could feel it pounding as he relived that hideous night.

'Go on,' she said softly, and he let his arm curl round
her shoulders and draw her closer against him, her warmth
reassuring.

'She came to the restaurant. She'd left Ella at home,
six weeks old, and she'd driven down to the restaurant to
tell me she was leaving me. It was a filthy night, sheeting
down with rain, the waves crashing over the prom, and

she'd been drinking. I took the car keys off her and told her to go home and wait for me, but she started swearing and screaming in front of the customers. I called her a taxi, told her to wait, but she walked out of the restaurant into the lashing rain and straight into the path of a car. The driver didn't stand a chance, and nor did she. She died later that night in hospital, and all I felt was relief.'

Amy's arms tightened round his waist, hugging him gently, and he turned his head and rested his cheek against her hair. 'I didn't love her, Amy, but I didn't want her to die. I just wanted the whole situation to go away, but not like that.'

'Is that why you're ashamed? Because you wanted her gone, and when she was you were secretly relieved? Do you think you're to blame in some crazy way?'

'I *am* to blame,' he told her emphatically, pulling away slightly. 'I should have made it clearer to her what our life was going to be like, but I knew she'd got pregnant deliberately, knew that she'd set a trap for me that weekend, so I suppose I felt she'd got what she deserved. But she didn't deserve to die, and I didn't deserve to have to go through all that, and Ella certainly had done nothing to deserve anything that either of us had done. Nor had my family, and the media had a field day with it. Don't tell me you didn't know that because I don't believe it.'

'Oh, Leo. I read things, of course I did, and I was worried about you. I tried to call you several times, but you weren't taking any calls, and your parents were really protective so I couldn't get through to you and I gave up. I shouldn't have done. I should have come and seen you.'

Her voice was soft, filled with anguish for him, and she turned her head and lifted her face to his, touching her lips gently to his cheek. 'I'm so sorry. It must have been dreadful for all of you.'

Her lips were inches away. Less. All he had to do was

turn his head a fraction, and they'd be there, against his mouth. He fought it for seconds, then with a shuddering sigh he turned his head and moved away from danger. Not far. Just enough that he could still rest his head against hers but with his lips firmly out of the way of trouble.

'Leo?'

'Mmm?'

'I wasn't trying to seduce you earlier,' she said, her voice a fractured whisper. 'I really wasn't. I was just concerned about you.'

He sighed, his breath ruffling her hair, and his arm tightened around her. 'I know. But things are changing between us, and I don't want them to. I love you, Amy. I love you to bits, but I'm not going to have an affair with you, no matter how tempted either of us might be—'

She pushed away, tilting her head to stare up at him, her eyes wide with something that could have been indignation. Or desperation? 'When have I asked you to do that? *Ever?* When have I *ever* suggested that we—?'

'You haven't. Not in so many words. But it's there in your eyes, and it's in my head, and I'm not doing it, I'm not going to be drawn in by it, no matter how tempting it is to turn to each other for comfort. Because that's all it is, Amy. Comfort. And it would change everything. We've been friends for ever, and I don't want to change that. I need it, I treasure it, and I can't bear to think I could do something stupid one day to screw it up, because I will. I'll let you down—'

She moved abruptly, shifting so she was facing him, holding his face in her hands and staring intently into his eyes.

'No, you won't,' she said slowly and clearly. 'You've never let me down, Leo. I've let myself down, plenty of times, and I expect you've done the same, but you'll never let me down. You've just stopped me making the biggest mistake of my life—'

'Yes, I have, and I'm not going to let you—or either of us—make another one when your emotions are in chaos and you're clutching at the familiar because your life's suddenly going to be so different from what you'd planned.'

He took her hands in his, easing them away from his face and closing his fingers over them, pressing them to his lips before he let them go. He tucked a damp strand of hair behind her ear and gave her a rueful smile. 'You just need time, Amy. Time to let the dust settle and work out what you want from life. And it isn't me. It really isn't. I'm no good for you—not in that way. You don't really want me, you just want what I represent—the familiar, the safe, but I'm not safe, and I can't replace what you've lost by not marrying Nick. I know what you want, what you've lost, but I'm not it.'

She nodded, shifting away a little, turning her head to stare out over the valley. After a moment she gave a shaky sigh.

'I know that—and I know I'm not ready for another relationship, especially not with you. I mean, how would that work?' she said, her voice lightly teasing now, but he could still hear the hurt and confusion underlying it. 'I wouldn't have my sounding board any more, would I? How would I know it wasn't another awful mistake? I made the last mistake because I didn't talk to you. I don't want to do that again.'

She turned back to him, throwing him a sweet, wry smile. 'Thank you for telling me about Lisa. And don't blame yourself. It wasn't your fault.'

'It was. I should have driven her home instead of calling a taxi—handed the restaurant over to the team and left, taken care of her, but I didn't, I didn't realise she was that fragile, that unstable, and because of that she died.'

'No, Leo. She died because she got drunk and did something reckless, with far-reaching consequences. Everything else stemmed from that. You were her husband, not her keeper. She was an adult woman, and she made bad decisions. And on the last occasion it killed her. End of.'

'Except it's not the end, is it? I've got a motherless child and a career I've neglected for the past nine months—more, really. And there's nothing I can do about it. What's done is done. All any of us have to do is take care of the future, and I have no idea how. All I can do is survive from day to day and hope it gets better.'

'It will.'

'Will it? I hope so, because I can't go on like this.'

He stood up, tugging her to her feet and wrapping her in his arms and holding her tight, his face pressed into her hair. 'Thanks for listening to me. And thanks for being you. I don't know what I'd do without you.'

'You aren't without me. You won't be without me.'

'Promise?'

'I promise. Just keep talking to me.'

He nodded, then eased away. 'I will. Now go to bed. You need some sleep and so do I. I'll be up at the crack of dawn with Ella.'

'Well, good luck with that,' she said ruefully. 'Look at the sky.'

They stared out across the network of fields and hills, still leached of colour by the moon, but on the horizon there was the faintest streak of light appearing in the sky.

'It's a new day, Leo. It *will* get better.'

He looked down at her, her eyes shining with sincerity, the one person he could truly trust with all his hopes and fears. He bent his head, touched his lips to her cheek and then, as he breathed in and drew the scent of her into his body, he felt his resolve disintegrate.

He let his breath out on a shuddering sigh and turned his head, as she turned hers, and their lips touched.

They clung, held, and with a ragged sigh of defeat he pulled her closer, feeling her taut limbs, the softness of her breasts, the warmth of her mouth opening like a flower under his, and he was lost.

He couldn't get enough of her. One hand slid round and found her breast through the slippery silk of that tormenting gown, and he felt her nipple peak hard against his hand.

She moaned softly, arching against him, her tongue duelling with his as he delved and tasted, savouring her, learning her, aching for her.

Her hands were on him, learning him, too, their movements desperate as she clung to his arms, his back, cradling his head as he was cradling hers, her fingers spearing through his hair and pulling him down to her.

He groaned, rocking his hips against hers, needing her for so much more than this, and she whimpered as his hands slid down and cupped her bottom, lifting her against him.

Amy...

Amy! No, no, no, no!

He had to stop. She had to stop. One of them had to stop. He uncurled his fingers and slid his hands up her back, but he didn't let go. He couldn't. He needed her. Wanted her. He had to...

His hands cradled her face, the kiss gentling as he fought with his warring emotions. And then she eased away and took a step back, out of reach, and he felt bereft.

Their eyes met and locked, and after an agonising second he dragged a hand down over his face and tried to step back, to put more space between them while he still could, but his feet were rooted to the spot, his chest heaving with the need that still screamed through him, and he tilted his head back and stared blindly at the pale streak of sky that promised a new tomorrow.

Could he trust it? Could he trust her?

She reached out, her hand finding his, their fingers tangling, and he lowered his head and met her eyes again, and saw nothing in them but honesty.

'Make love to me, Leo,' she murmured, and the last vestige of his crumbling self-control turned to dust.

CHAPTER EIGHT

AMY LAY ON her side, one leg draped over his, her head pillowed on his chest, her lips tilting into a smile of utter contentment and wonder as his hand stroked idly over her back.

So that's what the fireworks were like. The chemistry she'd dismissed. The 'amazing' that she'd never, ever found before.

His lips brushed her hair, his breath warm against her scalp, and she turned her head so she could reach his mouth.

He kissed her slowly, lazily, shifting so he was facing her, his hand sliding round her ribcage and settling on her breast, and she snuggled closer, feeling the jut of his erection against her body as her leg curled over his hip and drew him up against her.

He groaned, deep in his chest, the vibrations resonating through his breath and into her like the faint tremors of an earthquake. 'I want you,' he breathed raggedly. 'I need you—so much. Oh, Amy—'

He rolled her onto her back, their bodies coming together instinctively, surely, and she felt the first quivers of another shattering climax ripple through her body. 'Leo...'

'I'm here. I've got you...'

His head fell forward into the curve of her neck, his mouth open, his breath hot against her skin as he said her name over and over again while she fell, spiralling down and down, reaching out, clinging to him as his body caught up with hers and took them both over the edge.

Their muted cries tangled in the soft light of dawn, their bodies blurring into one, and as their hearts slowed and their breathing quietened, he rolled to the side, taking her with him into sleep.

Leo lay beside her, staring at the ceiling and trying to make sense of his tangled emotions.

All these years, he'd been so careful to preserve their friendship, to keep it platonic, to treasure the bond they had without crossing the invisible line between them. It had been so vitally important to him, his respect for Amy's friendship so deeply ingrained that it hadn't ever occurred to him to muddy the waters by sleeping with her. Other women had fulfilled that need for him, women who didn't trust him or depend on him or need him, women who wanted from him only what he wanted from them. Women who weren't Amy, or anything like Amy, because Amy was sacrosanct, untouchable.

Well, he'd certainly touched her now, the line well and truly crossed, and there was no going back. What he didn't know was what lay ahead, because he had nothing to offer her except the few scraps of himself that were left over from work and from caring for his daughter. And it hadn't been enough for Lisa, so why on earth did he imagine it could be enough for Amy?

He groaned silently.

He should never have kissed her, never have let her lead him into her bedroom, never peeled away the flimsy barriers of their clothing and with them the protective layers of their friendship, exposing the raw need and desperate hunger that lurked beneath.

He'd made a catastrophic mistake by doing that, but what an incredible, beautiful, exquisite mistake it had been.

Because he loved her, in every way, without reservation, and what they'd done had felt so right, so good, so pure and simple and innocent and—just *right*.

Oh, Amy. His lips moved silently on the words, his eyes drifting shut against the tears of joy and regret that welled in them. *Don't let me hurt you. Please, don't let me hurt you.*

But he knew he would. Somehow, some time, sooner or later it would happen. And it would break his heart, as well as hers.

Ella woke her, the baby's wail cutting through her dream and dragging her back to reality, and she stretched out to Leo but he was gone.

Oh.

She stretched and yawned and lay there for a moment waiting, sure he must have gone to her, but there was no sound from him and the baby was still crying, so she threw back the covers, found her nightdress and went to investigate.

'Hello, sweetheart. Where's your daddy?' she murmured, lifting the baby out of the cot and cuddling her close.

'I'm here. Sorry, I was in the other kitchen but there was something I couldn't just drop. Come here, poppet.'

He took her out of Amy's arms, his eyes brushing hers fleetingly, warm and gentle but troubled, and she gave an inward sigh.

'I know what you're thinking,' she said, sitting down on the bed while he put Ella down on the changing mat at her feet and knelt down. 'But don't.'

He shot her a sideways glance. 'How do you know what I'm thinking?'

'Because I know you inside out, Leo. You might have changed a little, grown older and wiser—'

His snort cut her off, but she just smiled and carried on, 'But you're still the same over-protective person you always were, and you're beating yourself up at the moment, taking all the blame, wishing you hadn't done it—'

'No.' He sat back on his heels and looked up at her, his eyes burning. 'No, Amy, you're wrong. I'm not wishing I hadn't done it. I just wish I could give you more, wish I could offer you a future—'

'Shh.' She leant forward and pressed a finger to his lips, silencing him. He kissed her finger, drew it into his mouth, suckled it briefly before he pulled away, and she nearly whimpered.

'You were saying?'

'I can't remember.'

His eyes were laughing. '*Shh* was the last thing.'

'So it was.' She smiled, and carried on. 'Forget about the future, Leo. It's far too soon to think about that. Forget everything except the here and now. We've got a few more days. Let's just enjoy them, get to know each other better, the people we are now, and have some fun with Ella. Have a holiday—'

'I have to cook.'

'You have to cook one meal.'

'And try out their stuff.'

'You're making excuses. I thought it was supposed to be a simple lunch?'

He smiled crookedly. 'I don't do simple, apparently. I want to do something that tastes amazing.'

'All your food tastes amazing.'

He arched an eyebrow. 'What happened to my critic?'

'Oh, she's still here, she'll come out when necessary,' she said with a laugh, and then sighed and threw up her hands. 'OK. I concede. Cook, play in the kitchen, and Ella and I'll play with you when we can, and you'll play with us when you can, and I know when they get back you'll be in meetings, but we'll still have the nights.'

She heard the suck of his indrawn breath, saw the flaring of his pupils as he straightened to look at her again, the jump of a muscle in his jaw. 'And then?'

She shrugged. She didn't know. And maybe it was better that way. 'What happens in Tuscany stays in Tuscany?' she said softly, and their eyes held.

'OK. I'll buy that for now.'

'Good. Oh, and by the way, you were amazing last night,' she said casually, and stood up to walk past him.

'So were you. Incredible.' His arm snaked out, his hand sliding up under the short hem of her nightdress and curving round her naked bottom, drawing her in against him. He rested his head briefly against her, his breath hot on her body through the fine silk, and then he let her go, his hand sliding down her leg and leaving fire in its wake. She sat down again abruptly.

'So, what are you doing today?' she asked when she could speak, but her voice was breathy and he tilted his head back and speared her with his eyes.

'I don't know. I know what I'm doing tonight. That's as far as my thoughts have gone for now.' A lazy, sexy smile lit up his face, and she felt heat shiver through her.

'OK,' she said slowly. 'So—assuming we're going to do something a little more practical in the meantime, shall I shower first, or do you want to?'

'I've showered. You were sleeping the sleep of the dead,' he told her, that lazy smile still lingering on his delectable and clever, clever mouth. 'If you could shower now and take Ella from me so I can get on, that would be great. I'll make us all breakfast if you like.'

'I like. I definitely like. I'm starving.'

He rolled his eyes and got to his feet, Ella cradled in one

arm, and he turned Amy and pushed her gently towards the bathroom door. 'Shoo. I've got a lot to do.'

'So, little Ella, what are we going to do while Daddy's busy this morning?' she asked. 'A walk? That sounds like a great idea. Where shall we go? The olive groves? OK.'

Ella grinned at her, a toothy little grin with a gurgle of laughter that made her heart swell in her chest until she thought it'd burst.

'Was that funny?' she asked, and Ella laughed again, so that by the time she was strapped in her buggy they both had the giggles.

'What's the joke?'

He'd stuck his head out of the kitchen door, and she turned her head and grinned at him. 'No joke. She just started laughing, and it's really infectious.'

'Tell me about it. Are you off for a walk now?'

'Mmm. Ella thought we might like to go down to the olive groves.'

'Did she now?' he asked, coming over to them and crouching in front of Ella.

'She did.'

He chuckled softly, bent and kissed the baby and then, as he straightened and drew level with her, he kissed Amy. It caught her by surprise, the sure, gentle touch of his lips, the promise of heat in his eyes, the lingering warmth of his hand against her cheek.

'Have fun. I'll see you later,' he murmured, and waggling his fingers at Ella he headed back to the kitchen to carry on.

They had a lovely walk, the air full of the buzzing of bees and the scent of the olive blossom as they strolled along beneath the trees, and predictably the rocking motion of the buggy sent Ella to sleep, so Amy's mind was free to wander.

And of course it wandered straight to Leo, and stayed there.

Not surprising, really, after last night. She'd never felt like she had then, but it wasn't because of anything in particular that he'd done, it was just because it had been him—his touch, his kiss, his body. It had just felt—right, as if everything in the universe had fallen neatly into place when she had been in his arms.

And today the sun was brighter, the grass greener, the birdsong louder. A smile on her face, she turned the buggy round and headed back up the hill to Leo. It was time she went back, anyway. She'd been out in the sun too long and her shoulders were burning.

She left the buggy with Leo and went to put after-sun lotion on, and when she got back Ella was awake, so they played outside the kitchen until Leo called them in for lunch, then Amy took her back in the garden under the shade of the pergola until she yawned again.

'I'm going to put her down in her cot,' she told Leo. 'Do you need any help?'

He shot her a warm but distracted smile. 'No, not really.'

'I'll sort some more photos, then,' she said, and going up on tiptoe she kissed his cheek and left him to it.

She couldn't quite believe how many pictures she'd taken of Leo.

Leo cooking, Leo swimming, Leo laughing, frowning, smiling, winking at her cheekily—hundreds. Hundreds and hundreds. Lots of Ella, too, and the two of them together. They brought a lump to her throat.

There were others, of the family, of the *palazzo* and its grounds, the olive groves, the vineyards, the chestnut woods—anywhere he'd gone and she'd been with him, she'd taken photos. And she'd lent him the camera so he could take some when she wasn't there, and she scrolled through those with interest.

He'd certainly have plenty to choose from for his blog, she thought with relief, so she didn't need to feel she owed him anything, not by the time she'd added in the babysitting this week and for the eight weeks of the filming.

Eight weeks in which they'd do—what? She'd said what happens in Tuscany stays in Tuscany, but if they were together, at home, would that still apply? Or would it be awkward?

Was their relationship going to end when they left Italy? She didn't know, and she didn't want to ask him, because she wasn't sure she'd want to hear the answer.

Then Ella cried, and she shut down her laptop and went to get her. She was sitting up in her little cot, rubbing her eyes and wailing sleepily, and she held her arms up to Amy.

'Hello, baby,' she murmured. 'It's all right, I'm here.'

She scooped her up gently and hugged her, and Ella's little arms snaked round her neck, chubby fingers splayed against her sunburnt shoulders. The tousled little head snuggled down into the crook of Amy's neck, and she squeezed the baby tight, deeply touched by the little one's affection. She'd formed a real bond with her in this short time, and it would be such a wrench not to see her again every day, not to be part of her life when this was done.

She was such a sweet child, and it was so sad that she would grow up without her mother. How would that feel? For all her gentle interference, Amy's mother was a huge part of her life. How would it have been never to have known the security and warmth that came with being so deeply, unreservedly and unconditionally loved by the woman who'd given you life? Even the thought of it made Amy ache inside for her.

Could she take that woman's place? In a heartbeat.

Would she be invited to? As his wife?

'It'll be a cold day in hell before that happens.'
Oh, Leo...

She gave a quiet sigh and changed Ella's nappy, put her back in the little sun dress she'd been wearing in the morning, picked up her pretty, frilly sun hat and went to find him.

There was no sign of him in the kitchen, but there was a bit of paper propped up on the table with 'In veg garden' scrawled on it in Leo's bold hand.

She plonked the sun hat on the baby's head, went out through the open French doors onto the terrace and followed it around until she spotted him on the level below, in a sheltered spot amongst the orderly rows of vegetables.

She went down the steps and walked towards him. He was crouched down, balancing on the balls of his feet as he studied the lush mounds of greenery all around him, and he turned and squinted up at her in the sun. It would have made a brilliant photo, but for once she didn't have her camera.

'Hi, there. Everything okay?'

'Yes, fine. We just wondered what you were doing.'

Ella lunged towards him, right on cue, and said, 'Dadadad,' her little face beaming, and of course he couldn't resist that.

'Ciao, mia bellisima,' he said, his face lighting up with a smile for his little daughter. He straightened up, his hands full, and bent his head to kiss Ella, his eyes softening with a love that made Amy's heart turn over.

He was standing close enough that she could smell him, her nose tantalised by a slight, lingering trace of aftershave overlaid by the heady scent of warm male skin, and he turned his head and captured her mouth with a slow, lingering kiss. Then he lifted his head, and she took a step back and pointed in the direction of his hands.

'What are those?'

He glanced down. 'Zucchini flowers—courgettes. They're so pretty, and they're delicious stuffed. I thought I might do them as a vegetable. Heaven knows, Lydia's going to have enough of them,' he said, waving a hand at the rows of rampant plants he'd been inspecting.

'I'm sure she'll think it's worth the sacrifice. So what are you going to stuff them with?' she asked, trying to focus on something other than the scent of his skin in the warm sunshine, and the lingering taste of him on her lips.

'I don't know. I've got a few ideas. I'll try them out on you this evening.'

He picked up a basket overflowing with the things he'd raided from the garden, plucked the baby off her hip, settled her on his and headed back to the kitchen, nuzzling Ella and blowing raspberries on her neck and making her giggle.

He was so good with her. Good enough that the loss of her mother wouldn't matter? And what about when they got back to England and *she* wasn't around any more? Would that matter to Ella? Would she even notice?

Don't borrow trouble.

Amy followed them, the taut muscles of Leo's tanned calves in easy reach as he walked up the steps in front of her. His long shorts clung to his lean hips, giving her a tantalising view of muscles that bunched and stretched with every step, and she wanted to reach out her hand and touch them, feel their warmth and solidity, test the texture of rough hair over smooth tanned skin. Taste the salt on his skin—

Later...

He crossed over to the kitchen, dumping the basket of vegetables on the big table. 'Tea or coffee?' he asked, turning his head to look at Amy over his shoulder.

'Something cold?' she said, and he pulled open the

fridge and took out the spring water. 'So what's the plan for the rest of the afternoon?'

He shrugged, those broad, lean shoulders shifting under the soft pale blue cotton of his shirt, the cuffs turned back to reveal strong, tanned forearms. He'd always tanned really easily, she remembered, part of his Latin heritage.

'I don't know,' he said, jiggling Ella on his hip. 'It rather depends on madam here and what she'd like to do.'

'I'm happy to look after her, if you want,' Amy volunteered, but he shook his head.

'No, it's okay, I haven't seen her all day and I'm going to need you tomorrow morning so I'm keeping you sweet for that,' he said with a grin. He unscrewed the bottle and poured two glasses of fizzy water, added a slice of lime to each and handed her one. 'Has she had her bottle?' he asked, and Amy shook her head.

'No, but it's in the fridge there. I thought I'd come and find you first, see what you're doing.'

'This and that.' He took the bottle out, hooked out a chair with his foot and sat down with the baby. 'So how have you been getting on?' he asked as he gave Ella her bottle. 'Did you look at the photos?'

'Yes. There are some really good ones that'll be great for your blog. They're on my laptop. There's a ton of dross as well, of course, but you can have a look later.'

'I'd love to, but probably not until after tomorrow. I've got enough on at the moment.' He gave her a wry grin. 'I hate to ask, but would you be able to keep an eye on Ella for a while later on so I can do some more prep? You can stay in here so she can see me, but I could just do with an hour or two to make up a marinade and get some risotto under way. I'll put her to bed.'

'It's why I'm here, Leo.'

His mouth softened into a smile. 'So you keep saying. I tell you what, how about a swim first?'

* * *

She wore the bikini, and when Ella grabbed the top again, he just smiled and gently disentangled the baby's fingers, which of course involved his own getting nicely into the mix.

He eased Ella away, met Amy's eyes and winked at her, and she blushed, which made him laugh softly.

'Later,' he promised, and her mouth opened a fraction and then curved into a smile that could have threatened his sanity if he hadn't already lost it.

And before he knew what she was doing, she slipped beneath the surface and swam towards him, nudging his legs apart with her hands before twisting through them like a mermaid. She'd done it before, hundreds of times when they were growing up, but not now, when he was so aware of the brush of her body against his.

'Boo!' she said, surfacing right behind him, and Ella squealed with laughter, so she did it again, and again, and again, and every time her body slid past his, grazing intimately against him until he called a halt.

'Right, enough. I need to get on.'

'We'll come out, too.'

She went first, reaching down to take Ella from his arms and treating him to the soft, lush swell of her breasts threatening to escape from the bikini that was proving so rewarding.

Never mind mermaid. She was a siren, luring him onto the rocks, and tonight was so far away…

'Are you sure you don't mind?'

'Positive,' she said patiently. 'Leave her with me and go and make a start, and I'll change her nappy and then we'll follow you. I can take photos of you cooking, and give you the benefit of my considerable expertise as a guinea pig while I play with her. And at least that way

I'll get something to eat, because I know what you're like when you start something like this. You get totally focussed and forget everything else, and supper will just go out of the window.'

He smiled, as he was meant to, and went.

'So what's that you're doing now?' she asked, carrying Ella into the kitchen a few minutes later and peering over Leo's shoulder.

'Broad bean, mint and pecorino risotto—it's the stuffing for the zucchini flowers, a variation on what we had last night.' He stuck his finger into the pan, scooped out a dollop and held it out to her lips. 'Here. Try it.'

He'd done it so many times before, and yet this time seemed so different. She opened her mouth, drew his finger into it and curled her tongue around the tip, sucking the delicious, creamy risotto from it without ever losing eye contact.

'Mmm. Yummy. You've put more mint in it. So are they going to be cold or hot?' she asked.

Leo hauled in a slow, quiet breath and tried to concentrate on anything other than the sweet warmth of Amy's mouth, the curl of her tongue against his finger, the gentle suction as she'd drawn the risotto into her mouth all too quickly. He turned away to check the seasoning of the risotto and gave his body a moment to calm down.

'Warm. Things taste better that way, often, and they need to be deep fried in tempura batter and served pretty much immediately, which rather dictates it.'

'They'd go well with the lamb,' she suggested, and he nodded.

'They would. And I could cook them at the last moment when everything else was ready to go. Here, try this. I've been playing with the topping for the bruschetta.'

He handed her a dollop—on a spoon, this time, since

he really couldn't afford to get that distracted, but it was nearly as bad. 'OK?'

'Lovely. Really tasty. So what do you want me to photograph?'

He shrugged, his shoulders shifting under the shirt, drawing her attention yet again to his body. 'Anything you like. You tell me, you're the photographer.'

'I don't know. What are you doing now?' she asked, casting around for something to take her mind off his body, because even framing the shots for the camera wasn't helping. If anything, it was making it worse because it meant focussing on him and she was having trouble focussing on anything else.

'Marinade for the mutton.' He'd set the vegetables on one side and was pounding something with a pestle and mortar, grinding garlic and herbs together with a slosh of olive oil and a crunch of salt and pepper, his muscles flexing as he worked. 'I'll smoosh it all over the meat, leave it till later and put it in the oven overnight so I can shred it and shape it first thing in the morning.'

He stopped pounding, to her relief, pulled out the shoulder of mutton from the fridge, stabbed it all over with a knife and smeared—no, *smooshed*, whatever kind of a word that was—the contents of the bowl all over the outside of the meat, dropped it back into the oven tray on top of the chopped vegetables, wrapped it in foil and stuck it back in the fridge.

'Right. Mint jelly.'

She watched him while Ella was playing contentedly with some stacking blocks, clicking away on the camera to record it all for his blog. Most of the shots were probably underexposed, but she didn't have any lights or reflectors so she was relying on the natural light spilling in through the open French doors to the terrace, and the under-cupboard lights that flooded the work area with a soft, golden light that worked wonders with his olive skin.

And as a perk, of course, she got to study him in excruciatingly minute detail.

The mint jelly setting in the fridge, he moved on, pulling together the ingredients for a dessert that made her drool just watching him.

'Tell me it's going to be your panna cotta?'

He threw her a grin over his shoulder. 'Was there a choice?'

Of course not. It was one of his signature dishes, and she'd never eaten a better one anywhere. Technically difficult to produce reliably—or for her to produce reliably, at any rate; she doubted Leo had any problems with it—he was making it with the ease of long practice, talking as he worked, and he was a joy to watch. But then, he was always a joy to watch...

'I'm going to turn them out and serve them with a compote of freshly sliced home-grown strawberries in their cousin's balsamic vinegar. I'm hoping I can talk them into letting me have a few bottles a year. It's amazing. It's almost a syrup, and it's—oh, it's just lovely with fruit. Beautiful. Works perfectly with it. I'll make a few spares. If you're really good, I'll give you one later.'

'I'll be really, really good,' she vowed, and he turned, holding her eyes for a second or two.

'Is that a promise?' he murmured, and it turned her legs to mush.

He finished the panna cotta, poured it carefully into the moulds and slipped the tray into the fridge.

'This kitchen's a joy to work in,' he said, and turned back to her with a grin that wiped the promise of dessert right off the menu and made her think of something much, much sweeter, powerful enough to blow her composure right apart.

And his, if the look in his eyes was anything to go by. Which was not a good idea when he was busy.

'I'll take Ella out in the garden in the shade. She's bored, and she loves the little sandpit.'

And scooping up the baby, she headed for the French doors to give him space.

Leo watched her go, let his breath out on a long sigh and braced his arms on the worktop. Why was he suddenly so intensely aware of her, after so many years? What was it that had changed for them? She wasn't a child any more, not by a long shot, but she'd been a woman for some considerable time, and it had taken this long for the change to register on his Richter scale.

And how.

But it wasn't for long. They only had a few more days here in Tuscany, by which time he would have sealed the deal with the Valtieri brothers.

Because he was going to. He'd decided that on the first evening, but he'd needed to know more about them and what they produced. And now he did, they could sort out the small print and he could go home.

He just had no idea where that would leave him and Amy.

CHAPTER NINE

'So I WAS RIGHT, then,' she said, trying to keep it light. 'No supper.'

'Don't worry, you won't starve.'

'I didn't think I would for a moment, but I have no doubt I'll have to sing for it.'

He gave a soft huff of laughter and carried on fiddling at the stove. 'Did she settle all right?'

'Yes, she's fine.'

'Good. Thanks. Here, try this.'

He put some things on a plate and set it on the table in front of her. Several slices of bruschetta—with the new topping, she guessed—and a couple of the stuffed zucchini flowers, dipped in the most delicate batter and briskly deep fried, then drained and drizzled in more of the heavenly olive oil.

'Try the *bruschetta*. I think this topping works better.'

She picked it up and sank her teeth into it, and sighed as the flavours exploded on her tongue. 'Gorgeous,' she mumbled, and looked up and caught his cocky grin.

'Did you expect anything less?' he said, with a lazy smile that dimpled his right cheek and an oh-so-Italian shrug that nearly unravelled her brain. 'Try the zucchini flowers. I tweaked the risotto filling again. Here—rinse your mouth first.'

She obediently drank some of the sparkling water he

passed her, then bit the end off one of the little golden parcels and groaned. 'Mmm. Yummy. Mintier?'

He nodded. 'I thought it might work with the main course as you suggested, instead of potatoes.'

'I don't suppose you've cooked any of the meat yet, have you, so we can try them together?' she said hopefully, and he chuckled.

'Not a prayer. It's going to take hours.'

He picked up the second zucchini flower and bit into it, and a little ooze of the risotto filling caught on his lip and she leant over, hooked her hand around the back of his neck to hold him still and captured it with her tongue.

He swore softly in Italian and shook his head at her.

'How am I supposed to concentrate now?' he grumbled, putting the rest of it in his mouth, but he was smiling as he took the plate and slid it into the dishwasher.

'I don't suppose the panna cotta's set yet?'

'You want some, I take it?'

'Absolutely. With the strawberries. And the balsamic. I want the whole deal. A girl has to eat. And you wanted my terrifying honesty, anyway.'

He sighed and rolled his eyes, muttering something about demanding women, and she smiled. It was just like old times, but not, because now there was something new to add to the mix, and it just made it even better.

She propped her elbows on the table and watched as he dipped the mould briefly in hot water, tipped the panna cotta out, spooned some sliced strawberries in dark syrup over the edge and decorated it with a mint leaf and a dust of vanilla icing sugar, and then shoved the plate in front of her, his spoon poised.

'I have to share it?' she joked, and then nearly whimpered as he scooped some up and held it to her lips.

It quivered gently, soft and luscious, the strawberries smelling of summer. She let it melt on her tongue—the sweet, the sour, the sharp, the…fiery?—and let her breath out slowly. 'Oh, wow. That's different. What's it got in it?'

'Pink peppercorns. Just a touch, to give it depth and warmth, and mint again for freshness. So what do you think of their balsamic? Good, isn't it?'

'Lovely. Beautiful. The whole thing's gorgeous.' She took the spoon from him and scooped up another dollop and felt it slide down her throat, cool and creamy and delicious, with a touch of lingering warmth from the pink peppercorns and the fresh richness of the ripe strawberries soaked in the glorious balsamic vinegar waking up every one of her taste buds. She groaned softly, opened her eyes again and met Leo's eyes.

And something happened. Some subtle shift, a hitch of breath, a flare of his pupils, and she felt as if she'd been struck by lightning.

For long seconds they froze, trapped in the moment, as if the clocks had stopped and everything was suspended in time. And then he leant in and kissed her, his mouth cool and sweet from the panna cotta, a touch of heat that lingered until he eased away and broke the contact.

'OK, I'm happy with that. Happy with all of it, so that's it for the testing,' he said, backing away, his voice a little rough and matter-of-fact, and if it hadn't been for the heat in his eyes she would have thought she'd done something wrong

'Can I give you a hand to clear up?'

'No, you're fine. I'll do it. I've got more mess to make before I'm done.'

'Shall I wait up for you?'

He shook his head, and a slow smile burned in his eyes. 'No. You go to bed. I'll come and find you.'

She hadn't even made it to the bedroom before he followed her in. 'I thought you had more to do?' she said softly.

'It'll keep. I have more pressing concerns right now,' he murmured, and tugged her gently into his arms.

She heard him get up, long before the sun rose, when the sky was streaked with pink and the air was filled with birdsong. She propped herself up on one elbow and groped for her phone, checking the time.

Five thirty.

He must be mad. Or driven. This meal was important to him, a chance to showcase his skills to the Valtieri team, and of course he was driven. There was a lot riding on it, and he wasn't going to derail it just because they'd fallen into an unscheduled affair. Even if it was amazing.

At least she didn't have to get up yet. She could sneak another hour, at a pinch, before Ella woke up. She flopped back onto the pillow and closed her eyes again, and the next thing she was aware of was the sound of knocking, then something being put down on her bedside table. She prised her eyes open and Leo's face swam into view.

'Tea,' he said economically, his voice gruff with lack of sleep. 'Ella's up and I need to get on. Can I drag you out of bed?'

She blinked to clear her eyes. 'Time?'

'Nearly seven.'

Rats. 'Give me five minutes,' she mumbled, and closed her eyes again. Mistake. She felt a wet trail across her forehead and opened them again to see Leo dipping his finger in her water glass again.

'Noooo,' she moaned, and forced herself to sit up. 'You're such a bully.'

His smile was strained, his eyes tired. 'Sorry,' he said, sounding utterly unrepentant. 'I really need you. Five minutes,' he repeated firmly, and went out, closing the door softly behind himself.

She looked longingly at the pillows, then sighed, shoved

them up against the headboard and shuffled up the bed. Five minutes, indeed. She groped for the mug, took a sip, then a swallow, and gradually the fog cleared from her brain. She had to get up. Now. Before temptation overwhelmed her and she slithered back down under the covers.

With Leo?

'Don't distract him,' she growled, and dumped the empty mug down and threw off the covers, just as Leo came back in.

His eyes flicked to her legs, then up again, and he zoomed in for a hot, quick kiss. 'Just checking you weren't asleep again.'

'I'm not,' she said unnecessarily, trying not to smile. 'Shut the door on your way out and go back to work.'

He backed out, pulling it to as he went. 'I'm taking Ella to the kitchen to give her breakfast while I carry on. That should give you time for a shower.'

The latch clicked, and she sighed and went over to the French doors and stared out at the valley.

Today was a big day for him, but it was also nearly the end of their stay. She knew Leo needed far more from her than a random fumble when he was too tired to think straight, but if she was going to be there for him for the next few weeks at least, to help him through the disastrous fallout from his doomed marriage, then her feelings and his had to remain on an even keel, which meant playing it light and not letting herself take it too seriously.

And certainly not distracting him when he needed to work, even if it killed her.

She showered rapidly and pulled her clothes on before heading for the kitchen. It was still only half past seven. How on earth was he functioning on so little sleep?

She found them in the kitchen, Ella mashing a soldier of toast all over the tray of the high chair, Leo doing something fast and dextrous with a knife and a rack of lamb.

There was a pile of zucchini flowers in the middle of the table, and the air was rich with promise.

'Smells good in here,' she said.

'That's the mutton,' he said tersely. 'I got up at three and put it in the oven, and I've shredded it and rolled it up into sausages in cling film and it's chilling, and I'm just prepping the racks. She could do with a drink and a handful of blueberries. They're in the fridge.'

She opened the door and was greeted by shelves crammed with goodies of all sorts, including the lovely, lovely panna cotta. 'Which shelf?'

He turned and pointed, then went back to his prepping, and she gave Ella the blueberries and put a slice of bread in the toaster for herself.

'Do you want a coffee?'

'I've had three,' he said. 'Not that it's helping. I'll have another one.'

'Or I could give you a glass of spring water with lemon in it and you could detox a bit for half an hour?'

'Just give me a coffee,' he growled, and gave an enormous yawn. 'My body's finally decided I'm tired. Talk about picking its moments.'

She laughed a little guiltily and handed him a coffee, weaker than he would have made it, longer, with a good slug of milk, and he gave her a look but took it anyway.

'Thanks.'

'You're welcome.'

He took a gulp and carried on, and she sat down with Ella, leaving him to it while she ate her breakfast and tried to stop the blueberries escaping to the floor.

'Tell me if there's anything you need me to help with,' she said, and he nodded.

'I'm fine. You're doing the most useful thing already.'

'I've brought my camera.'

'To catch me at my worst?'

She turned her head and studied him. His hair was tousled and spiky, his eyes were bleary and he had on yesterday's shirt and ancient jeans cut off at the knee, showing off those lean muscular calves that she'd recently realised were irresistible. His feet were bare, too, the toes splayed slightly as he leaned over, strong and straight and curiously sexy. Why had she never noticed them before?

She dragged her eyes off them.

'I think your fans will be able to cope,' she said drily, and pulled out her camera. One for her personal folder...

The family arrived back at eleven thirty, and Lydia came straight into the kitchen to ask if he needed help.

'No, I'm fine,' he said. 'All under control.' Unlike his emotions. 'What time do you want to eat?'

'Twelve thirty?'

He nodded. 'I thought we should eat in the garden under the pergola, unless you'd rather be in here?'

'The garden would be lovely. So, can I ask what's on the menu?'

He told her, and her eyes lit up. 'Fabulous,' she said. 'Bring it on—I'm starving! And I *will* be picking your brains later.'

He couldn't help but laugh. 'Feel free. Now leave me alone so I can concentrate.'

Not a chance. The kitchen became party central, but it didn't matter. He was used to working in chaos, and Lydia made sure they all stayed out of his way and she helped him unobtrusively, taking over the stuffing of the zucchini flowers while he checked on the other things.

Which was fine, except of course Amy was there, and his eyes kept straying to her, distracting his attention from the core business.

He forced himself to focus. The last thing he needed was the lamb rack overcooked or the zucchini flowers burnt in the hot oil when he started to cook them in a few minutes.

But it seemed that although she was pretty much ignoring him, Amy was very much aware of what he was doing, and with twenty minutes to go she chivvied them all outside into the garden to leave him in peace. He stopped her as she was following them.

'Amy?'

'Do you need me?'

What a choice of words, after all that had happened last night. He held out a serving plate piled high with bruschetta.

'Could you give them these—and try and make sure you don't eat them all yourself,' he added, grinning.

She took the plate from him with an unladylike snort and a toss of her head, and he chuckled. Still the same old Amy. 'Thank you,' he called after her, and she relented and threw him a smile over her shoulder as she went out of the door.

She checked her watch. Any minute now, she thought, and leaving Ella in Lydia's care she slipped back into the kitchen.

'Anything I can do?'

'Take the plates out and make sure they're all sitting down ready and then help me ferry stuff in a couple of minutes? I'm just frying the last of the zucchini flowers and everything else is done. The lamb's resting, the mutton's keeping warm and the veg are steaming.'

He was working as he talked and she glanced at the clock on the kitchen wall. Twelve twenty six. Bang on time. She felt her mouth tug in a wry smile. He'd never been on time for anything in his life until he'd started cooking professionally.

'OK. Nothing you want me to do except ferry?'

'No, I'll be fine. And, Amy?'

She turned and met his eyes.

'Thank you. For everything. I couldn't have done it without you. You've been amazing.'

She felt his warmth flood through her.

'You're welcome. And I know you'll be fine. They'll love it. You have some serious fans out here. Just don't burn the zucchini flowers.'

He *was* fine.

Everything was fine. More than fine, and he was in his element.

The food was amazing, and everyone from the babies upwards loved it. The zucchini flowers he'd finally chosen as the starter were beautiful and utterly delicious, and once the lamb two ways—*agnello in due modi* as Leo called it for the benefit of their Italian hosts—was on the table, he looked utterly relaxed. And by the time he brought out the panna cotta and strawberries, he was Leo at his best.

This was his dish, the thing he'd made his own, and Lydia, who by now was muttering things about how on earth she was expected to feed the family after this, was begging him for a master class or at the very least a recipe.

'Any time. It's so easy.'

'Easy to make, but not easy to make taste like *that*,' Lydia pointed out, and he laughed

'But it's nothing without the right ingredients.' His eyes swung to Massimo.

He was leaning back in his chair, wine in hand, his eyes on Leo, and he nodded slowly. 'We need to talk. Heaven knows my wife's an excellent chef, and I'm used to amazing food on a daily basis, but you've taken our ingredients and lifted them into something incredible. We have to do a deal. I want our produce on the table in your restaurants.'

For a moment Leo said nothing, but then a slow smile

started in his eyes and lit up his whole face. 'Thank you. I was going to say the same thing. I don't know what it is about your produce—maybe the care you take, the land, the generations of expertise, but I've been able to find a depth of flavour that I've never found before, and I really want to work with you. And I want that *balsamico* on the list,' he added with a wink.

They all laughed. 'I'm sure that can be arranged. Nine o'clock tomorrow. We'll sort out the fine print,' Massimo said, and drained his glass.

She was sitting on the terrace nursing a cup of tea and watching the swallows when he appeared. Ella was in bed and the families had all gone their separate ways, and they were alone.

He dropped onto the other end of the bench and let out a satisfied sigh. 'Well, that went OK.'

She laughed softly. 'Did you ever doubt it would?'

'Absolutely. There are always doubts, but it looks as if I've achieved what I'd come for.'

'With bells on. They really like you, Leo. And if they hadn't, it wouldn't happen.'

'I know. Tell me about it. And I really like them, too. I trust them, and I couldn't have wanted more from this trip.' He turned his head, his eyes seeking hers. 'And I couldn't have done it without you.'

She looked away, suddenly awkward. 'I haven't done that much—'

'Yes, you have,' he said sincerely. 'I needed to know that Ella was all right, and she was, which left me free to see everything there was to see and take my time getting to know them. It's an important deal, and I wanted to be clear about what I was getting.'

'And are you?'

'Oh, yes. I imagine they'll want to tie up the loose ends

tomorrow, but we're pretty much done. Time to go home. I've neglected my business long enough.'

Home.

Whatever that meant.

Amy stared out over the rolling hills and felt a stab of apprehension mingled with regret. She'd always known this was just for a short time, but it had been a wonderful time, cocooned in a dream world of sunshine and laughter and playing happy families. And now it was almost over. Eight weeks with Leo and Ella, and then she had to find something to do, some way of earning a living until her photography took off, and she had no idea where to start.

Whatever, it meant an end to her time with them in this magical place, and the thought left a hollow ache in the centre of her chest. Things had changed now for ever and, whatever the outcome of their affair, it would never go back to that easy, loving friendship it had been.

'So, what's next for you?' he asked, as if he could read her mind, and she gave a little shrug and dredged up a smile.

'Oh, you know. This and that. I'm sure something'll crop up. I imagine there'll be wedding stuff that still needs dealing with, and I've got a lot of work to do on the photos for your blog, and pulling a portfolio together. I'll need to do some studio shots, clever things with lighting, that sort of thing. Arty stuff. Maybe I can do that while they're filming and the lights are there. And then I'll have to market it. Or myself.'

He nodded thoughtfully. 'I just wondered—I've been thinking I ought to do some cookery books ever since you first nagged me about it, but it's never seemed like the right time before.'

'And it does now?'

'Yes, I think it does. It will be a lot of work, but it might tie in well with Ella. And if I do, of course, I'll need a photographer.'

'You will. And you're right. I told you years ago you should do it but it just wasn't right for you at the time.'

'I don't suppose you want to take it on?'

'Being the photographer?'

Would she? It would mean seeing him again. Over and over again. Which would be fine if they were still together, but torture if they weren't. 'Mind if I think about it? I don't know where I'll be or what I'll be doing.'

'No, I understand that, but bear it in mind. I'd be really grateful. Your photos are amazing.' He gave a huff of laughter. 'There's just the small matter of a publisher, of course.'

'Now there I can definitely help you. I've got contacts, remember?'

'Great. Sound them out, by all means.'

He smiled at her, and her heart flipped over. Could it work? It would mean working with him again, spending time with him, helping him move on with his life. And moving on with hers. She knew a cookery book by him would fly off the shelves, and it would ensure her success, too, but more than that it would give them a better chance to find out if they could forge a future together.

'I'll see what I can do. I'd have a vested interest, of course, in getting this off the ground,' she reminded him. 'Always assuming I'm free.'

'I know. There's no rush. I've got the TV contract outstanding, and that'll have to come first.'

'They might want to tie them together—launch the book of the series, as it were. They do that a lot. Ask them.'

'I will. I'll sound them out, but they're getting impatient. The producer wants to see me like yesterday. I've told him I should be back by Tuesday and I can't deal with it until then.'

'Assuming tomorrow goes to plan.'

'That's right. So we need to fly out on Tuesday morning at the latest. Earlier if we can. I'd rather go tomorrow.'

'Another posh plane?' she asked drily, ignoring the sinking feeling in her gut, and he laughed.

'Probably. It's less stressful than killing time at an airport with Ella, and we need to pick the car up. It's easier. But we'll get whatever we can whenever we can.'

'See how it goes,' she said. 'I'll make sure all our stuff's packed ready first thing in the morning.'

'OK.' He reached out, threading his fingers through hers. 'I think we ought to turn in now. It's been a busy day and I need my business brain working for the morning.'

'Don't you trust them?'

He laughed, his eyes creasing up at the sides, that fascinating dimple flirting with her near the corner of his mouth. 'Of course I trust them, but they'll want the best deal and so do I. I need to be able to think clearly. I'm not going to sign my life away without realising it.'

He got up.

'Come to bed,' he said softly, and she nodded.

'Just give me a couple of minutes. You go first in the bathroom. I want to say goodbye to the valley.'

'Crazy girl,' he murmured, but his voice was full of affection, and he crunched softly over the gravel and went in through the French doors.

She let her breath out slowly. Less than forty-eight hours ago, they'd sat there together while he'd poured his heart out. And then he'd kissed her. Or had she kissed him? She wasn't sure, but she knew that from that moment on everything had changed.

Could she work with him on a cookery book? Maybe, maybe not.

She sat there a little longer, knowing they'd most likely be leaving in the early afternoon and this would be her last chance to soak up the time between day and night, that wonderful time when the swallows went to bed and the bats woke and took over the aerial display in a carefully orchestrated shift change.

She'd miss this. Miss all of it, but most especially the family, Lydia in particular. The warmth of their welcome had been amazing, and she knew it wasn't just because Leo was a celebrity. It was because they were lovely, decent people with a strong sense of family and loyalty, and she'd miss them all.

But most of all she'd miss being with Leo and Ella in this stolen moment in time. The little girl had crept into her heart when she'd least expected it, and Leo...

She sighed softly. Leo had always been massively important to her, but this holiday had changed things, shifted the delicate balance of their friendship from platonic to something she'd never anticipated.

She had no idea what the future would bring, but she knew it would be a long time before she'd be looking for any other man. Her emotions were a mess, her judgement was flawed, and it was far too soon for her to be thinking about another relationship, even with Leo.

Not that he was in any better shape than her emotionally, and probably a whole lot worse. The pair of them were a lost cause. Could they save each other and build a future together?

She desperately hoped so, but she had a feeling the answer would be no, once reality intruded.

She watched the swallows depart, watched the bats dart in to take their place, and when her eyes could hardly make them out in the darkness, she got to her feet and went inside to Leo.

Tomorrow would be here all too soon. It was time to go back to the future.

CHAPTER TEN

'Soon be home.'

She glanced across at him and found a smile. 'Yes. Not long now.'

Not long enough. He'd booked another charter, not getting the benefit of the empty leg rate this time but there were bigger fish to fry, she guessed, like the meeting with the TV series producer tomorrow.

She wasn't complaining, though. This flight, like the last, had been seamless, the car ready and waiting when they arrived, and they were cruising steadily towards Suffolk as the light faded, Ella fast asleep in her car seat behind them.

She glanced over her shoulder at the little girl she'd somehow fallen in love with, and felt a sudden pang of loss at the thought of parting from her. From both of them.

Leo's face was expressionless, his hands relaxed on the wheel, his eyes on the road. He flicked a glance at her and smiled. 'You'll get a lie-in in the morning,' he said, with something like envy in his voice, but she'd swap her lie-in for a cuddle with Ella any day.

'Yes, I will,' she said evenly, trying not to dwell on how much she'd miss those special moments. She'd be going back home to her mother and he to his parents, at least until his house was finished, so at the very least their affair was on hold for now.

'So, when do you want to look at the photos?' she asked, clutching at straws. 'Shall I download them onto a memory stick for you? Obviously they'll need some work before you can put them in your blog, but you'll want to choose some initially for me to work with.'

'Yeah, that would be good. Maybe we could go over them one evening this week? I need to write it, too. I made some notes while we were over there, but to be honest I've had so much to think about my mind hasn't been on it at all. Not to mention certain other distractions,' he added, and she could hear the smile in his voice.

'Going through the photos will help,' she said. 'Will you be staying with your parents?'

'Initially, which'll make life easy when I go to London tomorrow and have to leave Ella behind. I guess you'll be with your mother?'

She would, at least for a little while, and they'd be next door. Her heart gave a little leap of joy. 'Where else?' she said, trying to keep it light. 'In case it's slipped your mind, I no longer have a home.' Or a job, after the next eight weeks. Or Leo?

'It hasn't slipped my mind.'

His hand reached out and found hers, his fingers curling around it as it lay on her lap. 'It'll be all right, Amy. Everything'll work out, one way or the other.'

Would it? She desperately hoped so, but she didn't like the sound of 'other'. The uncertainty of her future was thrown into sharp focus by the raw reminder of her homelessness. And joblessness. Not to mention the touch of his hand.

'Does that apply to you, too, or is it only me you've sprinkled fairy dust on?'

He gave a short huff that could just have been laughter, and put his hand back on the steering-wheel. 'I'm a lost cause,' he said, which was just what she'd thought last night, oddly, but hearing him say it gave her a hideous sinking feeling.

'You're not,' she argued gently, her own situation forgotten because his was far, far worse. 'You've just been in a bad place, Leo, but that'll change. It's already changing. You need to start working again, doing more at the restaurant, getting back into the filming, focussing on your USP.'

'Which is what, exactly?'

She shifted in the seat so she could study him. He hadn't shaved today—or yesterday, probably, either—and the stubble darkening his jaw gave him a sexy, slightly rakish air. How on earth had she never noticed before this week just how gorgeous he was?

'You have great media presence,' she said truthfully, avoiding the obvious fact of his sex appeal in the interest of their mutual sanity. 'Everyone loved your first two television series. Another one will raise your profile, and you can cash in on that with the cookery book. You're a great communicator, so communicate with your public, charm the punters in your restaurant, flirt with the camera, sell yourself.'

His brow crunched up in a frown. 'But I'm not the product. My food's the product.'

How could he really be so dense? 'No. You're inseparable. You, and your enthusiasm for food, your quirky take on things, your energy—that's what people love.'

What she loved. What she'd loved about him since she'd been old enough to be able to spell 'hormone'. She just hadn't realised it until now.

'Well, how on earth would I market that?' he asked, and she laughed. He really didn't get it.

'You don't have to market it! You just have to be you, and the rest will follow. The TV, the cookery book idea, your blog—all of it showcases you. The food is secondary, in a way. You were doing all the right things already. Just keep doing them and you'll be fine.'

He grunted, checked over his shoulder and pulled out to overtake. 'Right now I'm more worried about where we're going to do the filming. The plan was to do it in my new house, in my own kitchen, but it's not ready and time's running out. I won't do London again, and they want more of a lifestyle thing, which will fit round Ella, but that's no good without the house.'

'So how long will it be before it's done?'

'I have no idea,' he said, and he sounded exasperated. 'The builder's running out of time, even though there's a penalty clause in the contract, but of course I've been away over a week so I haven't been on his case and I don't know how well they've got on.'

'What's left to do?'

'It's mostly done, it's just the finishing off. They were fitting the kitchen, which is the most important thing as far as filming's concerned, and it should be straightforward, but every time I think that it all goes wrong, so who knows?'

'Could you use the restaurant kitchen in Yoxburgh?'

'Not without disrupting the business, and it's going well now, it's getting a name for itself and it's busy. I don't want to turn people away; I have to live in the town, it's where I'll be working, so it's the flagship restaurant, and that makes it hugely important to the brand. It would be career suicide and I'm doing pretty well on that already.'

'So push him.'

'I will. I'll call him in the morning, on my way to London, see how far off finishing he is.'

He turned off the main road, and she realised they were nearly home—if family homes counted, and at the moment they both seemed to be homeless, so she guessed they did count. He drove slowly through the village, turned into her mother's drive and pulled up at the door.

He didn't cut the engine, presumably so he didn't wake Ella, but he got out and by the time she'd picked up her bag and found her key he was there, holding the car door open for her.

'I'll get your stuff. I won't stop, I need to settle Ella and I've got a million and one emails to check tonight. I've just been ignoring them.'

He opened the back of the car and pulled out her bag, carrying it to the door for her. She put her key in the lock and turned to thank him, but he got there before her, reaching out a hand and cupping her face, his thumb sweeping a caress across her cheek.

Her eyes locked with his, and held.

'I don't know what I would have done without you, Amy,' he said softly, his voice a little gruff. 'You've been amazing, and I'm so grateful.'

Her heart thumped, her face turning slightly as she looked away, her cheek nestling into his hand so his thumb was almost touching her mouth.

'Don't be,' she murmured. 'You saved my life, getting me out of here. I don't know quite what I would have done if you hadn't.'

'You would have been fine. Your mother would have seen to that.'

She felt her mouth tip in a smile, and she turned her head again and met his eyes. 'Yes, she would, but it wouldn't have been the same. Thank you for rescuing me for the umpteenth time. I'll try not to let it happen again.'

And without checking in with her common sense meter, she went up on tiptoe and kissed him. The designer stubble grazed her skin lightly, setting her nerve endings on fire and making her ache for more, but before either of them could do anything stupid, she rocked back onto her heels and stepped away.

'Good luck tomorrow. Let me know how it goes.'

'I will. Enjoy your lie-in and think of me up at the crack of dawn with my little treasure.'

Think of him? She'd thought of very little else for the past week or more. 'You know you love it.' She turned the key in the door, pushed it open and picked up her bag. 'Goodnight, Leo.'

''Night, Amy. Sleep tight.'

It was what he said to Ella every night, his voice a soft, reassuring rumble. *'Goodnight, my little one. Sleep tight.'*

She swallowed the lump in her throat, walked into the house and closed the door behind her.

Time to start sorting out her life.

Her mother was pleased to see her.

She was in the sitting room watching the television, and she switched it off instantly. 'Darling! I didn't hear the car, I'm sorry. Is Leo with you?'

'No, he's got to get Ella to bed and he's got an early start in the morning.'

'Oh. OK. Good journey?'

'Yes, fine. It seems odd to be home.'

Odd, but good, she thought as her mother hugged her tight and then headed for the kitchen. 'Tea? Coffee? Wine?'

She laughed and followed her. 'Tea would be great. I've had a lot of wine this week. Wine, and food, and—'

Leo. Leo, in almost every waking moment, one way or another.

'So how was Tuscany? Tell me all about the *palazzo*. It sounds amazing.'

'Oh, it is. I've got a million photos I've got to go through.

I'll show them to you when I've had time to sort them out a bit. So how's it been here?' she asked, changing the subject. 'I'm so sorry I ran away and left you to clear up the chaos, but I just couldn't face it.'

'No, of course you couldn't, and it's been fine. Everyone was lovely about it. I went next door and spoke to them all, and the family came back here and it was lovely, really. We had quite a good time, considering, and Roberto made sure we had plenty to eat, so it was fine.'

'What about the presents?' she asked.

'No problem. I spoke to the store, and they agreed to refund everyone. They just want to hear from you personally before they press the buttons, and people will need to contact them individually, but it'll be fine. Nothing to worry about.'

That was a weight off her mind. There was still Leo's gift, of course, but she'd done what she could about that, and there was more to come. Looking after Ella for a week had been a joy, and photographing Leo had been a guilty pleasure, but she'd promised her help for eight weeks to help during the filming, and if that didn't come off, for any reason, she could give him those photos, edit them until they were perfect for what he needed, so even if she couldn't help him with a cookery book, he shouldn't come off too badly from their deal.

'Mum, are you OK with me staying here for a while?' she asked, before she got too carried away with the planning. 'Just until I get my life sorted out?'

Her mother tutted and hugged her. 'Darling, it's your home. Of course you can stay here. You're always welcome, and you always will be. And don't worry. Things will sort themselves out. I just want you to be happy.'

Happy? She felt her eyes fill, and turned away.

'I don't suppose there's anything to eat?'

'Of course there is! I knew you were coming home so I made curry. I'll put the rice on now.'

Ella wouldn't settle.

He couldn't blame her. She'd been trapped in her baby seat for a long time today, one way and another, and she'd slept for a lot of it. Not surprisingly, she wanted to play.

With him.

Again, he couldn't blame her. She hadn't seen nearly as much of him as usual in the past week, and she'd been in a strange place, with a strange carer. Not that she'd seemed to mind. She adored Amy.

His daughter had good taste. Excellent taste.

He covered his eyes and wondered how long it would take to get her out of his system. A week? A month?

A lifetime?

'Boo!'

Ella giggled and crawled up to him, pulling his hands off his face again and prising his eyes open. He winced, lifted her out of range and opened them, to her great delight. Another giggle, another bounce up and down on his lap, another launch at his face. She was so easily pleased, the reward of her smile out of all proportion to the effort he was putting in.

He reeled her in and hugged her, pushing her T-shirt up and blowing a raspberry on her bare tummy and making her shriek with laughter.

His email was squatting in his inbox like a malevolent toad, and he had phone calls to make and things to do, but he didn't care. The most important thing was checking in with the restaurant, but they were shut on Monday nights so that wasn't a problem for today.

She pulled up her little T-shirt again and shoved her tummy in the air, and he surrendered. Ella wanted her father and, dammit, he wanted her, too. The rest would keep.

* * *

She stood at her bedroom window, staring across at Leo's family home. The light was on in his bedroom, and through the open window she could hear Ella's little shriek of laughter and Leo's answering growl.

They were playing. That wouldn't please him, with all he had to do, but they sounded as if they were having fun, or at least Ella was.

She couldn't help smiling, but it was a bitter-sweet smile. She already missed them so much. Watching him playing with Ella, focussing all that charismatic charm on his little girl, not caring at all that he was making an idiot of himself.

Oh, Leo.

It was warm, but she closed the window anyway. She didn't need to torture herself by listening to them. It was bad enough without that.

She turned and scanned the room.

Her wedding dress was gone, of course, hung up in another room, she imagined, together with the veil and shoes. And her ring? She'd left it on the dressing table, and that was where she found it. Her mother had put it back in the box, but left it out for her to deal with.

She'd send it back to Nick, of course. It was the least she could do, it must have cost him a fortune. Not that he was exactly strapped for cash, but that wasn't the point.

She got out her laptop, plugged in the memory card from the camera and propped herself on the bed against a pile of pillows. She'd have a quick look through the photos before she went to bed, but she wasn't even going to attempt her emails. No doubt her inbox was full of sympathetic or slightly sarky comments about the wedding fiasco, and she might just delete the lot. Tomorrow.

Tonight, she was looking at photos.

* * *

'Are you busy?'

Busy? Why should she be busy? All she'd had to do today was draft a letter to all the guests, hand-write them and take them to the post office. Preferably not in the village so she didn't have to stand in the queue and answer questions or endure sympathetic glances. And sort through the photos.

So far, she hadn't even got past first base.

'No, I'm not busy. Why?'

'I just wondered. I'm back, I've put Ella to bed and I've got a site meeting with the builder in half an hour, but then I thought we could go through the photos.'

Ah. She hadn't got far last night. About five minutes in she'd been reduced to tears, and she'd had to shut her laptop. 'I haven't had time to go through them yet and delete the dross.' Or extract the ones that were for her eyes only. There were a lot of those. And it had been nothing to do with time.

'That's fine. We can do it together.'

'Here, or yours?'

'How about the new house? The builder said it was habitable, pretty much, so we could take the laptop over there.'

She could always say no—tell him she was tired or something. Except that so far today she'd done almost nothing. A bit of laundry, a lot of wallowing in self-pity and kicking herself for being stupid didn't count. And at least it would deal with the photos.

'Fine,' she agreed, dying to get a look at his house and too weak to say no.

'Great. Come round when you're ready, and we'll go from here.'

That meant seeing his parents, and they'd been the ones with the marquee in the garden, the catering team crawling all over the place, the mess left behind afterwards. And all for nothing.

She'd been going to take them something by way of apology, but now he'd short-circuited her plans and she wouldn't have a chance.

She shook her head in defeat.

'OK. I'll be round in a minute.'

'We're in the kitchen. Come through the fence.'

So she did. Through the gate in the fence that their fathers had made together years ago, and into their back garden where just over a week ago there had been a marquee for her wedding. You couldn't tell. The garden was immaculate, a riot of colour and scent. The perfect setting for a wedding.

She turned her back on it, walked in through the kitchen door and straight into Mrs Zacharelli's arms.

'Welcome home, Amy,' she said, and hugged her hard.

Amy's eyes welled, and she swallowed hard and tried not to cry. 'I'm so sorry—' she began, but then the tears got the better of her and Mrs Zach hugged her again before she was elbowed out of the way by her husband. He hauled Amy into a bear hug and cradled her head like a child.

'Enough of that,' he said. 'No tears. It was the right thing to do.'

'But you did so much for me,' she protested.

'It was nothing. Sit. Drink. We're celebrating.'

He let her go, pushed her into a chair and thrust a glass into her hand. Prosecco? 'Celebrating what?'

'Leo hasn't told you? They're starting filming the new television series next week.'

She turned her head and met his eyes. 'Really? So quick? What about your house?'

'We'll see. The builder says it'll be ready. Drink up, or we're going to be late.'

* * *

It was beautiful.

Stunning. She vaguely remembered seeing the cliff-top house in the past, but it had been nothing to get excited about. Now—well, now it was amazing.

While Leo poked and prodded and asked the builder questions about things she didn't know anything about, she drifted from room to room, her eyes drawn constantly to the sea, wondering how on earth she'd thought that Palazzo Valtieri could trump this. Oh, it was hugely impressive, steeped in history and lovingly cared for, but there was none of the light and space and freedom that she felt in this house, and she knew where she'd rather live.

He found her upstairs in one of the bedrooms. 'So, what do you think?'

'I think you need to give me a guided tour before I can possibly judge.'

His mouth kicked up in a smile, and he shook his head slowly. 'Going to make me wait? I might have known it. You always were a tease. So...' He waved his arm. 'This is my bedroom.'

'I see you chose the one with the lousy sea view.'

He chuckled and moved on. 'Bathroom through there, walk-in wardrobe, then this is the principal guest room—'

'Another dreadful view,' she said drily, and followed him through to Ella's bedroom.

'Oh! Who painted the mural? It's lovely!'

He rubbed his hand over the back of his neck and gave a soft laugh. 'I did. I wanted her room to be special, and I thought it was something I could do for her, something personal. I'm sure I could have paid a professional to do it much better, but somehow that didn't seem right.'

Her eyes filled, and she ran her fingertips lightly over the intertwining branches of a magical tree that scrambled up the wall and across the ceiling, sheltering the corner where she imagined the cot would go.

'It's wonderful,' she said, her voice choked. 'She's a lucky little girl.'

'I wouldn't go that far, but I do my best under the circumstances.'

He turned away, walking out of the room and down the stairs, and she followed him—through the hall, a sitting room with a sea view, a study fitted out with desk and shelves and storage facing the front garden and the drive this time, a cloakroom with coat storage and somewhere to park Ella's buggy—and then back across the hall into the main event, a huge room that opened out to the deck and the garden beyond.

Literally. The far wall was entirely glass, panels that would slide away to let the outside in, and right in the centre of the room was the kitchen.

And what a kitchen! Matte dark grey units, pale wood worktops, sleek integrated ovens, in the plural—and maybe a coffee maker, a steam oven, a microwave—she had no idea, but a bank of them, anyway, set into tall units at one side that no doubt would house all manner of pots and pans and ingredients as well. There was a huge American-style fridge freezer, still wrapped but standing by the slot designed to take it, and he told her it was to be plumbed in tomorrow.

'So—the verdict?'

She gave an indifferent shrug, and then relented, her smile refusing to hide. 'Stunning. It's absolutely stunning, Leo. Really, really lovely.'

'So who wins?'

She laughed softly and turned to face him. 'It grieves me to admit it, but you do. By a mile.'

His eyes creased into a smile, and he let out a quiet huff of laughter. 'Don't ever tell them that.'

'Oh, I wouldn't be so rude, and it's very beautiful, but this...'

'Yeah. I love it, too. I wasn't sure I would, because of the circumstances, but I do. I started planning it before Lisa died, but she had no interest in it, no input—nothing. And it's changed out of all recognition.'

'So she's not here.'

'No. And she's never been here. Not once. She wouldn't set foot in it. And now I'm glad, because it isn't—'

He broke off, but the word 'tainted' hovered in the air between them.

She took a breath, moved the conversation on, away from the past. 'So, will it be ready for filming on Monday?'

He shrugged, that wonderful Latin shrug that unravelled her every time, and his mouth quirked into a smile. 'He tells me it's done, all bar the fridge-freezer plumbing and the carpets, which are booked for tomorrow. I've gone over everything with him this evening to make sure it's OK, and I can move in whenever I want.'

'Oh. Wow. That was quick,' she said, and was appalled at the sense of loss. She'd thought they'd be next door with his parents, but now they wouldn't. He and Ella would move into their wonderful new house a few miles up the road, and she'd hardly see them.

Oh, well. It had to happen sooner or later.

'It had to be. The series team liked the Tuscany idea, by the way, and it's a brilliant opportunity to showcase the Valtieri produce, so they won't be unhappy with that. I just need to knock up some recipes, bearing in mind the schedule's pretty tight.'

'So you're going to be really busy setting it all up this week. Do you want me to look after Ella from now on?'

He ran his hand round the back of his neck. 'Yeah, I need to talk to you about that. We'll be filming all day from Monday, and I need to spend some time in the restaurant in the evenings, and I can't do that and look after her. She loves you, she's happy with you—but I don't know how you'd feel about moving in.'

'Moving in? Here? With you?'

He shrugged. 'Not—with me. Not in that way. I just think it would be easier all round if you were here, but you don't have to do it. You don't have to do any of it. It was never part of the deal.'

'I changed the deal. And you agreed it.'

'And then we moved the goalposts into another galaxy. You have every right to refuse, if you want to.' His face softened into a wry smile. 'I'm hoping you won't because my parents need a holiday and I'd like to cut them some slack. They've been incredible for the past nine months, and I'm very conscious that I've taken advantage, but I know that moving in with me is a huge step for you, and I'm very conscious of what you said about what happened in Tuscany—'

'Stays in Tuscany?' she finished for him. 'That's not set in stone.'

'But we could still do that. Keep our distance, get to know each other better before we invest too much in this relationship, because we're not the people we were.'

'So what do you want to know about me?'

'Whether or not you can live with me would be a good start.'

'We seem to have done a pretty good job of it this week.'

'We haven't shared the toothpaste yet,' he said, his mouth wry.

'We've done everything else.'

'No, we haven't. We haven't been together while I've been running the business, which takes a hell of a lot of my time, and what's left belongs to Ella. And that's not negotiable.'

'I know that, Leo, and I can handle your schedule. I've

already proved that. I'm not a needy child, and I'm not Lisa. I haven't been transplanted into an alien environment. I've got friends and family in the area, a life of my own. Don't worry, I'll find plenty to do.'

'I still think we need to try it. And to do that, I'd need you living here, at least while my parents are away, and preferably for the whole time we're filming. If you could.'

She hesitated, part of her aching to be there helping him and spending time with Ella, making sure she was safe and happy, the other part wary of exposing herself to hurt.

No contest.

'So how long is it? Is it eight weeks, as you thought?'

'I don't know. They're talking about eight episodes. Probably a couple of days for each, plus prep and downtime for me while they cut and fiddle about with it. I reckon a week an episode. That's what it was last time. Or maybe six, at a push. It's a serious commitment. And it's a lot to ask—too much for my mother and father, even if they weren't going on holiday.'

Eight weeks of working with him, keeping Ella out of the way yet close enough at hand that he could see her whenever he had a chance. Eight weeks of sleeping with him every night? Maybe. Which meant eight more weeks to get to know him better, and fall deeper and deeper in love with both of them.

And at the end—what then?

She hesitated for so long that he let out a long, slow sigh and raked his hands through his hair.

'Amy, if you really can't, then I'll find another way,' he said softly. 'I don't want to put you under pressure or take advantage of you and it doesn't change things between us at all. I still want to get to know you better, but if you aren't sure you want to do it, I'll get a nanny—a childminder. Something. A nursery.'

'Not at such short notice,' she told him. 'Even I know

that. Anyone who's any good won't be able to do it, not with the restaurant hours as well.' She sighed, closed her eyes briefly and then opened them to find him watching her intently.

'So where does that leave us?' he asked.

'With me?'

'So—is that a yes?'

She tried to smile, but it slipped a little, the fear of making yet another catastrophic mistake so soon after the last one looming in her mind. 'Yes, it's a yes. Just remind me again—why it is that you *always* get your own way?' she murmured, and he laughed and pulled her into his arms and gave her a brief but heartfelt hug.

'Thank you. Now all I have to do is get the furniture delivered and we can move in and get on with our lives.'

Well, he could. Hers, yet again, was being put on hold, but she owed him so much for so many years of selfless support that another eight weeks of her life was nothing—especially since it would give them a chance to see if their relationship would survive the craziness that was his life.

She'd just have to hope she could survive it. Not the eight weeks, that would be fine. But the aftermath, the fallout when the series was filmed, the crew had left and he'd decided he couldn't live with her?

What on earth had she let herself in for?

CHAPTER ELEVEN

THEY WERE IN.

He looked around at his home—their home, his and Ella's and maybe Amy's—and let out a long, quiet sigh of relief. It had been a long time coming, but at last they were here.

Ella was safely tucked up in her cot in her new room, his parents had stayed long enough to toast the move, and now it was all his.

He poured himself a glass of wine, walked out onto the deck and sat down on the steps, staring out over the sea. He was shattered. Everything had been delivered, unpacked and put in place, and all he'd had to do was point.

In theory.

And tomorrow the contents of the store cupboards in the kitchen were being delivered and he could start working on some recipes.

But tonight he had to draft his Tuscan tour blog. Starting with the photos, because they hadn't got round to them on Tuesday night and he hadn't had a spare second since. Amy was coming round shortly with her laptop, and they were going through them together. Assuming he could keep his eyes open.

The doorbell rang, and he put his glass down and let her in. He wanted to pull her into his arms and kiss her, but with what had happened in Tuscany and all that, he really wanted to give their relationship a chance.

'Did she go down all right?'

He smiled wryly. Typical Amy, to worry about Ella first. 'Fine. She was pooped. I don't know what you did with her all day, but she was out of it.'

She laughed, and the sound rippled through him like clear spring water. 'We just played in the garden, and then we went for a walk by the beach, and she puggled about in the sand for a bit. We had a lovely day. How did you get on?'

'Oh, you know what moving's like. I'll spend the next six months trying to find things and groping for light switches in the dark. Come on through, I'm having a glass of wine on the deck.'

'Can we do it in the kitchen, looking at the photos? There are an awful lot. And can I have water, please? I'm driving, remember.'

'Sure.' He retrieved his glass, poured her water from the chiller in the fridge and sat next to her at the breakfast bar overlooking the sea. 'So, what have we got?'

'Lots.'

There *were* lots, she wasn't exaggerating. And there were gaps in the numbers, all over the place.

'What happened to the others? There are loads missing.'

'I deleted them.'

He blinked. 'Really? That's not like you. You never throw anything out.'

'Maybe you don't know me as well as you think,' she said.

Or maybe you do, she thought, scrolling down through the thumbnails and registering just how many she'd removed and saved elsewhere.

'Just start at the top,' he suggested, so they did.

Him laughing on the plane. She loved that one. Others in their suite, in the pool—still too many of them, although she'd taken bucket-loads out for what she'd called her private collection.

Self-indulgent fantasy, more like.

She knew what she was doing. She was building a memory bank, filling it with images to sustain her if it all went wrong.

There were some of her, too, ones he'd taken of her shot against the backdrop of the valley behind their terrace, or with Ella, playing. She'd nearly taken them out, too, but because nearly all of them had Ella in, she hadn't. He could have them for his own use.

'Right, so which ones do you want me to work on?'

He didn't hold back. She got a running commentary on the ones he liked, the ones he couldn't place, the ones he'd have to check with the Valtieri family before they were used.

'How about a *short*list for the blog?' she suggested drily, when he'd selected about two hundred.

He laughed. 'Sorry. These are just the ones I really like. I'll go through them again and be a bit more selective. I was just getting an overview. Why don't you just leave them with me so I'm not wasting your time? Did you copy them?'

She handed him the memory stick with the carefully edited photos that she'd deemed fit to give him. 'Here. Don't lose it. Just make a note and let me know.'

'I will. Thanks. Want the guided tour?'

'Of your furniture? I think I'll pass, if you don't mind. I still have stuff to do—like writing to all my wedding guests.'

'Sorry. Of course you do. And I've taken your whole day already. Go, and don't rush back in the morning. I should be fine until ten, at least.'

She moved in on Sunday, and the film crew arrived on Monday and brought chaos to the house—lights, reflectors, a million people apparently needed to co-ordinate the shoot, and Ella took one look at it all and started to cry.

Amy ended up taking her home for the day more than once, which would have been fine if they'd stopped filming at her bedtime, but sometimes it dragged on, and then she'd be unsettled, and he'd have to break off and read her a story and sing to her before she'd go back to sleep.

'I'm sorry, this is really tough for you both,' Leo said after a particularly late shoot. 'I didn't know it would disrupt her life so much. I should have thought it through.'

'It's fine, Leo,' she assured him. 'We're coping.'

And they were, just about, but it was like being back in Tuscany, tripping over each other in the kitchen in the morning, having breakfast together with Ella, doing all the happy families stuff that was tearing her apart, with the added bonus of doing it under the eyes of the film crew.

And because of the 'what happened in Tuscany' thing, the enforced intimacy was making it harder and harder to be around each other without touching and she was seriously regretting suggesting it.

Then one night Ella cried and she got up to her, but Leo got there first. 'It's fine. I'll deal with her, you go back to bed,' he said, but the fourth time she woke there was a tap on her door and Leo came in.

'Amy, I think she needs the doctor. She must have an ear infection or something. I have to take her to the hospital. They have an out of hours service there, apparently.'

'Want me to come?'

The relief on his face should have been comical, but it was born of worry, so she threw her clothes on and went with him. It took what felt like hours, of course, before they came home armed with antibiotics and some pain relief, and Leo looked like hell.

'I feel sorry for the make-up lady who's going to have to deal with the bags under your eyes in the morning,' she said ruefully when the baby was finally settled.

'Don't you mean later in the morning?' he sighed,

yawning hugely and reaching for a glass. 'Water? Tea? I've given up on sleep. Decided it's an overrated pastime.'

She laughed softly and joined him. 'Tea,' she said.

'Good idea. We'll watch the sun come up.'

Which wasn't a good idea at all. Tuscany again, and sitting on the terrace overlooking the valley with the swallows swooping. Except here it was the gulls, their mournful cries haunting in the pale light of dawn.

'Thank you for coming with me to the hospital,' he said quietly.

'You don't have to thank me, Leo. I was happy to do it. I was worried about her.'

She stared out over the sea, watching it flood with colour as the sun crept over the horizon. It was beautiful, and it would have been perfect had she been able to do what she wanted to do and rest her head on his shoulder, but of course she couldn't.

'How's the filming going?' she asked, and he sighed.

'OK, I think, but I'm neglecting the restaurant, and I haven't even touched the Tuscany blog. On the plus side, we're nearly two weeks in.'

Really? Only six more weeks to go? And when it ended, they'd have no more excuse to be together, so it would be crunch time, and she was in no way ready to let him go. She drained her tea and stood up.

'I might go back to bed and see if I can sleep for a few more minutes,' she said, and left him sitting there, silhouetted against the sunrise. It would have made a good photo. Another one to join the many in her private collection.

She turned her back on him and walked away.

The filming was better after that, the next day not as long, and Leo had a chance to catch up with the restaurant over the weekend. Ella was fine, her ear infection settling quickly, but she'd slept a lot to catch up so Amy

had helped him with the blog over the weekend, edited the
photos, pulled it all together, and she showed it to him on
Monday night after Ella was in bed.

'Oh, it looks fantastic, Amy,' he said, sitting back and
sighing with relief. 'Thank you so much. The photos are
amazing.'

'Better than your selfies?' she teased lightly, and he
laughed.

'So much better!' He leant over and kissed her fleetingly, then pulled away, grabbing her by the hand and
towing her into the kitchen. 'Come on, I'm cooking you
dinner.'

'Is that my reward?'

'You'd better believe it. I have something amazing for
you.'

'That poor lobster that's been crawling around your
sink?'

'That was for filming. This is for us. Sit.'

She sat, propped up at the breakfast bar watching him
work. She could spend her life doing it. What was she
thinking? She *was* spending her life doing it, and it was
amazing. Or would be, if only she dared to believe in it.

'The producer was talking about a cookery book,' he
told her while he worked. 'Well, more a lifestyle-type
book. Like the blog, but more so, linking it to the series. It
would make sense, and of course they've got stills they've
taken while I've been working so it should be quite easy.'

So he wouldn't need her. She stifled her disappointment, because she was pleased for him anyway. 'That
sounds good.'

'I thought so, too.'

He was still chopping and fiddling. 'Is it going to be
long? I'm starving,' she said plaintively.

'Five minutes, tops. Here, eat these. New amuse-bouche
ideas for the restaurant. Tell me what you think.'

'Yummy,' she said, and had another, watching him as she ate the delicious little morsels. The steak was flash-fried, left to rest in the marinade while he blanched fresh green beans, and then he crushed the new potatoes, criss-crossed them with beans, thinly sliced the steak and piled it on before drizzling the marinade over the top.

'There. Never let it be said that I don't feed you prop-erly. Wine?'

He handed her a glass without waiting for her reply, and she sipped it and frowned.

'Is this one of the Valtieri wines?'

'Yes. It goes well, doesn't it?'

'Mmm. It's gorgeous. So's the steak. It's like butter it's so tender.'

'What can I say? I'm just a genius,' he said, grinning, and hitched up on the stool next to her, and it would have been so natural, so easy to lean towards him and kiss that wicked smile.

She turned her attention back to her food, and ignored her clamouring body. Let it clamour. They had to play it his way, and if that meant she couldn't push him, so be it. He was turning his life around, getting it back on track and she wasn't going to do anything to derail his rehabili-tation. Or her own.

And Leo was definitely derailing material.

'Coffee?' he asked when she'd finished the crème brûlée he'd had left over from filming today.

'Please.'

And just because they could, just because it was Leo's favourite thing in the world to do at that time of day, they took it outside on the deck and sat side by side on the steps to drink it.

He'd turned the lights down in the kitchen, so they were sitting staring out across the darkened garden at the moonlit sea. Lights twinkled on it here and there.

as the lights had twinkled in Tuscany, only here they were on the sea, and the smell of salt was in the air, the ebbing waves tugging on the shingle the only sound to break the silence.

She leant against him, resting her shoulder against his, knowing it was foolish, tired of fighting it, and with a shaky sigh he set his cup down, turned his head towards her and searched her eyes, his arm drawing her closer.

'Are we going to be OK, Amy?' he asked, as if he'd read her mind. His voice was soft, a little gruff. Perhaps a little afraid. She could understand that.

'I don't know. I want us to be, but all the time there's this threat hanging over us, the possibility that it won't, that it's just another mistake for both of us. And I don't want that. I want to be able to sit with you in the dark and talk, like we've done before a million times, and not feel this…crazy fear stalking me that it could be the last time.'

She took a sip of her coffee, but it tasted awful so she put it down.

'I'm going to bed,' she said. 'I'm tired and I can't do this any more. Pretend there's nothing going on, nothing between us except an outgrown friendship that neither of us can let go of. It's more than that, so much more than that, but I don't know if I can dare believe in it, and I don't think you can, either.'

She got to her feet, and he stood up and pulled her gently into his arms, cradling her against his chest. 'I'm sorry. Go on, go to bed. I'll see you in the morning.'

He bent and brushed his lips against her cheek, the stubble teasing her skin and making her body ache for more, and then he let her go.

She heard him come upstairs a few minutes later. He hesitated at her door and she willed him to come in, but he didn't, and she rolled to her side and shut her eyes firmly and willed herself to sleep instead.

* * *

The film crew interrupted their breakfast the next morning, but she didn't mind. The place stank of coffee, and she couldn't get Ella out of the house fast enough.

She strapped her into the car seat, pulled off the drive and went into town. They were running short of her follow-on milk formula, so she popped into the supermarket and picked up some up, and then she headed for the seafront. They could go to the beach, she thought, and then they passed a café and the smell of coffee hit her like a brick.

She pressed her hand to her mouth and walked on, her footsteps slowing to a halt as soon as they were out of range. No. She couldn't be. But she could see Isabelle's face so clearly, hear her saying that she couldn't stand the smell of coffee, and last night it had tasted vile.

But—how? She was on the Pill. She'd taken it religiously.

Except for the first day in Tuscany, the Sunday morning. She'd forgotten it then, taken it in the afternoon, about four. Nine hours late. And it was only the mini-pill, because she and Nick had planned to start a family anyway, and a month or so earlier wouldn't have mattered. And she'd hardly seen Nick for weeks before the wedding. Which meant if she was pregnant, it was definitely Leo's baby.

She turned the buggy round, crossed the road and went to the chemist's, bought a pregnancy test with a gestation indicator and went to another café that didn't smell so much and had decent loos. She took Ella with her into the cubicle which doubled as disabled and baby changing, so there was room for the buggy, and she did the test, put the lid back on the wand and propped it up, and watched her world change for ever.

He hadn't seen them all day.

The filming had gone well and the crew had packed up early, but Amy and Ella still weren't home.

Perhaps she'd taken Ella to her mother's, or to a friend's house? Probably. It was nearly time for Ella to eat, so he knew they wouldn't be long, but he was impatient.

He'd been thinking about what Amy had said last night, about their lives being on hold while they gave themselves time, and he'd decided he didn't want more time. He wanted Amy, at home with him, with Ella, in his bed, in his life. For ever.

Finally the gravel crunched. He heard her key in the door, and felt the fizz of anticipation in his veins, warring with an undercurrent of dread, just in case. What would she say? Would it be yes? Please, God, not no—

'Hi. Have you had a good day?' he asked, taking Ella from her with a smile and snuggling her close.

'Busy,' she said, heading into the kitchen with a shopping bag. 'Where are the film crew?'

'We finished early. So what did you do all day?'

'Oh, this and that. We went to town and picked up some formula, but it was a bit hot so we went to Mum's and had lunch in the garden and stayed there the rest of the day.'

'I thought you might have been there. I was about to ring you. Has she eaten?'

'Not recently. She had a snack at three. Are you OK to take over? I've got a few things I need to do.'

He frowned. He couldn't really put his finger on it, but she didn't sound quite right. 'Sure, you go ahead. Supper at seven?'

'If you like. Call me when you're done, OK? I might have a shower, it's been a hot day.'

She ran upstairs, and he took Ella through to the kitchen, put her in her high chair and gave her her supper. She fed herself and made an appalling mess, but he didn't care. All he could think about was Amy, and what was wrong with her, because something was and he was desperately hoping it wasn't a continuation of what she'd said last night.

What if she turned him down? Walked away and left him?

On autopilot, he wiped Ella's hands and took her up to bath her.

'Amy?'

'Yes?'

He opened her bedroom door and found her sitting up on her bed, the laptop open on her lap. She shut it and looked up at him. 'Is supper ready?'

'It won't take long. Can you come down? I want to talk to you.'

'Sure,' she said, but she looked tense and he wondered why.

'Can I go first?' she said, and he hesitated for a moment then nodded.

'Sure. Do you want a drink?'

'Just water.'

He filled a tumbler from the fridge and handed it to her, and she headed outside to the garden, perching on the step in what had become her usual place, and he crossed the deck and sat down beside her.

She drew her breath in as if she was going to speak, then let it out again and bit her lip.

'Amy? What is it?'

She sucked in another shaky breath, turned to look at him and said, 'I'm pregnant.'

He felt the blood drain from his head, and propped his elbows on shaking knees, the world slowing so abruptly that thoughts and feelings crashed into each other and slid away again before he could grasp them.

'How?' he asked her, his voice taut. He raised his head

and stared at her. 'How, Amy? You're on the Pill—I know that, I watched you take it every morning.'

'Not every morning,' she said heavily. 'The first day, I forgot. I didn't take it until the afternoon.'

'And that's enough?'

'Apparently. I didn't even think about it, because it didn't matter any more. I wasn't on my honeymoon, and we weren't—'

He was trying to assimilate that, and then another thought, much harder to take, brought bile to his throat.

'How do you know it's mine?' he asked, and his voice sounded cold to his ears, harsh, uncompromising. 'How do you know it isn't...?' He couldn't even bring himself to say Nick's name out loud, but it echoed between them in the silence.

'Because it's the only time I've taken it late, and because of this.'

She pulled something out of her pocket and handed it to him. A plastic thing, pen-sized or a little more, with a window on one side. And in the window was the word 'pregnant' and beneath it '2-3'.

A pregnancy test, he realised. And 2-3?

'What does this mean?' he asked, pointing to it with a finger that wasn't quite steady.

'Two to three weeks since conception.'

The weekend they'd been alone in the *palazzo*. So it *was* his baby. Then another hideous thought occurred to him.

'When did you do this test?'

'This morning,' she told him, her voice drained and lifeless.

'Are you sure? Are you sure you didn't do it a week or two ago?'

Her eyes widened, and the colour drained from her face.

'You think I'd lie to you about something as fundamental as this?'

'You wouldn't be the first.'

She stared at him for what seemed like for ever, and then she got to her feet.

'Where are you going?'

'Home. To my mother.'

'Not to Nick?'

She turned back to him, her eyes flashing with fury. 'Why would I go running to Nick to tell him I've been stupid enough to let you get me pregnant?' she asked him bluntly. 'If you could really think that then you don't know me at all. It's none of Nick's business. It's my business, and it could have been yours, but if you really think I could lie to you about something so precious, so amazing, so beautiful as our child, then I don't think we have anything left to say to each other. You wanted my terrifying honesty. Well, this is it. I'm sorry you don't like it, but *I am not Lisa!*'

He heard her footsteps across the decking, the vibrations going through him like an earthquake, then the sound of the front door slamming and the gravel crunching under her tyres as she drove off.

He stared blindly after her as the sound of her car faded into the evening, drowned out by the cries of gulls and the soft crash of the waves on the shore below, and then like a bolt of lightning the pain hit him squarely in the chest.

Her mother was wonderful and didn't say a thing, just heard her out, hugged her while she cried and made them both tea.

'Do you know how wonderful you are?' she asked, and her mother's face crumpled briefly.

'Don't be silly. I'm just your mother. You'll know what I mean, soon enough. It'll make sense.'

Her eyes filled with tears. 'I already know. I'm not going to see Ella again, Mum. Never.'

'Of course you will.'

'No, I won't. Or Leo.' Her voice cracked on his name, and she bit her lips until she could taste blood.

'That's a little difficult. He has a right to see his child, you know.'

'Except he doesn't believe it is his child.'

'Are you absolutely certain that it is?'

'Yes,' she said, sighing heavily. 'Nick was away, wasn't he, for five weeks before the wedding. I only saw him a couple of times, and we didn't…'

She couldn't finish that, not to her mother, which was ridiculous under the circumstances, but she didn't need to say any more.

'You ought to eat, darling.'

'I couldn't. I just feel sick.'

'Carbs,' her mother said, and produced a packet of plain rich tea biscuits. 'Here,' she said, thrusting one in her hand. 'Dunk it in your tea.'

Was it really his? Could this really be happening to him again?

He'd sat outside for hours until the shock wore off and was replaced by a sickening emptiness.

The pregnancy test, he thought. Check it out. He went up to her room and opened her laptop, and was confronted by a page of images of him. Images he'd never seen. Ones she'd lied about deleting. Why? Because she loved him? And he loved her. He could see it clearly in the pictures, and he knew it in his heart.

He searched for the pregnancy test and came up with it.

As accurate as an ultrasound.

Which meant if she *had* just done it, the baby was his—and he'd accused her of lying, of trying to pass another man's baby off as his.

And he knew then, with shocking certainty, that she hadn't lied to him. Not about that. As she'd pointed out at several thousand decibels, she wasn't Lisa. Not in any way. And he owed her an apology.

A lifetime of apologies, starting now.

But he couldn't leave Ella behind, so he lifted her out of her cot, put her in the car and drove to Jill's. Amy's car was on the drive, and he went to the front door and rang the bell.

'Leo.'

'I'm an idiot,' he said, and he felt his eyes filling and blinked hard. 'Can I see her?'

'Where's Ella?'

'In the car, asleep.'

'Put her in the sitting room. Amy's in her room.'

He laid her on the sofa next to Jill, went upstairs to Amy's room and took a deep breath.

'Go away, Leo,' she said, before he even knocked, but he wasn't going anywhere.

He opened the door, ducked to avoid the flying missile she hurled at him and walked towards her, heart pounding.

'Get out.'

'No. I've come to apologise. I've been an idiot. I know you're not Lisa, and I know you wouldn't lie to me about anything important. You've never really lied to me, not even when you knew the truth was going to hurt me. And I know you're not lying now.' He took another step towards her. 'Can we talk?'

'What is there to say?'

'What I wanted to say to you when you got home. That I love you. That I don't want to wait any longer, because I do know you, Amy, I know you through and through, and you know me. We haven't changed that much, not deep down where it matters, and I know we've got what it takes. I was just hiding from it because I was afraid, because I've screwed up one marriage, but I'm not going to screw up another.'

'Marriage?' She stared at him blankly. 'I hate to point this out to you, but we aren't exactly married. We aren't exactly anything.'

'No. But we should be. We haven't lost our friendship, Amy, but it has changed. Maybe the word is evolved. Evolved into something stronger. Something that will stay the course. We were both just afraid to try again, afraid to trust what was under our noses all the time. We should have had more faith in each other and in ourselves.'

He took her hand and wrapped it in his, hanging on for dear life, because he couldn't let her go. Let them go.

'I love you, Amy. I'll always love you. Marry me. Me and Ella, and you and our baby. We can be a proper family.'

Amy sat down on the edge of her bed, her knees shaking.

'Are you serious? Leo, you were horrible to me!'

'I know, and I can't tell you how sorry I am. I was just shocked, and there was a bit of déjà vu going on, but I should have listened to you.'

'You should. But I knew you wouldn't, because of Lisa—'

'Shh,' he said, touching a finger to her lips. 'Lisa's gone, Amy. This is between you and me now, you and me and our baby.'

'And Ella,' she said.

'And Ella. Of course and Ella. She won't be an only child any more. I was so worried about that.'

'You said it would be a cold day in hell before you got married again,' she reminded him, and his eyes filled with sadness.

'I was wrong. It felt like a cold day in hell when you walked out of my life. Come back to me, Amy? Please? I need you. I can't live without you, without your friendship, your support, your understanding. Your atrocious sense of humour. Your untidiness. The fact that you do lie to me, just a little, on occasions.'

'When?' she asked, scrolling back desperately.

'The photos,' he said with a wry smile on the mouth she just wanted to kiss now. You told me you'd deleted them, but you haven't. They're still on your laptop. I saw them just now. I opened your laptop to check up on pregnancy tests and I found them. Photos of me. Why?'

She closed her eyes. 'It doesn't matter why.'

'It does to me, because I know why I would want photos of you. Why I took them. So I can look at the images when you're gone, and still, in some small way, have you with me. Amy, I'm scared,' he went on, and she opened her eyes and looked up at him again, seeing the truth of it in his eyes.

'I'm scared I'll fail you, let you down like I let Lisa down. My lifestyle is chaotic, and it's not conducive to a happy marriage. How many celebrity chefs—forget celebrity, just normal chefs—are happily married? Not many. So many of their marriages fall apart, and I don't want that to happen to us, but I need you in my life, and I'll have to trust your faith in me, your belief that we can make it work. That I won't let you down.'

'You already have, today. You didn't listen.'

He closed his eyes, shaking his head slowly, and then he looked up, his eyes locking with hers, holding them firm.

'I know. And I'm sorry, but I'll never do it again. I love you, Amy, and I need you, and I've never been more serious about anything in my life. Please marry me.'

He meant it. He really, truly meant it.

She closed her eyes, opened them again and smiled at him. She thought he smiled back, but she couldn't really see any more. 'Yes,' she said softly. 'Oh, yes, please.'

He laughed, but it turned into a ragged groan, and he hauled her into his arms and cradled her against his heart.

'You won't let me down,' she told him. 'I won't let you. Just one more thing—will you please kiss me? I've forgotten what it feels like.'

'I've got a better idea. Ella's downstairs with your mother, and she needs to be back in bed in her own home, and so do I. Come home with us, Amy. It doesn't feel right without you.'

It didn't feel right without him, either. Nothing felt right. And home sounded wonderful.

'Kiss me first?' she said with a smile, and he laughed softly.

'Well, it's tough but I'll see if I can remember how,' he murmured, and she could feel the smile on his lips...

EPILOGUE

'ARE YOU READY?'

Such simple words, but they'd had the power to change the whole course of her life.

Was she ready?

For the marriage—the *lifetime*—with Leo?

Mingling with the birdsong and the voices of the people clustered outside the church gates were the familiar strains of the organ music.

The overture for their wedding.

No. Their *marriage*. Subtle difference, but hugely significant.

Amy glanced through the doorway of the church and caught the smiles on the row of faces in the back pew, and she smiled back, her heart skittering under the fitted bodice that suddenly seemed so tight she could hardly breathe.

The church was full, the food cooked, the champagne on ice. And Leo was waiting for her answer.

Her dearest friend, the love of her life, who'd been there for her when she'd scraped her knees, had her heart broken for the first time, when her father had died, who'd just— been there, her whole life, her friend and companion and cheerleader. Her lover. And she did love him.

Enough to marry him? Till death us do part, and all that?

Oh, yes. And she was ready. Ready for the chemistry, the fireworks, the amazingness that was her life with Leo

Bring it on.

She straightened her shoulders, tilted up her chin and gave Leo her most dazzling smile.

'Yes,' she said firmly. 'I'm ready. How about you? Because I don't want you feeling pressured into this for the wrong reason. You can still walk away. I'll understand.'

'No way,' he said, just as firmly. 'It's taken me far too long to realise how much I love you, and I can't think of a better reason to marry you, or a better time to do it than now.'

His smile was tender, his eyes blazing with love, and she let out the breath she'd been holding.

'Well, that's a relief,' she said with a little laugh, and he smiled and shook his head.

'Silly girl. Amy, are you sure you don't want my father to walk you down the aisle? He's quite happy to.'

'No. I don't need anyone to give me away, Leo, and you're the only man I want by my side.'

'Good.You look beautiful, Amy,' he added gruffly, looking down into her eyes. 'More beautiful than I've ever seen you.'

'Thank you,' she said softly 'You don't look so bad yourself.'

She kissed his cheek and flashed a smile over her shoulder at her bridesmaids. 'OK, girls? Good to go?'

They nodded, and she turned back to Leo. 'OK, then. Let's do this,' she said, and she could feel the smile in her heart reflected in his eyes.

'I love you, Amy,' he murmured, and then slowly, steadily, he walked her down the aisle.

And when they reached the chancel steps he stopped, those beautiful golden eyes filled with love and pride, and he turned her into his arms and kissed her.

The congregation went wild, and he let her go and stood back a little, his smile wry.

'That was just in case you'd forgotten what it's like,' he teased, but his eyes weren't laughing, because marrying Amy was the single most important thing he would ever do in his life, and he was going to make sure they did it right.

* * * * *

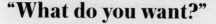

LET'S TALK
Romance

For exclusive extracts, competitions
and special offers, find us online:

 facebook.com/millsandboon

 @millsandboonuk

 @millsandboon

Or get in touch on 0844 844 1351*

For all the latest titles coming soon, visit
millsandboon.co.uk/nextmonth